ABOUT THE AUTHOR

CHRISTOPHER M. PURRETT

Christopher attended college at Central Michigan University, graduating with a degree in Broadcast & Cinematic Arts. There he met his wife,

Misty, with whom he had two daughters, Lea & Kyra. The Phillip & Whizzy characters were born when he began telling bedtime stories to his daughters. In his spare time, Christopher loves music, movies and sports, especially hockey and football. He lives in Michigan with his family.

Keep up with him at www.Purrett.com
Twitter
www.Twitter.com/CMPurrett
Facebook
www.Facebook.com/CMP_Author

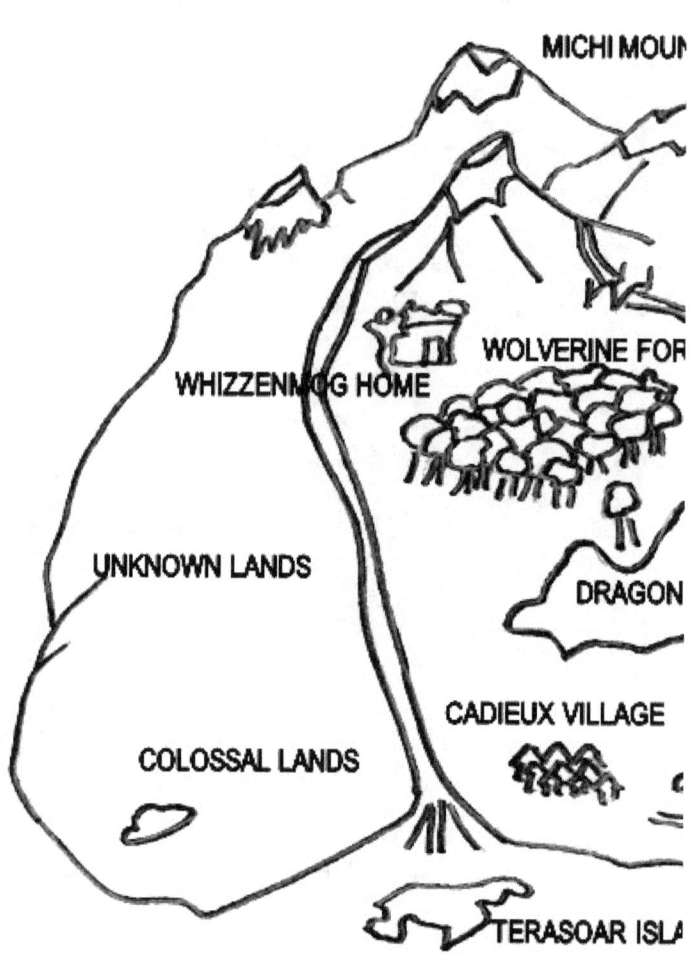

MICHI MOUN

WHIZZENMOG HOME

WOLVERINE FOR

UNKNOWN LANDS

DRAGON

CADIEUX VILLAGE

COLOSSAL LANDS

TERASOAR ISLA

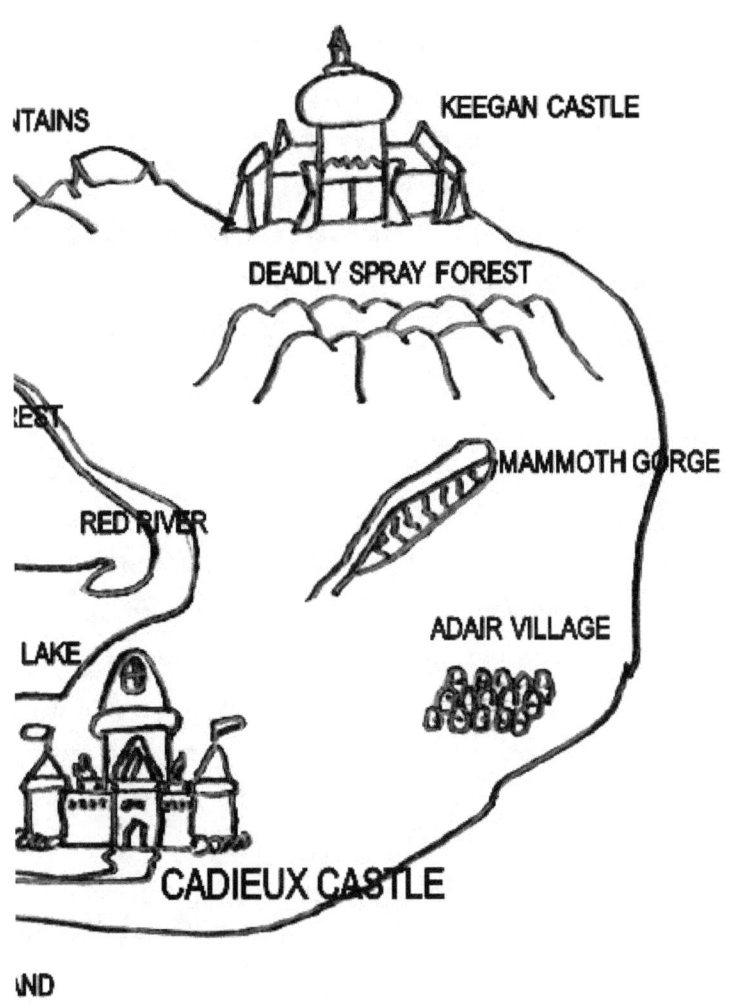

NTAINS

KEEGAN CASTLE

DEADLY SPRAY FOREST

REST

MAMMOTH GORGE

RED RIVER

LAKE

ADAIR VILLAGE

CADIEUX CASTLE

ND

ISBN 978-0-9833278-6-8
[1. Fantasy — Fiction. 2. Science Fiction — Fiction. 3. Wizards — Fiction. 4. Heroes — Fiction.]
Released in United States of America
Paperback format
First Edition, November 2014

WHIZZENMOG
BETRAYAL

Christopher M. Purrett

www.Purrett.com

CHAPTERS

ETHAN WHIZZENMOG

1

Standing before me was the shadowy figure of my brother. His back was to the light of the full moon, which hung large in the dark, star-filled sky. His usually red-colored fur was nearly black. His eyes were intense and fixed on me.

My heart pounded in my chest. It was hard to breathe. I held my arm outstretched with my wand gripped tightly in my right paw. My yellow fur seemed to glow against the brightness of the full moon making it quite difficult to hide.

"Don't do it, Rainer!" I pleaded as the tip of his wand lit up. "No!" I screamed in fear.

A bolt of light dashed toward me and slammed into my chest before I could jump out of the way. My body went numb and I fell on my back. I was now staring into the Mistasian night sky. The blades of grass wrapped around my long fox ears. I wanted to get up and run away, but nothing moved. My big brother had just paralyzed me with a spell. It was the same thing every time. We would begin to practice our spells and one way or another it would end with me losing.

"Great job, Rainer. You have really developed into a premier wizard, son." The voice of our father, Glyndon Whizzenmog, proudly proclaimed. "The King and Queen will be truly impressed with your skills."

"Thank you, father!" my brother gleefully replied.

"Tomorrow I will present you to the King. You are ready to join me in protecting the throne, Rainer."

Then our father turned his attention to me as I still remained motionless in the cool grass. "Ethan. I'm disappointed," He said with a deep exhale. "Your brother has defeated you with the exact same spell three days in a row now. Will you ever learn?"

Even in the dark, I could see the disapproval in my father's eyes. Rainer was so much stronger and quicker than me. It was unfair. We weren't the same wizard.

I watched as my father patted my brother on the back, "Great job!" Then he turned and walked away leaving me paralyzed in the grass.

My heart sank. I don't know why it still bothered me...my father had always been that way. He was embarrassed of me.

Rainer pointed his wand at my chest again. It lit up sending a warmth surging through my body as if the blood suddenly flowed through my veins again. I took a deep breath. When my brother reached out his hand to help me, I pushed it away.

"I don't want your help!" I shouted in disgust. "Why do you have to do that?" I angrily yelled at him once I was back to my feet.

Rainer was taller than I was too. I had to stand on my tip toes to see eye to eye with him.

"Cut that out, Ethan." Rainer shoved me in the chest and laughed. I stumbled backwards and tripped over a rock, falling back into the grass again. Rainer quickly realized he had pushed too hard.

"Hey, I'm sorry. Let me help you up."

"I don't need your help, brother!" I was fuming. My left paw was bruised, but not as deeply as my ego. He just didn't understand what it was like to feel small...weak. I wanted to show him so badly, but knew I would never match up to him...our father's favorite son.

"Come on. Let's go back to the house." Rainer turned and started walking, but then stopped when he noticed I wasn't following. He was used to me following him everywhere. I had always been envious of him, but now I was just angry. "Ethan?"

"You go," I calmly replied. "I want to be alone."

"But father is waiting for us?" Rainer ignorantly stated.

"No, Rainer." I held back tears. "Just you!"

WOLVERINE FOREST

2

The air was crisp and cool as it swept across Dragon Lake and floated into Cadieux Village. I started to walk along the shore just thinking to myself and not really paying attention to the village behind me in the distance. When I finally stopped to pick up a crescent-shaped rock at my foot and toss it into the lake I noticed the torches from the village were no longer visible.

Should I go back?, I questioned myself.

"No," I answered aloud and tossed the rock into the lake. "They'll never notice I'm gone."

So I continued to walk along the shore. Dragon Lake was the calmest water anywhere in Mistasia. It looked like it was frozen as the moonlight reflected from the top of the steady water. In the distance I could make out the treetops of Wolverine Forest.

Why is he so mean to me? Images of my father's disappointed expression haunted me all night long. The farther I got from the castle, the more I realized I could never go back. There was no reason for me to return.

I should just keep walking, I thought to myself. Behind me I heard a snort. When I turned, I gasped.

Staring at me was a very large wolverine. The beast growled. Its fangs hung down from its upper lip. The Wolverine had snuck up on me. I could hear my father's voice, "You will never learn!"

Suddenly, I realized I had my wand in my paw and pointed it at the beast. The Wolverine grunted loudly and bent down to attack.

"No, don't do it!" I yelled in my deepest voice, which sounded more like a whimpering child.

The wolverine charged. I fired the first spell I could think of in a panic. It completely missed because my hand was shaking so badly. The spell hit a small tree causing it to drop all its leaves and acorns, leaving it naked. I ducked to avoid the wolverine, but it still grabbed me. Now, I was dangling in the air by my ankles. I dropped my wand, which the beast quickly snapped up from the grass. It pushed its big, ugly face into mine. Its warm, smelly breath burned my nostrils.

I'm in so much trouble. I cried in my head. I hoped this hungry beast wasn't going to eat me for a snack. I closed my eyes. Then, we were moving again. When I opened them I realized the wolverine was running back toward the forest. Where there were more wolverines!

I hit the ground with a thud, rubbing my neck as it throbbed with pain. Then, I heard a voice that would change my life.

"What brings a Whizzenmog to the Wolverine Forest?" The crass voice challenged me.

I hesitated to look up and see who was speaking.

"Answer me, fox!" He yelled.

I shuddered at the anger in his voice. It reminded me of my father. I tried to answer his question, but when I moved my lips nothing came out.

"Stubborn...just like his father!" The voice replied.

"No!" I suddenly found my voice. For the first time I looked away from the dirt-covered forest floor and saw the elven man that sat before me. He was old and thin. He had short white hair, and a long braided white beard. The elf glared at me. "I mean...I am not like my father." I clarified.

The man smiled and sat upright in his throne. It was a beautifully carved wooden throne made from the root of a massive tree. Two wolverines stood at his sides like guards.

"Who are you?" I mustered up the courage to ask.

The elf scoffed as though he was offended that I didn't know.

"My name is Pierre LaCroiux, and I ask you again young Whizzenmog. What brings you to my forest?"

"Well...I...well," I stammered as I tried to figure out how to explain my situation.

Then LaCroiux stood from his throne and walked toward me. My heart skipped a beat, and I had to remind myself to breathe. My paws trembled as I began to recoil. The elder elf put out his hand and placed it on my shoulder. Then he knelt before me. Our eyes met and a strange sensation overcame me. It was calm. My paws no longer trembled, my heartbeat returned to normal.

"You can tell me...Ethan," Pierre LaCroiux spoke in a friendly voice.

"How...how did you know my name?" I didn't know if I should be fearful or honored by his knowledge.

"I make it my business to know the names of the King's wizard guardians," he smiled. "Word has come to my ear that you and your father are...not seeing eye to eye." He suddenly stopped. He appeared to be awaiting my answer.

"Ah...yes Lord LaCroiux," I responded.

"Sorcerer," He corrected. "You have yet to explain why you have come to my forest, young Whizzenmog?"

"I was walking along Dragon Lake when I ran into one of your guards," I replied feeling silly. The guardian of the king would always be on his guard and not so easily captured by his foe.

"So you are my prisoner then?" LaCroiux chuckled. "A Whizzenmog wizard as my prisoner? Now that is something." His laughter became a roar as the Wolverines around him began to laugh with a raspy voice.

I felt a pit in my stomach.

"Do you really want to be my prisoner, Ethan?" The elven sorcerer questioned as he again knelt before me.

I shook my head no. I most definitely didn't want to be a sorcerer's prisoner.

"But you don't want to go back home either?"

"My father doesn't want me anyway. My family is better off without me." I replied in disgrace.

"Then you are welcome to stay here...in Wolverine Forest. I can teach you the way of a sorcerer. You will never again feel the shame your father has created in you. I can lead you to a greater purpose. You will become stronger than you ever dreamed possible."

I began to smile. I wanted so badly to be important. To be strong and powerful. Maybe sorcery was the way that I can be great?

"Yes." I responded. It was the quickest decision I had come to in my lifetime.

I remained in Wolverine Forest and became Sorcerer LaCroiux's apprentice. He showed me things that I never even dreamed possible. As a wizard your powers are limited to what you can do by your wand; however, as a sorcerer there seems to be no limitations. Whatever my mind can imagine I can conjure into reality...both beautiful and frightening.

I never felt so alive, and so powerful. Sorcery definitely had its advantages over wizardry. LaCroiux brought a twenty-foot tall tree to life. It pulled its roots from the ground and began walking around. The tree snatched up a wolverine and tossed it like a pebble. Another time, LaCroiux showed me how to control fire. He set fire to a small bush and then made the flames dance and stretch on his command, even making shapes out of the flames. He grabbed a sword right from the powerful grip of a Wolverine Soldier with the arm of a flame creature.

For the first time in my life I believed I could challenge my brother. He would be no match for my sorcery.

One windy night, I walked at the edge of the forest staring across Dragon Lake. I couldn't see Cadieux Castle, but I knew where it was in the distance. The moon was full this night and it reflected off the lake the same way it had the first night I arrived here. For a brief moment, I wondered if my father had even noticed that I was gone.

He has Rainer. My mind answered in a rage. It didn't matter whether I was there or not. A surge of anger overtook me and I snapped the branch from a nearby tree and flung it far across the lake. Dragon Lake swallowed it quickly with almost no wake in the water. A slight ripple rolled outward. I followed it with my eyes until it landed along the narrow sandy beach at my paws.

A noise came from behind me. I figured it was another wolverine. When I turned around there was no one.

I furrowed my brow. I knew that I had heard something. I reentered the forest and searched for what could have made the noise.

Footprints? In the dirt was a trail of footprints most definitely not wolverine in origin. I followed the prints through the winding and sometimes narrow spaces between the trees until they vanished at the base of a very wide tree trunk. I folded my arms across my chest.

Where did they go? Footprints don't just stop. There had to be an explanation. This forest was full of surprises. What happened next shouldn't have been so shocking. After walking around the tree a couple of times in frustration I again stopped next to the last set of footprints just in front of the tree. I stepped inside them, placing my paws exactly. The footprints were larger than mine. I stared at my paws for a few moments and exhaled deeply. Then I glanced up at the tree and noticed something new, a unique shape in the bark of the tree's trunk. It appeared to be a handle. I reached out and grabbed hold. Then the front of the tree swung open revealing a staircase leading up.

I moved inside and the door shut behind me. It was extremely dark. I used my paws along the wall to guide myself up the winding staircase. I worried that if I used my wand to light my way whoever had made those tracks would know that I had figured out my way inside. Finally, I reached another door. Light peeked out from around its frame. I could hear voices. One was very familiar...my teacher, Sorcerer LaCroiux, and the other sounded like someone I knew. I tried to place the voice.

"Do you believe that this is the way you want to resolve your issues with your brother?" I heard LaCroiux ask harshly.

Brother? I wondered. It couldn't be. **Rainer?**

The second voice responded, "My brother has held his position for too long. Together we can rid this kingdom of his ignorance."

Prince Cragon Cadieux? I was shocked.

"And when King Steven is gone, you will assume the throne?" Sorcerer LaCroiux crassly questioned. "I don't see how that is worth the trouble for me. What do I gain from this, Prince Cragon?"

"You would become my advisor. Live in the castle," the evil prince responded hoping to persuade the sorcerer to join his side. "You would no longer have to live in the wild with these animals," he said, referring to the wolverines.

"I want control over everything outside Cadieux Village," LaCroiux demanded.

"Everything? But..." Cragon sounded stunned at the request. "That sounds like a hefty request, friend."

The sinister sorcerer responded with a snicker, "So does asking me to eliminate the King and Queen."

Their conversation frightened me, so I quickly escaped from the hideout and dashed back into the forest toward my makeshift home in the base of a large hollow tree.

It wasn't long before Sorcerer LaCroiux returned. He glided across the forest floor like a ghost. His robe dragged along the dirt making it appear he had no feet.

"Ethan!" LaCroiux anxiously called. "Where are you? I have something to share with you."

I took a deep breath and stuck my head out from my home.

"Oh, there you are. Come here, Ethan." The sorcerer carried a wide smile upon his normally weary face.

That sent a shiver of fear down my spine. If the thought of eliminating the King and Queen made him happy, I wanted no part of making him unhappy.

"Ethan, we have a proposal from the Prince of Cadieux." LaCroiux twirled his braided beard in his fingers. His smile had increased.

My throat was so dry it hurt to swallow. I rubbed my paw across my wet nose nervously. "What is it?" I asked, careful not to reveal that I already knew the plan.

"How would you like to test your newly learned skills?" The sorcerer goaded.

"My skills?" I asked. The dryness in my throat had wiggled its way all the way down into my stomach, which now ached with each breath.

The elven sorcerer's eyes were piercing. It was like he could see straight through me, and knew just how to control me.

"Ethan." He softly whispered. Sorcerer LaCroiux looked around before he continued, as if he thought someone else would overhear, but the only other beasts in this forest were the Wolverines and they didn't speak so who would they tell what they heard?

"You were destined for this moment. The day you arrived at my throne crying for a purpose, wishing you were more than the son of a wizard. That was the day I gave you a purpose...power and sorcery. You can do so much more than your lowly brother. Ethan Whizzenmog, today is the day you make the choice to remain a meager wizard from the family that serves a weak King, or claim your place as a powerful and majestic sorcerer that stands by the side of the true and mighty ruler of Mistasia." Pierre LaCroiux reached out and placed his large, skeletal hand on my paw.

I felt the adrenaline surging through my fur. It reached the ends of my body. I inhaled sharply.

"Imagine it, Ethan. You're standing beside the throne of Cadieux, as your family bows at your feet."

A smirk invaded my once fear-driven face. The worries of the meeting between LaCroiux and Cragon Cadieux had vanished. A feeling of clarity had overcome me. It was my choice. I was here for a reason. I could have gone home at any time in the past, but I choose to stay here in Wolverine Forest with Sorcerer LaCroiux to teach me the dark powers of sorcery. I wasn't going back to a family that hated me...that thought I was inferior.

"I'll show them," I finally spoke.

LaCroiux stood tall at the opening to my new home in this secluded forest.

"So I guess that means you're looking to demonstrate your skills, apprentice?"

I quickly sprung into action. I heard the snap of a twig behind me and spun around. My arm swung out and across my body like a swinging sword. I felt it crash to a stop against the chest of a Wolverine. Lifting him up, I flung the heavy and muscular beast into the air and over my head with ease. It crashed to the forest floor with a sickening thud.

Sorcerer LaCroiux had an approving smile on this elderly face when I again met his glance.

"We need to begin to prepare!"

THE RETURN HOME

3

A cool breeze flowed through the Wolverine Forest, as the moonlight crept in with each gust. I knelt on the limb of a tree perched high atop the forest's edge overlooking Dragon Lake. On the far side of the lake, was Cadieux Castle. The sky glittered as millions of stars shown above the peaceful castle below. I had forgotten how mesmerizing the nighttime sky was in Mistasia. Lately, all I had seen was the deep-colored leaves of the Wolverine Forest hanging over my head like a cloud.

I had in my hand a small wooden cylinder given to me by Sorcerer LaCroiux; he called it a "magnifinder". It was his creation and it looked like a simple small branch except at one end was an opening. I held the contraption with the open end to my eye. The device allowed me to see a great distance; with it, Cadieux Castle was easily visible.

Day after day, I would return to the same position in the trees and watch the King's guards as they moved around the castle. My master, Pierre LaCroiux, had spoken of a mystical item that the King's guards would be transporting to the castle.

"King Steven's guards discovered an emerald," LaCroiux had revealed to me before sending me high into the trees where I now spent most of my time awaiting the moment I could catch a glimpse of them bringing it into the castle.

Emeralds were powerful jewels that allowed its beholder to wheeled great power. To have this green gemstone would give them the power to rule all of Mistasia. If this was an emerald, it would be the last of its kind and extremely valuable.

In the early dawn, I began to dose. My yellow furry head grew heavy. I leaned against the tree trunk and slowly closed my eyes. I just wanted to sleep a few moments...I was so tired. Relaxation began to sweep through my body as all my tired and sore muscles released the night's tension. It felt great.

My eyes suddenly opened wide as I felt myself slipping. I gripped the tree branch that had been under me as I fell. Now, I found myself hanging extremely high in the air dangling above an obstacle course of branches that would batter me to a bloodied pulp if I let go. With all my strength, I pulled myself up.

Holding the branch tightly, I attempted to regain my composure. My heart was still racing and I felt sweat on my brow.

"The magnifinder!" I shouted as I realized it was gone. If I dropped it, it would surely be destroyed. "LaCroiux is gonna kill me," I said as I looked back down into the maze of branches that the magnifinder would have fallen through to the forest floor below. Fortunately, I found it behind me wedged between the tree branch and a smaller branch growing out.

I felt it was time to go back home and get some rest before returning tonight. LaCroiux had believed that King Steven would attempt to move the emerald into the castle at night to avoid a commotion. If the word spread that an emerald had again been found in Mistasia, it would become a special event drawing everyone within the Kingdom and beyond.

I held the magnifinder securely as I began to descend. I took one last look through the open end, mostly to make sure I hadn't cracked the glass when I almost fell.

"What's that?" I said as I discovered two elves in Cadieux Village. I caught a glimpse of a green light as the sun, which had risen above the castle behind them, shown across the object in a female elf's hands. "The emerald!"

I dashed back to speak with Sorcerer LaCroiux.

"The emerald," I shouted after entering LaCroiux's chamber deep within Woverine Forest. I needed to catch my breath before continuing. "I saw the emerald in the village, Master!"

"Good." LaCroiux's head lifted, and a sharp chuckle emerged. It was startling. I had not heard him laugh very often. The sound was full and aggressive...much like his demeanor. "You have done well, my apprentice. Are you ready for your journey?"

When I entered he was working on a new contraption. It was a small, square box. It was made from a material similar to that of the elven warriors' shields. I had caught myself staring at his work and didn't answer, which was angering him.

"Ethan!" My master shouted to regain my attention. "It is now time for you to return to your family," he stated matter-of-factly.

A sudden sinking feeling appeared in my gut. "What? I..."

He interrupted me, "This is not up for discussion." He quickly returned to working on his project as if I wasn't standing shocked in the same room.

"You want me to leave?" LaCroiux didn't respond immediately. Finally, I turned to leave.

"Ethan, your opportunity to prove that you are the strongest Whizzenmog has arisen. It is time to claim your place in Cadieux Castle beside the rightful ruler of Mistasia. You will see me again soon when we are reunited at the throne, my apprentice. First, you must steal the emerald, Ethan."

I had just assumed that when Sorcerer LaCroiux requested that I observe the daily routine of the guards around Cadieux Castle, it was for the planning of an attack against the king to find out when the king might be vulnerable. Now, I am charged with reentering the castle and stealing its most prized possession...the last emerald.

I now found myself walking away from what had become my home, The Wolverine Forest, and back to the place I had dreaded I would someday have to return...Cadieux Castle. I shuffled my paws along the grass leaving a trail behind me. My wand gripped tightly in my left paw, I glided my right paw across its smooth edge toward the tip. Never before had I felt this uneasy...this nervous. Not even the night I was carried away to LaCroiux's hideout by a Wolverine. Today, the sun hung high in the sky over Dragon Lake. It looked like a giant pancake atop the perfectly still water, which reminded me that I was hungry, but I didn't want to eat. My stomach was too upset right now to tolerate any food.

"My father won't be happy to see me," I muttered.

I reached Cadieux Village just before night fall. The moon had switched places with the sun. It aided me in my journey to the edge of the small village where most of the elves lived. These elves were extremely loyal to King **Steven**. They worked around the castle performing any jobs necessary for the kingdom, including protection, when called upon.

As I walked up the narrow pathway between the small houses I could feel eyes watching me. The farther I travelled up the path the stronger that sensation became.

I stopped. Someone was behind me. When I turned around, no one was there. I searched for figures in the darkness. I saw what looked like a slender elven warrior, but as the wind blew, I realized it was nothing more than the shadow cast by a nearby tree.

Quickly, I moved toward the castle's back gate at the edge of Cadieux Village. The front of the grey stone structure was actually on the opposite side facing the ocean.

At the door, were two elven warriors, and they weren't very happy to see me approaching.

"Stop right there, Ethan Whizzenmog!" The elf to my right barked. "You are not welcome here any longer."

"But this is my home," I coyly replied.

"Your father claims that you abandoned your home to live with the evils of the Wolverine Forest," the second elf retorted.

I growled at him and pointed my wand at his chest. "Summon my father. We will let him decide." I don't know what had come over me, but I had suddenly developed the courage of a Whizzenmog.

The elf to my right dashed into the castle and quickly returned. "You are clear to pass!"

I stared down the two elves as I walked past them in through the open door of Cadieux Castle. The familiar smell of wet stone and mildew entered my keen nostrils. I looked to the ceiling as I passed under the large opening. There between the inner and outer stone walls hung large black metal chains that controlled the gate. Many other elves glared at me as I walked past. It was more than obvious that my return was not welcomed.

"Ethan!" a familiar voice shouted. Before I could turn my head and see who called my name, a pair of reddish orange arms wrapped themselves around me and lifted me into the air.

It was my brother, Rainer Whizzenmog, who clutched me tightly and spun me around like a spinning top.

"Please, put me down, Rainer," I cried thanking the heavens that I hadn't eaten anything today.

"You have returned," Rainer stated with glee and the biggest smile I had ever seen. His eyes were wide and his ears pointed straight up. "Oh, brother, I missed you, Ethan!" He said and then hugged me once again.

I attempted to hold back my emotions, but couldn't. A sudden swell of happiness to see him came over me. It felt strangely good to once again be in Cadieux Castle, but I had yet to see my father, who would most definitely react differently.

Rainer hastily whisked me away to meet up with our father. We dashed past the tall wooden doors bearing the crest of the king, Steven Cadieux, and stopped just outside the next set of doors.

These doors were far smaller and darker in color. They were very old, but still in good condition. Rainer brashly flicked his wand and the doors opened. He waved me inside the room...a room in which my father would surely be awaiting me.

My stomach turned and I inhaled deeply. I felt my brother's paw against my back as he began to lightly push me in the right direction. He again motioned for me to walk inside. It felt like a trap. I felt like I would walk in there and the door would close behind me, then a giant troll would snatch me off the ground and bite my head off.

"Come on, Ethan," Rainer urged as he dragged me in by my arm.

The room was poorly lit. Only a few candles hung along the walls in this circular room. A small bed was at the far end. In the bed I could see the figure of my father under his covers. I had forgotten just how late it was.

"Is father asleep?" I asked Rainer, who continued to drag me across the stone floor.

"Yes. He will be so surprised to see you, Ethan!"

"Wait!" I pulled my arm back from Rainer's strong grip.

"You told them to let me into the castle?"

"So what!" my brother replied.

"Our father doesn't even know that I am here...does he?" I suddenly felt a panic setting in. This was a trap.

"Everything is just fine, Ethan. Calm down."

"Ethan?" I heard my father call in a drowsy voice. He now sat upright in bed. "Is that really you my son?"

I watched as my father reached for his wand at the side of his bed. He grasped his perfectly straight wand within his paw and turned toward me. The tip began to glow. My heart raced. Was my father about to zap me to death? His wand brightened and lit the room.

My father's face instantly exploded with a smile as he dashed from his bed, tossing away the covers, and running to me. He grabbed me by the shoulders and pulled me closely. My father, a man that had never shown any affection toward me in my entire life, was hugging me.

My father walked around the castle with a smile on his face for the next few days. He didn't look like himself. I was used to a scowl or frown.

Rainer and I spent most of our time together. He was just as excited about my return. We went out to the village and sat down on two tree stumps.

"Thank you, Ethan."

"For what," I nervously laughed. **What does that mean?** I thought.

"For coming home. Father has been very upset since you left. He blamed me for you leaving."

I didn't reply. How do you reply to something like that?

"If you don't mind me asking...where exactly did you go?" Rainer wondered.

I inhaled deeply. It must have sounded like he had upset me, because Rainer quickly retracted his question.

"Just forget it. I'm just glad you came home." Rainer rubbed my back.

"It is good to be home, brother."

A few weeks later, I walked alone along the edge of Dragon Lake. It was night. Torches burned in Cadieux Village just behind me, but along the calm waterfront I could feel the chill in the air. Stars lit up the sky. I had wandered out here without realizing where I was going. This walk had begun inside the castle grounds, but I just kept going as if something was drawing me away.

A snapping sound hit my ears, like a branch breaking. It was followed by another. If someone was attempting to sneak up on me they were doing a very poor job. I searched the darkness for signs of motion, but couldn't see anyone.

"Whizzenmog!" A curt voice startled me.

I still couldn't see where it was coming from.

"Behind you, Ethan."

Standing behind me was a frightening sight. A tall slender and hideous looking creature was directly behind me. It was a vampire bat. Its wings were outstretched giving it a grand appearance.

"Who are you?" I cowardly questioned.

"It is I, Sorcerer LaCroiux," The voice sounded very familiar to that of my master, yet the figure standing before me didn't resemble him in the slightest.

"Master? How can that be?"

"I cast a spell on this dimwitted soul in order to reach you. I believe you have forgotten your task, Ethan. The emerald?"

"No...no. I haven't forgotten, master. I just am trying to gain their trust."

"Stop wasting time and get the emerald. It is everything." LaCroiux snapped through the razor-sharp teeth of the Vampire bat. Then, almost as quickly as he had appeared, he vanished by leaping skyward and flying into the darkness.

A rush of wind blew across my face signaling his departure. I searched through the sky for him, but he was gone.

Now it was apparent that Sorcerer LaCroiux was watching my every move waiting for me to steal the Last Emerald of power.

I struggled to open my eyes the next morning. My head was pounding like someone had been hitting me with a rock all throughout the night. Sitting up was difficult. My stomach felt nauseous.

The sunlight pierced through the window like a knife stabbing me in the eyes. I placed my furry forearm across my eyes to block it. This didn't help.

A rustling sound came from the far side of my room as the heavy wooden door swung open. The rusty hinges squealed. A thud echoed when the door reached the stone wall.

"Ethan? Are you okay?" Rainer asked.

I attempted to open my eyes. They burned. "No. I have a monster headache."

"Let's get you something for that," Rainer said as he now surprisingly stood next to me.

It startled me to hear his voice in a different area of the room since I couldn't see him. I felt the small tip of his wand rest against my forehead. I shrunk away.

"Hey, what are you doing?" I barked.

"Just sit still, Ethan."

I had to admit I was a bit nervous, since not that long ago I considered my brother my enemy. Well, technically he still was. A warm sensation entered my head just below my ear. It spread across my forehead. It felt like a fire had been lit between my ears, yet it didn't hurt. The warmth slowly moved down between my eyes. Tears formed and then began to stream down my checks. I could feel them moving through my fur.

"Open your eyes," Rainer said. My vision had been restored and, even more amazingly, my headache was gone.

"That's amazing."

"You're welcome, Ethan." Rainer patted my back with his strong paw. "Come on, I want to show you something."

We walked through the bustling castle, passing Elven Warriors at every turn until we reached the far end of Cadieux Castle. This was a very darkened and private area. Candles lit the hallway just enough to allow me to see a short distance.

"Where are we, Rainer?"

Rainer placed his paw over his mouth, motioning to be quiet. His usually orangish-red fur was almost black in the dimly lit hallway. He began walking and I followed. Rainer used his wand to replace the candle light as we moved farther down the hall. Rainer stopped at what appeared to be a dead end. He moved his wand attempting to find something.

"Hold this," Rainer said as he handed me his wand.

"No, like this," My brother directed. I had allowed the lighted wand to point at the floor. He showed me where to direct the light. In the lower corner, was an oddly-shaped stone.

Rainer pushed against the stone and it easily moved. The wall split and swung open.

"Hurry!" Rainer said. He grabbed my arm and pulled me inside the blackened room. I heard the stone wall close behind us, but I couldn't move. I was completely focused on the object perched on a golden pedestal in the middle of the room glimmering against the light produced from my brother's wand.

I only spent a few moments with it, but my life changed completely. I had never felt such a pure adrenaline charge like when I placed my paw on the green emerald. In an instant I knew exactly what I had to do. I would steal the emerald...not for Sorcerer LaCroiux, but for me. It would make me stronger than anyone in Mistasia. No wizard or sorcerer would stand in my way. My father would soon be bowing to a new king, but it wasn't going to be Cragon Cadieux...it would be me!

MORNING OF TRUTH

4

My mind had become overrun with thoughts of the emerald. Its beauty. Its power. Now all that remained was how I would steal it.

Rainer came to get me the following morning. I was eager to see where he would take me today...hoping it was to see the Last Emerald again. To my disappointment, he took me to the Proving Grounds just outside the castle. It was where Rainer and I used to battle while practicing our wizardry. Therefore, this was a place of bad memories for me. It was the last place I had been before running away, and since my return I had avoided it.

"Why did you bring me here Rainer?" I said with shortness in my tone.

"Father asked me to meet him here this morning. He has a very important assignment for me."

"So why am I here?"

"I hoped you would join me," He said it with such heartfelt sincerity I almost believed him.

I scoffed. My brother's reaction showed that he actually meant it. I suddenly felt uncomfortable.

"You really want me with you?" I asked.

Rainer smiled and nodded.

I smiled back but didn't respond. Rainer had been trying very hard to repair our friendship since I returned, but I continued to keep my distance. It would only make what would happen easier for us all.

"Rainer, are you ready?" Our father's voice joyously rang out into the Proving Grounds. He hesitated upon noticing me standing next to

Rainer. "Ethan, good morning, son. I didn't know you were going to be here." The surprise in his voice seeped forth like the smoke from an uncontrolled flame. It hung over my head casting a dark shadow. This was the father I'd expected upon my return to the castle. Loveless and ashamed.

"I asked him to join me father," My brother replied.

Our father's eyes moved sharply between us as though he was attempting to figure out if I had some sort of spell cast over Rainer. Surely, my brother couldn't be acting of right mind to invite me. After a moment, he cleared his throat in what appeared to be an attempt at ridding himself of whatever he actually wanted to say, but he thought better of it. Then proceeded to address Rainer and ignore me.

"Rainer, the king and queen will be making a journey to the northern territory of Mistasia and I need you to join them as their protector."

My brother's face was overjoyed. It was a great honor to be the keeper of the royal family's protection.

"I must remain here at the castle." My father suddenly stopped his explanation. He was unaware that I knew about the last emerald being here and that Rainer had shown me its location. It was obviously the reason he wasn't joining the King and Queen on their trip. He was always at their side.

"I'm trusting you with their safety."

"Thank you, Father." Rainer bowed his head.

Our father glanced in my direction for a moment. The emotion he had shown me the night I had returned was nowhere to be recognized. Then he turned and left.

Rainer was excited. "This is amazing. Brother, you must promise to come with me. It would mean a great deal to have you by my side."

"I don't think that is such a good idea, Rainer." I was referring to both the fact that our father obviously didn't want me to go and the fact that I would be away from the castle, which made it more difficult to steal the emerald.

He placed his strong paw on my shoulder and looked me in the eyes. He looked down upon me, standing a full head taller.

"Please, Ethan. It would be good for us to spend time together. I have missed you so much, brother." Then he pulled me close and hugged me so tightly it became hard to breathe.

I agreed to go with him but quickly regretted my decision.

"Great. We leave tonight!"

Rainer dashed off to collect supplies and weaponry for the journey. I stood stuck in the grass...not literally, but just unable to move my feet. I hoped that if I didn't reenter the castle I wouldn't have to go tonight. It also meant that I would have to wait until my return to steal the emerald.

The air had cooled since Rainer and I were in the Proving Grounds earlier in the day. The wind had picked up. It blew through my fur and cut into my skin like a thousand tiny arrows. Fires from the village where doused. I watched as a few elves scrambled to relight them, but the winds made it a worthless attempt. Most gave up and returned to their homes.

I stood alone in the field between Cadieux Castle and the village. Closing my eyes I could see the glowing green emerald hidden away within the castle.

"Ethan," A voice whispered in my ears. I opened my eyes, but no one was around. My gaze fixed in the distance...the exact place where I knew Sorcerer LaCroiux's hideout was deep within the Wolverine Forest. The tree tops were barely visible beyond Dragon Lake. Again I closed my eyes, when I heard my name repeated whistling in the winds. My master was calling to me.

Then, something landed on my shoulder. I jumped and brandished my wand.

"Ethan, it's me!" Rainer yelled.

"I'm sorry, Rainer. You just startled me."

Rainer smiled at me. He was so excited about our journey. I on the other hand, was dreading the next few days. We walked through the village making small talk, but discussing nothing important. I found myself drifting in and out of the conversation until we stood before a large pile of wood sitting next to the lake.

I didn't say anything right away, just looked at my brother waiting for the explanation, because his expression showed that he was not surprised to see the enormous pile of trees cut and laying on their sides in a triangular stack.

"I had the elves gather wood for us."

"Really? Do we have enough?" I sarcastically asked while looking into the sky to see the top of the pile.

Rainer chuckled slightly and slapped me in the chest lightheartedly. "Come on, Ethan."

"Are we building a fort?" I asked.

"Ah...no. We are building a boat for the king and queen to use on their journey up Red River tonight." He said this as though it was a small feat. Just create a ship that by the look of the wood pile would be able to transport every elf living in the kingdom.

"Well, you have fun with that." I replied jokingly.

Rainer held his wand out and began motioning the wood to move. In just a short time, Rainer had moved most of the wood into smaller piles and had begun molding and shaping them like pieces of clay.

"Are you just going to stand there?" Rainer questioned while flattening one tree trunk into a plank board that he used to create a small section of the ship's deck.

I scoffed and shook my head in disbelief that I found myself building a boat for two people that I planned to remove from the throne.

It only took the two of us a little over two hours, but by the time the royal family began to gather with their assembly at the edge of Cadieux Village, we placed the finishing touches on a magnificent vessel worthy of carrying the king and queen along Red River. The boat was tall and narrow with sails made from woven tree leaves and cattails from around the lake.

We quickly set sail.

The air remained cool as the sun completed its journey over the edge of the world. Stars slowly began to emerge one by one like creatures peeking out from their homes and looking to see if it was safe to venture out and play with one another. A calm settled into my body like I had never felt before. The smell of the salty water rushed below us and mixed with fragrances from the Wolverine Forest.

"Ethan," A voice whispered.

My heart quickened its pace, energizing my body. A surge of adrenaline burst through my veins to my paws. It was the unmistakable voice of my master calling to me from the Wolverine Forest which was laid out before us.

"Be prepared," his voice commanded.

"Ethan," Rainer's voice rang out clearly breaking LaCroiux's hold over me.

"Yes," I responded while attempting to swallow my fear.

"Are you okay?"

I nodded, but could tell that it really hadn't satisfied Rainer's worry.

"Is there something wrong? Do you sense something?"

"No. That is ridiculous," I awkwardly laughed at the thought hoping he didn't really know the truth and was just waiting for me to admit it. I was becoming paranoid. "Do you?"

"No, my brother, I wasn't gifted with such senses." Rainer replied.

It couldn't have been more than a few seconds after he finished when I heard it for the first time in my life. It was a sound that I would never forget. The dreadful screeching of Sorcerer LaCroiux's new pets...Vampire bats. The soulless creatures from the Deadly Spray Forest descended upon our ship with wings spread, claws drawn and fangs exposed. Even in the moonlight they were mightily frightening.

Two crashed down on the deck. Their wings spanned over both sides of the ship. They were much taller than our Elven Warriors, and so quick.

I drew my wand, as did my brother. We each blasted a Vampire bat. Rainer's spell landed directly on his target's chest flinging the retched beast from the ship and into Red River. My shot was not so precise. It hit the vampire bat's left wing, which caused the beast to screech at us. The high-pitched wail stabbed my ears like a million knives. I covered them with my paws, but it gave little relief. Rainer fired again sending the other vampire bat off the ship and into the dark waters below.

There were dozens more buzzing above us like pesky bugs. We ducked when one swooped in and sliced at us with its razor-sharp claws. The deck of the ship was in chaos as the Elven Warriors battled the Vampire bats. Some used bow and arrow, picking off the bats as they dove in for a chance to knock an elf into the waters below. I watched as a young elf met just that fate and tumbled over the rail into the darkness.

"Watch out!" Rainer barked as another winged creature dove toward us.

I raised my wand, but found myself frozen, unable to cast a spell to save myself. The creature closed in fast, but my brother tackled me just as its claws missed my furry face.

"What are you doing?" I asked slightly annoyed.

"Saving your life!" Rainer quickly stood up and began searching for something in the chaos of our ship.

"What are you looking for, Rainer?"

"The King and Queen!" he replied.

A bright flash of light exploded at the far end of the ship, which was now rocking violently back and forth.

"What was that?" Rainer asked. He ran off before I could venture a guess, but I was pretty certain that I knew what had just happened.

I followed my brother as he moved through the battle like a maze, ducking and dodging arrows and swords. A Vampire bat jumped in front of him, but Rainer blasted the beast out of the way without hesitating. It was actually pretty impressive to see his courage.

When we reached the far end of the ship where we had seen the light, I caught my first glimpse of our plot taking form. Sorcerer LaCroiux held the queen around the neck as the king pleaded for her release. LaCroiux wore a long gray robe with a hood to guard his face, but I could feel his presence.

"Release her!" Rainer demanded. He held his wand at the ready. After standing there looking back and forth between LaCroiux and Rainer for a moment attempting to figure out who I should be pointing my wand at I chose Rainer...and then quickly swung it over to LaCroiux before my brother noticed.

Am I supposed to reveal I'm a bad guy yet? I thought.

"Let her go, now!" my brother barked. He looked so calm and courageous. I found myself proud of him just when I should have wished for Rainer to crumble under the pressure.

I could barely see the glimmer in my master's eye hidden in the shadow of his hood, but it was there. Everything was going according to his plan, and now it was time for his next move.

LaCroiux released the queen, who rushed back into King Steven's awaiting arms. Just as he grabbed her and pulled her close LaCroiux struck.

"Portio!" He yelled. A bright orange light escaped his hand. It moved through the air like it was riding a wave into shore before reaching the king and queen and engulfing them. It grew brighter by the second until it hurt my eyes to watch.

I closed my eyes and turned away. When the brightness diminished they were gone. The only thing remaining was the wicked yellow smile of Sorcerer Pierre LaCroiux, which gleamed from his shadowy face.

"NO!" Rainer cried. His panicked voice sent a chill up my spine. He reacted so quickly, firing spell after spell in a dazzling array of light directly at my master.

LaCroiux calmly deflected each spell seemingly sorting them by color into certain directions. Then, when he seemed to have grown tired of this sad attempt at an attack, he mustered up a fireball and hurled it into Rainer's chest. My brother collapsed.

"Rainer," I ran to his aid. He was breathing, but was unconscious and very warm to the touch, yet not burned. "What are you doing?" I angrily questioned my master.

"Ending this," LaCroiux removed his hood. His long braided beard emerged first against the moonlight. He walked toward my wounded brother like an animal stalks its prey. There was a glint of red in his eyes.

"No," I began to say when LaCroiux grabbed me by the neck and lifted me up. My paws dangled in the air, and I couldn't breathe.

"Retrieve the stone, Ethan." Then, he flung me down on top of Rainer. Another flash of orange light burned my eyes and then it was completely dark.

BATTLE OF BROTHERS

5

"Ethan!" My brother called "Ethan, get up!

I knew when I opened my eyes I would no longer be on the ship, just like the king and queen vanished. Sorcerer LaCroiux had transported them somewhere using his powers. I also had a pretty good idea where Rainer and I ended up...Cadieux Castle. "Retrieve the stone, Ethan," LaCroiux's words echoed in my head. He would have to send us back to the castle for me to retrieve the last emerald of power. I was alarmed at what I saw outside the castle when I opened my eyes...a battle!

"Get up, NOW!" Rainer yelled as he pulled me up off the ground.

My eyes were definitely wide open. The castle was under attack. Sorcerer LaCroiux had given me assistance in the form of hundreds of wolverines and a few large trolls. The Elven Warriors valiantly defended the castle, as did our father. He was directly in the middle of the battlefield fending off two or three wolverines at a time.

"We have to help father!" Rainer said as he continued to pull me toward the action.

I personally didn't want any part of this battle. I wanted to find a way through it and into the castle. Searching through the groups of Elven Warriors and wolverines, I found a path to the back gate. Rainer stopped me.

"Where are you going?"

Do I zap him or play along? I wondered. Then I remembered that I would need his help to enter the room where the emerald was hidden so I played along. I picked the first wolverine I saw and blasted him in the back.

"Great shot, Ethan!" my brother cheered.

A smile crept across my face. I blasted two more. It felt good. **Don't shoot the elves.** I reminded myself. Besides they would be my servants soon.

I suddenly realized that my father, brother and I had formed a triangle defense so no enemy could sneak up behind us. We were easily fending off LaCroiux's mighty henchmen.

"Rainer! Ethan!" our father called. "I need you both to get to the castle."

I immediately began searching for the safest route.

"I can help, father!" Rainer replied.

"I need you two protecting the princess."

That seemed to be all Rainer needed to hear, and we were off toward the castle. Once we reached the back gate we slipped inside and quickly found the princess. The castle shook as the monstrous trolls hammered away on the walls with their meaty fists trying to punch a hole through the stones. Fortunately, this castle was well built and would keep them at bay long enough for me to steal the emerald and end this insanity.

The young princess was crying when we arrived, and her uncle Cragon Cadieux was in the room. I gasped at the sight of him.

"Thank goodness you have arrived. I fear for the princess's safety," The strong, young elven prince claimed.

"Yeah, sure," I muttered, but no one seemed to hear me.

"Why are you not with my brother?" The prince questioned.

Like you don't know, I sarcastically thought. The prince sure seemed to be laying this act on thick. He knows exactly what happened on the boat, and outside the castle. He's behind it all. But, he doesn't know how I'm going to ruin his well thought out plans.

The castle shook violently again and again. With each thunderous boom, the princess cried out. A young elven girl named, Grace Tallon, held her against her chest attempting to sooth, Princess Merran Cadieux...who was now the rightful heir to the throne.

"Rainer Whizzenmog, how will your father stop this attack?"

Rainer ignored Prince Cragon. He appeared to be in deep thought, maybe trying to figure out his next move. I could almost feel his torment while he helplessly waited in the castle for the battle to end outside.

"We are losing the battle!"

"NO!" Rainer screamed. He was panting heavily trying to control his rage. I had never seen him like this before. He appeared torn.

"We have a secret weapon that could change our fortune, Rainer."

I immediately knew exactly what the prince was referring to...the last emerald.

"It is truly our only hope," Prince Cragon pleaded.

Rainer snapped his head at the prince and looked him up and down struggling to maintain eye contact. My brother was fighting within himself whether to open the hidden chamber and release the power within the emerald to save the castle, or hope that our father could stop the onslaught before it was too late.

That is when I decided to enter the fray with the good prince...for now. I calmly placed my hand upon my brother's shoulder. "Rainer, you have already failed father once tonight." I said reminding him that Sorcerer LaCroiux had kidnapped the king and queen under his guard. "Don't do it again."

A tear formed in Rainer's eye. "Let's go!" He gave in.

I instructed Grace to lock the door from the inside and hide until we returned. Something I had no intention of doing. Prince Cragon and I followed Rainer as he ran through the castle to the secluded wing where the emerald was hidden. He opened the secret doorway and we entered. I reached for the glowing green gemstone, but it magically lifted into the air and over my head. When I turned around, it was firmly in the grasp of my brother's paw. He sternly glared at me. Prince Cragon's face lit up with excitement at the very sight of the emerald.

"It's astonishing," Prince Cragon commented. A reflection off the emerald shown in his eyes.

I caught myself staring. It had grown uncomfortable in the small room, when the prince reached out for the emerald. I don't think he realized he was doing it. The gemstone was drawing him to it. Rainer pulled it away. I saw an opportunity and snatched it from his grasp. We all began to struggle attempting to pry the emerald from one another's grip. I freed it, when Prince Cragon punched me square in the snout. My eyes instantly began to tear, and I dropped the emerald. My brother snagged it using his wand and was off running. I zapped the prince with a freezing spell for socking me, and followed Rainer into the hallway.

As I turned the corner, a flash of light blinded me. Then I saw my master. He stood across from me with Rainer between us trapping him. By now, he had probably figured out that I was not playing on his team anymore, but if he wasn't certain, I was going to make it crystal clear.

"Give it to me, brother." I demanded.

Rainer responded by pointing his wand at me. He began to back into the wall feeling

LaCroiux's presence creeping up behind him. We converged on my brother. Rainer frantically swung his wand between us, pointing it at me, then LaCroiux and back again.

I reached out for the emerald and Rainer swatted at me. When our paws collided I felt a warm sensation again as the orange light reappeared. This time I heard a loud snap and everything again went black.

When we reappeared, I again found myself in a familiar place, but I knew that Rainer would not recognize our location. We were deep within the Wolverine Forest...my new home.

It was eerily quiet within the forest, as it should be since most of its inhabitants were currently at the castle. A calming sensation settled into my previously rigid body. I felt my paws relax and conform to the dirty forest floor. Inhaling deeply, the aroma of the forest zoomed through me. An evil smile overtook my face. One

I couldn't resist even if I tried. I now realized that only my brother stood between me and the emerald. Sorcerer LaCroiux made certain of that by sending us here alone.

"Rainer? Where are you, my brother?"

I listened to the forest talking to me. Birds chirped, leaves rustled against the slight breeze. Then, a sound. Something produced only by another stepping on a twig. I spun around. My wand at the ready

"I don't want to hurt you, Rainer. I only want the emerald."

A rustling sound rose from my left. "Never!" Rainer yelled as he ran toward me. He leaped and crashed into me, knocking my wand into a pile of leaves. We rolled along the forest floor throwing punches, which is an odd way for two wizards to settle anything, but our brotherly spat went much deeper than just this emerald. I grabbed hold of Rainer's fur and flung him against an exposed root. He yelled out in pain as I pinned him down.

"Where is the emerald?"

We were both breathing heavily. He struggled to free himself. "I have hidden it in the woods. You'll never find it."

Angered, I slammed his head against the ground. The ground trembled as my powers began to boil. As a wizard, I needed my wand to channel my powers into use, but as a sorcerer I was free to twist the elements around me.

I began to laugh. It was unexplainable. There was no good reason for laughter at this moment, but I couldn't control it. Fear had taken over Rainer's face. He had begun to realize just how much danger he was in.

"How could you do this, Ethan? How could you betray your own family?"

"My family?" My laughter ceased and was replaced with rage. The swell of emotions caused me to tear down a nearby tree. It crashed to the ground only a few feet behind me. "You ask me how I could betray my family? This family? I was never a part of the Whizzenmog family, Rainer. Our father never accepted me for what I wasn't."

"And what's that?"

I hesitated briefly deciding whether or not to answer truthfully, then I did, "You, Rainer. I was never as good and strong as you." I summoned more roots from the ground. They burst out tossing dirt into the air, which landed on Rainer's face and body covering his reddish-orange fur. I directed the roots to entangle his body and hold him to the ground.

"I will find the emerald, Rainer."

"Why are you so angry?" Rainer questioned.

I scoffed at the thought that he was unaware of the reason. "Do you remember the night I left? What you did to me? Humiliating me again! The look in our father's eyes that night said it all. I knew that I would never be as good as you in his eyes. That was the day he choose you, Rainer."

"That's not true."

"LIAR!" I screamed so loudly that the chirping birds leapt into the sky and flew away. "Liar," I repeated in a whisper.

"He was crushed when you didn't return, Ethan."

"Well...father won't have to worry now, because when I find that emerald, I am going to be the most powerful sorcerer in Mistasia. And you will call me King."

Rainer didn't respond. He just stared at me shocked, like I had just slapped him in the face.

"Now where did you hide the emerald, Rainer," I asked while searching around the forest.

When I turned my back, a bright blue flash caught my eye, followed by a snapping. I turned to see Rainer had broken free and escaped into the forest. I followed him forgetting about my wand in the leaves. It didn't matter. I had left that life behind now. I was a sorcerer and in this forest there were all the weapons I would ever need to defeat my brother.

First, I pulled the ground up under his feet causing him to trip. Rainer gathered himself and ran again. Next, I snapped a nearby limb free and flung it like an arrow. My brother blocked it with a charm and continued to flee. He hid behind a large tree, but I just yanked it from the ground, roots and all, before tossing it aside with a tremendous crash which crippled at least two more trees nearby.

Rainer attempted to slow me down with a freezing spell, but I pulled the dirt before me up like a shield. It froze, but I kicked my leg through and continued stalking him.

"Give me the emerald, Rainer!" I demanded.

Rainer started to run again, but I had had enough. A tree branch lodged into the ground blocking his path. He turned to the right and another landed in front of him; then two more encircled Rainer in a wooden prison.

"There's no escaping this forest, Rainer!" I stuck my face between two branches. "For so long, I envied you. Now, I pity you. I will not ask you again."

Rainer pointed to a bush located between two trees just a short distance away. Underneath, I could see a green glow. My heart began to quicken as I reached underneath and grabbed hold of the solid stone. I pulled it out and focused on the object in my hand. It was green in color, but was not the emerald...just a mere rock.

"Rainer!" I yelled in frustration, but when I turned around he was gone again. He had escaped from my trap and disappeared into the forest. I closed my eyes and knelt to the ground. Placing my paw along the forest floor I calmed myself. I could feel the vibrations flowing to me from my right side. I dashed off in pursuit.

The forest quickly thinned and I found myself at its edge. Before me was a clearing. In the distance, Rainer ran for the shelter of a small house. I dashed toward him running faster than I had ever gone in my life. Just before I reached him, Rainer gripped the emerald tightly in his hands and was chanting something.

I didn't have the time to reach him, when the ground began to tremble. I skidded to a halt. That was when I noticed our family's crest upon the large wooden door. This was our old family home from centuries ago, before we became the protectors to the king. The land had claimed most of the house; only this door remained visible under the green vines, and tall grass.

The emerald began to glow brightly in Rainer's palms. The wooden door began to change. It started to swirl around and around. Flashes of light spun at great speed. Rainer glanced at me for a single moment and then jumped into the portal. He had vanished.

I had to follow. I ran the short remaining distance and jumped, crashing into the decaying wooden door. I burst through into the dark and dirty room behind. The portal was gone, Rainer was gone, and most importantly...the emerald was gone with him.

I was crushed. My hope for greatness had just vanished before my eyes. I pulled myself out of the wreckage and stepped out into the grass. Standing at the edge of the forest was my master, Sorcerer LaCroiux. Fear overtook me.

PUNISHMENT

<u>6</u>

Sorcerer LaCroiux's eyes were fixated upon me. **How much had he seen? Did he know that my brother had escaped? Did he know Rainer had the emerald?** All these thoughts raced through my mind. My head was swimming, my stomach flipped with fear. I quickly got my answer.

The elder elven sorcerer lashed out. He lifted me into the air. I floated above the ground as the wind carried me toward my master. LaCroiux briskly guided me to the edge of the forest and then released his grip on me. I crashed, landing hard on my side. My elbow lodged into my ribs knocking the wind from my lungs. I gasped for air as LaCroiux picked me up by my neck with his bony fingers sticking into my fur. He still hadn't spoken to me.

Our eyes meet for a brief moment. It frightened me to see into his devilish soul from such a close distance. I struggled to speak causing LaCroiux's head to tilt in an odd fashion. A smug grin invaded his old slightly wrinkled skin.

"Speak up, Ethan." Then he released his grip and I fell back to the ground. "Where is the emerald you ignorant fool?"

"It is gone." I braced for an attack, but he didn't strike.

"Gone?"

"My brother stole it from me and then vanished into some kind of spinning portal. I chased after him, but it disappeared before I could follow."

Sorcerer LaCroiux stared at the broken door in the distance where he must have witnessed my brother's disappearance.

"You have failed me, Ethan. You're father was right. You are a disappointment."

My body trembled. I couldn't bring myself to look at my master. All the strength and power I had felt just a few short moments ago was now gone. I was left cowering like a small child.

"You will have to pay for your failure, Ethan." The powerful sorcerer didn't hesitate.

He tossed a bright blue fireball at me. It engulfed me. At first it actually felt cool around my body, but at the snap of his fingers the color changed to a scorching white and the intense heat ripped through my body. I could smell my skin burning. The pain was excruciating. I screamed for him to stop, but he continued. My fur began to burst into flames and crumble from my body. The skin underneath was covered in heat blisters, which began to burst and then boil under the tremendous heat directly on my skin. Sorcerer LaCroiux was cooking me alive. My skin began to peel and stretch revealing a scaly layer underneath. I couldn't take much more. I wished for death, but then the pain stopped. My vision began to blur and fade to black. I collapsed to the ground and passed out.

When I awoke, we were no longer in Wolverine Forest. LaCroiux had taken us back to Cadieux Castle. He had let me live. I found myself on the stone cold floor of my father's bedroom. I was alone. I struggled to my feet and stumbled into a wooden chair, barely catching myself before I fell to the floor. I pulled myself along the wall to the bed. My chest felt tight and my side hurt. I began to cry when I saw the skin on my arms. There was no longer any fur. It was completely gone. My skin was scaly and had a brownish-yellow color, like I was sickly. I lifted my head slowly almost too afraid to glance in the mirror and see my reflection. I gasped aloud at the sight of myself.

"NO!" I screamed. I now resembled some hideously deformed creature, a cross between a snake and an elf. My eyes were deep red and bulging from the sides of my head, with two large fangs and a forked tongue.

LaCroiux had exacted his punishment for me losing the emerald of power. I would forever remember my failure.

I sat alone in my father's room. The sun had risen and begun to set again, when the door creaked open and three elven warriors entered with swords drawn. They stepped to the side as

Sorcerer LaCroiux swooped in with a gleeful smile and joyous tone in his voice as though he had never been mad at me.

"Ethan! You are going to miss the celebration!" His demeanor was a far cry from our last encounter. His appearance had changed drastically too, as he now wore royal robes; a long white robe with gold and purple designs along one side and a metal staff with an empty place in the top which looked like it was made to hold something specific. "Come Ethan, we are requested at this celebration!"

I followed LaCroiux to the upper most part of the castle that overlooked the village. Gathered below was the entire population of Cadieux. I stood quietly beside my master as we waited patiently, but I dared not ask why. I was afraid to even look in his direction, so I just stared at the ground allowing me to notice that even my feet had changed. They now looked like lizard claws of the same color as my skin. One tear streamed down my scaly cheek.

Music began to blare. The crowd began to make noise, some cheered, some gasped and other cried as I did.

Then Cragon Cadieux walked from the opening out onto the balcony joining LaCroiux and me. He was wearing the king's robes. Long, thick black material with the royal colors woven in all around the edges...purple and gold just like LaCroiux's. Cragon wore a smile that beamed from ear to ear. He had won. The plot against his own brother had materialized almost exactly the way he and my master had planned...except for the emerald, for which I paid dearly.

Grace Tallon emerged behind Cragon. She looked distraught as she carried the young elven princess in her arms. Her uncle turned and removed Princess Merran from her care giver's unwilling release. Grace was quickly pulled back and escorted away. The crowd erupted in a chaotic array of yelling, with some cheering mixed in. Then the moment every inhabitant of Mistasia would regret took place. Sorcerer LaCroiux carefully placed the crown of King

Steven on the top of his brother's head. At that instant, King Cragon Cadieux emerged victorious before all of Mistasia.

REDEMPTION

7

It was extremely difficult for me to live in Cadieux Castle for many years after my father's death at the hands of my master's Wolverine Army. I knew I was mostly responsible for his demise. I was forced to spend my nights in my father's old room. I slept very little, and when I would drift off, I'd awake from terrible nightmares. In each terrifying dream I was the one that killed my father, even though I wasn't sure how he had died. I never saw him after Rainer and I left him in the fields between Cadieux Village and the castle. The lack of sleep made me uncomfortable in my tight, dry skin. It itched all the time. Some nights I wouldn't even make it to the dreams about my father because my skin would burn so badly, just as it did the day LaCroiux turned me into this...this thing.

Rainer never returned. Sometimes I would sneak away and watch from the edge of the forest with the magnifinder LaCroiux made hoping to see my brother return...with the emerald in hand.

I spent my existence in servitude to my master and the king.

Recently, LaCroiux returned to the castle in a flash as he did on most occasions, but this time with a vibrant smile. He called to me immediately. He pulled me inside the castle and into a secluded room in a far wing.

"Do you recognize this room, Ethan?"

I searched the small darkened room for any clue as to where we were. Then suddenly, an image of the emerald glowing brightly in the center of the room emerged in my mind.

"The emerald!"

"Yes," LaCroiux acknowledged my wide-eyed recognition. "I have located your brother, Ethan. Here is your opportunity to redeem yourself."

"Yes, I'll do anything, master?"

"I have discovered a way to reopen the portal that your brother created using the emerald of power so many years ago. Now, you will go through the portal and lure him here," LaCroiux said as he grabbed me by the arm and led me back into the hallway.

An orange flash of light meant we were travelling. Now we were in the Wolverine Forest.

"Aren't I to steal the emerald?" I asked

"I doubt very much that Rainer will carelessly leave it laying about for you to steal, so we need to make him want to return...and return with the emerald."

"What must I do?"

"You will go through the portal and steal something from him. His family."

"What?" I responded.

"His grand child, a girl. You will kidnap her, Ethan, and bring here to Mistasia."

LaCroiux explained how I would need to enter the portal, travel through the woods and then enter a house just beyond. Inside would be a young girl. He handed me a white pouch, within it was a powder that would reopen the portal allowing me to return to Mistasia with the girl.

He grabbed a handful of the powder from the pouch and tossed it at my feet. The ground began to shake and tremble. Then it started to spin and swirl. I had seen this once before, when my brother disappeared forever. **Was LaCroiux tricking me? Was he punishing me one last time? Would the ground open up and I be sucked down into the depths never to be seen again?**

I would soon find out. I felt a tugging on my feet, and I began to sink into the portal. LaCroiux smiled.

Just as I began to feel the portal pulling me in, Sorcerer LaCroiux hit me with a blast of ferocious wind and knocked me to the ground.

"We have company," he pointed to two Elven Warriors tracking through the forest. "Despose of them. Then use the powder to reopen another portal." He pointed to the portal as it closed. Sorcerer LaCroiux vanished in a flash with a single tap of his staff upon the ground.

I tracked through Wolverine Forest. I stopped and inhaled deeply. The scent of elves was unmistakable upon the air, sweet and fruity as it entered my reptilian nostrils. They were easy to find.

I slithered up behind them; Grace Tallon, guardian to Princess Merran Cadieux, and Mecca Begron, an elven warrior.

"Just two elves? I am hurt to know your princess thinks so little of me that she believes it takes only two Elven warriors to defeat me." I mocked.

Grace spun aiming her meager arrow directly at me. I felt laughter begin within my tainted heart. She truly believed she could stop me with a single arrow? It would take hundreds. I faked a panic and placed my hands in the air.

"I surrender."

"Really?" Mecca blurted out in astonishment.

"No," I replied with a laugh, confusing the simple-minded elf.

Grace's temper flared. She fired her arrow, but I summoned a burst of wind with a wave of my hand directing the arrow toward Mecca.

The muscular elven warrior wore armor, yet jumped out of the way just in time. It pierced the ground where he had been. Mecca brandished his sword and slashed at me.

I danced away from each attempt while laughing. **These two were the best warriors the princess could send to stop me? What a joke.** I had a task to perform. This battle was becoming bothersome. I gritted my teeth and blasted Mecca with a gust of wind knocking him to the ground. Then, I summoned tree roots around the fallen warrior. Roots burst free from the soil wrapping themselves around Mecca, trapping him.

"Grace, run!" Mecca shouted as he struggled to free himself.

I spun toward Grace. She ran.

For a moment, I wondered if I should chase.

"Dispose of them!" my master's voice echoed in my head.

I chased the fleet-footed warrior through the forest. Grace ducked under roots and between the trees. Her sweet scent led me directly to her. I discovered her hiding behind a group of intertwined tree trucks.

"Tell me, Grace Tallon." I whispered in her ear after slinking up beside her unnoticed.

She turned to face me and raised her bow and arrow.

"How do you think you're going to stop me? Do you really believe you alone can defeat me? I've already defeated your weak friend."

"Just give me one good shot, Whizzenmog. That's all I need." Grace defiantly replied.

We glared at each other. I stalled her as my next attack approached. A rhythmic rustling emerged in the distance. A wicked smirk overcame my scaly face. A new scent reached my nostrils. Wolverines. Their strong, pungent odor was distinctive and overpowering in small numbers. This approaching scent was nearly deadly to those not accustom to it.

"This is my cue to leave, my dear. Tell the princess I'll take care of everything. It was good to see you...for the last time."

I moved with great haste back toward the Whizzenmog dwelling just outside Wolverine Forest.

There would be the perfect place to reopen the portal. My large reptilian feet stood firmly in the short wet grass at the edge of the forest. The sun was setting with a pink glow changing the color of the sky around it to light purple.

I closed my eyes to compose myself for a moment. The excitement of my redemption was overwhelming. My heart pulsed at great speed, racing my blood through my body.

A sudden rush stabbed the air behind me. I turned just in time to block an arrow that would have struck me in the back.

"Tallon!," I hissed.

The two elven warriors had somehow survived and raced toward me.

"Don't move, Whizzenmog!" Grace barked. "It's over!"

"Over?" I questioned the crazy thoughts of a diluted warrior. "You are too weak to defeat me?"

"I am far from weak, Whizzenmog. You are weak. Your whole family was nothing but thieves and betrayers," The angered elf scolded.

"My family betrayed me!" I screamed in pain. "It was my brother who turned out to be weak."

"I heard you helped him steal the last emerald," Grace replied arrow now pointed at my chest.

"No, but I will retrieve it from him." I removed the small pouch given to me by LaCroiux and poured a sand-like powder into my palm. I leapt back into the air and tossed the powder on the wooden door of the old Whizzenmog home.

A bright light flashed followed by rushing winds.

The elven warriors struggled in the tall grass.

The wooden door had changed. It was now a spinning vortex of colors. The colors slowly faded as did the powerful wind. When the colors had completely faded, all that was left in the doorway was a spinning black portal that resembled the nighttime sky.

Mecca stood up in the grass and yelled, "Grace, stop him! He's entering the portal to Greenville!"

I leapt into the portal, but Grace Tallon latched onto me as I entered the spinning black hole. We entered together and spun violently. She released her grip on me inside. The dizziness forced my eyes to shut.

When I reopened my eyes, I was alone. Grace wasn't near me. The forest was enormously tall. The blades of grass blocked my vision. I lifted my head. **That's better**, I thought. I was very low to the ground. It was quite disorienting. The trees were so tall here. I tried to move my legs, but felt my hips slide to the side. I looked back and noticed I had no legs, but my scaly body stretched out into the grass and disappeared. I lifted my hind end and there was a tail, with the white pouch at the very end. I shook with fear and heard an odd sound. I did it again and the sound returned. It was coming from me. My tail was rattling. I realized I had transformed into a snake.

I panicked. I needed to return to Mistasia as quickly as possible. I slithered through the grass. It wasn't very long until I reached the edge of this forest. Here it was open and raining. The grass was now shorter. In the distance was an elven-like figure sitting. She was holding a unique object above her head deflecting the water away from her body. Behind her was a home, quite a bit larger than the ones the elves called home in Mistasia.

A voice called out to her. She didn't respond. I couldn't understand what they were saying, because the rain was running down my head and across my back. I could smell the fresh water along my nostrils. I lapped at it with my forked tongue.

This was the girl that I was to retrieve. This was Rainer's grandchild. The one I must steal. It was my redemption. She stood up and walked toward the opening in the side of the home. I began to thrash my tail back and forth propelling myself across the slick grass. I was gaining on her. She entered the home and disappeared into the darkness. I slid off the grass and scratched my underbelly along a stiff rocky substance just before the door. I heard more voices calling out, but I ignored them. I was completely focused on her. I could see the funny-looking object still above her head, but her body was hidden behind a dark material. I now found myself gliding across a new substance. It was like grass, but darker and itchy. I lifted my head again as I move around to see the young girl sitting and crying.

Here was my opportunity, my redemption. I just needed to wrap myself around her and she would be mine! I sprung forward. My fangs exposed and tongue lashing. She screamed.

Sweat Redemption.

Phillip & Whizzy Trilogy

LAND OF MISTASIA

Christopher M. Purrett

www.Purrett.com

CHAPTERS

PHILLIP HARPER

1

My name is Phillip Harper. I live in a small town called Greenville. I am your average 14-year-old boy; my body feels weird, I'm afraid of girls and am terrified of school...mostly because of Billy Lawton, but that's another story. But you'll never even guess what happened to my friend and me this summer. It's the most amazing story and I'll tell you all about it, if you want me to.

We saved the world...well not our world, but Mistasia. "Mistasia?" you ask...never heard of it? Well neither had my friend, Whizzy, and me, but it exists. Really...I swear.

It all started at the end of last school year...

SUMMER COULDN'T COME SOON ENOUGH

2

It was the last day of 8th grade and my mom was driving me to school. I only lived a block away on Violet Lane, but it was raining out and my mom didn't want me getting wet.

So I jumped into the back of our dirty, black car, set my worn out backpack in the seat beside me and buckled up.

"All buckled up, Phillip?" My mom still treated me like I was in Kindergarten sometimes. I think it's because I'm an only child...so to her I will forever be her little baby boy. The one problem with that was now I was nearly six feet tall and closer to driving the family car to school myself than learning how to walk or go potty. Most of the time I just let it go. She didn't mean any harm.

"Yes, mom." I replied trying not to sound too annoyed.

She started up the engine, which sounded a little rough. This car was nearly as old as me, but we couldn't afford a new one. We weren't very wealthy...that was why I had also been using the same backpack all through middle school and most of my clothes were too short. I had gone through another growth spurt this school year and now most of my shirts looked like I had no sleeves and my pants showed my ankles.

The school bully, Billy Lawton, always teased me. "You expectin' a flood, Harper? Looks like you're worried about getting' your pants wet." I hated Billy! He picked on me everyday, but today would be his last shot until high school. We were about to start summer vacation and it couldn't come soon enough.

It didn't take very long for us to arrive, only a minute or two. My mom turned right onto Orange Avenue...the one main road directly through Greenville. All the schools for our town sit next to each other on Green Circle. The high school, where I will go next year is in the middle with the elementary on the left and the middle school on the right. These buildings were pretty old. My mom and dad both went to school here too.

As we pulled up in front of Greenville Middle School the sun tried to peek out from the massive dark gray clouds that had consumed the sky. For a slight instant a sliver of sunlight dashed toward the ground like a spotlight on a stage. It only lasted for a few seconds and then the sun was swallowed up by another uniquely shaped cloud. It looked like a taco, which reminded me that I had forgotten to eat breakfast this morning and was hungry.

I always had a hard time eating breakfast because my stomach was turning in knots.

"Bye, Mom!" I yelled as I started to open the door. The car door bumped the car next to ours. My stomach flipped. I hurried out to check the beautiful, expensive, white car for damage. Somehow there was no mark, just some dirt. "Thank God!" I was relieved.

"Everything alright, Phillip?" My mom questioned through the passenger window. She had a worried look on her face.

"Fine. Everything's fine."

"Please, be careful." She always worried about me. Especially since I was quite clumsy. "Sometimes I pray that you will just come home in one piece, honey." She smiled at me and waved goodbye.

I stood on the sidewalk as she drove away. Then I remembered that there was some crackers in my backpack; I was hoping food would cure my stomach pains. I rummaged around inside my bag as it started to rain harder. Fumbling around, I dropped my notebook on the wet sidewalk. A gust of wind began blowing the pages open. "Darn It." Quickly. I gathered my notebook and backpack and ran towards the school. Running was a problem for me. My big feet and general lack of coordination seemed to end any attempt at speed or grace. Today was no different. A long strap from my backpack dragged on the ground, and of course...I stepped on it. I tumbled like a twisted ballerina, which for a 14-year-old-boy isn't the way to go. I landed very ungracefully on my belly. I could hear laughter rise out of the entryway. I looked up to see three 7th grade girls who had just witnessed my non-athletic moment. My stomach turned like someone was ringing out water from a sponge. "This day can't end soon enough."

A loud voice from behind barked at the giggling girls, "What are you geeks laughing at? Huh? Oh, thanks for the help!" I didn't need to turn around to recognize his sarcastic voice. It was my best friend, Michael Whizzenmog the third, but I called him "Whizzy". "You alright, Phillip?" He asked while helping me get back to my feet. He shot another evil look at the girls who now moved inside.

"Thanks, Whizzy." I moaned.

"Man, you are all wet. Did you bring another shirt?"

"No," I replied. "Don't worry about it. I'm fine."

We walked inside Greenville Middle School for the last time. It would have probably been a good feeling had I not looked like I showered in my clothes. Everyone stared even more than normal as I walked down the hall toward my locker. You see I'm the tallest kid in our school...that is why I can't wait to go to the high school next year. I stick out like a tree in a field of shrubs. It doesn't help that my best friend is on the shorter side.

Whizzy has always been rather small. He only comes to my chest. Even his twin sister, Rachel is taller than him. That hasn't helped his demeanor either. You know how the smallest dog barks the loudest? That's Whizzy. You would think that I would be the one protecting him, but it's always been the other way around.

After collecting my stuff, Whizzy and I went to his locker. While he cleared out junk from the past school year, I watched the usual daily gatherings in the hallway. It was the same everyday.

A group of 6th grade girls stood together in a huddle, yet no one talked. Laughter would erupt periodically as they texted one another on their cell phones. The blonde-haired girl with braces held her hand over her mouth so no one would notice her smile, but everyone knew she had braces. Her friend wore the same ponytail. It never changed. I wondered if it was real hair or just a wig that she put on every morning.

"Did you study for the math exam?" Whizzy asked.

"Yeah. It should be pretty easy."

"I don't know. I just don't get it."

"Whizzy, we have been studying this all year. How can you still not get it?" I didn't believe that Whizzy had even attempted to look at the study guide for this exam. He hated math...well mainly our teacher Mr. Quinch. "You should have asked me for help."

"I know."

I laid my head back against the lockers waiting for Whizzy to gather his book when I saw his sister, Rachel Whizzenmog, walking toward us with a group of her friends.

She was beautiful. Her reddish-brown hair came down to her shoulders. She had emerald green eyes and had developed a young woman's figure over the past year. The whole school had noticed that. Unlike Whizzy and I, Rachel was very popular. The funny thing was that Rachel and Whizzy almost didn't even talk.

They ignored each other most of the time, and when they did talk it was more like arguing. I never understood them. How could twins dislike each other so much?

I watched her almost glide up to the locker beside her brother's. As she walked past, I pulled my head forward to watch not knowing my hair was caught in the locker hinge. I pulled a tuft of hair out. It hurt.

"What are you doing? Are you checking out my sister?" He slapped me in the chest. "You traitor." Whizzy walked away quickly leaving me at the lockers with Rachel and her entourage.

"Hi." I said to Rachel with a smile.

She laughed. She had always considered me a dork, partly because I was an awkward klutz and partly guilt by association. Being Whizzy's best friend hadn't endeared me to Rachel.

My stomach flipped again. Luckily, I hadn't eaten my crackers because I probably would have thrown up. I dashed off behind Whizzy.

We sat in our 1st hour math class awaiting the bell to ring. It hadn't been the worst start to a day this year, but it hopefully wouldn't get worse.

"Only seven hours left. Summer couldn't come soon enough!"

ATTACK OF THE BULLY, BILLY LAWTON

3

The school day was almost over. I had made it through my math, science and French tests without any major disasters. It was the last hour, and we were being released to the football field for our year-ending assembly.

Every year before summer our Principal, Mr. Deters, would talk to us about responsibility and safety. Nobody ever paid any attention.

I walked out through the gym doors and followed the other kids to the football bleachers. Sitting at the top was Whizzy. He waved at me.

The gray clouds had moved on and now it was very sunny and quite hot.

I noticed that Whizzy was standing when I reached the top of the bleachers.

"Hey, Phillip, watch this." He pointed at a couple of 6th grade boys. As they started to sit, Whizzy let out a strange giggle. He grabbed my arm in anticipation. The boys lowered their butts and sat on the metal seats. They burst back up like being ejected from a toaster and grabbed their backsides. Whizzy exploded into laughter. "Did you see that?"

"Whizzy" I scolded.

"Come on, Phillip. That's funny. They burned their butts."

I just shook my head, and then proceeded to sit down and burn my butt.

Whizzy laughed even harder. I think he may have actually cried, but he hid his face.

Principal Deters began his speech, "Students. Thank you!" No one was clapping. "We have had another wonderful year here at Greenville Middle School. I want to congratulate this year's 8th grade class. You will be moving on

to our high school next year..." he continued to
assault us with his speech for the next forty-five
minutes. His bald- head reflected so much
sunlight that it appeared that his body was a
candle and his head a flame. I watched in
amazement thinking he was going to have the
worst sunburn tomorrow. Whizzy would probably
find that hysterical. I found it quite sad.
Boredom reigned, and I watched the different
groups of students...all not paying any attention
to Principal Deters either. Two boys in the
corner of the bleachers were slapping each
other's hands in some random punishment game.
The same group of 6th grade girls was texting on
their cell phones and snickering. They were most
definitely making fun of Principal Deters. I
continued to keep myself occupied watching the
other students when I noticed something strange.

   "Whizzy, look. Isn't that Billy Lawton
with Rachel?" I pointed directly below us about
twenty rows.

   "What the heck? No way!" You could tell
by the expression on Whizzy's face that he wasn't
happy. He never got along with his sister, but

having our biggest enemy becoming friends with Rachel wouldn't be in Whizzy's best interest. Or mine for that matter.

Billy made some peculiar gesture with his face, I assumed he was mocking Principal Deters, but I couldn't see Deters's face from all the sunlight beaming off his head. Rachel laughed. Way too hard I might add. Billy wasn't funny...believe me. Mean...yes. Funny...not at all.

Whizzy stood beside me stewing in anger. I swore his reddish hair had turned a little brighter. He gritted his teeth and clenched his fist.

"Calm down, Whizzy. There has to be an explanation."

"Billy Lawton...and my sister!"

He never really finished his thought aloud, but I figured it had something to do with inflicting pain and a lot of bad words.

Fortunately, Principal Deters had apparently finished his speech and announced that summer had started, because the student body erupted and everyone had leapt off the bleachers so quickly you could feel them sway forward.

Whizzy and I went back into the building to clean out our lockers and get our backpacks. The hallways were covered in papers that kids had tossed onto the floor. It had become something of a tradition at Greenville Middle School, but I wasn't quite sure why. Janitor Findley swept the papers into a pile as we went past. He gave a crooked smile. "Good summer boys."

We said thank you and walked out to where our moms would be picking us up.

Standing in front of the school, Whizzy and I planned our first day of summer vacation...baseball, bike riding and swimming!

"Hey, Wasn't!" a cruel voice blast. Then Whizzy shot forward and stumbled to keep his balance. It was Billy Lawton. He had pushed Whizzy from behind, but Whizzy quickly regained his balance. I, however, would have hit the pavement for sure.

Billy was quite large...not tall, but thick. His was between Whizzy and I in height, but probably weighted as much as us combined. His arms were so big that they stretched his sleeves. The girls at Greenville Middle School fawned over him...apparently including Rachel who was draped around one of Billy's large arms. It looked like she was hugging a tree branch.

"That's not his name, Billy" I responded. I could immediately tell that Whizzy wished I hadn't.

"He knows that, Phillip. Billy just isn't smart enough to pro-nounce it pro-per-ly." He over-enunciated.

Billy wasn't stupid, though we wished he were. The vein in Billy's neck pushed outward and his nose shrugged. I was well aware of what that meant. Whizzy had the unfortunate ability of pressing Billy's button's, which I still am not completely sure why he would want to...but Whizzy did it anyway.

Billy lunged at Whizzy and snatched him up in the air by his shirt. "Listen here, Wasn't! You keep that up and it's gonna be a long summer for you. We're gonna be seein' a lot of each other." He tossed Whizzy into me and we fell to the ground. "I'll see ya' round, Wasn't"

Then Billy did something I wished I had never seen. He kissed Rachel...ON THE LIPS! I almost vomited.

"Rachel!" Whizzy yelled. He struggled back to his feet. "Rachel, you cannot be serious? Billy. Billy Lawton?"

The Whizzenmog twins continued to argue until their mom picked them up.

"There's mom!" Whizzy bolted for the car, nearly getting run over.

I could faintly overhear Whizzy animatedly describing the kiss.

"Mom, he's lying!" Rachel yelled back as she entered the car.

I stood on the sidewalk and watched as the Whizzenmog family car drove away with them arguing inside.

"Bye, Whizzy." I said out loud. Standing next to me was a small girl. She gave me a sad look as if she felt sorry for me. "That's my best friend. He had to go."

I normally felt uncomfortable. I was used to that, but I wished the earth would open up and swallow me whole right about now. Then the bottom of my backpack broke open and spilled onto the ground. "Great day!"

I SPY WITH MY LITTLE EYE
4

The only day that tops the last day of school is the first day of summer. I was so excited when I awoke that I nearly bolted downstairs without changing clothes. I rummaged around my room looking for my favorite green t-shirt with a frog face on it. Then I pulled up my orange, brown and white checker-plaid shorts and began to move toward the door again, but out of the corner of my eye I noticed something move under the pile of clothes in my open closet.

My mom consistently hounded me about my closet. You see I used it more as a laundry hamper than a closet. There was only one shirt hung up. It was a bright yellow perfectly brand-spanking new shirt with stars and a rainbow on it that my parents had purchased at some cheap store in the Greenville Mall. I never wore it all school year. Beside it were a dozen empty hangers.

My eyes caught movement in the pile to the left again. My heart skipped a beat. *What is that?* I thought. It seemed really large. I hoped it was too large to be a spider. A chill shivered up my spine at the thought of a big, ugly, hairy spider with beady red eyes focusing on me. I looked around the room for something to move the clothes from a distance. A baseball bat would work...maybe a hockey stick.

In the far corner of the room between the window and my bed sat the large glass case for my pet frog, Sampson. The lid was ajar just enough for the slippery guy to escape.

"Sampson." I said with a sigh of relief. Reaching into the closet I moved the pile to find my plump brownish-green frog. He leapt into my hands. Ironically, he did have red beady eyes. "Hey, buddy. What you doing out of your case?

You need to be careful. I could have squashed you with a baseball bat." I petted him as I placed him back into the glass case and closed the lid.

Then I dashed downstairs.

Our home was pretty modest. Two bedrooms upstairs: mine and my parents. On the ground floor, a living room, small den, bathroom and the kitchen. Our kitchen was pretty small. The dining table took up much of the room, and it wasn't that large. It only seated four.

While I ate breakfast, my parents gave me a present.

"Here you go, Phillip. We are so proud of you!" My mom beamed. "I can't believe you are going into high school already. Then she wrapped her arms around me causing me to spill milk and cereal onto the table. Worse yet... she started to cry.

"Mom." I struggled to free myself. "Mom. It's not like I'm leaving."

"Alright, honey." My father interjected. "Leave the poor kid alone." My father always seemed to understand when my mom was being too...mom-like I guess is the best way to describe it. He just smiled at me and went back to work on his laptop computer. He wasn't home very much. He worked long hours in an office outside Greenville. I usually only saw him on the weekends.

"So." My mom exhaled deeply as she tried to compose herself. "Open your gift, Phillip." She was excited. My father even stopped typing on his computer to watch.

The box was rectangular in shape and wrapped in a purple paper. My mom had long thought that purple was my favorite color...it's blue. I think she might be color blind, because when she gave me the yellow shirt up in my closet last summer I recall her claiming it was white.

I began to pull back the wrapping paper and notice it was a shoebox. I started to get excited. I had been asking for new shoes for nearly the entire school year. The ones I had now were so tight that my toes were nearly permanently curled up from getting crammed into them everyday. I started to open the box with enthusiasm. Inside was a pair of dark blue sketchers.

"Oh, wow!" I jumped from my seat. "Thank you, Mom!" I gave her the biggest hug. Then ran to my father on the other side of the table. "Thanks," I said. He gave me a one-armed hug with a slight pat on the back. That was pretty good for him. My father wasn't the most affectionate man.

My father quickly changed the subject. "So what are your big plans for the first day of summer?"

"Whizzy and I are gonna play baseball, ride bikes and maybe go swimming." A rush of excitement came over me as I again realized that it was summer vacation.

While I changed into my new dark blue sketchers, my dad looked outside.

"It's not looking very good to the west. We're going to get some rain, Phillip."

I had a sinking feeling like letting the air out of a balloon. Leaning back in the chair I gave a sigh. "Well. I guess we can play some video games."

"I'll give you a ride, Phillip," My mom added.

I slid into the backseat of our dirty black car and buckled up. The engine roared and we started off.

Whizzy lived a couple blocks from me. My mom turned left onto Orange Avenue and headed up the road. I sat impatiently. The rain clouds moved in quickly. We hadn't even reached Scarlet Lane, the next block up, when the rain began to pelt our car. By the time we reached the next block, Golden Lane, it was all out pouring.

I watched the rain as it ran down the window. It split into two separate streams about halfway down. In the distance, outside the window was Umber Forest. As we approached Burgundy Drive, where Whizzy lived, something emerged from the treetops. It was huge. I couldn't tell what it was, but it seemed to be following us.

"That can't be," I said aloud.

"What was that, Phillip?"

"Oh. Nothing, Mom." I didn't want her to
think I was crazy. Looking out the window and
through the rain I wasn't able to locate the flying
object in the treetops again.

We turned right onto Burgundy Drive
and headed to the Whizzenmog's. This was the
place where the wealthy families of Greenville
lived. The homes were all recently built and
beautiful. I'll admit I dreamed of living in one of
these houses. They were three times the size of
ours, but still didn't compare to Whizzy's.

At the end of Burgundy Drive was the
oldest house in Greenville. Whizzy told me that
the house was older than Umber Forest. I am not
sure if I believe him though. It was certainly old,
and monstrous. I actually mean that it looks like
a monster. When you drive up to it at night and
the lights are on upstairs the house appears like
it has two large eyes staring you down while you
approach. It's was very unsettling the first time I
came over. I wouldn't even spend the night until
we were in 6th grade. They had a half circle
driveway at the end of Burgundy Drive.

When we got to the front doors it was raining so hard I struggled to open the car door against the wind.

"Have a good time, Phillip. Call me when you're ready to come home."

"Thanks, Mom!" I yelled as I dashed away. I am not sure if I would have been drier had I walked, but I certainly splashed enough water onto myself that I definitely wouldn't have been any wetter.

A large wooden canopy hung over the front doors. Two heavy wooden doors like you might see on a castle from the middle ages, with a large circular metal handle on each stood before me. I grabbed the handle on the right and banged it against the door. It was heavy. The house spanned out a great distance on either side from where I stood. I could barely make out the edges of the house against the rain.

Finally, the door creaked and then opened. My heart was already beating quickly due to my anticipation, but when the door opened and Rachel Whizzenmog was standing there, I almost fainted. She was glowing. Her hair pulled back in a ponytail showed her graceful neck.

Rachel was obviously not thrilled to see me. "Whizzy!" she yelled up the staircase directly behind her. Well not directly behind her...it was about ten feet behind her. "Whizzy, Phillip is here!" She yelled again. "Are you coming in or not?" She snapped and then walked away from the door.

I was mesmerized. *Move! Step inside!* I yelled at myself. My legs just wouldn't work.

Whizzy came bounding down the stairs skipping three at a time. "Phillip, get in here." He wasn't the most patient person. It must run in the family. "You are soaking wet." He exclaimed.

"Yeah! I didn't bring an umbrella."

Whizzy just laughed. "Cool shoes."

We had to change our plans because of the rain, but Whizzy didn't mind. He loved video games particularly a game called "Wizards and Sorcerers." We played...correction, he played and I sat and watched after he destroyed my wizard five minutes after we started. Whizzy continued on against beasts, demons and sorcerers for nearly two hours before ending in a fiery blaze of glory. He threw the controller to the ground and yelled, "Darn it! I can never get past this part."

I just shrugged my shoulders, because I hadn't ever made it past the first battle.

Whizzy's room was huge. It was bigger than my living room at home. He had posters hung covering nearly every last inch of the walls. I don't think his bed would even fit in my entire room. That is why we always played at his house..., which I didn't mind because he had the most awesome basement on the planet.

"What now?" Whizzy said with anger still in his voice. He picked up a red rubber ball and tossed it against a "Transformers" poster. It sped back to him, but he caught it easily. He continued to bounce it directly off "Megatron's" head while we talked.

I really wanted to play baseball. I had been waiting all school year for summer...mainly for that reason. From Whizzy's bedroom window I could see the Umber Forest. Remembering the image in the treetops, I began searching to find any motion. A black winged silhouette raced past the window. I jumped backward and tripped over a chair falling down on my butt. My chest felt like someone had just pulled my heart out.

"Phillip!" Whizzy yelled as the red rubber ball smacked into his face knocking him and his chair over. He fell on his back, legs in the air. "Ouch." Whizzy rolled over and stood up quickly hoping no one would notice he had fallen. "Ah, what the heck are you doing, Phillip?"

Whizzy had a red mark on his forehead. I didn't have the heart to tell him. He looked pretty upset, and I could tell he was blaming me for his injury. His eyes burned with the Whizzenmog fury. He had never fought with me, but I had seen those eyes directly before every altercation he had ever been in. He raised his arms in the air as if saying... "explain!"

"Something just flew past your window, and it was huge."

Whizzy pushed his face against the glass. "I don't see anything. You must be imagining."

He turned around to face me and the shape reappeared. I could feel my breath escape me. The expression I must have shown Whizzy had to prove that I was witnessing the image again.

He whirled back around, but the image had vanished again. "Stop foolin' round, Phillip. Come on; let's go to the basement." Before I could even respond Whizzy dashed past me and left the room. I heard him call me from down the hallway again.

I stood up and slowly walked toward the door. Before I left I had to look one last time. Nothing there. I exhaled deeply. I was glad. *AH!* Suddenly the thing was back. Just outside the window hovering. It was an eagle. It was very large. Bigger than the window...and that is saying something, because the windows in this house were twice the size of mine. It shrieked at me.

"What do you want?" I yelled out of fear.

"For you to come to the basement," Whizzy sarcastically replied from the bottom of the staircase.

I looked away from the window for a split second, but when I glanced back the eagle was gone.

BLACK-HOLE IN THE BACKYARD
5

Running as quickly as I could I bolted past Whizzy and headed straight for the basement door. Whizzy yelled for me to wait up, but I was gone.

I felt like I was going crazy, as if scientists had drilled into my head and were playing around inside to see what would happen. *'So Dr. Crazy if you press this part of the brain Phillip will see strange flying objects. Great Dr. Mental! If you press this part of his brain he will shout in pig-Latin and pass gas uncontrollably!'*

Once I entered Whizzy's basement everything changed.

"This is the coolest place ever!" I announced as if I had never been here before.

Standing at the bottom of the stairs, I gawked in amazement. To the left were a humongous flat screen 3D-televison and all sorts of cool electronics. Whizzy had at least three different types of gaming consoles, a blue-ray player and an audio system that could shake the walls when something blew up in a movie. In the middle of the room was possibly the most comfortable couch I had every sat on. Beyond that were a billiards table and a bowling alley...that's right an actual life-size bowling alley. In the opposite corner from the bowling lane was a basketball hoop and hockey goal. It was like the Whizzenmog's had an entire gymnasium in their basement. Now you see why I never minded that we always played at Whizzy's house instead of mine?

"What'cha wanna do?" Whizzy questioned. I could tell Whizzy didn't care what we played.

Where to start? I thought. There was so much excitement built up inside me I was about to burst.

"What's that smell?"

"I didn't do it!" I quickly denied any possible connection to the smell Whizzy was referring to. "At least I think I didn't." Maybe something could have slipped out during my feverish anticipation of actually having some fun.

"No. I don't mean THAT smell! It smells like wet dog down here." Whizzy noticed that the sliding glass door was wide open.

It was still raining...hard, and the carpet had gotten wet. Whizzy and I walked over to see who had left the door open. Rachel was standing in the grass, her burgundy colored umbrella above her with rainwater cascading off its sides. It looked like she was standing in an amusement park ride.

"Rachel," Whizzy yelled.

She didn't respond. He yelled again, but much louder this time. Rachel's face was somber. She must have been crying, but I had never seen her cry in all the years I had known her so I wasn't sure what that would look like. She slowly walked past us back into the house still carrying her umbrella, which just missed gouging out my eyeball. Rainwater drizzled off the tips of her umbrella and ran onto the carpet as she sat on the couch facing the television. Whizzy and I waited for some sign of life, but all we could see was her burgundy umbrella, still over her head, and the back of the couch.

"Should we go talk to her?" Whizzy whispered.

I wasn't equipped to deal with my own emotions, let alone a 14-year-old-girl's; I could only imagine what insane things were swirling around in her head...and I didn't want involvement in any of them.

"She's your sister," I responded.

"Yeah, but you like her," Whizzy snapped back. He had been saving that for the perfect time to throw it in my face.

"I...I don't. That's...not true," It was the best response I could come up with...I know it's lame.

But before Whizzy and I could decide who would lose this battle and have to confront Rachel, she blurted out, "Billy stood me up!"

Whizzy's eyes almost popped from his tiny head. I had an odd feeling of relief. Mostly because that meant she wouldn't be dating Billy anymore, but that also meant she was free to be my girlfriend. I started towards the couch to sit with her when she screamed. Then something yanked her by her feet off the couch. Her umbrella flew into the air.

Whizzy and I ran to help her. You'd never believe what we saw. Wrapped around her ankles was a thick, scaly, brownish-yellow snake. I followed its body along the carpet, but its head wasn't visible behind the couch. The snake was dragging Rachel across the carpet and around the couch. Whizzy reached her first and screamed like a little girl when he came face to face with the large diamond-headed snake with its golden sideways shaped eyes, forked tongue and sharp venomous fangs. He jumped backward and landed on my left foot. He weighed a lot for a small kid. I stumbled from the pain causing the both of us to crash to the carpet. Whizzy landed in my lap, which was both uncomfortable and awkward. The snake lurched at us, then continued to slither forward pulling Rachel behind it.

Everything was happening so quickly. The snake was almost to the open door. Rachel's mouth frantically moved, but I couldn't hear her. My mind was racing, and I felt nauseous.

Whizzy began angrily belching out questions, "Where did that snake come from? How did it get in here? What is it doing? Where is it taking her?"

The last question seemed the most ridiculous of them all. *Where was it taking her?*

Whizzy continued to uncontrollably blurt out questions, "Snakes don't eat people...do they? Is it gonna eat Rachel?"

I finally pushed Whizzy off me. He landed face first next to Rachel. She grabbed on to him, and then they locked hands. The snake continued to pull both of them. *This snake is really strong.* I thought.

Outside the rain started to wane. Suddenly, the eagle I had just seen at Whizzy's upstairs bedroom window swooped down and landed on the cement patio just outside the open sliding-glass door. It shrieked.

The venomous snake hissed and then shocked us all. It lunged forward and grabbed the door handle in its mouth and swung it closed before the eagle could enter.

The eagle spread its massive wings, which took up the entire frame of the door and shrieked again. Then it began pecking at the glass.

I grabbed Whizzy's legs. Now we made a strange train of interlocked bodies from the snake to Rachel, then Whizzy and finally me. I attempted to wrap my legs around the arm of the couch but couldn't. The snake released its scaly grip for an instant and smashed its tail into the glass. It scared me.

The glass fractured but didn't break. The fractures continued to splinter like a spider's-web streaking out in all directions across the doorframe until I couldn't even see the eagle outside any longer.

For some reason none of us used this opportunity to get up and run away from this obviously crazy snake. Instead we laid there motionless in complete shock watching the glass splinter.

The brownish-yellow, diamond-headed snake hissed once more and the glass turned an evil dark gray. It looked like a black hole from outer space consumed the doorway as it began swirling viciously.

I felt the pull and grabbed Whizzy even tighter.

The snake pivoted back toward us and snapped at Whizzy's face. He screamed and instinctively released his grip on Rachel to protect his face. The heinous snake seized the opportunity to wrap himself around Rachel again and quickly dragged her into the vortex.

"No," Whizzy yelled. "Rachel!"

I couldn't even speak. This couldn't be happening. I must be dreaming.

Then as quickly as the vortex started it exploded in a flash of white light blinding us both.

I don't know if we were knocked unconscious or how long we were laying there on the carpet, but it couldn't have been more than a few minutes.

The familiar sound of rain crept back into my ears. Then the rhythmic tapping on glass, and finally Whizzy springing up into a seated position.

"RACHEL!" my friend frantically ran for the sliding glass door, which was magically repaired. He checked it over before slinging it open and bursting outside into the wet grass. He didn't even acknowledge the massive eagle standing on the cement patio outside the door.

As I approached, the eagle tilted its head at me in a very peculiarly human way. I waited for a moment to see if it would speak, but that was absurd.

"Where is she, Phillip? Where did that thing take her?" Whizzy was twitching with rage. His eyes had transformed from blue to a fiery red. "I have to help her."

"You can, Whizzenmog!" a harsh female voice replied.

I instantly looked directly at the eagle standing beside me. Whizzy gave me an inquisitive look. I think he believed I had answered him. I pointed at the eagle, which didn't make Whizzy any happier.

"Stop foolin' around, Phillip."

"But I," I started to defend myself, but was interrupted by the same voice.

"You can save your sister, Michael Whizzenmog, but only if you listen to my directions."

I watched as the eagle's beak moved in exact sync with the words I could hear.

"That's just not right!" I said in amazement. "Did you just talk to us?"

"Yes, Phillip Harper, and we don't have much time. You both must listen to me if you are to save Rachel! We must go inside and close the door. It is the only way the portal will reopen. Please, you must hurry." The bird stood tall on its legs and flapped its massive wings leading us back into the basement. "Now close the door."

Whizzy did. The eagle shrieked in a unique pattern. The glass began to fracture the same way it had when the snake hit it with its tail.

Just seconds later the glass turned dark gray again and the vortex returned.

"Michael Whizzenmog, you must jump now." She demanded.

Whizzy's expression was hard to read. It was a mesh of confusion, anger and fear that really isn't a good look for anyone. He hesitated at the vortex.

Wind swirled around the room. My shirt billowed like a flag, and my hair stood off the side of my head.

Whizzy stepped up to the vortex, his back facing me. He turned slightly to look at me. Just then the eagle pushed Whizzy from behind with her giant wings. He fell into the vortex and disappeared.

"You are next, Phillip Harper!"

My stomach sank. I felt sick. She grabbed me and tossed me into the vortex. Then everything went black.

WHAT'S WRONG WITH ME? I'M ALL GREEN

6

I don't remember much except the frightening feeling of falling to my death. It was what I imagine it would be like to be flushed down the toilet...not something I recommend. It all happened in a few moments. A tiny dot of light appeared. It rapidly expanded. I landed softly on my back in plush, thick, green grass.

The sunlight was so bright I could barely open my eyes. Once my eyes adjusted they saw a colorful and beautiful place.

Before me was a field of tall bright green grass waving against the blowing wind. In the distance were enormous reddish-brown trees. They must be one hundred feet tall, because they seemed to reach to the sky, which was a pale shade of blue. Only a few sparse clouds hung in the sky.

"It's beautiful."

"Phillip?" Whizzy said in a surprised tone. "Is that you?"

"Yeah, of course it's me. Don't you...know...your...best fr-" I stammered at his appearance, because standing before me wasn't my best friend Michael Whizzenmog the third. It was a red, furry fox. "AHHHH!" I tried to run away, but my legs didn't respond. I slipped and fell on my face.

"What's happened to us?" Whizzy questioned. I could hear the concern in his voice. "She did this to us! I knew we couldn't trust her!"

"Who?" I asked with a mouth full of grass.

"That eagle."

The eagle! I had forgotten. How I am not quite sure, but it had been an eventful few minutes in my life. I started to push myself up when I noticed something weird. My hands were webbed...and green. I followed them up my arms to my chest and then down to my legs. ALL GREEN!

"What the...! Whizzy what's wrong with me? I'm sick! I think I'm dying!"

"No, Phillip Harper. You are a frog. An unusually large frog I might add."

Standing in the field thigh high in grass, was a slender white-haired girl. She wore tattered light brown pants and a flowing pale green shirt.

"Who the heck are you?" Whizzy demanded. It was apparent that his impatience hadn't altered like his physical appearance.

"My name is Grace Tallon, Whizzenmog, and lose the attitude. Or I won't help you find your sister."

Whizzy confronted her, "You took my sister?"

Grace pulled a sword from her side and pointed it at Whizzy's chest. "No, Whizzenmog. I did not. I was sent to save her."

"Save her?" I asked. "From the snake?"

Grace nodded. "I was sent to your world to save her from the King's treacherous henchmen, but I was too late."

"Where is it taking her? You better tell me." Whizzy clenched his furry paws into a

143

balled fist of rage. His black tipped tail even stood up.

"Or what Mr. Fox? You'll jump on my sword? In case you haven't noticed you are unarmed and standing at the tip of the blade of an Elven warrior."

"Elven warrior!" I was impressed and confused at the same time. I hadn't noticed her pointed ears until now. I remembered that in every story I had ever read about elves they had pointed ears. They also usually lived with Santa Claus at the North Pole and wrapped gifts for Christmas.

"Fine Elven warrior, where did that slithery twerp take my sister?...Please." Whizzy attempted to be nice. That was actually pretty good for him."

"And why am I green?" I added.

Grace stowed away her sword and helped me to my wobbly webbed feet.

"You have entered the Land of Mistasia, Phillip the Frog," She harshly replied. She wasn't the friendliest elf.

"Mistasia?" Whizzy and I both responded.

"Yes. King Cragon had your sister captured. I still do not know why. I was only sent to try and stop it, so I have no more information as to why. I do know that she has been taken to Cadieux Castle. Which rests beyond the Wolverine Forest, and past Dragon Lake. I am to lead you two there."

"But why aren't we human?" I really needed to know. It was driving me crazy.

"Just as I could not be Elven in your world, you cannot be human in mine. The reasons for your forms are your own. I cannot tell you why you have transfigured into a frog and a fox. That is for you both to discover on your own."

Whizzy and I shared a quick glance. This had been the strangest day of our lives. Should we believe Grace and follow her to Cadieux Castle to save Rachel or smack ourselves silly and hope that we wake up in Whizzy's basement?

"What is your decision? Do I lead you to Cadieux Castle or send you back to Greenville?" Grace Tallon coldly asked. She had a stern expression on her face.

"Lead the way, elf," Whizzy bravely answered.

I'LL SAVE YOU FROM THAT MUDDY SWIMMING POOL!

7

The Land of Mistasia didn't seem to be much different from our quiet hometown of Greenville at first glance, but I would soon discover Mistasia isn't all that it appears.

Whizzy and I kept pace behind the swift moving Elven warrior. I quickly understood why her name was Grace, she moved with an easy fluid motion, yet at a very rapid speed. It was very difficult for me. These webbed feet didn't grip well on the wet blades of grass. Whizzy on the other hand didn't have the same problems. He was, however, complaining about the heat. His furry body wasn't helping as we moved through the open field under the blazing sun.

It wasn't as hot as I would think it should be though. It must be fall in Mistasia. The tree leaves were reddish in color, which always meant that fall had arrived in Greenville. Was it the same here?

Grace reached the forest line first. There she waited for us. Whizzy reached next. He sat down on a stump. It was a couple of minutes before I arrived. I wasn't tired, just struggling to walk.

"Sorry. I keep slipping."

Grace smiled. "You will be better off on the dirt floor in the Wolverine Forest, Phillip the Frog. If not, you will not survive."

"Oh, that is reassuring."

"Before we enter, you both must understand the dangers that lay inside this forest. We are still a good distance from Cadieux Castle, but this forest is under the control of King Cragon's Wolverine Army-sinister, evil and ravenous beasts with razor sharp claws and teeth. They have unmatched endurance. These beasts are not to be fooled with."

Grace was funny in a unique way. She just said whatever was on her mind...whether it would scare us out of our minds or not. At this point I wasn't sure if I should cry or wet myself, but I also wasn't sure if I could do either of those things. How does a frog go to the bathroom?

"Are you ready?" She asked us as if we had any choice.

We both nodded.

Grace started to turn into the forest when we heard a loud rumbling in the sky. Grace yelled for us to run. In the distance, storm clouds swooped in at great speed. The winds kicked up and began swirling around us. Leaves and branches were thrown through the air.

We dashed between two extremely tall and large trees and into Wolverine Forest. At the beginning the trees were about ten feet away from each other, but as we moved deeper into the forest they began to creep closer. Ahead appeared to be a wall of bark. The trees were so close together that it was difficult to see the spaces between them.

The rain began to trickle and suddenly opened into a torrential downpour. It didn't help visibility any. Lightning flashed and thunder echoed through the trees so loudly that it sounded like my head was inside of a drum.

We scrambled for cover. Grace had disappeared. Whizzy was just ahead of me. The rain soaked my new skin. I could feel it absorbing through me. The sensation was strange, but I started to feel different. Better. I had an unfamiliar strength in my legs. I was normally a pretty skinny kid in Greenville so muscles had never been a trait of mine. The wetter I became the stronger I felt.

"Phillip," I heard Whizzy shout. His voice was shaky. I couldn't see him through the rain, but knew he was in trouble.

"Whizzy where are you?" Everything around was dark, like the rain had washed away the brilliant colors of the forest. I closed my eyes and listened for Whizzy's voice. I hopped through the muddy forest floor. Finally I found him lying in a huge puddle. It was the size of the swimming pool at Greenville Middle School.

Whizzy looked awfully tired. His once brilliantly red fur was matted to his face and almost black. His eyes had faded too.

"Whizzy what happened?"

"I slipped and fell. It was like the forest floor opened up and tried to swallow me. My legs are stuck in the mud, Phillip." Whizzy struggled to speak. He was exhausted.

"Phillip the Frog!" Grace's voice echoed in my head. "You must hurry."

"Why? Where are you?" I tried to see her, but there was no use. The rain hadn't let up any, and I could barely see Whizzy directly In front of me.

"Phillip?" Whizzy responded.

I realized he didn't understand whom I was talking to. He must not have heard her talking to me.

"Don't worry, Whizzy. I'll get you out of there." I pulled with all my might. He slid slightly forward, but as soon as I stopped his body fell backwards even deeper into the growing puddle. "Whizzy!" I dug my heels into the mud, squatted down low and leaned back.

150

"Come on, Whizzy!" His grip on my webbed hands was weakening by the second. If I didn't get him out now he would drowned.

I pulled again. Whizzy didn't even move.

"NO! I screamed. I suddenly got very angry. This must be what Whizzy feels like all the time. I made some deep-throated yell and pulled with all my strength.

The next few seconds were a little fuzzy, but I remember a loud popping sound like when you open a can of soda, and when I opened my eyes Whizzy was lying next to me in the mud. It had worked. And my legs were suddenly very sore.

I shook him. He smiled at me and said, "Thank you, Phillip!"

"Run, Phillip the Frog!" I heard Grace Tallon's voice in my head again. I hadn't seen her since the heavy rains began, but somehow she knew where I was.

Whizzy and I stood up. We still couldn't see very well.

"Which way, Grace?"

Whizzy gave me a peculiar glance. I think he thought I was going crazy. By now I realized that Grace was only speaking to me. Whizzy couldn't hear her.

"Straight ahead. Run for the first tree."

I grabbed Whizzy's sopping wet furry palm. It felt really gross. Then I ran, nearly dragging my best friend all the way.

"There will be a small hole in its truck. Hide inside. Hurry!" She directed.

The rain began to hurt my skin. It felt like pebbles pelting me at a million miles an hour. And they started getting larger.

"Hail!" I muttered to myself. *That couldn't be good.*

The hailstones doubled in size almost every second.

We reached the tree and found the opening. I pushed Whizzy's almost limp body inside and then jumped in myself. A golf ball size hailstone smashed into my leg, and I tumbled through the opening and slid down a wet, slimy wooden slide. I fell backwards sloshing and bumping on the uneven amusement park-style ride until I slid to an uncomfortable stop. My entire body was sore, and nearly completely covered in mud. I had gone from a green frog to dark brown.

"Not bad, Phillip the Frog. You survived our first test. And because of you, so did he." She said with resentment while pointing at Whizzy slumped against the wall.

She held out her hand. Grace had a firm and powerful grip. I stood directly in front of her. I hadn't realized how small she really was. I looked down at the top of her white- haired head with her pointy Elven ears sticking out like antennas. She was the same height as Whizzy. Our eyes locked. There was a fury similar to Whizzy's. We were silent. The awkwardness swept over me like in school. Girls just made me uncomfortable, apparently Elven girls too.

"That was quite a storm, huh?" I said to break the silence.

Grace just walked away without answering. She started dumping water out of her backpack. Arrows were laid out in a perfect row at her feet. She acted like someone in the military...oh, wait, I guess she was kinda in the military. *Grace Tallon, Elven Warrior.* That was how she had introduced herself.

Whizzy was sleeping now. Probably best. I was starting to feel tired too. I sat down next to him and closed my eyes.

"Does it storm like that often in Mistasia?" I asked Grace while fighting not to yawn.

She spoke while refilling her backpack with the arrows from the ground. "No. Only when you're being attacked by a Sorcerer!" She replied.

My left eye shot open. "Sorcerer?"

IS HE A SNAKE OR A MAN?

8

The diamond-headed, brownish-yellow snake slithered across the black rectangular cement floor. It hissed with anticipation. Down the corridor the snake swept across the floor toward an old wooden door at the end of the poorly lit hallway. Behind it the serpent dragged a wooden board, which magically hovered in the air. Lying upon it was Rachel Whizzenmog.

The snake stopped just outside the solid door with no handle. Small candles hung on the wall and dripped leaving a pool of molten wax like lava from a volcano on the floor. The snake stretched for the ceiling. A flash of light burst from it.

Rachel gasped.

It appeared as though the snake had exploded. Swirls of golden light shot higher and higher in the hallway, reaching the ceiling. Then disappeared. Left standing in the hallway was a disfigured serpent man. His body was covered in a smooth skin the same color and pattern as the snake that had kidnapped her. The head was smooth with two ridges just behind its eyes, which were set to the side of its head and elongated. They were exactly the same as the snakes. He wore a long brown trench coat, which flowed down past its feet...if it had feet. However snake-like this man appeared he did possess two strong arms and a staff in his right hand.

The serpent man gazed at Rachel with hatred and contempt. She coward before him. He didn't speak. He only reached out his staff and motioned for her to rise. She floated in the air. Another bright flash blinded her. Then she reappeared in a dark room.

The room smelled horribly like rotting watermelons and stinky cheese...but not the kind you would actually eat. She heard trickling of water and little feet scurrying across the stone floor. Her eyes struggled to focus in the darkness.

Where am I? She thought. Rocking back and forth in fear she could only wait for something to happen. She had no idea where she was or why she had been taken.

"Phillip the Frog wake up," Grace yelled.

"Rachel!" I cried. I felt sadness and fear. My mouth was dry and my stomach was performing Olympic summersaults.

Whizzy and Grace each gawked at me, yet with different expressions. Whizzy looked tired and unsure of my sanity. Grace, however, seemed to be waiting for more. She didn't respond, but pried at me with her eyes.

Finally, she spoke to me. "Did you see her, Phillip the Frog?"

"Yes!"

Whizzy's head kept flopping back and forth between Grace and me.

"You saw Rachel Whizzenmog? Are you certain?" She asked in my head. Grace seemed to want to understand if I was completely positive.

"Yes, I'm sure it was her, Grace!" I empathically croaked. "The snake...guy had her. He locked her in some dark room."

Whizzy continued to swing his head like watching a tennis match. His frustration level was growing as rapidly as the hailstorm did. Finally he popped like a cork.

"Is somebody gonna explain this to me? What the heck is going on?" His fur was frizzy and whiskers twitching.

"I just saw Rachel in my dream, Whizzy."

"You're insane!" His voice cracked. "You are absolutely bonkers, Phillip."

"I am not joking. Whizzy I really saw her. She is alive. The snake man is holding her prisoner."

He processed this for a minute. Grace just waited patiently for Whizzy the Fox, as she called him now, to catch up with us.

Grace raised her eyebrows.

Whizzy scoffed in her direction, and then looked back at me.

I almost began to laugh, but held back. It would not have been the best reaction. Whizzy's temper might have gone nuclear.

"Who has Rachel?"

"The snake man that captured her in your basement."

"Wait. The snake...man? Is he a snake or a man?" Whizzy demanded.

"Ah..." I wasn't sure how to explain, but before I could he continued on.

"And how did you see her?"

"In my dream I guess." I looked at Grace for an explanation.

Whizzy leaned closer and intensely inspected my Froggy eyes. A deep line formed between his eyes. I had seen that same line on Michael Whizzenmog the human for years. It appeared whenever he was really thinking about something. After a few moments a sly smile appeared on his face. It scared me, when his fangs emerged. His eyes immediately softened. Now he turned to confront Grace.

Her expression was still stern, and she folded her arms.

"You did this to him didn't you?"

She didn't reply.

"You messed with his mind? Screwed up his marbles didn't you, Grace?" Whizzy walked right up to the Elven warrior. And yes they were the same height.

I shot up. My skin felt extremely dry and tight. I was now covered in dirt instead of mud as it had dried overnight. I walked over beside Whizzy. I had a bad feeling that this argument wasn't going to end well.

"What did you do?" Whizzy yelled. His rage boiled.

Grace just stood calmly. She took a deep breath and then exhaled before she spoke. She frightened me far more than Whizzy did. Grace reminded me of a balloon filled too full of air ready to explode at any second...you just didn't know when and most certainly hoped it wasn't in your face.

I grabbed Whizzy by the arm, but he pushed me away.

Grace reacted. She pulled her sword out and pointed it directly at Whizzy's right ear.

He was shocked. I thought I even heard him whimper. "Okay...okay!" He backed away from her.

"Sit down and shut up, Whizzenmog. Don't make me end this here." The venom in her voice was unmistakable. She definitely disliked Whizzy.

Whizzy and I went back to the spot we had slept. Grace stowed her sword. She was not happy. Whizzy was upset and I...well I had questions.

I patted Whizzy on the shoulder and then approached Grace. She hadn't broken her stare from Whizzy.

"Grace?"

"Yes, Phillip the Frog?" She answered in my head.

This seemed to be the only way she would talk to me now. I didn't exactly like it because Whizzy could hear everything I said and nothing she said so I sounded like a crazy person, but I needed answers.

"Why can you talk to me...like this?"

"You have the ability of telepathy."

I must have just blankly stared at her, because she began to explain.

"You can communicate with others through your mind. That is how I can speak to you in your mind. As for the dream about Rachel...you are also clairvoyant. This means that you can see events that are either happening somewhere else or in the future." She explained.

"Wow. That is really cool." I childishly responded.

"Yes, Phillip the Frog. It is a great gift that few have. You are just learning to develop these gifts. They will be very useful to us in our journey."

"But what about, Whizzy? What can he do?" I asked hoping to hear something amazing.

Grace watched Whizzy pouting for a moment before responding, "Presently...nothing!"

TELEPHATHY FINDS A WIZARD

9

What did that mean? Presently nothing! I wondered why she said that about Whizzy. That must mean he had some ability. He couldn't just be a fox. If I had powers he most certainly would too. Whizzy was the stronger human. He had confidence, something I lacked. Maybe here in Mistasia I was stronger. I had already discovered that water helps my strength, and that I am both telepathic and clairvoyant. Whizzy just hadn't discovered his powers yet or why he was a fox. Come to think of it I still didn't know why I was a frog.

"Grace. Why am I a frog here in Mistasia?"

"I do not know. There are many possibilities. It could be your family's past, or your surrounding back home. Something you love or hate." Grace explained as she used a knife to sharpen the tip of an arrow.

"Then why are you an eagle in my world?"

She stopped working on the arrow. "It is my family's crest. Elves are the only creatures in Mistasia that are close to humans. We have a very close connection to this land...unlike your kind." Her answer sounded coarse. I could tell she was trying not to offend me, but I knew that if she were talking to Whizzy it would have come out much harsher. "We take honor in our form, and my family long ago chose the eagle for its beauty and strength in mobility."

I sat and wondered what would have made me a frog. Was it some long family tradition? I had never eaten frog legs, and was really glad about that right now. I would feel awful. My stomach began to churn at the thought of a steaming plate of fried frog legs.

Suddenly, I thought about my pet... "Sampson!" I blurted out.

"What?" Whizzy replied.

"Sampson. My pet at home; he is a frog, Whizzy." I was excited to have finally figured it out. A smile would have grown from ear to ear, but since I was now a frog I had no ears in the human sense. "That has to be why I became a frog. I held him this morning and then I put that frog shirt on. It's my symbol!"

Whizzy nodded at me with his eyes widened. "That's good, Phillip. I was really worried about why you became a frog." He snapped in a snotty tone.

"Come on, Whizzy. Don't you want to know why you became a fox?"

"Not really. I just want to find Rachel and go home." He growled.

"You should listen to your friend, Whizzy the Fox. He is far smarter than you give him credit for." Grace told him.

"Leave me alone!"

"While you sit here and pout, your sister is in the hands of the King's minions. These are not creatures to take lightly, Whizzy the Fox. The sooner you come to grips with yourself and realize your true potential the better." She was challenging Whizzy. "Or it will be too late for your sister. Phillip the Frog can help you, but Rachel needs you! You are her...hero," Grace seemed to have to choke that last word out.

"Hero? I'm no hero. I am a stupid fox."

"I believe you're right. Unfortunately, the one I serve believes otherwise," Grace said.

"Who do you serve, Grace?" I asked politely.

Grace stood at attention as though she were preparing to salute. "Princess Merran, the heir to the thrown of Mistasia. She is to be Queen at Cadieux Castle on her next birthday. She believes that this whinny fox will save us all from her uncle, King Cragon."

"Oh yeah! And why would she believe that, Elf?" Whizzy growled while standing up.

The two combatants closed in on each other again. They stood only a few feet from one another now.

"Why, Grace? What would make me so important? Phillip can read minds and see dreams. I can't do anything!" Whizzy was almost in tears, but he was still fighting. "Huh, so what makes me so important?"

Grace hesitated. I could see the resentment in her eyes. She was holding something from us. I searched her mind. Grace looked at me, and I saw it in her gaze. She exhaled.

"You're a wizard!" I said in astonishment. "You are a freakin' wizard, Whizzy!"

WE'RE NOT THE ONLY THING IN THE WOLVERINE FOREST

10

"A wizard?" Whizzy replied. "Is that true?"

"Yes." Grace turned and walked away from him.

Whizzy and I were speechless. How do you respond to something like that? Well, apparently with silence because that was what we did.

Grace reached down and picked up her backpack from the dirt. More than a dozen sharp-tipped, wooden arrows stuck out from it. She unbuckled a side pouch and pulled out a stick. Grace hesitated for a moment. She must have been deciding whether or not to actually give it to Whizzy, but she did.

Whizzy stretched out his paw and held the slightly crooked stick. It was not very long, and had a jagged tip, not what I imagined a wand would look like at all. Whizzy grasp the twig and inspected it.

"Is this a..." Whizzy started to ask but Grace interrupted before he could complete his thought.

"Wand? Yes, it is the wand of the last Whizzenmog protector to the King. Your family used to honor this land with its bravery. For centuries the Whizzenmog's were the strongest wizards in Mistasia."

"Were? What happened?" I asked as Whizzy continued to play with his new toy. He probably should have been listening to Grace's story, but I don't think he was.

"Sorcerer LaCroiux!" She emphatically answered, and that was the end of her tale.

Again I felt like she was leaving out some important information. I knew she was hiding something. I tried to read her mind, but she was too powerful.

"Get out of my head!" She barked.

The noise was so loud it caused me to collapse to the ground. Whizzy stopped playing with his wand and helped me back to my feet.

Grace Tallon tossed her pack over her shoulder and said, "It's time to leave."

Outside it was peaceful again. The warmth of the day had made it very misty from the rainwater burning off the ground. Grace led us between trees and over enormous entangled roots. These trees had grown for so long and to such heights that their roots had run out of room on the forest floor. Many had burst out of the ground and begun to intertwine with each other.

We didn't walk through the forest we climbed up, over and even under branches and roots. It was also dark despite being afternoon...or at least that was what Grace said when I asked her what time it was.

Time seemed different in Mistasia. There was no "2 o'clock p.m." or "7 o'clock a.m." like back in Greenville. It was just Morning, Afternoon or Night.

"How much further?" Whizzy asked our guide.

"Three miles."

That wasn't too bad I thought. It was about three miles from the Whizzenmog's house back home to Greenville Middle School. Whizzy and I had ridden our bicycles that far a bunch of times.

I could hear birds calling, and the wind rustling through the leaves just like back home in Umber Forest. I was as peaceful as I had been in a long time, yet whenever I started to feel comfortable in Mistasia...something bad happened!

Grace stopped walking. She turned and motioned for us to stop. I waited for any sound. A bird called from the tree above us, but Grace ignored it. She was definitely listening to something in the distance. Slowly she reached back for an arrow and readied her bow.

My heartbeat started to quicken.

Whizzy held his crooked wand like a sword...he looked silly, but I wasn't going to tell him that. At least he had a weapon. What was I going to do? Think happy thoughts and make whatever it was go away?

Wait. I can speak to Grace. "What's wrong?" I asked in my mind.

"Something is tracking us." She responded.

"What?"

"Wolverines. Cragon's army. Don't move." She warned.

Ah...the Wolverine Army. I had conveniently forgotten about the vicious, ravenous army set out to hunt us by the evil

King. I felt woozy. My head began to swim. Then a stroke of good fortune. It had begun to rain and this one appeared to be natural, not sorcerer created. How could I tell? Grace hadn't told us to run. The raindrops landed on my Froggy head. They ran down my back and across my skin. I felt a surge running through my body. It felt great. My strength was returning.

"Grace, what do we do?" I asked her.

She didn't respond. She was tracking something with her bow and arrow. I watched as she slowly moved the target and then fired her arrow.

"RUN!" she yelled.

A ferocious, pained roar thundered through the forest.

We ran. Grace passed us quickly. We followed her on a narrow winding path between the trees. It shrunk down to almost a sliver. We had to turn sideways to continue. When we had reached a point that we could go no further, I thought we were in serious trouble. Then she grabbed hold of a branch and began to climb. I looked up and noticed a series of branches like a ladder raising far into the treetops. Whizzy and I followed her lead. We climbed very high almost one hundred feet above the ground. At this height I saw my first glimpse of Dragon Lake beyond Wolverine Forest. I didn't realize its beauty just now...mostly because I was absolutely terrified.

"Are we safe up here?" I asked.

"The King's Wolverine Army can't reach us here, but they aren't the only enemies we have in this forest."

"What now?" Whizzy blasted. "Stop lying to us. We can't protect ourselves from something we don't know about!" He continued yelling.

"You can't protect yourself anyway, Whizzenmog! You don't even know how to use your wand." She scolded the new wizard. "To you it's as useful as to those beasts below. It's a stick!"

"You told me it was a wand!"

"It is a wand...to a real wizard!"

They continued yelling at each other. A group of Wolverines gathered in the distance. They were far too large to maneuver between these trees, but they continued to watch us intently...even from a good distance. One placed something to its mouth.

"What is it doing?" I said aloud.

Grace stopped arguing immediately. She didn't say anything verbally, but I think I heard her swear in elfish in my mind.

Suddenly, the forest rung out with the sound of a horn blowing a war cry. You know the sound you never want to hear, like your mother telling you you're grounded for life.

Grace pulled out an arrow and hastily tied a knotted rope to its tail. Then she tied the loose end to a small branch sticking out of the massive tree limb we stood on. She aimed and shot into another tree.

"Phillip, grab hold." She demanded.

"No way!"

"Do it NOW!" She yelled. I was too afraid to argue any more.

I grabbed hold of the rope with both webbed hands and then wrapped my Froggy legs too. She placed her hands on my shoulders and pushed...hard.

"AHHHH!" I screamed like a little girl. I flew through the air moving at great speed. The other tree was quickly approaching and I wasn't quite sure how to slow down, let alone stop. I closed my eyes and braced for impact. I crashed legs first into the hard bark and flipped off the rope landing on my stomach. It hurt really badly.

Grace and Whizzy were still on the other tree, along with a very big purplish dragon. It had spikes on its tail and swung it around. I saw three more different colored dragons land in nearby trees. Whizzy jumped and grabbed the rope. He was whizzing toward me. Grace had pulled out her sword and thrust it at the purplish dragon. Why doesn't she leave? What if the dragon blasts her with fire? Whizzy landed next to me. He turned to watch Grace battle the dragon.

"Come on, Grace!" He yelled.

She lunged at the dragon again. It screamed in pain and raised its wings. Grace used that opportunity to dash away. She flew through the air holding the rope with one hand and her sword in the other.

The other dragons began to shriek. It was so loud. My head rang. Whizzy covered his large fox ears. He yelled in pain.

Grace had almost reached us when the purplish dragon took flight and attempted to bite her. It missed Grace but clipped the rope snapping it clean. Grace started to freefall toward the ground. She held the rope tightly and slammed into the tree nearly twenty feet below us.

"Grace!" I yelled.

She was hurt and in grave danger. The purplish dragon swung past her as she dangled along side the tree. The rain had continued to fall and the rope was too slippery for Grace to hold. She inched closer to the bottom. It would be over seventy feet to the ground. She wouldn't survive!

"Do something, Whizzy!"

"What? What do I do?" Whizzy yelled to Grace for instructions.

"Use your wand, Whizzy. Please help her!"
I urged him but knew Whizzy didn't know what
to do. What does a wizard do in an instance like
this?

The dragon circled back around. I
panicked. My only chance to help was distract
the dragon.

"Whizzy you can do this. You save Grace."
"What are you gonna do, Phillip?"
I could hear him ask as I leapt off the
branch and into the air. My frog legs thrust with
power. The rain gave me a strength that I
couldn't explain and a confidence I had never
had. I flew through the air directly for the
unsuspecting purplish dragon. I landed on its
head and slipped back. Now I was on its back like
a rider. Two spikes protruded from its head. I
reached out and grabbed them using them like
handlebars to steer the beast like a bicycle.

The dragon shrieked, but I managed to
redirect it away from Grace.

Whizzy must have figured out some way
to save Grace, because she was up on the branch
with him when I circled back around on the

dragon. Its friends had remained in nearby trees, but didn't attack. I thought that was strange, but was more concerned with figuring out how to get off this dragon. I steered it back to the tree and jumped.

I landed next to Whizzy and slid to a stop. It was awesome. The coolest moment of my life. Too bad the kids at school didn't see it.

The dragons bolted, and we were alone in the treetops.

Now we had to figure out how to get down and out of the Wolverine Forest alive.

THE FRIENDLESS TREE

11

I was so geeked about my recent battle with the dragon that I couldn't stop talking all the way down. I think most of the time I was talking to myself, but I didn't really care. I had never done anything that brave. Not even close.

Whizzy didn't want to talk. I think he was jealous? Back home it had always been Whizzy doing all the cool and daring things. I couldn't even perform any tricks on my bike, but Whizzy did spins and jumps with ease. I have always been too afraid. Today, I just jumped!

I tried to get Whizzy to talk to me as we had finally finished our climb down to the forest floor. "Hey, Whizzy. What spell did you use to save Grace?"

He only shook his head in disgust and gave me a dirty look before walking away.

I walked over to Grace. "What's wrong with him?"

"He's your friend. You tell me."

"Hey, wait, Grace! Did he use magic to save you?"

"Magic. No. He used his brain. It's better than nothing."

"What do you mean?" I asked

"He just pulled me up with the rope." She replied.

Grace carefully moved through the forest. She said that the Wolverine Army was still out there. She could hear them breathing. Apparently elves have exceptional hearing. Grace said she could hear fruit fall from a tree nearly thirty miles away on a quiet night. I'm lucky if I could hear Mr. Quinch, my 8th grade math teacher, from across the room.

She told us we needed to move quickly because the Wolverines used their strong sense of smell for tracking and would find us if we stayed still for too long.

"We are not far from the southern edge of the forest. The King's army cannot leave this forest. We must get beyond the friendless tree." She explained while peeking around the tree before her.

"Friendless tree?" I questioned.

"There," she replied.

Grace pointed to a lone tree in the distance. It was bright and colorful. It didn't appear as large as the other trees within the forest either.

"Okay lets go!" Whizzy said suddenly energetic.

Grace grabbed him by his furry arm. "You must wait. I don't know if it's safe."

He pulled his arm away roughly. "Then let's go find out." Whizzy pulled himself up onto a outstretched root and climbed over.

"Is he insane?" Grace asked.

I didn't consider answering. I think Grace had already answered her own question.

She leapt into the air and over the root with out touching it. I was impressed. I struggled to climb as I slipped and fell backward onto my Froggy behind and into a small puddle.

"Roar!"

A ferocious angry blast sounded from beyond the tree root.

My legs, now wet, surged again. I leapt just as Grace had a moment before. Once I landed on the other side I wished I hadn't.

Two muscular, black-haired beasts with thin legs and strong arms growled and sneered at the three of us.

Grace held her sword tightly, pointed directly at one of the Wolverines. Whizzy copied her stance with his crooked wand in his hand. I still had no weapons. I searched the ground around us and found a large circular piece of bark to use as a shield, and a branch about the same length as Grace's sword. Now I had weapons...but I wasn't feeling any better about our situation.

I noticed that we were only about the length of Whizzy's driveway back home away from escaping the forest. Grace had said that the Wolverines couldn't follow us outside their realm. They only attacked whoever was inside the forest. The friendless tree was our safe zone...like playing freeze tag. You reach your safe zone then no one could touch you.

I must have been daydreaming too long because the next thing I knew the Wolverines attacked.

They were nearly nine feet tall. Whizzy and Grace looked like dwarfs as they only came up to the beasts bellies. I watched as Grace swung her sword just missing her target's hand. It lunged at her again, but Grace stuck the tip of her sword into its forearm. It screamed in pain like nothing I had heard before.

Whizzy's attempt didn't go as well. He still didn't have any idea how to use his wand.

The Wolverine swung and slashed at Whizzy. My friend ducked and rolled away from each attempt until the beast clobbered him with a backhanded swat. Whizzy was flung through the air and bounced into a nearby tree. He slid to the ground and slumped over.

I grew angry. The surge in my legs had just traveled through my entire body. I started bouncing and leaping all around the Wolverine. It kept growling and swinging, but I just dodged every strike. It was like the beast was moving in slow motion. I blocked him with my shield and struck him on the head with my branch sword, which was more like a club. It staggered backwards. I jumped and kicked the black-haired monster in the chest. It crashed to the ground.

Grace continued to battle with the other monster. "RUN FOR THE TREE!" She commanded.

"But Whizzy's hurt," I yelled back. I dashed to my best friend. He was awake, but dazed. "Whizzy! Whizzy are you alright?"

"Yeah. I...no. I'm going to be sick." Whizzy fell sideways and spewed out a strange colored liquid.

"Oh, gross." The smell was awful. "I hope that's not blood."

Another painful scream sounded from behind me. Grace had struck the beast in the stomach. It stumbled away crying in pain.

"Come on. Now is our chance." She demanded. And she was right.

"Come on, Whizzy!" I helped him to his feet and put his arm around my neck. Grace did the same on his other side.

We ran as quickly as we could nearly dragging Whizzy across the damp thin grass. We nearly reached the friendless tree when I felt a strong tug on my shoulder. Whizzy was gone.

The Wolverine I had clubbed in the head was awake and extremely angry. He held Whizzy above his head like a championship trophy. I didn't know if the beast was going to kiss him or eat him. I wasn't thrilled about either option. The monster's gold eyes locked on me, and then it screamed. Its razor sharp teeth normally would have made me faint, but I wasn't myself. I was Phillip the Frog and in the Land of Mistasia; I felt like a hero.

I leapt into action, and Grace joined me. We attacked from both sides. The beast tossed Whizzy at me.

His furry feet struck me in the chest, and we both crashed to the ground. The air escaped my lungs like a deflating balloon. My vision was blurred. I could see three Wolverines now. Shaking my head I regained my sight.

Grace continued to swing her sword at the angry beast. I pushed Whizzy aside and joined her. We continued to battle the Wolverine. It was so strong, and we began to tire. The longer this fight stretched on I was more certain that other Wolverines would appear. That would be deadly.

What happened next was frightening and amazing. The beast struck me with its muscular forearm and tossed me through the air. I bounced on the ground and slid just a few feet from Whizzy. He still lay unconscious with his back to us.

Then Grace went down with a kick to the chest.

I was exhausted. I needed water. I struggled to get back up. I could hear the beast walking toward me.

Whizzy began to stir. He pushed himself up, but his back was still to our enemy.

It came up on us so quickly. The Wolverine grabbed me by the neck and lifted me into the air. It screamed into my face and then reached out to pick up Whizzy.

Whizzy was startled by the monstrous scream and jolted around. His right hand extended in slow motion, and when it touched the beast a bright blue flash exploded.

The Wolverine dropped me and flew through the air. It slammed head first into forest.

I landed hard on my back but still managed to roll on my side to see Whizzy, his arm still extended with his wand in his paw and an astonished expression on his face. Then I turned to find the Wolverine and noticed Grace in the distance with the same expression that Whizzy had.

I smiled. I don't know how he did it, but his magic had just saved us.

We all dashed for the safe zone of the Friendless tree and finally escaped the Wolverine Forest and King Cragon's Army.

WHAT OTHER CREATURES ARE IN MISTASIA?

12

The sun had changed colors from bright yellow to a pale red as it began to set to the West. It hung in the distance like a glowing dodge ball. It was unnerving. This land had thrown us a number of curveballs. I only hoped nothing pulled the flaming sun out of the sky and tossed it at us because I was always the first kid knocked out at dodge ball in gym class.

We hadn't gone very far, when we reached Dragon Lake. I asked Grace why it was named that, and she said that from the air it was shaped like a dragon. I just took her word for it.

The water was calm, like it was frozen. There were no ripples. The air began to cool. It pushed against my skin lightly. I felt a shiver. I reached out to place my webbed finger in the water.

"Don't!" Grace yelled and grabbed my arm. Her eyes were very intense and beautiful. "This water is enchanted. There are many creatures that live within this lake. Creatures that you do not want to awaken."

"Is there anything in Mistasia that doesn't want to hurt us?" Whizzy snapped.

"I'll let you know when I find anything," Grace said.

I wasn't sure if I saw it because I was so tired, but I thought Grace had just smiled. It was the first expression besides anger that she had shown.

"So how do we cross?" I asked.

"By boat."

My stomach lurched. I always got seasick on boats. The swaying back and forth. I was not looking forward to this trip.

At the side of the lake, behind a large bush was a ten-foot long wooden boat. It was very slim and had two small oars on either side.

Slowly we moved along the water. Grace didn't use the oars to paddle, only steer the boat when needed. The boat cut through the water so smoothly we left almost no ripples behind us.

The sun had nearly set now. A chill had overtaken the air. There was no breeze either. Along the lakeshore were small bushes, but almost no trees. I could see for a good distance in all directions. Whizzy sat at the front of the boat examining his wand. He must have been trying to figure out how he defeated the Wolverine. Grace was the most peaceful I had seen her. And I didn't feel seasick. Maybe this boat ride wouldn't be so bad after all.

It was peaceful on Dragon Lake. The sun was gone and the stars had appeared in the clear night sky. It didn't look any different than the nighttime in Greenville that I could tell. I saw the "Big Dipper" and "Little Dipper" as well as other constellations we had learned about in science class this past year. I would have shown Whizzy, but science wasn't really his subject. He was always so bored that he fell asleep most of the time and got into trouble.

We floated for what felt like hours. I would have asked Grace, but I remembered that she didn't understand time. To her is was night...and that was it.

I struggled to keep my eyes open. My big froggy melon was bobbing around like a balloon in the wind.

Whizzy finally broke our silence, "How exactly did I do that?" He asked as if the battle in the Wolverine Forest had just happened.

For some weird reason he looked at me first. I didn't know. He stared at me, so I shrugged my shoulders in response. He finally looked to Grace.

She still sat at the back of the boat holding the oars steady. "Whizzenmog, I am an elf, not a wizard."

"So you don't even know anything about wizards?" He replied.

"I told you that your family used to protect the King." Grace barked.

"Were my family the only wizards in Mistasia?" Whizzy asked.

"No. You're family were the King's protectors. They were the strongest wizards, yes. Not the only."

Grace lowered the oar in her left hand and steered the boat to turn slightly.

"If there are other wizards than we must find them so they can train me." Whizzy demanded.

"No," was Grace's short reply.

Whizzy was getting frustrated so I intervened.

"I thought you said that Whizzy would need to save Rachel. Shouldn't he be trained to use his powers?"

"Yes." She said.

Whizzy and I both waited for an explanation, but she didn't give one. I was confused, and Whizzy was...well mad.

"Grace. If we should train Whizzy then why won't you let us find a wizard?"

"There are none remaining in Mistasia. Whizzy is the last." She stated staring at Whizzy. She seemed unhappy about that.

"No more wizards," I muttered.

"How can that be, Grace?" Whizzy blurted out.

"A Whizzenmog turned on your family. He became a sorcerer and destroyed the remaining witches and wizards in Mistasia." Grace's nose twitched.

I couldn't tell if she was going to cry or explode.

"My family?" Whizzy was shocked. "Who...who would do that?"

"A treacherous snake. You know him, Whizzy." She crassly remarked. "You met him in your family's basement."

"The snake?" Whizzy and I replied in unison.

"Ethan Whizzenmog," She revealed. He is your great uncle, Whizzy. Once a great and powerful wizard, he fell into debt to the heinous Sorcerer LaCroiux."

"The one who created that storm in the forest?" I asked.

She nodded. "Ethan Whizzenmog became so evil that he's no longer able to regain his previous form. He is snake-like."

"Then he is the snake man I saw in my dream. He did take Rachel!" I shouted.

Grace motioned for me to be silent. "Words travel far in the night of Mistasia. Cadieux Castle will most certainly be listening for us." She paused for a moment, before continuing. "Your great grandfather Whizzy was one of the most powerful and noble wizards this land has ever encountered. When he learned of his son's treason he was crushed. Ethan attacked your great grandfather, but wasn't successful. The story is that your great grandfather asked his second son, Rainer to keep the Whizzenmog family alive. He was sent to your world to hide until the time that the savior of Mistasia was born. No one could ever find out how your great grandfather sent Rainer to your world...until now. Sorcerer LaCroiux discovered the portal and sent Ethan to find the savior."

"What is the savior supposed to do?" I asked.

"Stop King Cragon and his minions and restore power to the true and just of this land!" Grace calmly replied.

"I'm the savior?" Whizzy muttered.

Grace scoffed. "No. You're sister is!"

Whizzy looked crushed. I was certain that he hadn't realized yet that meant Rachel was a witch...and probably a more powerful one. He wasn't going to be happy. This would be one more thing in which Rachel was better than Whizzy. It was the whole reason they didn't get along. She was taller, more popular, and now the savior of Mistasia! This day couldn't get worse for my best friend.

"What is that in the water?" I asked as I saw two emerald green circles peering up through the water at me. They couldn't be eyes.

Grace carefully looked over the side of the boat. She gasped softly.

"Mermen!"

MERMAN VS. MERMAIDS

13

We had traveled through the portal to Mistasia, been transformed into a frog and fox, nearly been crushed in a hailstorm, battled dragons and fought off an attack from giant Wolverines...but I was about to be more terrified than ever.

The emerald green circles under the surface of the water flashed. Then a man burst out of the water and let out a booming roar.

The man was young, strong, and had short dark brown hair, which appeared dry even though he had just been submerged in Dragon Lake.

"What is that?" Whizzy yelled

"A Merman!" Grace replied.

"What?" He questioned again.

Grace didn't answer. She grabbed the oars and pulled back hard. She tried to push the boat away from the angry Merman.

It charged and rammed the boat. We spun sideways, but remained upright.

I screamed like a little girl. "What do we do?" I hoped Grace had a plan.

Whizzy held his wand tightly within his right paw. "We need to get to shore!" He yelled as he pointed.

I noticed just ahead was the shoreline.

Suddenly, the boat began to move towards shore. It moved quicker with each passing second.

The Merman swam for our boat again, but just missed.

"Awesome, Grace!" I praised.

"It's not me."

"What?" I replied

"I'm not paddling!" She yelled back.

She held the oars in her hands. They weren't in the water. I didn't understand immediately, but realized it must have been Whizzy. He was still holding his wand at his side.

"Whizzy did it," I muttered in surprise.

Grace gave me a disapproving glance. Then she glared at Whizzy.

"How? He doesn't know what he's doing!"
She said attempting to remind me that Whizzy
still needed training.

"It must have been when he pointed his
wand and said we needed to get to shore. The
boat responded. He used magic on accident!" I
was so excited. Then I realized the Merman was
gaining on us. His grayish-blue tail glimmered in
the moonlight as it pattered back and forth
propelling the sleek swimming Merman toward
us like a torpedo. "It's back!"

Grace snapped around and pulled an
arrow from her pack. She raised her bow, aimed
and fired. The arrow just skipped off its scaly fin.

"Oh, that is not good," I remarked.

Whizzy started to steer the boat with his
wand. He would point in a direction, and give a
command and the boat would respond. He
dodged the Merman's attempts to strike our
boat multiple times.

Then the Merman leapt from the water.
It jumped into the air like a dolphin and dove
below, but slammed its muscular grayish-blue
tailfin into the back of the boat.

The wooden boat splintered. A large section was gone. The back end began to sink, but we traveled so quickly that the boat remained afloat.

Another booming roar echoed across the water. My heart skipped a beat and my stomach felt like I had swallowed a rock.

The next few seconds were a blur. The boat exploded, and we were flung into the air. The Merman must have struck us from beneath. As I fell back to the water, I saw Grace then Whizzy splash and disappear into the water as if they were swallowed whole.

I landed just seconds after. The water was warm. It was very dark and murky. Pieces of wood were scattered all around me. I couldn't see Grace or Whizzy. I felt the water swirl around me. Then I saw the Merman's tail out of the corner of my eye. I spun to find him, but he had vanished. I found it quite easy to maneuver in the water, I was very glad to be a frog right now. The familiar surge of strength that overcame me when water touched my amphibian skin was back. I searched around for

my best friend and our Elven guide one last
time. There was no sign. I thrust myself upward
with my legs and reached the surface.

I saw Whizzy first. His fur was almost
black and matted to his face. He was coughing
and struggling to stay above water. I swam to
him and grabbed hold. It wasn't long before I
noticed Grace. She was gripping a large section
of the boat to remain afloat. I brought Whizzy to
her.

"Where did he go?" I asked Grace.

She shook her head. She didn't know. I
went below the surface to look for him. It was
very hard to see. I searched around, and thought
I saw the Merman's tail directly in front of me.
Then it disappeared. I rejoined Grace and Whizzy
above.

"I saw him! I saw him!" I yelled in a
panic.

A splash behind me signaled the Merman's
return. I spun around to see him leaping from
the water directly toward us.

His seemingly normal human face was
twisted with rage. We braced for impact. Then

an object sprung from the water and smashed into the Merman knocking him sideways.

"What was that?" I screamed. It was so quick I didn't realize it was another Merman.

The two bobbed up and down like apples as they fought. The second Merman was slender and had longer Blonde hair.

We watched helplessly as the two struggled with one another. Finally the slender Merman sprang from the water and struck the first with its aqua colored tailfin. That was when I noticed it wasn't another Merman...it was a Mermaid.

The Merman dashed away. The Mermaid raised herself high in the water with only her fins submerged and blasted a high-pitched scream that hurt my ears.

I didn't know what to expect next. Should we swim for safety or prepare to fight? I really hoped it wasn't going to be fight, because I was afraid of the Merman and she just kicked his rear and sent him home cowering.

The Mermaid gracefully lowered herself into the water and swam to us. "Whizzy the wizard Fox and Phillip the Frog you are in great danger here. I am Lynthma. I am a friend to Princess Merran and I will protect you."

The Land of Mistasia was like an amusement park with no safety rails. Everything was so beautiful, yet dangerous.

Our hero Mermaid, Lynthma, fit that description. She was probably the most beautiful woman I had every seen. Her sparkling eyes matched her aqua colored tail. Her creamy white skin glowed against the moonlight. She was gorgeous, yet maybe the most dangerous creature we had encountered.

Only later did Grace Tallon explain to Whizzy and me that Mermaids were the dominate species in Dragon Lake, and that Mermen were their servants, but that Sorcerer LaCroiux had convinced a small band of Mermen to rebel against the Mermaids in order to attack us.

It seemed that King Cragon's minions would stop at nothing to keep us from reaching Cadieux Castle. Yet we had survived both

Wolverine Forest and Dragon Lake, and now only a small stretch of open field separated us from our destination and more importantly...Rachel Whizzenmog.

THERE IS ANOTHER WAY
14

Sitting in the dark, smelly room Rachel Whizzenmog cried. She didn't know how long she had been locked away with no food, water or light. The room had no windows and the door closed so tightly that no light came through except a small sliver at the floor. It was her only reference point.

The frightening snake man that had trapped her hadn't returned either. Rachel was afraid he would return at any moment.

She wrapped her arms around her legs and tucked her head between her arms. Curling up into a ball, she felt a small bit of security.

"Rachel," A familiar voice echoed inside her head.

She gasped. It was the first words she had heard while in this room.

"Who's there?" She questioned in a scared voice.

"Rachel are you okay?" The voice continued.

"Who are you?" She demanded.

"Phillip Harper."

"Phillip? Is that really you? Where are you? I can't see anything." She tried to search the room using her hands.

"We are coming Rachel. Whizzy and I are coming for you."

"What? I...I don't understand. Aren't you here?"

"No. I can't explain now. Just know that we are coming for you," I said.

Rachel Whizzenmog began to cry. "I must be going crazy."

"No, Rachel. You can hear me. I am talking to you. Trust me. We will be there soon," I explained.

I opened my eyes. Sitting in the wet grass, under a small tree Cadieux Castle was in the distance behind me.

Grace Tallon and Whizzy the Wizard Fox gawked at me waiting for answers.

"I was able to speak to her. She is okay for now. She is very scared." I explained.

"Then let's go!" Whizzy started to hastily leave.

"Wait!" Grace demanded and grabbed Whizzy's arm. "We must be careful how we approach the castle. Sorcerer LaCroiux will be waiting for us. He will no doubt have a trap waiting.

"A trap?" Whizzy said with a sly grin.

I knew what that meant. Whizzy had an idea that no one else was going to like very much.

He explained that one of us would need to be captured, distract Sorcerer LaCroiux and the other two could sneak into the Castle, save Rachel and escape.

"Who gets captured?" I asked thinking Whizzy would nominate Grace.

He paused for only a second and then with the biggest smile I had ever seen he replied, "Me!"

"You are going to get yourself captured?" Grace Tallon's elfish mind was trying to process Whizzy's plan. "I don't understand how you think that is going to help us save your sister?"

"It would be the easiest way into the castle. Then I'll use magic to escape." Whizzy replied.

"You accidentally move a boat and you believe you are ready to challenge a Sorcerer and his apprentice? Either you are the bravest Whizzenmog I have ever met or the most foolish." Grace turned to face me, "I bet it's the latter." Then she winked at me.

The sun began to rise in Mistasia. I watched the brilliance of Cadieux Castle as its stone façade glimmered. It was massive, maybe three times as large as Whizzy's house back in Greenville.

"Your friend's plan is insane, Phillip the Frog." Grace stood beside me now.

She startled me when she spoke. After I caught my breath I began to laugh.

"Whizzy is pretty self-confident," I replied.

"Are you certain? I would call it naïve. He has no idea what he is walking into. I believe we need to stay together," Grace suggested, but really meant it as a directive.

The thing was that I believed she was correct. Whizzy was putting himself in danger. We knew nothing about Sorcerer LaCroiux or his apprentice, Ethan Whizzenmog. How could we possibly battle against them? How would we defeat them?

She read my thoughts. She knew I was concerned for my best friend's safety. Grace used that to her advantage.

"You should talk to him. There is a safer way to enter the castle," She pleaded. "We cannot defeat them without Whizzy the Wizard Fox."

THE HOODED FIGURE AT GRACE'S HOUSE

15

We walked through the fields leading to the Village of Cadieux, a group of twenty modest homes that sat just outside Cadieux Castle.

Grace and I stayed together, and Whizzy slowly walked behind us. He seemed to be deciding the best way to get caught.

Grace, on the other hand, definitely had a plan. She went straight to the last house on the left. It was a small red brick home with two windows, one on either side of the front door.

The people of Cadieux must be poor. I thought after seeing their homes.

"Their homes are not very big, Phillip the Frog. They do not need the spacious houses you live in," Grace replied. She must have been reading my mind.

I felt ashamed to have even thought it. I didn't mean any harm. These houses were just tiny. I expected homes the size of the one's back home on Burgundy Drive, where Whizzy lived.

Grace continued to scold me, "They do not have the things you have in your world. Therefore, they only need a home for shelter. These are humble elves who live off this land."

"Elves?" I replied aloud. I hadn't noticed that these people were elves. Most of them wore hoods or hats. "Are these elves...I mean is this where...?" Grace interrupted me before I could finish.

"I live?"

The tone in Grace's voice made me believe that I had offended her.

"Yes, it is my home, Phillip the Frog."

We stood before the red, bricked house.

"This is my home."

"This is your home, Grace?" Whizzy said finally joining the conversation. He sounded impressed.

I was suddenly confused. Why would Whizzy be impressed? I thought he would be making fun of her.

"Yes, Whizzenmog. It is my home." Grace replied with an air of resentment in her voice.

"Cool," was all he said.

A small slender hooded figure came out from the front door.

Whizzy and I waited for Grace to introduce us. She didn't speak. She appeared to be waiting for the shadowy figure to acknowledge her.

Grace approached slowly and then bowed.

"Well done, Grace," A soft young female voice spoke.

"Thank you, Princess Merran," Grace replied still bowing.

The princess removed her hood. She was much younger than I expected. Grace had said that Princess Merran would become queen at her next birthday, but this Elven girl was very young. I knew that I had to be older than her. Her long blonde hair was pulled back tightly. Her bright blue eyes gazed at Whizzy and me. She had rosy-colored cheeks and an impish smile.

"Princess Merran," I felt myself saying. Then I bowed just as Grace had before.

Whizzy just stared at the young Elven princess. Finally he spoke, "You're just a kid!"

I wished he hadn't spoken. I think Whizzy felt that way too shortly after realizing that he had just offended her.

"I'm sorry. I mean...I guess I thought." Whizzy stammered.

I quickly placed my webbed froggy hand over my best friend's mouth hoping to shut him up. He continued to mumble for a moment and then finally stopped.

"I apologize, Princess. Whizzy the Wizard Fox is an...," Grace searched for the proper word. I knew that if she weren't talking to the princess, she wouldn't have chosen so carefully. I believe the word she was looking for was idiot.

"That is alright, Grace. Thank you." Princess Merran turned to face Whizzy. She was shorter than him, which made her appear even younger. "If you must know I will become thirteen at my next birthday. Then I will be Queen of Mistasia and rule at Cadieux Castle."

"Congratulations," Whizzy said trying to sound impressed, but it came out more sarcastically.

Princess Merran bowed slightly toward us. "Well that may depend upon you, Whizzy."

"Me?" Whizzy replied. "I thought I was here to save my sister?"

"Yes, and in turn stop my uncle, the king, from overtaking these lands. He plans to keep me from the throne."

"How?" I asked. I didn't quite understand the connection.

A low rumble sounded in the distance. Dark gray clouds had formed and quickly made their way toward the Village of Cadieux. The wind started to push the grass at our feet. Whizzy's fur was blowing around, and Grace's hair too.

"The Whizzenmog family has long been the protector to the throne, as I am sure Grace has told you. The King believes that your sister is the savior that your great grandfather spoke about restoring the glory to your family's name and the throne. My uncle knows that the throne will no longer be his at my next birthday. He wants to keep me from obtaining my rightful place as queen and your sister stands in his way."

Every time Princess Merran referred to Rachel as the savior, Whizzy clenched his paw into a fist. At one point, I thought he seriously considered socking the princess in the nose.

"Princess Merran another storm approaches. We must go inside," Grace stated.

We all gathered inside the modest home of Grace Tallon. We didn't stay for long.

"If we can help you, how do you plan on us getting into the Castle unseen?" Whizzy questioned, his ire still up.

Grace swiftly moved through the main room and down a narrow corridor. Princess Merran motioned for us to follow. I watched as Grace stopped at the end of the hallway. She reached toward the ceiling and grabbed a metal candleholder on the wall. She gave it a turn and a clicking sound rang out from inside the walls.

The wall moved slightly. Grace leaned against it
and pushed it aside.

"A hidden doorway?" I replied in
astonishment. "Where does it lead?"

"Cadieux Castle," replied Princess Merran.

THE DOOR IN THE FLOOR

16

The corridor was small. I had to hunch
over to avoid hitting my head on the ceiling.
Everyone else was the perfect size. It was obvious
that it was built for elves. The floor, walls and
ceiling were plain dirt. It was cooler and smelled
funny like it does just after it rains and all the
worms crawl from the ground.

We walked for a while; how long? I
wasn't sure. It was so dark. Grace led the way,
followed by Whizzy and the princess. I brought
up the rear.

Princess Merran explained that the
corridor was actually an escape tunnel built for
her when she was a baby. Her parents believed

that her uncle wasn't trustworthy so they built this tunnel from the castle into the village.

"So the king doesn't know about it?" I asked as I hit my head against a root sticking out from the ceiling. I rubbed my head and realized how close it came to my eye.

"No, Phillip the Frog he doesn't. We are almost to the castle. Be prepared for anything. The king may not be aware of this passage, but he is definitely expecting our arrival." The princess sounded so confident.

"Aren't you scared?" I asked her. I was. My stomach had begun its usual round of somersaults. I felt like I was sweating despite the cool air, but it might have just been my amphibian skin.

"Fear is the unknown. Nothing more, Phillip the Frog!" The princess calmly responded.

I could hear Grace laughing in my mind. If it wasn't so dark, I bet you could see me blushing.

Whizzy had kept very quiet. That wasn't very Whizzy-like. Normally, he would be trying to be the center of attention. But the longer we were in this tunnel, the more I felt like he was trying to hide. I knew he was scared too.

Finally, we approached a door. This door was small too and had no noticeable handle. Candles on either side of the door lit the tunnel.

The princess gave us directions. Grace and I were to save Rachel, while she took Whizzy to find Sorcerer LaCroiux.

Whizzy looked sick. His face lacked expression. It was like someone had sucked the life right out of him.

Princess Merran could tell my best friend was scared.

"Whizzy you are much more powerful than you understand. A wizard's strength comes from within. Let your mind take control...it will know what to do." She placed her small hand on his furry, red shoulder. "The Land of Mistasia believes in you." The princess looked into Whizzy's eyes. "I believe in you, Whizzy the Wizard Fox."

Grace reached her hand inside an opening in the door I hadn't noticed before. Her arm disappeared nearly to her elbow before she stopped and grabbed hold of something inside.

She turned her arm to the left and unlocked the door. She removed her arm and placed both hands on the door to push. Struggling to move the door I rushed to help her. Together we pushed, but the door was heavier than anything I had ever felt. Whizzy joined us and finally we felt the door give way. It popped up slightly and then slid to the side.

Light washed into the tunnel like a river over-stepping its banks. My eyes stung. When I was able to see again, I realized that we were looking up into a room. I didn't know when we had started moving upward, but being underground had confused our senses. The door that was before us led up...not out.

We climbed out of the tunnel and into a bedroom. A huge four-post bed draped with purple and gold linens sat in the middle of the room. Normally, a bed this large would consume the entire bedroom, but not in this castle. Beautifully carved wooden furniture lined the walls: a dresser twice the size of my parent's car; three chairs that couldn't have been for the princess as they were big enough for a giant; and a large rectangular box with little elfish faces, symbols and creatures carved along its front.

"Wow!" I exclaimed.

"Shush!" Princess Merran retorted.

Whizzy used his wand to move the open door back into position. That was when I noticed it was covered in stones, as it was part of the bedroom floor. That explained why it was so heavy.

"We're in the princess's bedroom," I whispered to Whizzy. He didn't seem impressed.

"We need to move before they discover we are here," Grace barked at us. She grabbed my arm and led me to the bedroom door.

The wooden door squeaked as she pulled it open slightly to peek out into the hallway. It was empty. She looked back at the princess and they shared a strange glance.

Princess Merran nodded, and Grace and I were off down the hallway.

THEY HAVE A GIANT WHAT?
17

Grace and I dashed down the hallway. I
had forgotten how quick she was. I struggled to
keep pace. That must have been why she gripped
my arm so tightly. She knew that we had very
little time and room for error. That meant
Grace couldn't be waiting for me to catch up.

"Where is Rachel being held?" I asked
Grace in my mind.

She answered, "They locked her away in
the south dungeon. It is a place that is rarely
used by anyone in the castle. The king hoped the
princess or her servants wouldn't have
accidentally discovered Rachel."

Running down the hall we came to a
right turn. Grace was going so fast she ran up
the side of the wall. I couldn't quite manage that
trick. I slammed into the wall and stumbled.
Grace and I fell to the ground.

"Come on!" She yelled as she grabbed me
again and pulled me forward.

My knee was sore and my elbow hurt, but there wasn't anytime to worry about it now. Next we stopped at a dark staircase.

"Grace, are you sure this is where we have to go?" I whimpered while trying to regain my breath. She however was breathing normally.

She nodded.

"Maybe she is over there," I pointed down a well-lit hallway.

Grace began to move down the staircase. I reluctantly followed. As we descended, it became easier to see. The floor was wet and candles were hung on the wall. It was like my dream.

"Grace this is it. I saw this hallway in my dream...when I was Rachel. She is here!" I tried to whisper, but I was too excited.

Grace shot me a motherly look.

Then an awful sound emerged from the end of the hallway. It was a deep groan, like a dinosaur had just awoken from a million year sleep. It sounded hungry and angry all at once.

I whimpered again, and that was before I actually saw him. The biggest, ugliest person I had ever seen. Nearly twelve feet tall his shoulders rubbed against the ceiling. His head was oddly shaped like it had shrunk in the washing machine and was now too small for his body.

I couldn't stop staring at his melon. It was just awful.

His eyes were dark and sunken with warts sprouting thick, dark hairs on his chin and forehead. The beast's ears were misshapen and teeth crooked or missing.

I was so frightened that I couldn't even speak. I tried to ask Grace what he was but couldn't...not even in my mind. It was as if the hamster running the wheel that kept my brain turning had been so frightened it froze.

"Phillip the Frog!" Grace spoke up. "Now would be a great time to run!" She immediately dashed back to the staircase.

I was frozen in place with fear. I had never seen anything this large outside a cage in the zoo.

"Phillip!" Grace yelled again! "Run."

Snapping out of my trance, I realized it was too late. The giant, ugly man was right on top of me. Luckily, he was almost too big. He took up so much space in the hallway that he couldn't move very well. Lifting his giant club-like hand, he swung down like a sledgehammer. I hopped underneath and slid behind him. Without thinking, I leapt onto his back and placed my webbed froggy hands over his sunken eyes.

The giant roared. It sounded like he was speaking, but in another language. I couldn't understand anything he mumbled.

Grace took the opportunity and acted quickly. She took rope from her pack and tied it around his left leg while the giant stumbled around attempting to knock me off his back.

I was very grateful that he wasn't smart, because if he realized that backing into the wall would have basically crushed me into froggy flapjacks it would have been over. Grace finished lassoing the monstrous man's feet and launched full speed back down the hallway.

"Jump, Phillip!" She yelled.

I quickly followed her instructions. I leapt from his back and walked backwards away from him.

He struggled to turn around. It probably would have been very funny to watch his shoulders deflecting off the wall like a bouncy ball if he weren't doing so to try and squash me like a bug.

Back away, Phillip the Frog! Grace Tallon directed in my head.

As I stepped away, I could see Grace pulling on the rope tightening its grip. The giant finally righted himself and started to lumber towards me. He didn't even have the time to realize what was about to happen, when the rope unexpectedly snapped.

My heart sank, and I nearly wet myself...yet again I didn't know how frogs went to the bathroom.

"What do I do?" I screamed in absolute terror. My voice was about three octaves higher than normal.

Grace yelled something, but I couldn't understand over the heavy breathing from the monster.

He squatted down and tried to wrap his tree trunk-like muscular arms around me. I freaked out and dove head first, like a baseball player sliding into home plate, between his legs. His momentum took him down, crashing face first into the hard cement floor.

I now laid on my back looking back at the giant. He was unconscious. Grace wasted no time and sprung into action. She tied his legs again and then his arms. It took every inch of rope she had.

"Let's hope that holds him." She sounded a little nervous as to whether or not it actually would. "We need to move with haste."

No one in Greenville had ever used the word 'haste', yet today I knew exactly what it meant...speed!

"Grace, what was that?"

"It is a giant troll. One of Sorcerer LaCroiux's henchmen, but not very quick in feet or brains...just brawn," She replied as she started down the hall to the door behind which Rachel Whizzenmog was being held captive.

I was excited and nervous all at the same time. We were finally going to save Rachel, yet a giant troll was laying on the floor only ten feet behind us and he could wake up at any second.

Grace looked at the door and then me. "It has no handle. How do we open it?" She asked in slight panic.

I wasn't used to hearing that in her voice. She was always so calm and in control.

"Can you use your sword?" I asked. She didn't seem to think that would work. "I...I don't...wait!" I yelled startling her a bit. "I have an idea, but you're probably not gonna like it." I whispered it to her in my mind.

"I like it," she replied with a smirk.

We stood outside the door waiting for the giant troll to awaken. He stood up and growled in rage. Spit flung from his crooked teeth and hung off his wart-covered chin.

"Ibe eet u!" The angry beast yelled.

"I think I understood that!" I responded. "I'm not liking this plan."

"It was your idea, Frog!" Grace reminded me as though to say if it fails I blame you.

The giant troll stood tall; his ropes were gone...also my idea. He began to run toward us. He moved quicker than I expected. Closer and closer he came, but at the last second, I leapt between his legs again, and as he lunged down to grab me Grace jumped over him. The lumbering giant troll smashed head-first into the solid wooden door. It splintered and exploded into a million pieces. The giant was down and out again.

We ran over his limp body into the dark room.

I yelled, "Rachel! Where are you?"

THE KING'S CHAMBER

18

"Over here!" Rachel replied back. I could tell she had been crying. She appeared in the rectangular-shaped path of light that emanated from the open door. "Phillip, thank you." She wrapped her arms around my amphibian skin. I was so happy. I would have given anything to have her hug me like this in Greenville. Usually she just rolled her eyes and walked away. At the time I didn't realize how different she was...until we exited the room over the giant troll's back and into the hallway.

As we emerged I understood why her hand felt differently than I expected. She too was a fox just like Whizzy, but only a shade of beautiful bronze.

She gasped. The words in her head screamed in mine. *What's wrong with me?*

"I'll explain everything, Rachel. Please we need to go now and help Whizzy!" I urged her.

"Whizzy? How did you two get here? Where is here?"

I could see her mind began to swim.

"You can have this conversation later," Grace interrupted sounding as irritated as usual.

The giant troll startled us all as he snorted kicking up dust and dirt from the floor.

We all ran up the staircase and back to the Princess's bedroom. While we ran I tried to catch Rachel up on everything: That we were in the Land of Mistasia; that she had been kidnapped by King Cragon's henchmen; that Whizzy and I had fought our way to the castle; and that Rachel was a witch and thought to be the savior of Mistasia.

Rachel Whizzenmog has known me my entire life and always thought I was weird, but this may have sent me into another level of weirdness...if she wasn't a bronze colored fox and I a green frog.

The one thing I couldn't understand was why when I was in Rachel's dream I didn't see her as a fox? Grace explained that I had never seen her as a fox, so my brain made her appear as I remembered her, a young girl.

"Phillip, where is my brother?" Rachel said with a tear in her eye. This was the first time I could remember that she wanted to know were Whizzy was and it wasn't because she was going to yell at him. "Is he okay?"

"He isn't here!" Grace replied after looking into Princess Merran's room. She turned to me.

"The King's chamber," Grace and I said in unison.

The three of us bolted toward the King's chamber. Grace led the way of course, since she knew her way around Cadieux Castle.

We watched from across the hall as three Elven guards stood watch before the twin doors leading into the King's chamber. I motioned for her to go speak to them.

"They are Elven Warriors aren't they? They know you right?" I questioned Grace using my telepathy.

"Yes, but I would have no good reason to enter the King's chamber without the princess," She snapped back in my mind.

Rachel quickly realized that something strange was going on between us. "What is going on? Are we just going to stare at this door, Phillip?" That was more like the Rachel Whizzenmog I remembered.

"Oh, I forgot to tell you that I can read minds," I answered.

She stared at me with her foxy jaw open. Her small sharp teeth jutted out at me.

"And see dreams," I added. It didn't help the conversation between us so I went back to telepathy with Grace.

"Find Whizzy the Wizard Fox. Use your mind and locate him?" Grace instructed.

"I can do that?"

She nodded. "Close your eyes and think of him. He will come to you. You will see him."

I inhaled deeply and closed my eyes.

Whizzy the Wizard Fox and Princess Merran stood in a square room with large drapery panels hanging along the walls. A brightly glowing chandelier swung slightly in the middle of the room. Orange dots emanated like eyes around the room, they must have been candles because each light stood along. Standing before them were two tall figures. The first was a very old white-haired man. He had a white beard too that was braided. His face was weathered yet surprisingly happy...maybe snickering. He wore a long white robe that covered his entire body and held a long dark brown staff in his left hand. Beside him stood the second man. He too was tall and strong but far younger. It was apparent that he was King Cragon as he wore a four-pointed sparkling gold crown upon his slick black-haired head. He had a thick black beard as well, and a devilish grin. He wore dark purple robes with a golden stripe down the middle. The king was arrogant and patronizing toward Princess Merran. He looked down on her from his long, pointed nose.

At first I couldn't hear them speaking, but the sound began to increase like turning up the volume on your television.

"I know what you're planning to do, Uncle!" Princess Merran strongly protested.

"Do you now, my niece? I raised you. Prepare you to become Queen and this is how you repay my efforts? Accuse me in my own chamber. And of what do you accuse me?" The King smoothly responded.

"You have been keeping a secret from me."

"I have no idea what you mean, Merran." He quickly responded.

"You know who this is don't you?"
Princess Merran pointed to Whizzy.

The king turned his head slightly and
gawked at Whizzy. His dark eyes burning as he
looked Whizzy up and down.

"I am sorry, my dear, but I haven't any
idea who this ragged-looking fox is. Should I? Is
he someone of importance from another realm?"
The King deflected her questioning with verbal
taunts.

"LaCroiux holds his sister captive in this
castle," Princess Merran divulged.

The king gasped. He turned to his advisor,
the white-roped elder sorcerer Pierre LaCroiux
who stood beside him in the King's chamber.

"Is this true, LaCroiux? Would we be
holding this fox's sibling hostage in our castle?"

It looked like the King was attempting to
hold back laughter as he openly mocked the
Princess.

Sorcerer LaCroiux smirked and replied
simply with, "No, your Majesty."

"You see vicious rumors, my princess. This
fox has misled you. I do apologize for the

misunderstanding." He smiled the most crooked, fake smile I had ever seen.

"THIS IS OVER KING CRAGON!" Whizzy suddenly exploded. His paws balled up in rage. He held his wand so tightly that it shook.

The king glanced at the wizard fox's wand, which he hadn't noticed until now, and nodded.

"Very well. I have many stately things to attend to this afternoon. I leave you in the very capable hands of my advisor and his staff." And the King disappeared before anyone realized what had just happened.

Sorcerer LaCroiux stood patiently. He seemed to be awaiting something. A grinding sound, like sandpaper scrapping across wood, echoed below at Whizzy's feet. He saw the same brownish-yellow, diamond-headed snake from his basement slither past him.

A sinking feeling swept through Whizzy's body, I felt it too. It was fear.

The snake-man appeared next to Sorcerer LaCroiux after a violent explosion of light burst through the room. When the light was gone Ethan Whizzenmog, or what he was now, stood before them.

My eyes snapped open. Gasping for air and I stumbled to the floor. Grace Tallon and Rachel the Fox rushed toward me.

"What did you see?" Grace pressed.

"The princess and Whizzy are in danger. Sorcerer LaCroiux and Ethan Whizzenmog are in the King's Chamber." I was still trying to catch my breath. The fear I felt through Whizzy was tremendous. It attempted to squeeze my lungs like ringing out a wet cloth.

"We need to get in there now!" Grace said as she gritted her teeth. She dug inside her pack and pulled out another twig. This one was more like what I imagined a wand would look like. It was straight and slender with a rounded tip. She carefully extended it for Rachel. "Take this. It belongs to you."

Rachel's eyes grew wide. She smiled and grabbed hold of her wand. "I am a witch?" She questioned me.

"Yes, Rachel," I answered.

"Possibly the most powerful in all of Mistasia," Grace added.

"What can I do?" Rachel asked.

"Anything," Grace responded.

The smile nearly overtook Rachel's furry bronze face. She didn't hesitate like Whizzy. She jumped in with no remorse. Swinging the wand in a sideways motion a gust of wind whipped down the hallway and swept the three Elven guards from their posts at the King's Chamber doors.

"Cool," Rachel laughed.

We dashed to the doors and flung them open wide. Inside we saw the King's henchmen tossing Whizzy around the room. Now we would see just how powerful Rachel the Wizard Fox really was!

WHIZZENMOGS VS SORCERERS
19

She didn't say a word. Rachel just gave me a wicked smirk and then started off toward

233

the snake-man. She definitely had a score to settle with him. I started to follow her, but Grace held me back.

"What are you doing? We need to help them!" I yelled.

"This is their battle, Phillip the Frog. There is little we can do against two sorcerers. Leave this to the Whizzenmogs." She sounded quite certain that Whizzy and Rachel would be able to handle the King's evil henchmen.

I, however, was scared out of my mind.

Rachel flicked her wrist and blasted the snake-man across the room.

Whizzy saw Rachel. He smiled, "Hey sis. You alright!" He asked.

"Just fine," Rachel replied as she fired another shot, this time at Sorcerer LaCroiux. Whizzy joined in.

The sorcerer easily deflected each attempt. He laughed and then raised his arms before slamming down his staff onto the ground. The room shook like an earthquake. We all fell to the ground.

It felt like he had punched me in the gut. I rolled onto my side and began to cough. My stomach hurt like I had eaten something bad.

A burst of flames rose toward the ceiling in the corner where the snake-man, Ethan Whizzenmog, had disappeared into the shadows after Rachel attacked him. He walked toward the Whizzenmog twins wreathed in flames. He began to shoot fireballs at them. One whizzed past Rachel and nearly singed my face. I ducked at the last second and it exploded against the wall behind me. The purple and yellow drapery was now burning.

Grace was itching to join the battle. Another fireball zoomed toward us. It crashed into the chamber doors and punched a hole through them. She grunted in anger, then grabbed an arrow from her pack, raised her bow and fired at Ethan Whizzenmog.

The fiery sorcerer's apprentice was too concerned with Rachel and Whizzy to notice that Grace had shot toward him when the arrow punctured his scaly skin just above his right knee.

His flame extinguished immediately and Ethan collapsed on the floor in pain.

"Hey! I thought this was their battle?" I crocked at Grace.

She smiled, "I just couldn't resist."

Sorcerer LaCroiux retaliated for his fallen apprentice. Sending Grace flinging backwards against the stonewall. She hit her head hard and slumped to the floor. I ran to her side. She was unconscious. I panicked. I'm not sure if it was anger or fear that made me do it, but I grabbed her sword and pulled it from its sheath. It glowed in the dim light of the King's Chamber. In its beautiful silver blade I could see the reflected image of Sorcerer LaCroiux aiming at me. I hopped as high as my froggy legs would let me to avoid his spell. I flipped in the air and landed between Whizzy and Rachel.

"You children are foolish to believe that you stand a chance against me. The King believes that you are the legendary savior of Mistasia." Sorcerer LaCroiux pointed his bony finger at Rachel.

I could feel the cold presence of evil as his shadow crept closer. My hand rose quickly before I thought it through, pushing Rachel away. Somehow I knew that his touch, even from his shadow, was not something any of us wanted to experience. I raised Grace's sword and chopped down at the Sorcerer's shadowy arm reaching out for Rachel. It landed at his wrist.

Sorcerer LaCroiux screamed in agony and dropped to the floor. I saw deep red blood leaking from under his white robe. I had wounded him. He and his shadow were connected.

"His shadow," Rachel and I acknowledged together.

Rachel cast a spell that created a whirling tornado. It viciously spun around the wounded sorcerer. He dodged its pull for a moment. Then Whizzy blasted him sending him falling into its vortex.

"Get him, Phillip," Rachel yelled.

I raised the sword again taking aim at the sorcerer's weakness, his shadow.

Suddenly a hissing sound startled us. Ethan had transformed back into the brownish-yellow, diamond-headed snake and lashed out at me. He snapped at my arm with his venomous fangs. I stumbled backwards.

Whizzy attempted to push the snake away, but he was too strong.

Ethan Whizzenmog, now in his snake form, whipped Whizzy's legs from underneath him with a single snap from his tail. Whizzy crashed hard on the ground and lost his wand. It rolled between Whizzy and Ethan.

Rachel's vortex still held Sorcerer LaCroiux captive, but it also began pulling objects into its circular spin, including Whizzy's wand.

The Sorcerer yelled for his apprentice, "The girl, Ethan, get the girl!" He demanded.

His snake eyes locked in on Rachel, who still concentrated hard on keeping her prey held captive in her spinning spell.

"I can't hold him much longer," She warned.

Grace stirred behind us. She awoke to see the battle still raging on. I think she was surprised to still see us alive, and doing fairly well.

Ethan Whizzenmog focused on his main target, Rachel. With Whizzy's wand caught up in the vortex with Sorcerer LaCroiux and Grace's sword lying on the floor, Rachel had become the only true remaining threat in the room.

"Kill her," The sorcerer demanded. His voice sounded shrill and demonic.

The snake lunged at Rachel.

I dove for the sword, grabbed it and swung.

A heavy thud sounded as the evil brownish-yellow snake landed on the floor. A pool of green liquid began to form just under its diamond-shaped head. Ethan Whizzenmog, the snake-man and sorcerer's apprentice was dead.

Rachel had grown weak and the vortex holding the wounded Sorcerer LaCroiux dissipated. He collapsed to the floor and began to mutter words in another language. He cried out, "You will pay! I will have my revenge."

He raised his staff above his head, still holding his injured hand close to his body. The blood soaked through. He screamed angrily and slammed the staff to the floor again.

A blue spark shot up from the ground and encircled him. Wind rushed into the King's Chamber from all sides. Sorcerer's LaCroiux's hair and robes flapped against the wind. A bright flash lit the room and then he vanished instantly. Just when he disappeared a blast shot out through the room knocking us all down again. We slid backwards on our rears. The chamber doors burst open and the candles all were extinguished.

BANISHED FROM THIS CASTLE
20

Dust hung in the air around my face. It was stuck to my damp skin. I was drained, and my knee began to throb from my fall earlier. I pushed myself to my feet. In the middle of the room was the large deceased snake, Ethan Whizzenmog.

Suddenly, Rachel Whizzenmog wrapped herself around me again. She hugged me tightly and thanked me for saving her from the snake. If this whole trip had been a dream, I figured now is when I would awaken to find myself still the same old clumsy, awkward Phillip Harper wishing Rachel would just say 'Hello' to me. But it wasn't a dream. I was really here and I had just saved her. It felt great! For the first time in my whole life I was the hero...or at least one of the heroes. We had all done a great job!

It was obvious now that Rachel was a very strong witch, but that she alone wouldn't be able to defeat Sorcerer LaCroiux. She and Whizzy would have to work together against the far more experienced Sorcerer.

"Princess, are you alright?" A deep voiced Elven Warrior spoke. Standing in the open doorway were the three guards that Rachel had whisked down the hallway earlier. The expression on his face showed just how confused he and the others were.

Magic was rarely used in Mistasia nowadays...at least since the Whizzenmogs had left. The sorcerers that remained didn't have the same type of magic. They controlled the elements: water, fire, wind & earth. These elves were astonished and frankly scared at the newcomers. They held their bows and swords at Rachel, Whizzy and me until the princess explained.

"I am just fine. Thanks to our new heroes. I would like to introduce you to the Whizzenmogs; Rachel and Whizzy, and their friend Phillip the Frog." She smiled widely and bowed before us. The Elven guards did as well. Grace did too.

The look on her face afterward was different. She was happy...I think. She was smiling too, but it looked oddly painful.

"Where is my uncle?" Princess Merran asked the guards.

"We do not know, princess."

"I can find him," I offered.

At the western most section of Cadieux Castle, King Cragon paced through the hallways.

He was nervous and awaiting the return of his henchmen, Sorcerer LaCroiux.

He muttered under his breath, "Where is he?"

The King approached a unique door at the end of the hallway. It had a large golden symbol perched at his eye level. It was a snakehead, with ruby red eyes. Its mouth was wide open and forked tongue exposed.

A flash of light appeared from underneath the doorway. The King stuttered, then reached for the golden doorknob and opened the door. It creaked loudly.

The fireplace burst into flame. The King gasped with surprise. Sorcerer LaCroiux had returned. His robes still bared the bloodied stains from his wounds. He was in pain.

The King was shocked. "They did this to you?" The sorcerer didn't respond. "How did they discover your weakness?" King Cragon lashed.

"I don't know. It was a fearful stroke of luck. The frightened frog of Greenville struck me with a sword. He gained a momentary glimpse of heroism. I won't let it happen again!" The sorcerer sneered.

"Again?" They are still alive? All of them?" The King was unhappy. "You mean to tell me that these three children discovered your weakness and managed to survive a duel against two sorcerers?" His chin jutted out like he attempted to catch all the rage he wanted to spew toward LaCroiux.

His advisor didn't reply and certainly didn't look the King in the eyes. The King was the only thing in all of Mistasia that Sorcerer LaCroiux feared.

"Well!" Screamed the King.

"Yes, master!" He feebly replied.

"Where is your apprentice? Why is he not with you?" The king continued to yell.

"He is dead, your Majesty."

The king stormed at LaCroiux and grabbed him by the throat. He was seething. "You are banished from this castle." He exclaimed through gritted teeth.

I opened my eyes. My heart was pounding. Everyone stared at me in anticipation.

"He was arguing with Sorcerer LaCroiux. The King banished him from the castle," I stated.

YOUR BIRTHDAY IS TOMORROW?

21

Princess Merran led us through the castle to the room where I had witnessed King Cragon. She recognized the snakehead symbol on the door.

"He banished LaCroiux," Grace said. She was repeating it aloud...I guess to make it sink in. The fact that the king had banished his personal advisor and a powerful sorcerer didn't make sense.

"If King Cragon wants the throne, how does he expect to keep you from taking it at your next birthday?" Whizzy asked.

"He is getting desperate," Princess Merran replied. "In less than twenty-four hours I will become queen, and then..."

"Your birthday is tomorrow?" I interrupted. It wasn't like me to be rude, but I was shocked to find out that the princess's thirteenth birthday was tomorrow.

Grace gave me a vicious stare. *Be quiet!* She barked in my mind.

Rachel laughed.

I felt my cheeks turning a violent shade of red. "I'm sorry, Princess."

She smiled coyly and then continued on. "He desperately wants to keep control of Mistasia. For nearly a decade he has ruled these lands, and he has no intention of allowing his brother's daughter to regain control of the throne." She had become upset.

"What happened to your parents, Princess?" Rachel inquired.

The princess explained that her parents mysteriously vanished. She told us how there were many stories about what had happened, but no one really knew. She believed that her uncle had arranged for their disappearance, which allowed him to claim the throne.

"He can not be trusted!" Princess Merran expressed vehemently.

"Well, then let's go get him," Rachel said. She pointed her wand at the door and it burst open slamming into the wall.

We all ran inside. The room was poorly lit and smelled of sulfur.

"It stinks in here," Whizzy gagged. "Phillip did you..."

"No!" I denied. I most certainly didn't fart. I couldn't believe that Whizzy had even asked. Really! I hadn't even eaten. Just because you eat one bag of chili-cheese corn chips and have a bad night doesn't mean you're ALWAYS the one that made the room smell funny!

Rachel and Grace seemed to think that Whizzy was funny. I really wasn't happy about the fact that they both suddenly found him funny. *Didn't they both dislike him?* I thought.

"Where are you, Uncle?" Princess Merran demanded bringing us back to reality in a hurry.

A frightening chuckle echoed through the room.

"I can't see anything?" Rachel said.

"Me neither," Whizzy replied.

"I can help you with that," The King's voice bellowed. A flash of light exploded in the fireplace. A blaze crackled to life. His strong square jaw became visible in the corner as he sat in a small throne. He had removed his dark purple ropes that symbolized his status as King. Now he wore a black coat. The golden crown, however, remained firmly planted upon his devious head.

The five of us stood together. Princess Merran in the middle with Whizzy and Rachel to her left and Grace and I to her right. The Whizzenmogs each held their wands firmly in their furry paws. Grace had pulled out her sword and then handed it to me. She then grabbed her bow and arrow.

King Cragon didn't even flinch. He just leaned forward exposing his entire face against the light from the fire. A wide grin was present. The gray hairs in his mainly black beard glimmered. His eyes seemed even darker than before.

This man was pure evil. If the devil existed in Mistasia, King Cragon was surely his right hand man. That would explain why the powerful Sorcerer LaCroiux would fear him so.

"Why the need for the weapons, my child?" The King calmly questioned. He placed his elbows on his knees and folded his hands together under his chin.

"Your reign over this kingdom comes to an end tonight, Uncle. You know that tomorrow I will become queen, and it is too late for you to stop that from happening now. You have failed."

King Cragon began to laugh.

The pit in my stomach tripled in size. His laughter was horrifying. I had faced man-sized wolverines, dragons, a merman, a giant troll and two sorcerers, yet the sound of his voice made my knees quiver. His presence alone sent chills down my spine.

The look on Whizzy and Rachel's faces didn't make me feel any better. Rachel was in shock, and Whizzy was a cross between pain and having to go to the bathroom.

"Failed? I'm sorry niece, but I have no idea what you mean." He replied with a patronizing tone.

"I know you were going to keep me from the throne...don't lie," the princess yelled.

"No. I wanted you to be more prepared. Wait a few more years. Then when you were ready...you would take the throne," The King said while standing from his seat. He towered above us all. I being the tallest only came to the middle of his chest.

"Wait a few more years. Tomorrow, I will be thirteen," The princess began, but King Cragon interrupted.

"That is correct. Thirteen!" He yelled. "And what makes you believe that at the age of thirteen you are ready to rule this land, Princess? You are but a child."

Princess Merran didn't respond.

"We know you banished LaCroiux, King Cragon," Grace spoke which shocked even the princess.

Turning toward the fireplace, King Cragon hid his expression from us. He placed his hands over its warmth. I could almost feel him searching for the correct response like he was a game show contestant.

I leaned to the side attempting to see him. The flames danced in a rhythm as he moved his hands. It was as though he commanded their movement like a maestro leading his orchestra.

"Yes, I did." King Cragon finally answered. "I had heard about the unfortunate incident within my chambers earlier tonight." He looked back over his shoulder at the princess. "It was unacceptable."

"That he attacked us, or that he lost?" Whizzy blasted.

Grace smiled at him.

King Cragon turned back to the fire and took a deep breath. He sighed deeply before answering, "Well, that he lost!"

The King swirled around and a white-hot flame jumped from the fireplace toward Princess Merran. It reached for her like an octopus's tentacles.

Grace reacted by pushing the princess away, but the flame snapped across her back. Her pack of arrows caught fire.

Whizzy and Rachel attempted spells to knock him down, but King Cragon created a shield with the flame easily blocking both.

I helped Grace remove her pack. She had just one arrow, and I held her sword.

"He's a sorcerer?" Grace questioned in disbelief.

"That would explain why LaCroiux feared him so much," Princess Merran replied as I helped her to her feet. "He has been hiding this for a long time. Our people won't be very accepting of a Sorcerer King!"

Rachel continued to fire spell after spell trying to pierce his fiery shield, but each had the same result.

Princess Merran placed her hand upon Rachel Whizzenmog's shoulder.

"Stop," She calmly stated.

The King's shield evaporated in a steamy plume.

"I hereby banish you from this castle, Cragon Cadieux, for crimes against the throne."

"I will not give you MY THRONE!" The King spit with rage.

"Oh that can't be good!" I responded.

LET'S PLAY A GAME OF FREEZE TAG
22

King Cragon pulled the flame out of the fireplace and into the middle of the room. The fire swirled before transforming into three large members of his Wolverine Army.

Grace pulled her sword from my slippery froggy hand and lunged toward one of the wolverines. She slashed at its belly, but it sliced through without doing anything. The beast swatted her across the chest tossing her into the wall. She crumpled onto the floor. Her sword landed beside her.

Rachel and Whizzy started using different spells to fend of the advancing wolverines.

Rachel pulled the rug out from under one wolverine. It tumbled to the ground and then turned back into flames. Just seconds later the beast reformed.

Whizzy made a slicing motion using his wand as a sword at another wolverine. It cut straight through the beast. The two halves fell to the ground and exploded, but they too quickly reformed.

The Whizzenmog twins slowly backed away now using lightning bolts to push the wolverines away.

"What do we do?" Whizzy yelled.

"I don't know!" Rachel frantically responded, as she backed into the wall. They had run out of room and the wolverines closed in on them.

Princess Merran yelled to them, "Think! What stops a fire?"

"Water!" The twins said in unison. They didn't have any water.

"Wind?" Rachel asked.

"Maybe. Try it!" He yelled as he blasted their enemies again.

She tried to summon a gust of wind like she had to push the Elven guards away from the King's Chamber door earlier.

King Cragon swept his hand up and sealed the door tight.

The drift slammed against the door, but was unable to enter.

Every time they attempted to defeat the fiery wolverine beasts, King Cragon's sorcery foiled them.

I tended to Grace. She was bleeding from a cut on her forehead. She also had burn marks on her chest. I held her in my arms and pulled her close to me. I could hear her still breathing.

"Grace, can you hear me?" I spoke to her.

"Cold," Grace said.

"What? You are cold?" I thought I had heard her wrong. It was so hot that sweat had begun to pour off my skin and hers. The flames created by King Cragon made certain that it wasn't cold.

"The answer is cold," she weakly spoke aloud.

Suddenly I understood. I used my telepathy to tell Whizzy without King Cragon hearing.

"Whizzy, its cold! Make it cold to stop the flames."

Whizzy knelt down and pointed his wand at the wolverine's stomach. The beast changed from white to yellow to icy blue. Then Whizzy blasted it again and the frozen statue exploded.

King Cragon screamed in anger.

Whizzy then proceeded to do the same thing to the second and third wolverines. The red wizard fox marched toward King Cragon with confidence in his eyes, but the King allowed the door to open and a spinning vortex sped into the room and swept Whizzy away and pinned him against the wall opposite me.

The water that was now on my amphibian skin had begun to create that surge of energy that I had felt in the forest and at Dragon Lake. I laid Grace in Princess Merran's lap and leapt into action as a second twister entered the room.

Rachel deflected it away.

Just then I approached King Cragon from behind. He was distracted against the twins and I took the opportunity to strike. With Grace's Elven sword in my hand I jumped in the air and pulled the glimmering sword over my head. I swung with all my strength, but he turned and dodged my attempt. The sword sparked against the stone floor. King Cragon used his sorcery to punch me in the gut. A large stone shot from the floor and knocked the wind out of me. I toppled over and gasped for air on the floor.

Whizzy broke free from the first twister and rejoined his sister as they began to push the King into the corner. Rachel used the dirt from the floor to extinguish the remaining flames in the fireplace. Whizzy then blasted the crown from the King's head.

Cragon Cadieux lost focus for an instant. He turned to reach for the crown of Cadieux when Rachel and Whizzy each hit him with a freezing spell.

The once King of Mistasia was now frozen solid, crouched down and stretching for the crown.

The battle was over.

QUEEN MERRAN CADIEUX
23

That night I had the best sleep of my life.
I was completely exhausted.

The next morning I awoke in a large
room. The sun shined in through the open
window. I could smell the freshly cut grass and
flowers from outside. A smile overtook me.

I sat up and stretched.

Whizzy burst through the door. "Great
you're awake!" He yelled.

Rachel was behind him. She stayed at the
doorway though. We smiled at each other.

"Phillip, we have been invited to today's
ceremony. Isn't that awesome?" Whizzy seemed
surprisingly eager to attend.

"Yeah, sure." I laughed at my best friend's
reaction like a girl that had just been asked to
the dance.

"Do you think Grace will be there?" He whispered, so Rachel wouldn't hear.

"Yes," Grace answered. She now stood next to Rachel at the doorway. She heard him with her powerful Elven ears.

Rachel began to laugh at her brother.

If Whizzy's fur weren't so red I would have sworn that he was blushing.

"Ah! I just wanted to know if I should save you a seat; that's all," Whizzy stammered.

I patted him on the shoulder, "Nice try."

We all went to the dining room, which was more the size of a house in Greenville, to eat breakfast. Then we walked around the castle enjoying the beautiful day awaiting the afternoon's ceremony for the crowning of Queen Merran Cadieux.

I asked Grace what happened to Cragon Cadieux after last night's battle. She said that he had been moved to the dungeons and remained frozen. He would be held there forever.

That afternoon Rachel, Whizzy, Grace and I entered the grand ballroom for the crowning ceremony. Merran looked very pretty. She may only be thirteen, but she looked like a queen after they presented her with the crown and placed it upon her head. She grinned proudly.

It felt very good to know that I had a part in making it happen. I had never done anything heroic before.

That night a victorious party was held at Cadieux Castle to celebrate Queen Merran and the demise of her evil uncle. There were fireworks, music and dancing late into the night. As I watched the elves and creatures carelessly party, I felt at ease. The Land of Mistasia suddenly seemed a lot less frightening.

As I lay back in bed that night I thought of home and how much I missed it. We had been told that Grace would take us back there in the morning. I was so anxious that I couldn't sleep. I tossed and turned all night with anticipation.

When the sun rose in the morning at the castle it marked our fifth day in Mistasia. It would be our last.

THE PORTAL HOME

24

For the first time in our journey Grace didn't walk quickly enough. I stayed right next to her the entire journey, which seemed to annoy Whizzy, who was probably hoping to talk with her during our return trip. He had grown very fond of her in the last few days.

We backtracked from Cadieux Castle that morning: moving through the Village of Cadieux, crossing Dragon Lake, and traveling through the Wolverine Forest. Somehow we didn't encounter any creatures that attempted to eat, stab or burn us to a crisp along the way. Mistasia seemed very different, even brighter.

There were no clouds in the sky, which was a perfect shade of blue. The wind blew at our backs as if it was guiding us back home. The sun shined brightly, yet I never felt an uncomfortable heat.

I would have enjoyed it had I not been so focused on getting back to Greenville. My parents had to be worried.

It had been quite a while since anyone in our group had spoken. When we exited the Wolverine Forest and once again could see The Whizzenmog's house resting alone in the field, Grace spoke.

"You have been very jittery, Phillip the Frog. You worried about something?"

"My parents," I said without hesitation.

Grace understood immediately. "Your family won't be so concerned," She replied curtly.

I was hurt. How could my family not care? They loved me. Now I was getting angry. Why would Grace say that?

She must have been reading my mind because she suddenly answered me.

"For every day you spend in Mistasia, it is only an hour to those in your world. Your parents don't even realize that the three of you are missing," Grace explained.

"It's only been five hours in Greenville," Rachel replied in amazement.

"When you return to your world, you mustn't speak of this place. It would endanger our world...and yours." Grace looked the three of us in the eyes. She had that stern expression back. "Understand?"

"Yes," We all replied.

We had finally reached the Whizzenmog's home...or at least the version that appeared in Mistasia. It was the portal between our two worlds, and now it was time to go home.

Grace pulled out a small pouch from her pocket. She poured its powdery contents into her hand and tossed it against the glass door. A flash, then the familiar swirling vortex reappeared.

Rachel hugged Grace and thanked her before jumping into the portal. Whizzy was next. He looked like he too wanted to hug Grace but was afraid. He decided to shake her hand instead. It was very awkward. He said goodbye and jumped into the portal. Now only Grace and I remained.

"You must move quickly before the portal closes, Phillip Harper," She said.

The change in title signaled that our journey had come to an end. I smiled, " Thank you for everything Grace. Will we ever see you again?"

"I believe you will."

I hugged her and then jumped into the portal.

The wind tugged at my skin as I fell through the air spinning around in a circle. Before I realized it, I was back in Whizzy's basement...in Greenville.

The rain had stopped and the sun now shined just as it had in Mistasia. When I stood up, I noticed that Rachel and Whizzy were talking...nicely to each other. It looked like they may have even hugged each other.

I wasn't quite sure how I felt about that. It was still very new to see them getting along. Their parents would wonder if they were alien replicas...or something like that.

Rachel and I smiled at each other. She ran toward me and hugged me. I hugged her back. It was amazing. Then she thanked me again for saving her. Suddenly, I felt something warm on my cheek. She had kissed me. Her beautiful eyes looked up at me. Then she ran away.

Whizzy gave me a hurt look. "Don't get used to that, Phillip!" He said. "That's my sister!"

We both started to laugh.

BILLY LAWTON, BULLY NO MORE
25

When school started the following year, Whizzy and I were excited to begin high school. The summer had changed us both, Rachel too.

I stood outside my locker when Whizzy came up and slapped me on the back.

"Hey, Phillip. Ready for another year of great education," He said sarcastically.

We both began to laugh when we heard a familiar voice.

"Hey, Wasn't. I missed you." It was Billy Lawton.

My gut sank. I really didn't want to deal with Billy today. Whizzy, however, was unfazed.

"Morning, Billy. Have a good summer?"
Whizzy didn't really care whether Billy had a
good summer or not. He just liked to taunt him.
Something I never understood.

Billy pushed his large face up against
Whizzy's.

"Not as good as this school year will be.
I'm gonna see you everyday," He sneered.

Whizzy just smiled.

I reached out to grab Billy's arm, when he
pushed me.

Whizzy pushed him back.

Billy raised his meaty arm back to punch
Whizzy, when Rachel yelled.

"Lawton!"

Whizzy and I looked to see Rachel and her
friends standing in the hallway behind Billy.
Before the lug could even respond, she socked
him in the mouth.

"Leave my brother alone!" She yelled.

Billy's mouth bled and everyone in the
hallway laughed. The older students started
picking on him that a girl beat him up. Billy

Lawton left us alone for the rest of the school year.

"I guess it can't hurt to have a witch for a sister," I said to Whizzy.

Rachel smiled at us.

"She's a witch alright!"

Phillip & Whizzy Short

GRACE'S QUEST

Christopher M. Purrett

www.Purrett.com

CHAPTERS

GRACE TALLON

1

I felt the sharp edges of bark against my sensitive-skinned talons as I perched high in the trees overlooking the dawn of another wintry day in Greenville. The sun blazed through a gap in the dense grey clouds rolling in from the west, no doubt bringing another fresh fall of snow. From my vantage point, Greenville wasn't in need of any more. It piled up beside the Whizzenmog home, which had almost been swallowed whole.

A brisk breeze ruffled the feathers of my face. I spread my wings lifting myself into the air...gliding backward slightly. I pulled my wings in tight and darted back toward the ground. Snow kicked up behind me as I zoomed across it. Flying was exhilarating. I loved to move through the air as an eagle. I so rarely had the opportunity to enjoy this form as I only came to Greenville when Queen Merran requested. Since Phillip Harper and the Whizzenmog twins had returned from Mistasia, I had personally come back to Greenville on only a few occasions. The Queen usually sent others, but today she had honored me with this request... to provide protection for the heroes of Mistasia, Phillip, Rachel and Whizzy.

The window to Whizzy's room was empty as I swooped past. I fully expected him to be sleeping in bed as Rachel was when I passed hers. It was still early morning in Greenville and time seemed to be crawling. I would only be remaining here until the twins had awoken.

I settled into another tree that allowed me to watch Rachel. It was good to see her again. I felt a smile, just as a snapping sound startled me from below. My wings opened, and I launched myself toward the noise. It was still shrouded in darkness as the Whizzenmog's house blocked the morning sunlight from the world far below the tree tops.

Wind whistled across my face. I felt freedom like I could never imagine as an elf back home in Mistasia. Swooping into the darkness, my keen eyes quickly adjusted to the lack of light. A figure came into focus, hunched at the base of a tree...its back facing me.

I yelled out, "Don't move!"

The figure dashed away.

I angled to the right and followed the slender creature between the trees. It tossed acorns over its shoulders like grenades in an attempt to stop my pursuit, but I persisted. It was my duty from the queen to protect the twins from any assailants while they slept...and I refused to fail.

I quickly gained on the scurrying foe zipping between the trees and shrubs for cover. Up ahead it was trapped. I landed hemming my furry enemy in.

"Give up!" I shouted raising my wings in a threatening manner.

"AHHHHHH!!" screamed the ugly beast in a high pitched squeal. "Don't hurt me."

"What are you doing here?"

"I'm gathering nuts."

That wasn't quite the answer that I was expecting. It clearly became apparent that this creature was quite afraid of me as its bushy tail vigorously whipped around.

"Who sent you?" I eagerly pressed.

"My wife. She was really mad because I had friends over last night, and we ate the last of our winter nuts."

"What?" I knew that at some point I would encounter a creature that spoke in a language unfamiliar to me. This filthy looking one was it. "So you weren't sneaking up on the Whizzenmog twins?"

"Who?" It replied nervously.

"Yes!" I had a sudden realization. This creature was so small and daring it had gone unnoticed, even to me, until it made a vital mistake by snapping a twig. "LaCroiux believed he could deceive me."

"Who?" my foe questioned again, slightly shaking.

"What are you? A ferret from the Eastern Plains?"

"No...I'm a squirrel...from that tree." He pointed behind me to a thick, tall specimen that had a whole carved in its base.

"A squirrel? Are you sure you're not a ferret?" I questioned him.

"Yes?" He replied.

"And you don't know the Whizzenmogs"

"No."

A gust of wind rushed between the trees sending snow into my face. The squirrel used the opportunity to dash away and into its home.

Upon my return to the Whizzenmogs, I discovered my duty had been fulfilled. The Whizzenmog twins had awoken, and both now sat at their dining room table. I felt pride in seeing them safe, but sad too that I would again have to leave. I would not know when I would get to see them again.

I had returned to Mistasia and returned to my duties for the Queen. Later that night, I was restless...unable to sleep. I stepped up to my window and unlocked the shutters. Outside Cadieux Castle, the wind howled ferociously, sounding the charge of Mistasia's latest wintry blast. It rushed against my fair-skinned cheeks turning them a rosy red. My eyes watered from its sting, yet I remained standing there defiantly studying every cascading wave of snow, like a force of enemy soldiers attacking us. I felt hatred for each and every flake of snow that invaded the castle. A powerful gust pushed a wave of snow in through my window against my face. I ducked and covered. The snow pushed me backward. I braced myself quickly in order to keep from falling.

This is no ordinary snow, I perceived after watching it for nearly an hour. **There is something more sinister on these winds than Mistasia would bring alone.**

The small village just outside of the castle grounds wasn't even visible through the white wall of snow. Drifts crawled up the walls inching closer to the window just outside my room. I stared it down as though it were an approaching

Wolverine soldier. I was not going to allow it to enter the castle.

I must protect the Queen.

My charge was to guard the Queen and lead the Elven Warriors in protecting this castle and its lands. Yet, I felt helpless against the advancing winter storm. Watching it slowly work to trap us inside. I grew frustrated.

I couldn't recall a winter this tough in all my life. The snow had been falling for days. The air was brisk and relentless as it cut through my window, swept out the door and rumbled down the hallway.

I just wanted to battle the storm. My hand rested eagerly on the hilt of my sword. I hadn't used it much of late. There had been no need. The storm had deterred even our most stubborn enemies from venturing out. I wished for action...adventure, and I needed it soon.

I would regret those wishes sooner than I could have ever imagined.

DO DREAMS COME TRUE

2

I released a deep sigh. **This storm couldn't last forever,** I hoped. A faint sound fell to my keen ears. **Who would be walking the castle at this time of night? All should be asleep and the guards posted at the main entrances.**

I yanked my sword free and spun to face my attacker.

"You know, a healer could make you a potion to cure your jitters." Standing just outside my doorway unfazed by my brazen attempt to protect myself was my long-time friend, Mecca Begron. He smiled widely quite amused by me aggressively pointing my sword in his direction. I had to look ridiculous. "We don't want you to go stabbing the maid...accidently of course."

"Shut up, Mecca," I barked feeling embarrassed and annoyed. I wished it had been some assailant sent to attack me. I needed the practice. For a moment, I thought about smacking him in the face with the blunt side of my blade just to cure his sarcasm, but it was one of his very few redeeming qualities.

Instead, I stowed my sword at my side and turned back to face the quickly darkening view out my window. Many of the torches around the castle had succumb to the winds and been extinguished.

I rested my thin fingers upon the icy-cold stone window sill. A shiver flowed up my hands, through my arms and into my body. It set in deeply, nearly to the bone. This winter was affecting me more severely than any before.

"Persistent isn't it?" Mecca groaned as he now stood beside me. His smile was gone. It had been replaced by concern.

I didn't respond, nor did I need too. Mecca knew what I was thinking. We had been friends since childhood. We had developed a unique sense of one another's emotions. He was very aware of how restless I had become lately.

"Do you feel that?" I asked.

"Yah, it's really cold," Mecca jokingly replied as the wind burst into the room and ruffled his jacket. He pulled it closed again.

I frowned. My white-hair flowed with the stiff breeze catching Mecca's attention. I normally wore it pulled back and tied away from my face.

He reached out and pushed it away from my shoulder.

I shot him a disapproving glare. Mecca shook his head and gave a half-smile as he scoffed at me.

"You know, this is why you don't have any friends, Grace."

"You're my friend, Mecca."

"Ah, yes, I am."

I was confused by his response. He didn't sound so sure.

"What did that mean?"

"Well, I have known you for a long time. I've grown to understand you."

"Understand me?" I had a feeling I wasn't going to like the response to my latest question.

"Grace," Mecca started to become uncomfortable.

"What, Mecca? Understand me how?"

"You're just not...friendly toward others. You make them all...scared."

"Scared? But, my job is to protect them! Why would they be scared of me?" I suddenly realized that I was yelling, as Mecca put his hands out in an attempt to defend himself from my verbal attack.

We remained silent for a moment as I stewed in my anger. The wind continued to howl through the open window. My cheeks were now on fire from the burn, and my ears began to ache.

"You did pull a sword on me earlier," Mecca spoke softly.

A smile crept upon my face. "I'm sorry about that. I have just been on edge lately."

Mecca began to chuckle. His laughter grew with each second until it had become unruly. It was one of the greatest sounds in Mistasia. His laugh could change the mood of an entire hall. Elves would flock to him when he began to tell stories, because they knew he would start laughing at some point. It was infectious. It was why he had ascended to my second in command. He was a warrior they followed out of respect and admiration. I was the leader they feared, mostly because I had a tendency to pull out weapons for no apparent reason...like tonight.

He placed one arm around my shoulder, then reached out and closed the shutters upon my window. His strong arm pulled me in close. Mecca was like a brother to me.

"Grace, everyone respects you."

"They love you, Mecca."

"You are our leader. They don't have to love you. They must follow you." Mecca pulled me in as closely as possible. He stood nearly a full head taller than me with thick blonde hair and a strong jaw. He was smiling again. Mecca was never short on smiles.

I, on the other hand, was never short on worry; about the queen, about protecting the castle, about Mistasia, and most recently about my new friend, Michael "Whizzy" Whizzenmog. It had been sometime since he had returned to his world along with his twin sister, Rachel, and best friend Phillip Harper, but suddenly his image haunted me. It was one of the many reasons why I hadn't been sleeping. I had gladly accepted the queen's request to monitor them in Greenville last night, but it hadn't helped my mood any. Only a few hours of sleep a day will do that to you.

"You need some rest, Grace. That is all." Mecca attempted to comfort me.

I shook free of his grasp. "I've tried." I grumbled after moving to sit atop my bed.

Mecca sat beside me, the look of concern had returned to his face. It was not his best look. I preferred his smile.

"What is keeping you awake? Nightmares?"

I nodded, but felt silly replying.

"It's the fox again." Mecca's voice grew stern.

Mecca disapproved of my friendship with Whizzy. I started to walk away, but he grabbed my arm and pulled me back.

"Stop walking away from me, Grace."

"I'm not talking to you about it!" I barked.

"Then who will you tell? I'm your only friend!"

He instantly regretted those words. I could see it in his eyes, but my anger flowed too quickly. I shot up from the bed and screamed at him, "GET OUT!" I pointed to the doorway with one hand and grabbed the hilt of my sword with the other. "You know I'll use it."

Mecca stopped in the doorway with his back to me, "I'm sorry."

"Sorry for what, Mecca? Hurting my feelings?"

Mecca started to speak when I interrupted him.

"You're not my only friend, Mecca."

"Whizzy will bring you only pain, Grace."

"Good night!" I slammed the heavy wooden door.

I began pacing across the floor, fists balled in anger at my side. I had taken my sword off to avoid any unfortunate incidents...actually, I was

afraid Mecca would return to apologize, and I
would jab him with it.

There was a knock at my door. I stopped
pacing and stared at the closed door
flabbergasted. **Twice in one night he comes to my
door. Mecca, so help me.** I looked at the sword
lying across my bed and thought better of
retrieving it. Instead, I opened the door
unarmed.

To my surprise, standing there was Queen
Merran Cadieux.

QUEEN'S PLEA

3

"My queen, what are you doing here?
And without guards?" I scolded as I quickly
ushered her into the room and closed the door
tightly.

The young Elven Queen, Merran Cadieux,
wore an impish grin as she always did when I

fretted about her safety. There had been no attempts upon her life since the defeat of her uncle, Cragon Cadieux, and I planned to keep it that way. She was used to my overzealous efforts to keep her safe, and I had grown used to her regal smile and effortless dismissal of my brash tone of voice. No one else in Mistasia would be allowed to act this way in front of her, but I had been her guardian since she was an infant and that gave me some liberties.

The queen bowed slightly, once I had calmed down enough to address her properly. I bowed back respectfully. Queen Merran had arrived at a very peculiar time and with an ever-increasing smile.

She must have something important to tell me, I believed. It had to be important for her to travel the castle alone...and at night. She had been wary of nightfall since an early age.

"I gave strict orders for the guards to remain with you at all times, my Queen." I felt a sudden swell of anger and dishonor for allowing her to walk unprotected through the castle.

"Yes, Grace, I understand, but needed to dismiss them after two attempted to join me in the royal bathroom."

I felt myself staring at the queen. What exactly was she getting at?

"You do realize I would enjoy some privacy?" the queen smiled.

Her smile made me irritated. She could smile at almost any situation. How the heck was someone who had lost her parents so happy all the time?

"But they are just protecting you, my Queen."

"From what exactly...robbers in the potty?" Her voice sounded less friendly, more disappointed.

"But, I..." I began to defend myself when she put her hand up to stop me.

"That is not why I'm here, Grace." A smile returned to her rosy face. "My parents are alive!" She squealed.

"What!" I screamed, startling her. "That's impossible." I whispered, barely allowing the words to escape my lips, but she heard them anyway.

I've received word otherwise from the Outer Realm. The queen answered using our Elven telepathy. She could barely contain her happiness. It beamed from her face. I couldn't blame her. She could barely remember their faces. She was so young when they had been betrayed by her uncle, the very same elf who was currently imprisoned in the castle dungeon...frozen in time. The very thought of seeing her parents alive again must have become overwhelming. If she wasn't the queen, she would probably be crying with joy, but she had spent her whole life controlling her emotions.

I opened the door, searching for eavesdroppers in the hallway before securing the door and checking the lock multiple times. I worried that anyone who heard this conversation would claim the queen had gone insane and become unfit to rule.

"That is impossible, Merran." I empathically responded. "I tell you this as a friend."

"Do you? I would believe a friend would be more encouraging and less heartless, Grace."

"Heartless? Does the truth make me heartless? You would prefer I lie to you with a smile, my Queen?" I snarked. I was quite glad that my sword still lay upon my bed away from my reach at this moment. I felt naked without it. I was useless in a war of words, especially against someone so well trained as Queen Merran; therefore, I am fairly certain I would have drawn it out by this point.

The room had grown awkwardly silent. She saw me glance at my sword. Her bottom lip began to quiver. She was breaking down.

I was shocked to watch her crumbling before me.

"You, of all people, Grace, should know what this would mean to Mistasia." She began to sob. "...And to me."

It had been so very long since I had seen her cry, not since that horrific day when her parents disappeared. The day the castle fell to her uncle's rule so long ago.

That was until Whizzy arrived with his friend, Phillip the Frog, and sister, Rachel. They turned the tide and freed us from Merran's uncle. It was the reason why she was queen and Cragon was imprisoned in ice.

A smile formed on my face, as I had images of Whizzy on my mind. I had become lost in my own head.

"You find pleasure in my pain? You are not the friend I once believed you to be, Grace Tallon." The queen managed to speak through her tears. "I came to you, not because you are my guardian but because you were my friend."

My smile quickly disappeared, "I am your friend, Merran."

"I need to know if it is true. If they are alive." The young Elven Queen pleaded with me. I could see the pain in her eyes. It was so much deeper than I had ever known.

"What do you need from me?" I asked stepping to her as the guardian of a queen should.

"I have received word from the Outer Realm that my parents are being held captive in the Deadly..."

"...Spray Forest." I finished with her.

The Deadly Spray Forest was a place that had long been avoided by the Elves of Mistasia. Trolls, Vampire bats and many other terrible creatures were held within. It was far more dangerous than Wolverine Forest and the trees were believed to be toxic...and alive.

What could have taken them in there? I wondered. That thought alone frightened me.

"I need you to travel to the Outer Realm and rendezvous with Delza Yorne. She is the village guardian and will be able to guide you to the forest."

I nodded. Our eyes met. Queen Merran's sorrow waned as an intense determination had returned to her gaze.

"Grace, please, be careful."

I wrapped a thick woolen cover around me, tying it firmly across my waist to protect against the chill of winter's wind, and stepped out into the courtyard. Drifts of snow crawled up the castle walls along either side of me. The wind howled between the towers. I pulled my hood up to cover my stinging ears.

This trip could be treacherous on the best of days, but in the heart of Mistasian winter this trip would become deadly in a matter of moments. I couldn't do this alone, but only trusted one other to accompany me in this journey...Mecca.

He awaited me at my modest home along the edge of Cadieux Village. My best friend huddled from the cold, standing beside the majestic, broad-backed steed, Millessa, that would take us upon our journey. She was tall and strong, muscles bulging from her well defined limbs. Millessa had long been a key warrior in our battles against the evils of Mistasia.

I stroked her snout. She rarely spoke and tonight was no different. I felt her willingness and steadied resolve. Millessa was ready.

"Are you going to explain exactly why we are freezing to death instead of resting comfortably in the castle?" Mecca groaned. His usually happy demeanor was as distant as our final destination. I wasn't sure if it was because of our recent argument or the terrible weather.

I smiled. It hurt my cheeks. "We have a quest." I answered hoping to find a reaction, but the cold froze it within him. Mecca had no intention of wasting energy; he knew this was going to be an exhausting journey.

"Then we best be on our way." Mecca mounted Millessa, and stretched out his hand for me.

"We need Fraydorn."

"A second steed? Millessa is more than capable of carrying us both, Grace." Mecca replied.

"Our quest is to return with the king and queen," I revealed.

The expression upon Mecca's face was everything I expected. Confusion combined with a deep worry for my sanity.

"Fraydorn will be bringing home our lost royals...according to Queen Merran." I couldn't believe that I was speaking these words aloud to another living soul. I turned away from Mecca to avoid his glare.

"Sounds as though our queen has been sipping from the fountains of desperation," Millessa spoke in a deep feminine voice.

My Elven friend chuckled as he pulled his thick black woolen coat under his chin. His head buried under a hood, cheeks red from the wind. It gave him a sinister appearance, except for the light-hearted grin.

"Grace," he called to me.

I had started around my house to retrieve Fraydorn. Millessa followed like the faithful steed she had always been. Mecca watched me from her back, awaiting my reply.

I gave none.

Mecca tried again to gather my attention. "Grace, do you believe in this quest?"

I stopped walking and turned slightly. I could just make out his shadow in the dim moonlight from the corner of my eye.

"Well, do you?" He pressed.

Millessa's eyes were drawn to me. Her beautiful white coat glistened from the snowflakes that had melted upon her.

"I believe in our queen," I solemnly replied then started off again.

THUD! Mecca had leapt from Millessa's back, sprung into the air, flipped over my head and landed before me on the frozen trail. He placed his hands firmly upon my shoulders. That famous smile beamed from his face.

"And I believe in you, Grace," He empathically announced.

Millessa snorted.

Mecca glanced over at her.

"Elves," she spat crassly.

"Do you mind? I am trying to let my friend know that I'm with her until the end."

I swatted his hands free and barked, "You have no choice, Mecca. The queen has given me this quest, and I commanded that you accompany me. Now mount your horse and wait here for me to return."

I stomped off, mumbling under my breath about how irritating and annoying my friend had become. **Right now, I would prefer to be with my traitorous brother**, I muttered.

"Now, that's not very nice, Grace," my knuckle-headed friend replied.

Mecca, if you don't stay out of my head...I'll feed you to the first dragon that flies into our path. "Sometimes telepathy is a curse." I scoffed.

We rode out of Cadieux Village under the cover of darkness in order to avoid being noticed. It would be the talk of the town if the queen's two highest ranking guardians scrambled out of the castle in the dead of winter.

A slivered, crescent-shaped moon dangled in the sky, accompanied by its minions, millions of stars. The breeze had subsided lending to warmth under my woolen coat as we rumbled along the shore of Red River. Our journey would take a few days to reach the Outer Realm, the most northern Elven village in Mistasia.

Mecca pushed Millessa hard, forcing her to pull up alongside Fraydorn and me. We galloped side-by-side for many miles without speaking. He would glance my way occasionally awaiting me to speak, but I refused. There was nothing to say...for now.

ARROWS UPON US

4

I awoke to the sounds of rustling. Springing to my feet, I loaded an arrow into my bow, pulled back its string and aimed.

"I almost shot you through the heart!" I barked with irritation at Mecca, who stood beside a jittery Millessa, as he rearranged items in her side pack.

"I've grown used to you pointing deadly weapons at me," he replied with a snort. "You haven't harmed me yet." He had pulled a large green apple from Millessa's side pouch and fed it to her before reaching back in and grabbing another.

I let loose my arrow, piercing the apple dead center, ripping it from his thick fingers and pinning it against the tree which we took shelter underneath.

"Hey," Mecca protested as Fraydorn whinnied with glee. Fraydorn always enjoyed it when I taunted and tortured Mecca. "That was my breakfast...and what are you laughing at, horse face?"

The large golden-brown steed was slightly bigger than his sister, Millessa, and son to the royal horses that transported Queen Merran Cadieux's parents long ago. It was why I had chosen him for this journey even though his coat would be obvious in the white-wash of this snow covered landscape, except for the haven of Blue Elm that we currently used as cover. These sturdy trees had grown accustomed to the long harsh winters of Mistasia and nearly retained all of their deep blue leaves throughout.

Fraydorn was the strongest and most exceptional steed in the Cadieux family line, bred for endurance. Millessa was my usual steed and the bravest of them all, despite what her brother may claim. She had fought many a troll, wolverine and dragon in battle with me defending the castle. For this journey, I had chosen to ride Fraydorn instead, simply because

of my elven company. Mecca and Fraydorn
didn't exactly get along.

Their squabble had begun a few years ago
during battle, when Fraydorn claimed
Mecca...well, how did he explain it?

"The elf deadened my senses with his
bottom bomb," Fraydorn recalled with his sister
as Mecca roared with laughter at her side.
Millessa joined him for a moment until her
brother shot her a stern look. The uptight steed
huffed with offense.

"I told you I had just eaten a spicy
mushroom when those darn trolls attacked. All
that bouncing around...it got me stirred up on
the inside. You shouldn't have been jumping
around so much Fraydorn," Mecca could barely
finish his sentence as he laughed harder with
each passing moment.

"You blame me? I heard you ate them on purpose, Elf!" Fraydorn scolded.

"How was I to know those darn beasts would attack? Besides, Grace fed them to me." Mecca pointed in my direction to pass the blame, his eyes wide, tight lipped and attempting not to explode into laughter.

"I did not!" I shouted in defense. "Those mushrooms were on the table for my stew. I hadn't even cooked them yet."

"Oh, really?" Fraydorn moved closer to my friend, attempting to intimidate Mecca.

"That's why his gas was so potent, Fraydorn. He ate them fresh."

The golden-brown steed stuck his snout in Mecca's face. The Elven warrior's laughter returned.

"As I recall Mecca, you shoved about four large mushrooms in your mouth as we dashed out to battle. You said something about blowing up a few trolls with a 'riot of explosion'"

Everyone wailed, except Fraydorn; he was far too uptight for potty humor. Mecca did much of what he did to irritate Fraydorn...and me for that matter. At least this time his nonsense was directed upon someone else.

The sun had begun to set and we needed to move. Night time was the best chance for us to travel without being noticed by the terrors of Mistasia.

We were approximately one night's ride from the Outer Realm now. Our journey had been uneventful, which made me edgy. Mecca, as usual, had found a way to relax my tension, even if for only a few moments.

I led us from the cluster of Blue Elm trees that had served as our protection throughout the past day and into the vast open space between us and the Outer Realm. Being Elf gave me an advantage in these wild lands. I could see quite clearly even in the dark. My keen ears also allowed me to hear any enemies that might be attempting to sneak up on us...I just needed to remain focused.

However, my mind began to race, eyes searching the area for any movement that could provide signs that someone was out there. A pressure gathered between my eyes. My instincts were at the verge of cracking under the strain. I was worried about our safety but fearful of what we just might find when we reached the Deadly Spray Forest. **Would we really find King Stephan and his wife, Delia? Would they really be alive, trapped in the forest?**

Grace! A voice shouted in my head, startling me awake from my dream. **What is that?** Mecca's voice sounded unusually surprised.

Ahead of us, in the darkness, colors swirled in the sky. It cast shadows over the silhouetted image of the Outer Realm. We were almost there, yet after these past few days of hard travel, I had the sudden urge to turn around and head back to Cadieux Castle.

Grace, what in Mistasia is that?

I have no idea. I replied keeping the conversation between us Elves.

The wind pushed hard against my face flinging my hood back, exposing me ears to the harsh cold. Snow lifted from the ground, swept skyward by the winds. Fraydorn struggled against the powerful gusts.

We slowly approached the village along the Red River. The slender-crescent moon was all the light that showed our way, and it had nearly been blotted out by the snow.

Where did this snowfall come from? Mecca groaned as he rode up beside me.

"It's not snowing, Mecca. The snow is being pulled skyward by whatever that is above the village." I stared blankly at the violently swirling lines of blue, green and yellow light.

The wind suddenly stopped. All sounds vanished like a void. A stiff pressure filled my ears. Mecca's too, I could tell as he covered them with his hands. The colorful light flashed toward the ground and exploded tearing apart a series of small buildings. Fraydorn knelt down bracing for the sonic boom. It swept in from the village knocking Millessa back tossing Mecca to the snow.

I dismounted and rushed to Mecca's aid. My ears numbed from the blast, it took a moment to understand the noise coming from my friend, but I should have known...he was laughing.

"I'm fine," he chuckled. "Help me up."

Our horses had moved behind us allowing a full view of the village smoldering. Flames danced atop the blackened remains of the buildings that had just stood there moments earlier. The colorful storm above had mysteriously vanished too.

Dread filled my body. Fear began to invade my mind with full force. Every part of me body ached. I desperately wanted to turn and leave but was too embarrassed to admit it. **I am Grace Tallon, Elven Warrior and Guardian to the Queen.** That is what I said to myself attempting to reassure my mind.

"What was that, Grace?" Fraydorn asked.

I shook my head. I had no response.

"It wasn't a storm of nature. That's for darn sure." Mecca brushed snow from his woolen coat.

My heart thumped hard in my head. I was regretting coming on the quest and we hadn't even made it to our initial destination yet.

A familiar sound rang out in my wind-burnt ears. The sound of steel sliding from its home, Mecca had unsheathed his sword.

"I'm not going in there unprepared," Mecca announced.

"That sounds unfair. I can't hold a sword," Fraydorn whined.

"Just use your tongue."

I pulled my sword free and gripped the hilt tightly in my cold fingers. "Mecca!" I barked.

"Yeah?"

"Shut it!" I moved ahead, trudging one foot at a time through the thickening snow. The top layer was fresh and powdery, yet below it was crusty and hardened. Snow was past my knees in areas and quickly rising near my hips. Travel had become increasingly difficult.

We entered the village of the Outer Realm with great apprehension. Lit by the bright moonlight from above and the smoldering flames where much of the village once stood. A few small buildings remained, but those too had cracked and scorched walls.

A rustling noise emerged from a badly burnt building to my right. A rush of wind hit my face; it carried a familiar sound...an arrow. I swung my blade deflecting the arrow just enough that it only grazed my shoulder, tearing through my jacket. Standing in the doorway was a figure. A glint of light sparkled from the tip of another arrow pointed directly at me. Two ferocious eyes gazed upon me.

"Show yourself!" I commanded.

It let loose another arrow.

Mecca cut it in half before it could reach me. The arrows pieces dove into the snow at my feet.

"By order of the queen's guards...show yourself! Now!" Mecca barked.

I reached for my bow and arrow and aimed at the shadowed figure. I watched as it slowly emerged from the building into the moonlight. It wore a hood to cover its face.

"I will not warn you again. Show yourself!" I shouted with my arrow pointed at it.

The figure reached up and removed its hood.

OUTER REALM

<u>5</u>

Standing before us was a young elf, she was beautiful yet angry. Her intense, golden eyes darted between us with contempt. She appeared to be searching our minds for answers...if we were friends or foes. Her flowing, brunette hair flapped in the blustery winds.

I quickly commandeered her attention with arrow still raised. I needed to know why she tried to kill me...an elf like her.

"We do not harm our own kind without good reason." I raised an eyebrow in contempt.

She shot me a horrific stare. "Nor do we leave our own to perish alone," she spat.

I quickly lowered my arrow and released the tension on my bow. "No, we do not." I replied.

"Who has been attacking this village?" Mecca interjected as he witnessed the devastation.

"The sorcerer." She replied with furrowed brow. She quickly approached. "And you Commander Tallon have abandoned us. Where is your honor?" The young girl hissed.

Mecca grabbed her by the arm, and she kicked out his legs, knocking him to the snow. She removed her sword reached back and stopped mid swing. My arrow was only a few inches from her nose; once again I was ready to fire.

"Put down the sword." I calmly commanded. "I think you are misguided young one. Your anger is just, but directed improperly at me when it should be toward the one that brought this chaos to the Outer Realm." We stared at one another with unwavering resolve. "Tell me of this sorcerer. What is his name?"

"LaCroiux."

I felt a shiver run through my body. I quickly lowered my weapon, gazing at Mecca who shared my fearful expression. Sorcerer LaCroiux had returned. That meant awful things to more than just the Outer Realm in Mistasia.

She led us into the burnt building and through the charred remains of the home it once was...her home, Delza Yorne. She was the elf that Queen Merran had asked us to find here. Delza was to take us to the Deadly Spray Forest to find the lost King and Queen of Mistasia. We never expected to find this upon our arrival.

Delza took us briskly into a narrow passage that dipped below the floor and led through a dirt-walled tunnel that spiraled down into the depths below the village. At the bottom of the tunnel was a heavy wooden door. She knocked and awaited a response from within. After her coded reply, which neither Mecca nor I understood as any current form of Elfish language, the door slowly retreated. Inside was an underground world far more intricate than that beneath Cadieux Castle, and it was full of Elves.

"What is this place, Delza?" I asked.

"The Outer Realm has long been the furthest Elven village away from the castle. We learned long ago that we must protect ourselves from the beasts of Mistasia. This underground shelter provided us that protection from LaCroiux when you didn't." Delza's words stabbed at me.

"I had no idea that your village was under attack...that our people were in danger."

"Communication has been cut off for some time now. I hoped that you would have noticed and sent warriors to check up on us in the very least, Commander Tallon." Delza handed her sword to an elderly elf. "Please repair the edges, Elder Smorg.

He nodded and hobbled off to a work station nearby. Instantly, he set to work sharpening the edge of Delza's blade along a large stone wheel.

"I am sorry, Delza." I began when I was rudely interrupted.

"Chief Yorne," She brashly replied looking at me intensely.

I stopped in shock.

"Chief? Who named you chief?" Mecca mocked.

"The people of the Outer Realm," She soundly retorted. "When it became apparent that our Commander had abandoned us...they named me Chief Commanding Officer overseeing the village and its protection." Delza left, leaving Mecca and I standing alone.

"What is going on here?" I mumbled in frustration.

"Well, it appears that you can add Chief Yorne to the "*not-a-friend*" list," Mecca mocked.

"This isn't funny, Mecca." I watched as a group of villagers had gathered around Chief Yorne. They muttered and pointed in our direction with looks of disdain and hatred on their faces.

"She has turned them against us."

"How are we going to get her to help us?" Mecca questioned.

"That will be simple. She may be '*Chief* of the Outer Realm,' but she still is under the control of the Queen of Mistasia."

Day broke shortly after we had descended into the world under the Outer Realm. We would have to wait for nightfall again before we could venture out for the forest. There was little cover in the light of day between this Elven realm and the horrors of the Deadly Spray Forest.

I had grown eager and impatient, which was why I stood alone in the burnt out home of Chief Yorne peering through a hole in the wall at our objective in the distance. The trees in the Deadly Spray Forest were menacingly tall with branches that hung down like the tentacles of an octopus. They swayed in the wind as though dancing on the horizon, taunting me...laughing at my fear. Horrible creatures lived in that forest; trolls, vampire bats, and now apparently a sorcerer. It would make sense that LaCroiux had made this forest his home. He once lived in Wolverine Forest, but unable to head back there, he found a new place...one with far more hideous creatures to control. From there he could easily attack this village, without even leaving the safety of the trees.

The chill of the air had set into my bones. My breath was exposed as the warm air from my lungs turned to thick white puffs in the freezing air outside. I rubbed my hands together in a vain attempt for warmth. It lasted only a few seconds.

"Grace?" Mecca's voice called from the tunnel behind me. He wasn't alone. Chief Yorne walked beside him. They appeared to be in the middle of a conversation...a civil conversation. Mecca did have a way with elves...especially females. His smile entered the room first. I smiled back...I just couldn't help it. That seemed to catch Chief Yorne by surprise. She gave a forced smile in return and slightly bowed. I did as well out of courtesy, not respect.

The sun had begun to set. The sky was a brilliant array of colors; from pink to orange to purple.

"Chief Yorne, we will be leaving shortly." I paused for a moment wondering how exactly to broach the subject of her leading us to the Deadly Spray Forest.

"Please, call me Delza. I apologize for how I behaved earlier. I should not have shown you such disrespect."

"I understand, Delza. You and your people have been through a great deal. I am sorry."

"I will gather my belongings and be prepared to assist you, Commander Tallon. Mecca has informed me of our mission...ah 'quest'." She corrected as she turned to Mecca for reassurance. "At Queen Merran's request, I will accompany you to the forest." The Chief nodded again and left.

Mecca and I stood alone in the cold. It was silent. Mecca's smile was beaming brighter than the sunset.

"Come on, Grace; you can say it."

"Say what?"

"How good I am."

I chuckled. "Yeah, you're good alright. Now go get our friends."

"What would you do without me?" Mecca joked.

"Yes, Mecca I am glad you're here," I regretfully replied. He most certainly didn't need his ego stroked any further. His head might grow so large that he would fall over.

After he left the room, I returned my gaze upon the horizon. I exhaled deeply. The pit in my stomach grew heavier.

"But you, my friend, may soon not be."

I sat tall upon Fraydorn's back while Delza climbed up Millessa to join Mecca. Tightening the strap that held my sword, I inhaled sharply. The rush of cold air stabbed my lungs.

"Grace? Are you alright?" Mecca noticed my discomfort.

I nodded, but my chest still hurt. Shaking it off, I grabbed Fraydorn by the reigns and pulled tightly. He lurched into the air and roared. We were off into the darkness.

Just outside the village the winds began to intensify. Snow formed a wall before us, encircling us.

A tornado! Delza called out with telepathy.

She was correct. The snow whipped around us.

"Ahhhhh!" I yelled as Fraydorn charged into the vortex. I was knocked clear from his back in an instant. I heard Fraydorn's voice call to me as I was whisked away. I landed in a large pile of snow, but the tornado continued to push more on top of my body. It was burying me alive.

Mecca! I called for my friend. There was no answer. The snow kept coming. My legs were buried deep. The wintry wind storm had me pinned down and was now attempting to finish me. I kicked my left leg free, but an angry growl echoed from the tornado as it doused me with a huge wave of white powder. Now, only my face and right arm were free.

A figure suddenly emerged from the swirling winds.

Fraydorn!

He grabbed hold of my arm in his mouth. The sharp pain from his teeth was a small price to pay for my freedom. Fraydorn yanked me loose. Blood trickled down my arm and dotted the white snow. I slung myself onto Fraydorn's back and hunched down to avoid the wind knocking me off again.

Fraydorn burst through the vortex of snow and we were ahead of the roaring monster. Millessa rode up beside us with Mecca and Delza still on her back.

The chilling blast of wintry air kept the pain in my arm from throbbing as we raced ahead of the tornado. I turned back to see just how close it was. In the winds was the face of a monster.

"LaCroiux," I muttered in anger.

Delza noticed too and fired an arrow into his mouth. LaCroiux swallowed it and spat it back at her, narrowly missing. The tornado cackled as it chased us down. There was nowhere to go. We were easy prey for the sorcerer out in the open fields.

Suddenly, I realized our fate. LaCroiux knew that I wouldn't dare return to the village of innocent elves. The only choice would be to enter the Deadly Spray Forest for shelter. He was driving us right toward him. We ran directly for his trap.

DEADLY FOREST

6

The roar of the wind trampled the snow behind us like thousands of horses charging into battle...with us.

The Deadly Spray Forest sprawled out before us. The power from the tornado pulled the tree branches like arms reaching out to snatch us. It was a frightening sight.

LaCroiux cackled heartily, signaling his latest attack. I turned around to witness arms forming at the tornado's side. They swirled around above his head gathering tremendous speed. Then LaCroiux whipped them toward us.

The first snap landed between Fraydorn and Millessa. The second barely missed Millessa, sending a cascade of snow up across her back. Delza slipped, but Mecca grabbed her at the last second keeping her from falling into the tornado's vortex. Millessa bolted ahead of Fraydorn and me, kicking up a trail of powder in our faces.

We had almost reached the forest when the tornado vanished.

"It's gone!" Delza yelled.

Millessa skidded to a stop and turned to watch the sky clear. Fraydorn galloped up beside.

"Where did he go?" Mecca questioned, slightly out of breath.

"Is he gone?" Delza nervously inquired. She knew the answer though. LaCroiux had been attacking her village for months. It was a false hope that he had given up.

"No! LaCroiux will return. He always returns." I patted Fraydorn as he restlessly moved about. "We must enter the forest."

"I'm not going in there. We don't go into the Deadly Spray Forest," Delza was obviously concerned.

"What is that?" Mecca pointed into the darkness.

I squinted to look through the night. In the distance loomed a wall of snow barreling directly toward us.

"Move!" I shouted pulling on the reins and directing Fraydorn toward the forest.

The noise was terrible as the wall of snow closed in on us quickly.

"It's gaining on us!" Delza screamed.

It was the last words any of us would utter before the snow cascaded over us, pushing us into the forest. I was pulled free from Fraydorn. I tumbled through the snow unable to break free from its grip. Finally, I skidded to a stop, much of my body buried in snow. My eyes fluttered. It was so difficult to keep them open. My head throbbed. I searched the area for my friends, but dizziness overtook me. I grew ill and vomited upon the dirty snow, which was tainted by leaves, rocks, sticks and dirt. I couldn't stay awake. I felt my body slump into the snow around me and everything went black.

Grace? Grace can you hear me? Mecca's voice echoed in my head. **Open your eyes.**

I could feel the touch of his strong hands upon my shoulders. My body was in great discomfort. It took too much effort just to pull open my eyelids. I took a short painful breath.

"Grace, be careful. You may have broken a few ribs. It will be difficult to breathe normally." Mecca explained.

Delza sat beside me tending to a wound on her arm. The gash was nearly closed now. Tears streamed down her face, which showed the result of our entry into the forest. Scratches and cuts were along the side of her face and over her eye.

"Where are we, Mecca?" I mustered up the strength to ask. A pain shot down my side as I shifted to sit up right.

"Grace! Take it easy." Mecca had turned his attention back to helping Delza finish closing the wound on her arm. "We are inside the

Deadly Spray Forest. Fortunately, we found a place to hide among the trees. LaCroiux has had Vampire bats out looking for us."

"Where are Millessa and Fraydorn?"

It remained silent. Mecca wouldn't look at me.

"Mecca?"

"They were both unconscious, and too large for me to move on my own. I had to leave them. LaCroiux has them now." He wiped the remaining blood from Delza's arm as she winced in pain.

"I'm sorry, Grace. There just wasn't enough time to save everyone." The sound in his voice was heartbreaking. He wasn't accustomed to failure.

"LaCroiux has grown much stronger than the last time we faced him," I stated.

Mecca turned his attention to me. "We need to check your ribs." He placed his hands upon my side. A pain shot straight up into my chest knocking the air from my lungs. "It doesn't feel as though they are broken, Grace."

"Badly bruised," I replied. "Not much better. It will be nearly impossible for me to use my sword."

"Or your bow," Delza spoke as she leaned her head back against the tree behind her, eyes closed.

"I will have to try. It is far too dangerous in this place for me to walk about unprotected. Even if I just hold my weapon it may keep LaCroiux's monsters off me long enough to escape." I said it but wasn't even confident in those words myself. We were in real danger before our injuries, but now we entered a realm of evil. LaCroiux controlled everything here. We now played on his terms, and by his rules.

"You two have to rest. You'll need your strength...or what you can recover before we move on." Mecca began gathering our weaponry and laying it out before us. "This was all that I could recover from the snow." Two bows, a dozen arrows, three swords and a small dagger.

"It will have to do," I attempted to sound as confident as I could. "We shouldn't venture out during night here. We will have to wait until daylight to help guide us."

"Well, there is one problem." Mecca began. "I believe that it is day time now. It is slightly warmer, and I have witnessed some rays of light coming into the forest when the trees move with the winds. These branches are unlike anything I've ever seen, Grace. They act like a canopy protecting us from the snow and cold harsh winds, yet also block almost all sunlight."

"That would explain the dirt blanket," Delza snarled as she ran her hand along the bare forest floor. "Real comfy!"

Mecca half-smiled at her weak attempt at humor. There seemed to be a bond growing between them.

"It beats sleeping in the snow," I muttered. My clothes were still icy cold from my time beneath the snow. Thankfully, these trees kept the winds at bay. Hopefully, they could help keep Sorcerer LaCroiux's henchmen off our scent too.

"Alright you two, get some rest." Mecca stood up and began walking away.

"What if the Vampire bats find us?" Delza asked the question that weighed heavily on us all...she was just the courageous one to speak it aloud.

"Then we fight with whatever strength we have left." I replied attempting to hide the fear that struggled to escape me.

I lay on the hard ground trying to rest my aching body. It was difficult to remain still, especially my mind. I kept watching the trees swaying sometimes seeing figures in them. Closing my eyes didn't help either. Images of LaCroiux hovering over me entered my mind repeatedly. My eyes would snap open again. It was becoming harder to tell dream from reality.

The next time I opened my eyes I felt different. My pain was numbed. Stretching out I realized that I was no longer an elf...I was again an eagle like when I enter Greenville. I took to the sky and maneuvered up through the trees. It was dark and very cold.

"Greenville?" I said in surprise after finding the Whizzenmog house in the distance. I swooped down and perched in the same tree where I had recently watched Whizzy.

A warm sensation entered my chest as I saw him sleeping in his bed. I watched him through the window for a few moments. It was peaceful...too peaceful.

"I should check on Rachel," I extended my wings and prepared to leap from the branch when a strange light appeared in Whizzy's bedroom.

The white light spun with flashes of gold growing more intense with each swirl. It grew larger by the second...a flash lit up the room. It stunned my sensitive eyes. When my vision returned, I was frightened by what I saw.

Sorcerer LaCroiux stood beside Whizzy's bed. I tried to get air born, but my body aches had returned. That was when I realized I was no longer an eagle, but myself again grasping the branch.

LaCroiux turned his gaze upon me. A rumbling laughter exploded through the window, bursting the glass out upon me. The same white light glowed from his mouth and eyes.

"You can't protect him, Grace. You can't even protect yourself!" the sorcerer mocked.

I watched helplessly as LaCroiux stood up tall, arms raised. Flames began to dance in his palms, a ferocious expression upon his face like that of a Wolverine preparing to pounce on its prey. He fired a ball of flames into Whizzy's bed. It exploded, shooting flames out the broken window and against my skin. The heat instead felt like a rush of cold air across my body. I began to tumble from the branch. I was falling to my death when suddenly I awoke.

"WHIZZY!" I screamed.

"Grace!" Mecca yelled snapping me back from the horrible nightmare and into our real-life horror.

Mecca helped Delza to her feet.

My heart was still pounding so hard it hurt my head. I struggled to catch my breath amidst the pain in my badly bruised ribs. I rolled to my side, still unaware of just how much danger we were in. Mecca's strong arms wrapped around me and lifted me up.

I whimpered in pain, but held back the urge to scream. Mecca noticed the tears running down my cheeks. Thankfully, he would believe that it was because of the pain in my body and not in my heart after watching Whizzy being destroyed at the hands of our enemy. I had to tell myself it was a dream. I couldn't have actually been in Greenville. LaCroiux was just torturing me...leading me to believe he had done it.

I heard the familiar sound of a sword ringing as it was unsheathed. Mecca held his sword pointed directly before him.

"Think you can fire your bow?" He asked me.

"I don't know how accurately."

"Well, accuracy is gonna count."

For the first time I got to witness our enemies. In the trees were dozens of Vampire bats seething and drooling. Cracking and growling came from the branches. A tree bent forward causing a Vampire bat to flee. Another loud crack exploded into our hideout, followed by a massive meaty fist. The monstrously tall tree snapped in half and crashed to the ground as three Trolls entered.

"We are in serious trouble!" Delza yelped.

"Well, at least he didn't send four Trolls." Mecca looked at me. "Then we'd be outnumbered," Mecca sarcastically replied.

SORCERY

7

There was a strange pause from our enemies. They were awaiting something...a command perhaps. The Vampire bats would jump from tree to tree, but remained high above us as though watching a sporting event.

The Trolls just glared at us, each seemingly choosing its intended target. I found myself sharing eye contact with the apparent leader of the group. Trolls are slow in just about every aspect; their mind, movement and skills; however, in my current condition it was going to be very difficult to take this creature on alone. The Troll's broad shoulders dipped up and down with each massive breath.

"What are they waiting for?" Mecca barked. He was gripping his sword so tightly that his knuckles were pure white.

"Don't be so eager for this fight." That was normally my stance before battle, but this particular fight was not in our favor...even if we were healthy.

"Delza looks jittery," I said to Mecca

"Yes, I think we all are jittery just about now," He replied.

"What are those bats doing?" Delza nervously asked. She raised her bow toward the tree tops aiming her arrow at multiple targets.

"Don't worry about the bats, Delza," I commanded. "The Trolls will attack first. Those nasty flying beasts are probably here to make certain the dumb Trolls do their jobs."

"I don't wanna be eaten," Delza cried. "I can't go out like this." Blood began to trickle from her nose.

"What in Mistasia are they waiting for?" Mecca barked again as he stepped forward.

"No, Mecca wait...don't," I reached for his arm, but a sharp pain held me back.

"What do you wait for?" He yelled at the Trolls. "If this is the end, then let us begin already."

The lead Troll leaned forward; its face features shifting into something all too recognizable...the face of Sorcerer LaCroiux.

"Then we shall begin, little Elf," The sorcerer sneered.

I gasped. Mecca retreated, and Delza fired her arrow directly at the lead Troll hitting him in the cheek. LaCroiux's face was gone. What returned was the ugly features of the Troll, which growled in agony as the arrow pierced its skin. It raised its giant arm back and swung toward her swatting her into the trees behind us. Mecca and I were now left to face these monstrously powerful Trolls outnumbered.

"NOOOOO!" Mecca screamed with hatred, something very unfamiliar for him even in battle. He raised his sword and dodged a Troll's attempt to squash him.

Dirt escaped from the Troll's hand. Mecca leapt up and disappeared into the cloud of dirt and debris. He emerged running up the mountain of an arm toward the Troll's head.

The other two Trolls thundered around their leader and approached me. Panic coursed through my body. I was still too weak to fight them...so I ran into the heart of the forest.

As I entered the maze of entangled limbs and branches of the Deadly Spray Forest, I heard a great cry of agony followed by a tremendous rumble. The trees shook, the ground buckled and I fell to my knees.

"Mecca!" **Mecca, are you alright?** I called out to him using telepathy.

One down...two to go. He replied with determination.

It was then I mustered up the courage to reenter the fray. I took the deepest breath I could handle, readied my bow and arrow, and launched myself through the branches back into the opening. Lying lifeless was the lead troll. Mecca was now attacking a second. I looked up to find the Vampire bats...they were still there watching and jeering.

I slid to a stop and pulled back upon my bow. My first shot missed badly and worse than that it drew attention to the fact that I had returned. I aimed again, this time striking a troll in the neck. It howled in pain. Mecca dashed forward and slashed at its ankles while sliding underneath the giant creature. This troll joined its slain brother falling upon him in the center of the clearing.

Now only one troll remained. We flanked the ugly beast. The troll swatted at us, flailing about angrily. I could sense its fear. We had destroyed two trolls; he knew he didn't stand a chance.

I heard a rustling noise from behind me. Mecca's face beamed. When I turned, Delza stood just inside the clearing. She looked awful, but was still alive.

"You will pay for that," Delza sneered in an unusual voice.

She no longer had her bow, but brandished a short sword and came charging at me. I deflected her attack with my bow, but she swung again knocking my bow free. I winced in pain, grabbing my side as she continued to slash at me in rage. Her eyes were burning with anger.

"LaCroiux?" I muttered to myself. He had overtaken her mind. Delza was now the sorcerer's prisoner. "This is a new trick sorcerer." I grabbed a branch from the ground and swung.

Delza's sword sliced through, cutting the branch in two. "Delza, fight him!"

She reached straight back over her head, sword held high. I kicked her in the chest.

Meanwhile, Mecca finished off the remaining troll. I knew by the heavy thud behind me. All three trolls were now heaped upon one another. My friend strolled over toward me confidently, twirling his sword at his side. He attempted to sheath it when I stopped him.

"You may need that."

Delza lay unconscious sprawled out on the ground; her sword now in my hand. She looked battered and beaten. I only hoped that LaCroiux would now leave her alone.

The forest had grown very quiet; only heavy panting from the Vampire bats above could be heard. My ears began to hurt. Pressure building up inside them pushed all sound out like a void. The branches began to lurch inward toward us at all sides. Then a flash of light burst forth; the tall trees bent backward. Mecca and I were knocked to the ground.

I struggled to my knees. There standing atop the fallen trolls was the sorcerer. His strength was impressive. LaCroiux moved down the troll bodies and stopped just before me.

"Commander," he mockingly bowed, staring at me. "You have done quite well. I never thought, with all your injuries, that your group would have been able to destroy these trolls. I guess I was wrong."

"What have you done with the King and Queen?" I questioned through gritted teeth.

He snorted. "Well, you will be disappointed to know that they are not here."

"Where are they, LaCroiux?" Mecca shouted.

The sorcerer swung his arm, swatting Mecca high up into the air. A Vampire bat clutched him and flew off. Another swooped down and snatched Delza from the ground.

"You are all alone, Grace."

I wasn't about to go out without a fight. I gripped Delza's sword in my right hand.

"You wish to use that against me do you?" LaCroiux snickered. He had always been arrogant. "Do your best." His voice deepened.

I swung, and he dodged effortlessly. Pain shot across my chest. I swung again but missed. LaCroiux punched me in the chest with a spell. I flew through the air, landing on my back. He slowly strolled toward me. I rolled onto my side and struggled with all my might to get back to my knees. I had no strength remaining...at least not enough to fend off a sorcerer.

I swung again, but LaCroiux knocked the sword from my hand and lifted me up into the air with the flick of his wrist. He summoned the winds, which burnt as they swept across my face.

"You are now my prisoner," LaCroiux growled.

A forceful wind lifted me free from his grasp pushing me back until I collided with a tree...everything went black.

EVIL REVEALED

<u>8</u>

"Grace?" LaCroiux's voice echoed in my head. It drifted from ear to ear as though it passed through me.

It was pitch black, not a glimmer of light nor hope. I was Sorcerer LaCroiux's prisoner. I felt a tingling in my body and numbness as my legs were trapped up underneath me. My arms were bound tightly behind my back. My eyes were open, but useless in this prison. I was blind. Fear began to creep its way into my heart.

Where was Mecca? What had happened to my friend? I tried to call to him, but something blocked the sound. It was as though a cloth covered my mouth. There was nothing at all, like something was absorbing it. With my hands bound, I wasn't able to feel what covered my mouth. My lips felt like they were sewn together.

Mecca! I screamed using telepathy. No reply.

Delza! I waited impatiently for any sign from them, but no one answered.

I was all alone. LaCroiux had made sure of that. His torture for me would be solitude. No one would find me here. No Elves would venture into the Deadly Spray Forest...if that's where I was now. LaCroiux could have taken me anywhere.

My mind was overrun with questions.

Where am I?

Why had LaCroiux returned?

Why did he keep me prisoner?

Where was he now?

My heart was pounding like a large drum, echoing off the walls and back to me. The walls must be closing in. They will crush me. Suddenly, a force hit my chest like a Troll's punch slamming me against the wall. A cackling rose above the thundering of my heart.

I attempted to scream, "LaCroiux!" Nothing came out.

The thunder dulled, but was replaced with cold and stars. My stomach flipped as I rose from the ground and floated through the nighttime sky. Horror overtook me. I was weightless, tumbling uncontrollably through nowhere.

The laughter returned. A single dot of light grew before me, the light of a star exploding in space from a million miles away. It began to intensify and with it the sorcerer's laughter grew stronger and louder...the sound of victory. A brilliant flash burned my eyes, which were wide open. I was unable to close them, fixated upon the intense flame.

I screamed in pain as a wave of heat surged across my body. It felt as though my skin was burning away.

Then darkness returned.

I had never left LaCroiux's prison. He was torturing me, turning my own mind and senses against me. No stars, no lights, just darkness and pain. My eyes still stung, legs numbed from the weight of my body pressing down upon them, wrists ached from the binds that tied them together.

I had but one last question. **Why did I still live?**

"That, my dear, is the question." LaCroiux's face emerged in the darkness, shadowed and frightening. His eyes were blazing like the sun.

The sorcerer waved his hand across my face. I was able to open my mouth again. He had removed the spell that had made me unable to speak.

"Set me free, LaCroiux!" I immediately demanded.

LaCroiux laughed. "I don't think so, Commander Tallon. You see, you're a key piece to my game."

"What game?"

"I am playing a political game. You see, I am not completely happy with our current monarch," LaCroiux said.

"Queen Merran? You think that you can replace her on the throne?"

"No, no, no. I am not the ruling type. I prefer to hide in the shadows, place someone else in charge and manipulate them to do my biding." The sorcerer's entire body transformed from the darkness as the nighttime sky returned. He walked before me like a constellation...a God.

"Cragon?" I whispered.

A smile beamed across his face. "Since the former king's untimely departure from the throne, I have grown in my powers. I have used that time to enhance them, and perfect them. Now, I am far more powerful than Cragon Cadieux...this time I will rule through him."

"But the people of Mistasia have their queen!" I shouted in disgust.

"Ah, ah, ah. It would be unwise to speak that way to your new king." LaCroiux slowly waved his fingers in front of my face. I felt my lips tighten and close. He had recast the spell to quiet me. "Grace, the people of Mistasia have no right to decide who is to be their ruler. It is to be decided by whoever is strong enough to claim the throne."

I struggled to free myself, when he pushed me against the wall.

"You were a key acquisition in this plan. Now that I have you, it is time to proceed with the last phase. You will love this part too because it involves someone you hold very dear."

Three figures began to form in the darkness beyond LaCroiux. Fear struck me when I recognized their faces.

"Yes, Phillip Harper and the Whizzenmog twins. I intend to bring them back to Mistasia...using you as bait and then trap them here with you...forever."

Phillip & Whizzy Trilogy

RETURN TO MISTASIA

Christopher M. Purrett

CHAPTERS

MICHAEL WHIZZENMOG

1

My name is Michael Whizzenmog the Third, but my friends call me "Whizzy". I live in a small quiet town called Greenville, but last summer I found out that I am a wizard, and my twin sister is a witch. Apparently, our family is really from another world...or place, well whatever it is, called Mistasia.

My best friend, Phillip Harper, and I traveled to Mistasia to save my sister from an evil king, Cragon Cadieux, who was a sorcerer that had ruled Mistasia for nearly a decade.

Phillip was normally a scared, awkwardly tall boy, but in Mistasia he was a green frog with superpowers. Weird, huh?

Anyway, we traveled to Mistasia through a portal in my basement, saved my sister, defeated the evil sorcerer and helped Princess

Merran, Cragon's niece, become queen. That's the very short version.

After summer ended we had to go back to school, and now I'm a freshman at Greenville High School. The first couple of weeks were awful. New school! New teachers and new bullies! I hated being a freshman.

My sister Rachel stuck up for Phillip and me when she could...something she never would have done last year. I could tell she missed being a witch.

The first thing I got excited about all school year was Winter break! Just before it started I began having dreams about Mistasia. In the dream, I could see Grace Tallon, our elven guide and protector for Queen Merran. I wondered if we would ever be there again.

That day would come much sooner than I expected.

I DON'T WANNA GO TO SCHOOL
2

"Ugh! What is that sound?" I rolled over in my bed and opened my stinging eyes. My head spun like I had just been on an amusement park ride for days. My alarm clock buzzed its annoying tone. It was a cross between a fire alarm and an injured cat...mostly because I beat it viciously every time it went off. Swinging my arm like a hammer, I smashed into the clock and knocked it onto the floor. "I don't wanna go to school." I said that every morning...like it would magically change my fortune. It never did. I always had to go to school.

After struggling out of bed and getting dressed, I dragged myself to the bathroom to brush my teeth.

I stared into the mirror. My fiery hair wildly waved back at me with every movement. I hadn't had a hair cut in about three months and so it sort of resembled octopus tentacles hanging off my head. Each eye blinked independently, and my eyelids felt so heavy.

"Toothbrush...Toothbrush? Where the heck is my...?" I searched through the drawers without luck. After slamming the drawer to my right in disgust, a voice startled me.

"Michael, sweetheart? You're up early." It was my mother.

Early? I thought. I got up for school at this time everyday.

My mom stood in the bathroom doorway with a stunned look on her face.

"I'm getting ready, Mom," I snapped.

"Michael Whizzenmog, you watch your tone young man!" She didn't sound happy.

I didn't even want to look her in the eye. She had a way of making me feel guilty about my attitude. The sensation of her glaring down at me burned the side of my neck. She waited patiently for an apology. I couldn't take it any longer.

I exhaled, "Sorry, Mom."

"Thank you, Michael."

She disappeared from the doorway and walked down the hallway.

I opened the drawer to my left and found my toothbrush. As I reached for it, I heard my mom call to me from down the hall.

"Yeah, Mom?" I called as I poked my head into the hallway to hear her better.

"Michael, you know it *is* Winter break. You don't have school today!"

My shoulders dropped and my toothbrush fell out of my mouth and onto the floor. I muttered inappropriate things under my breath so she wouldn't hear. I had forgotten to turn my alarm off and now I was awake...way too early.

Two hours later my twin sister, Rachel, came bouncing down the stairs, happy and perky as usual.

"Morning, Whizzy!"

I just groaned as I lay with my head resting on the arm of the couch.

"Well! Someone's happy this morning," she responded.

"Your brother forgot to turn his alarm off," my mom interjected from the kitchen.

Rachel just laughed and went in to join her.

I rolled toward the back of the couch and buried my face in the cushion. **Shut up!** I yelled into the couch.

"What's wrong, Michael?"

"Nothing, Mom!" I quickly responded as I bolted up into a seated position.

Why does she have to be so happy? I wondered about my sister. I might still challenge the fact that we were actually twins. We don't even look alike. She had long straight reddish-brown hair, green eyes and was about four inches taller than me. That's right...my twin sister was taller than me. It is awful. People at school think she is pretty...Pretty? I don't even want to go there.

It didn't matter. She had been really nice to me this school year. We almost never talked in middle school. Now, after what happened in Mistasia last summer, she was different.

"Michael. Breakfast is ready!"

Well, at least Phillip will be here this afternoon!

WAYS TO AVOID MY SISTER

3

After breakfast I paced around my house waiting for Phillip to arrive. I was bored out of my mind. Sitting still isn't one of my best traits. I would sit on the couch in the basement for a couple of minutes. Then, I would walk around the couch before sitting back down again.

When the doorbell rang, I dashed upstairs leaping three steps at a time, which is a lot for my short legs.

"I got it! I got it! I got it!" I yelled at my sister as we both reached for the door handle. "I got it," I said in a little bit calmer voice.

"Alright," Rachel replied while giving me a peculiar expression. I think she was questioning my sanity at that point.

Rachel stood next to me waiting. I didn't open the door though. I glanced at her, then the door before looking back at her again.

"What?" She snapped. "Open the door."

"Are you gonna stand there?" I asked.

"Whizzy, what's wrong with you?"

"What? Nothing's wrong with me. Don't you have to go do your hair or something?" I sounded like an idiot. Then, the doorbell rang again.

"I wanted to say 'hi' to Phillip," Rachel replied. She seemed hurt that I was questioning what she was doing, like she was Phillip's best friend.

"Well, he's here to see me!" I almost couldn't believe I said it. I was fighting with my sister over my best friend...who just happened to like my sister.

"Whizzy, can you open the door?" Phillip's muffled voice came through. "It's really cold out here."

Suddenly, I snapped out of my haze and opened the door.

Phillip was bundled up in a light green jacket that had "GHS" embroidered on the chest in large white letters with a gold trim. The letters stood for Greenville High School. His floppy brown hair was hanging out from underneath his winter hat, which matched his jacket. He was now over six-feet tall and really skinny. I only came up to his chest.

Phillip had adjusted to high school much better than I did. I wouldn't be caught dead in our school's jacket.

"It's freezing out there," Phillip chattered. He rubbed his cold hands together.

Phillip Harper had been my best friend for as long as I could remember. He had also pined for my sister nearly as long.

"Hey, Rachel," Phillip smiled.

He wouldn't have been able to speak around her last year, but Mistasia changed him...all of us really. Last year Rachel wouldn't have been standing at the cold front door when Phillip got here either.

After a couple of awkward moments of them looking at each other I pulled him toward the basement and told Rachel she could talk to him later.

I spent most of the day attempting to avoid my sister. Every time Phillip and I would start something she would check in on us. First, we played bowling but only finished three frames. She came downstairs with sodas and pretzels, and the next thing I knew, her and Phillip were sitting on the couch together. Then, when we started watching a movie, "The Captain's Loot", an awesome story about pirates, she joined us. She even flopped right down between us. At one point, I thought she and Phillip were holding hands. Then, we played basketball...or maybe I should say dodge ball because I spent more time avoiding getting drilled in the face with the ball than anything. Phillip kept blocking all my shots. In my attempt to get Rachel to leave us alone, I had asked Phillip if he would play basketball...which I never do for two reasons. One, he is really tall, and two, he's on the high school junior varsity basketball team. Whenever we play, he kills me. Sometimes I don't even score. So technically, Rachel ruined my game with Phillip without even playing. Finally, I dragged Phillip upstairs to the one place that I figured my sister would never go...my bedroom. She says it smells funny, which I like because it keeps her away. However, our

alone time didn't last very long. It was
dinnertime.

MISTASIAN MATH
4

During dinner, I had talked my mom into
letting Phillip spend the night. She usually never
minded. It had been a few months since he was
on the basketball team now. Most weekends he
had had a game or practice, but now he had
more free time. I didn't quite understand why he
had joined the team...I guess it was because he
was tall. He thought it helped him fit in. Phillip
had somehow figured out how to work his body
in the past couple of months, too. If he had tried
to play a sport of any kind last year, it would
have meant total humiliation. He struggled to
walk and chew gum before, and now he suddenly
figured out how to run and dribble a basketball
without falling down.

Don't get me wrong...it's great! I go to
every game. I hate basketball really, but he's my

best friend. It just hasn't been the same since we got back from Mistasia...I almost wish we hadn't gone. Phillip and Rachel both had changed...for the better, but I still felt the same – small, angry all the time and ...well, I don't know.

Anyway, Phillip and I sat up watching television. We had moved back to the basement. Rachel hadn't come downstairs in a while, so I had started to relax. Neither of us talked. It was like there was nothing to say. When we did talk, it was about stupid things, like a commercial about shoes or some new video game. Then, Rachel startled me.

"Whizzy!" was all she said, but it scared the heck out of me. I almost fell off the couch.

"Jezz, Rachel! Don't sneak up on me like that."

Phillip started to laugh. I shot him a nasty glare.

"What do you want?" I snapped. My heart pounded in my chest. It echoed all the way into my ears.

"Sorry, Whizzy. I was just thinking. How long has it been?" She just looked at me as if I had any idea what she was talking about.

I could feel my frustration growing. Sometimes the slightest thing would get me going...and Rachel was at the top of the list of frustrations.

"Rachel, I have no idea what you are even asking me?

"Since when, Rachel?" Phillip asked trying to avoid my meltdown.

She sat down between us on the couch and looked behind us. I turned around to see what she was looking at. It was nothing...just the staircase. I thought she was losing her mind. Then, she unfolded a piece of paper in her hand. It had writing all over it. Maps, numbers, and drawings...it looked like Mistasia.

"Wow, is that Mistasia?" Phillip seemed overly interested.

Rachel nodded and then smiled. She pushed her hair back from her face and tucked it behind her ears.

I caught Phillip staring at her. He saw my expression and quickly refocused on the drawing in her hands.

"I can't figure this out. I hoped maybe you guys could help me."

"Sure!" Phillip answered.

"Fine," I replied out of disgust. I could see that my sister was never going to leave us alone.

"I was trying to do the math, but it just doesn't seem possible." Rachel pointed to a jumble of numbers in the upper right corner of the map she had sketched. Just next to the title "Mistasia", was her attempt to figure out something.

I had no idea what it was. "What are you doing? This is a mess." I barked and slid back on the couch.

Rachel shook her head in frustration. "If you would let me explain, Whizzy, I would tell you. I am trying to figure out how long it's been since we were in Mistasia."

"Well, it was right when we got outta school last year," Phillip replied eagerly.

"June 17th," I elaborated.

"Yes, I know. And today is December 15th. That makes two hundred and ten days," Rachel said as she refigured the math on her paper.

"Alright problem solved. Goodbye!" I quickly responded.

Phillip, however, got pretty upset. Sometimes I forgot that he liked my sister...apparently more than he favors our friendship. He didn't even look at me when he barked, "Shut up, Whizzy!" He never yelled at me. I was shocked and kind of angry actually.

"Guys, stop it!" Rachel pleaded before she continued. "I know it's been two hundred and ten days here in Greenville, but I am trying to figure out how long it has been for the people in Mistasia."

"Oh, well, how do we figure that out?" Phillip asked while he studied her math problem on the paper still in her hands. "Grace said that every day in Mistasia was equal to an hour here."

"Right!" Rachel responded. "That's what I thought she said, but that's impossible."

I sat up as I tried to do the Mistasian math in my head.

"No, we had only been gone for like a little more than five hours when we returned home remember," Phillip empathically responded.

"He's right, Rachel," I agreed. "It had only been five hours when we came back. The math would work."

"So what's wrong with that?" Phillip asked Rachel who seemed hesitant to give her answer.

"That would mean it's been more than thirteen years."

MOUSE IN THE WHIZZENMOG HOUSE
5

"Thirteen years!" Phillip and I replied in unison.

I turned the television on mute and tossed the remote on the floor.

"Does that mean Grace and Princess Merran are thirteen years older?" Phillip asked in astonishment.

"*Queen* Merran," Rachel corrected. "She became queen just before we left."

"That's unbelievable. It hasn't even been a year here. How does that happen?" I questioned. It made my head hurt to think about it.

"How did our sliding glass door turn into a spinning black portal to another world? None of it seems possible, but unless all three of us are having the same crazy dream, it happened." Rachel refolded her paper and put it in her jean pocket.

"What was that?" Phillip asked as if he had heard a noise.

"I didn't hear anything, Phillip," I said while listening intently.

"I thought I heard a squeaky giggle."

Rachel began to laugh. Then, I started laughing. Phillip seemed confused at first. Then, he joined us with a snort which made all of us laugh even harder.

But we quickly stopped. Standing on the carpet next to the television was a small black mouse. It stood on its hind legs and stared at us. It even seemed to smile.

Rachel screamed. I placed my hand over her mouth. It was almost midnight and our mom was sleeping upstairs.

"You'll wake up mom!" I whispered in her ear.

"It's a friggin' mouse, Whizzy."

"Phillip, get the sticks!" I demanded.

The mouse's expression changed violently from a smile to fear. Its eyes bulged and it yelped when Phillip handed me a hockey stick. We both dashed after the fleet-footed mouse as it darted around the basement's carpeted floor.

"Don't kill it, Whizzy," Rachel yelled. "Phillip, stop!" She started to cry.

"Are you kidding me? What do you want us to do with it?" I barked.

"Please, don't kill me!" A squeaky small voice echoed through the room. We all looked down at the black mouse as it was cowering in the corner.

"Oh no," I muttered. "Not again!"

Rachel exploded off the couch and ran between us almost knocking me down. "Are you from Mistasia?" She asked in excited anticipation.

"Yes, Rachel Whizzenmog," the black mouse responded.

She picked up the frightened creature and held him up in the air.

The three of us stared at yet another talking creature in our basement. This was the third in the past six months counting the snake that stole my sister for the sorcerer that worked for King Cragon and Grace Tallon who appeared as an eagle.

"I am Aevion. I am a servant to the Queen. Commander Tallon sent me here to ask for your help." The scared mouse pleaded. He rubbed his paws in a jittery fashion.

"Grace!" I responded. My heart jumped at the thought of her. I wanted to see her, and had always hoped she would return some day. "What's wrong?"

"Commander Tallon needs your
assistance. I do not know for what purpose. I am
only a humble servant to the Queen. I am not an
elven warrior. I only know that the commander
was headed to The Deadly Spray Forest after
sending me through the portal."

"What is it with the forests in Mistasia?" I
thought aloud. "Why can't there be a Happy
Cheerful Forest?"

"Aevion, how can we help?" Rachel asked.

"Do you have your wands?" He asked.

WHIZZENMOG WANDS

6

I rummaged through my closet. It was a
disaster. I had been tossing things in here all
school year. My mom had been yelling at me to
clean it up. Right about now, I wished I had
listened to her.

I grabbed my backpack and slung it over
my shoulder, nearly winging Phillip in the head.

Actually, it was a pretty good toss considering he was over six-feet tall now.

"Watch out, Whizzy!"

"Sorry," I replied while continuing to pull things from my closet. I found all sorts of things. My English paper about Edgar Allan Poe...it was due over a month ago. I never thought to look in the closet. Then, I discovered a half-eaten sandwich from like October.

"That is disgusting!" Phillip said. I thought I heard him gag just a bit.

"I know; it reminds me of you last summer, Phillip." I held up the now green piece of bread.

"This is going to take forever, Whizzy. We need to go...now!" Phillip was so excited. I think he even started licking his lips like a frog after eating a fly.

"I know. I thought it was in here."

"Are you sure?" Phillip asked. "I mean could it be somewhere else? I'll go look if you just tell me where?"

"Ah, ha!" I interrupted as I pulled out a woody colored object.

"You found it!" Phillip croaked.

"Ah...no I think it's an old hot dog."

Phillip didn't even respond right away. What do you say to someone who just found an old wiener in his closet?

"Whizzy. There is really something wrong with you."

"Did you find it?" Rachel yelled as she burst into the room. Aevion the mouse sat on her shoulder. I didn't think it was possible, but his eyes bulged out even more after seeing the disaster in my room.

"Are you referring to his wand or his wie..." Phillip began.

"Shut up, Phillip! Not funny," I snapped, and then smiled as I finished the sentence in my head. It was funny. "I can't remember where I put it. I thought I hid it in here to keep mom from finding it."

"And you, apparently!" Phillip barked. He was becoming unusually cranky.

"You lost your wand?" Rachel was shocked. "How could you be so...so...?"

"Irresponsible?" Phillip added.

"Stupid?" Rachel finished.

"Look! Are you going to help me find my wand or not?"

We split up and continued searching my room. Phillip looked under my bed, Rachel bravely checked in my dresser drawers, and I continued to claw my way through the closet.

"Phillip!" Rachel called in an uncomfortable voice. "I need you to check this one!"

"What's wrong?"

"It's Whizzy's underwear drawer."

I started to laugh. I had finally reached the back of the closet. Sitting in the right corner was a white sock. "I got it!"

Phillip gave a sigh of relief that he wouldn't have to search my underwear drawer.

Rachel and Phillip rushed to my side as I pulled the white sock out and held it up in the air.

"That's a sock, Whizzy!" Rachel crassly remarked.

"Duh!" I simply replied. "I stashed my wand in the sock and hid it in the closet.

"Why?" My best friend asked.

"I really don't remember why!" Quickly, I removed my wand and tossed the old dusty sock at Phillip. He attempted to dodge it, but the sock landed on his shoulder.

"Ah, Whizzy. Gross! It smells awful." Phillip looked hilarious as he brushed it off his shoulder, and then attempted to smell himself to see if the stink rubbed off on him.

Rachel and I now both had our wands and we were ready to make the journey back to Mistasia. My sister held Aevion the mouse in her hand as we quietly moved through the hallway trying not to wake up our mom. Once we reached the basement I began to feel an excitement overtake me. My heart pumped so hard it felt like it was coming through my chest. I watched Rachel as she held Aevion in her hands and extended him close to the sliding glass door in our basement. It usually led outside into our backyard, but we all waited for it to once again lead us to Mistasia.

Aevion held a small mushroom in his hand. I hadn't noticed it before. He crumbled it up and then tossed the tiny pieces against the glass door.

Just like it had last summer when Sorcerer LaCroiux's evil snake had slammed its tail into the glass, the door magically changed into a swirling portal.

Rachel was the first to enter with Aevion held tightly in one hand and her wand in the other. She was swept inside and quickly disappeared.

Phillip didn't hesitate for a moment. He was off directly behind Rachel.

I took a deep breath. It sounded like a drum was inside my head as my heart continued to pound. Gripping my wand tightly, I sprinted for the portal, leapt into the air and felt a gust of wind pull me in.

A DIFFERENT MISTASIA

7

Traveling in a portal is kind of like riding a roller coaster without the safety straps while flying through the air at great speed, twisting and bouncing. It only lasted for a few seconds... then silence. There was no movement.

My eyes were closed tightly, but I quickly realized that Mistasia would be much different than the last time we visited. I instantly thought about our conversation in the basement a few hours earlier. It was thirteen years in the future here...it would be different.

The ground was strange. I opened my eyes and realized I was lying on my back. The sky was gloomy and full of rough-shaped dark gray clouds. They overlapped each other like pancakes stacked on a plate. I couldn't see any blue...like the beautiful sky last time we had visited.

"Whizzy?" I heard Rachel calling for me.

I sat up in what used to be a tall green grass field. Now it was covered in deep snow. All around me was white, which made me stick out like a pimple on the big bully, Billy Lawton's, ugly face.

Once again I had transformed into a red-haired fox. Rachel now stood beside me. She was also a fox, but bronze colored. Phillip had changed, too. He was again a green tree frog with long arms and legs and bright red eyes.

"So, it's winter here, too," Phillip said with obvious disappointment in his voice.

I can't imagine that being a frog helps much in the winter. At least Rachel and I have furry coats to keep us warm. I wondered if the snow would make him strong like water did the last time. I guessed we would find out soon enough.

"Where is Aevion?" Rachel wondered aloud.

We all searched around not realizing that he wouldn't still be a small black mouse. Walking toward us was a shorter than expected, young dark-skinned boy. He was even smaller than me. His hair was short and curly, and he had big, bright green eyes. I think he's a midget.

"Hurry! Follow me," Aevion spoke and then quickly darted away in the opposite direction of Cadieux Castle.

"Where are you going?" I yelled as he swiftly separated from us. I was shocked at how fast he was. Everyone here in Mistasia must be really fast.

He stopped and turned. The snow almost came to his waist. It looked like he was sinking. He had a peculiar expression on his face. Aevion waved his arms urging us to join him.

"Wait!" I yelled to Aevion again. "He's in a hurry!" I crassly remarked to Phillip and Rachel.

When we caught up with him, Aevion explained, "I must take you across Red River and lead you in the direction of The Deadly Spray Forest. There you will meet up with Commander Tallon."

"So, we aren't going to the Castle?" Phillip asked.

"No, Phillip the Frog."

This guy is annoying I thought. He was really starting to bother me. I hoped we wouldn't have to spend much time around him. I might have to use a spell to change him back into a mouse.

Phillip started laughing.

I forgot that in Mistasia he was telepathic and could read our minds. He had just heard everything I thought. Honestly, that kind of bothered me, too.

Rachel looked at Phillip as if he was going crazy. She gave him that what-are-you-laughing-at look that she gave me every day. Usually, it was because I was laughing at something strange that she just didn't find funny.

I pointed at my forehead.

She now gave me the same look.

"Ah forget it...I'll tell you later, Rachel." Ever since we had landed in Mistasia I had become very agitated. My whole body felt wrong...I mean more wrong than the fact that I was a furry red fox with the ability to turn a tree inside out.

"Come on, Whizzy!" suddenly echoed inside my head. Phillip was yelling at me using his 'special' telepathic powers.

I snapped out of my daze just in time to notice Phillip's green-skinned frame disappearing over a hill. Rachel and Aevion were gone too.

I dashed off to catch them.

"Stay out of my head, Phillip," I barked. It didn't take someone with telepathic powers to realize that I was making everyone feel uncomfortable...especially our guide, Aevion.

No one spoke for a while. We trekked through the deep snow. Phillip hopped. Aevion lead the way with Rachel and Phillip right behind, like eager puppies following their master. I, however, was falling further behind. We reached another hill, which was lined with short evergreen trees. When they had ascended to the top, I had just reached the bottom.

"Come on, Whizzy," Rachel urged with a tone that sounded exactly like our mom. "You need to move faster."

I could feel the rage moving through my body. **I'll show you faster.** I thought, knowing that Phillip would hear me. He reached out and pulled Rachel towards him. I held my wand extended above my head, then jabbed it down toward the ground. My body was catapulted into the air. Before they could react, I was standing next to them on top of the hill.

"Fast enough for you, Sis?"

She never answered. I think Phillip told her to ignore me in his 'special' way.

Ahead of us was a small clearing at the bottom of the hill, which was much steeper on the back side. Then, Red River flowed briskly, with sharp rocks sticking out amidst the crashing water in the distance. Only a long, thin bridge stretched over the river for us to cross.

I burst into the air again and landed safely at the bottom. When I turned around, Rachel and Phillip were headed right for me. Trying to run away, I slipped in the powdery snow. Phillip missed me and landed softly to my left. Rachel, however, didn't. She crashed into me and we tumbled through the snow and slid to a stop about twenty feet away. I bolted up.

"You did that on purpose, Rachel!" I growled, but she didn't respond.

"Rachel, are you okay!" Phillip gulped. My tall green friend went to her side without even asking me if I was all right.

Her eyes fluttered for a few seconds as she tried to focus. Then, when she tried to get up, Phillip caught her as she stumbled.

Suddenly, I felt bad for yelling at her. "What were you thinking?" I knew it sounded bad the second I said it, but now the damage was done.

"Lay off, Whizzy," Phillip argued with a strange sound in his voice.

I thought he was going to cry.

"She landed on *me*, Phillip. Stop protecting her," I answered hotly.

"I'm not...she's hurt. Maybe if her brother actually cared I wouldn't have to protect her."

The argument would have lasted longer, but Rachel walked away. Then, Phillip followed.

"Some friend," I muttered aloud.

Aevion had made his way down the steep hillside and joined us mid argument.

"Whizzy is everything all right?" He asked. His eyes felt like they stared into my brain. It was really creepy.

"No, Aevion. My sister and her new best friend are starting to annoy me." I began walking for Red River. At this point, I really didn't care if they followed or not. Grace needed our help, so I was going to find her.

WHY IS IT CALLED RED RIVER?

8

It didn't take very long for me to reach Red River. Only moments later I heard Phillip's voice and this time it echoed through the air instead of my head, which was nice for a change.

"Whizzy! Wait up."

I took a deep breath to calm myself. Fighting with my best friend wasn't something I was good at. It hadn't happened often, but most of them were very recent...since we came back from Mistasia on our first journey.

"Hey, look I'm sorry I yelled, but she didn't mean it," Phillip started to explain when Rachel interrupted.

"Why are you so angry?" She barked.

I could feel the cool breeze against my sharp front teeth as I sneered at her. A deep growl escaped from me.

Phillip croaked, "Whizzy don't!"

It was too late. I roared at her and pounced on top of her. She landed on her back in the snow. Quickly, she kicked me up into the air. I flipped over and landed on all four paws.

Rachel and I stared at each other. I stood on my hind legs again and positioned my wand so it pointed directly between her eyes. She did the same.

"Try it," she dared me.

"What would you like me to turn you into...a slimy slug maybe?"

Rachel growled back, "You're not fast enough, Whizzy. I'll have you buried up to your eyeballs in dirt before you could blink."

Aevion stood paralyzed. He couldn't believe what he saw. Grace had sent him to get us because we were supposed to save Mistasia, but right now we couldn't save ourselves from...ourselves.

Phillip stood a couple feet behind Rachel. He didn't speak...which made me wonder what he and my sister were plotting against me.

"Shut up, Phillip!" I yelled. "You stay out of it."

"I didn't say anything!" Phillip lied.

"You're talking to her using your telepathy."

"No, I'm not," Phillip tried to defend himself.

"Don't lie! I can see it in her eyes. I can't trust either of you," I screamed.

"You've lost your mind, Whizzy," Rachel said as she slackened her grip on her wand.

Phillip turned his head toward the river. "What was that?"

Aevion scrambled to Phillip's side.

Rachel gave me a scornful glare and then joined them at the edge of the cold rushing riverbank.

I felt of shudder of frustration in my arms as I pulled them to my side. I wasn't going to join them. They were trying to trick me.

"What did you see?" I heard Rachel ask.

"What color was it, Phillip the Frog?" Aevion hastily questioned.

"Color?" I thought.

"It was bright red."

"Was it long and scaly?" Aevion seemed determined to rule out something.

"Yeah!"

"We need to cross the river now!" Aevion screamed and dashed for the narrow wooden structure.

Phillip and Rachel didn't hesitate to follow. The three sped over the bridge and safely reached the other side.

"Come on, Whizzy! Hurry!" Phillip spoke in my head.

"Fine," I replied in disgust. This seemed ridiculous, but I remembered that Mistasia did have the ability to turn ugly in seconds. As I began to cross the narrow bridge, I jogged slightly. I really wasn't in any hurry to join my sister on the other side. She would probably try and turn me into a football and then kick me back across the river.

A loud rushing of water rose up from below me. I slowed down to look over the side. Below was the clearest water I had ever seen. The water was like a pane of glass on an aquarium. Underneath were rocks of all different sizes and colors. Some had green moss growing on them. I could feel, against my fur, the cold air rising off the water. It was soothing. My muscles began to loosen. I felt the grip on my wand lessen. A fish swam out from under the bridge. It whipped its tail vigorously against the current. **Why would it be swimming against the water?** I thought.

Suddenly, a streak of bright red split the river and then disappeared. It left a wake behind. When the water settled, the fish was gone.

I searched around for any sign, but it had vanished.

"Whizzy!" Rachel yelled to me.

"What are you doing?" Aevion screamed. "You must cross the river!" He sounded frantic.

I looked away from the river for a moment. Everything seemed to slow down. I saw them standing at the edge of the bridge pointing up river. When I turned back, I saw a horrifying image.

Jumping out of the water was a bright red giant creature. It looked like a cross between an eel and a fish. Its mouth was wide open. Sharp fangs stuck out around a slender, pink forked-tongue. I ducked as the creature flew over the bridge and gracefully landed in the river on the other side.

I leapt to my feet and suddenly realized why this perfectly clear river was called 'Red'. Names in Mistasia aren't only descriptive, but important, like Wolverine Forest...because it's full of angry large wolverines that are out to kill you. Red River has a deadly bright red monster that will try to eat you.

I ran as fast as my fox paws would take me toward the end of the bridge. Phillip and Rachel began yelling at me as I approached, but I couldn't understand them. They were again pointing, which I knew meant only bad news so I didn't bother to look. I didn't really want to...I had already seen the hideous monster that apparently craved a large helping of fox for dinner. As I reached the edge of the bridge I dove for the snow.

Just then the creature crashed into the bridge jarring it loose. It bounced skyward before flopping onto the snowy riverbank. It slid sideways and crashed into a pair of small evergreens. The tree on the left bent over and slowly fell onto the creature. A branch pierced its scaly skin, trapping it.

"Whizzy, are you all right?" Rachel cried as she grabbed me and pulled me off the ground. Five minutes ago she was going to hurt me! Girls...I'll never understand them.

"Come on, before it gets free!" Aevion cried as he ran away.

None of us argued as we quickly followed him away from the river. In the distance, we could hear the creature screeching and thrashing.

I would say that I was glad to be getting away from that situation, but we were now headed directly for The Deadly Spray Forest, which doesn't sound much friendlier than the river we just left behind.

WINTER LASTS HOW LONG?

9

I was furious. Our guide hadn't mentioned the flesh-eating creature lurking in the river. What else was he hiding from us? His secretive manner was similar to Grace's from our last trip. He was reminding me of Grace with each passing hour...just not as pretty.

"When were you gonna tell us about the giant flying monster, Aevion?" I growled as I grabbed him by the arm.

He began cowering and hid his face.

I was shocked to see how frightened of me he had become. I was definitely never feared at Greenville High School. Suddenly, I felt like a bully, and the last thing I wanted was to be like Billy Lawton.

"I'm sorry, Aevion. I didn't mean to...I was just angry. I'm sorry."

Rachel sat down beside Aevion to comfort him. I walked away shaking my head. **How stupid.** I yelled at myself.

"Don't worry about it, Whizzy," Phillip tried to console me. "You've been really upset ever since we got here. What's wrong?"

I struggled to control my thoughts. The last thing I needed now was to fight with my best friend about how much it upset me that he liked my sister. He couldn't help it. Phillip had always liked my sister. I instead thought about Grace.

"Are you worried about Grace?" Phillip responded seconds later. "She will be just fine. She's an elven warrior."

A smile crossed my face. I missed Grace. She was amazing, pretty, strong, and angry. Everything I could ever want in a girl.

"Do you think she's okay, Phillip? Can you see her?" I wanted him to use his powers of clairvoyance to connect with her. Maybe he would be able to find her in his dreams and see if she was safe.

"I can try," Phillip said and then closed his eyes. He stood completely still.

Rachel joined us.

"Is Aevion gonna be okay?" I asked her.

"Yeah. He is really frightened by your anger. He is just sensitive. It's like his body can read your moods somehow. Aevion just knows when you are getting upset, which he said has been almost the entire time in Mistasia." Rachel gave me a motherly glance.

It was creepy how much she looked like mom when she was upset with me. "You look just like mom," I told her.

She smiled.

"No, Rachel, that's not good. Cut it out!"

She smiled even wider. "What is Phillip doing?"

"Trying to contact Grace for me. I asked him to use his powers and see if he could find her in the forest." I turned to look behind us. The Deadly Spray Forest loomed in the distance.

"It's not working, Whizzy," Phillip responded. He sounded distraught.

"Can you talk to her?" I asked.

Phillip tried, but I could tell immediately that he had no response.

"I'm sorry, Whizzy."

Rachel grabbed Phillip's arm. "I'm sure she's fine, Whizzy. She can take care of herself."

"I know." I walked away from the group. The moon began to show through a gap in the clouds. It was dull and colorless. The sun had finally set. It was nighttime in Mistasia...the time I dreaded most. This place was scary enough in the daytime; shadows only made it more terrifying.

It had begun to snow very lightly. Flurries dangled in the air in front of the dark green trees. It was amazingly beautiful. I just wished it were warmer. Even with this fur coat, I felt the stiff winter breeze.

"You're dang right it's cold," Phillip chattered. He had his thin amphibian limbs wrapped around his body in a vain attempt to stay warm. "Hold me, Whizzy." He said in a silly voice.

"I don't think so. You can get Rachel to do that. I'm the best friend...not the girlfriend."

"She's not my girlfriend," Phillip quickly responded.

Neither of us spoke for a moment. Then Phillip added, "I wish she was."

"I know, Phillip." I wasn't going to continue this conversation...although it would have probably started my blood boiling and warmed my body up.

Phillip shuttered as a chill went up his spine. "Darn it!" He yelled out. "I hope it warms up soon."

"Winter has just begun," Aevion's small voice answered.

We all gave him a strange glance.

"He's just wishing for warmer weather. He was kidding, Aevion," I explained.

"Yes, but winter has just begun."

"Right, it started last month," Rachel said meaning November back in Greenville.

Aevion laughed uncomfortably. He sounded like a child's squeaky toy. Then, he began to explain, "Last month. You are very funny, Rachel the Wizard Fox. It has been winter for over a year."

"A year?" Rachel, Phillip and I said in surprised unison.

"How is that possible?" Winter is only a quarter of the year. A little more than three months...from December through March," Phillip pleaded with Aevion as if he was going to change his mind on how long the winters in Mistasia were.

"I am sorry, Phillip the Frog, but winters here last for six years."

"What?" Phillip croaked.

"Six years!" I was floored. The winters in Greenville were pretty brutal...cold winds, heavy snow and freezing temperatures, but at least it only lasted for a couple months. Then, it would warm up and summer made us forget about how miserable the winters were.

"That's awful." Rachel sounded like she was going to cry.

I immediately imagined her trapped in an igloo, frozen solid with some dumb look on her face. Phillip punched me in the shoulders and then did some weird eye-blinking thing.

"What was that?" I laughed while rubbing my shoulder. I don't even think Phillip realized that his eyes were blinking independently but it was creepy.

"That's rude," Phillip responded referring to my image of Rachel frozen in the igloo. I really needed to control my thoughts around him.

Is six years of winter even possible? I thought.

"What?" Phillip responded.

"Will you cut that out? I am going to turn you into something that doesn't talk!" I barked.

"Whizzy, be quiet," Rachel demanded.

She was trying to figure something out in her head. I could always tell, because she would crinkle up her nose and furrow her eyebrows. It made her look really angry. It must be what I look like all the time.

Finally, she blurted out, "That sounds about right."

"What are we talking about?" I questioned. The last thing I was talking about was her being trapped in an igloo, but I was fairly certain that she wasn't in the same frame of mind...so I figured I'd ask.

"Remember we did the math and it had been about thirteen years here in Mistasia since we had left?"

Phillip and I both nodded.

"The math works out. It would mean that each year in Greenville would be approximately twenty-four years here! Each season lasts about one quarter of the year back home, so it must work the same way here. Therefore, winter or summer or whatever season would last six years!"

"That's ridiculous!" I blurted out.

"She's correct, Whizzy," My best friend said siding again with my sister.

"Well, I guess we're in for a long journey," I added as the snow began to increase.

"We had better get moving. It is only another ten miles to The Deadly Spray Forest," Aevion, our guide, urged.

ARE YOU GONNA GET SICK?
10

Each breath expelled from my mouth like a winding snake slithering out and curling up into a strange-knotted mess. The temperature in Mistasia had dropped quite a bit in the last hour. My whiskers drooped down under the weight of the icicles that had formed around my mouth. Snow had clumped up in my fur. I had white blotches all over my body as the snow attacked me.

Rachel looked the same. Phillip didn't have any snow on him at all. In fact he appeared to shine in the moonlight. As the sun completely disappeared, the once dull colorless moon had exploded. It was bright and large in the sky when it peaked between clouds like the eye of some ever-present creature watching us move through the snow. That light reflected off of Phillip's skin and glowed. The snow was melting against his skin and turning into water, which kept his froggy legs strong. It was another one of Phillip's powers here in Mistasia...water against his amphibian skin gave him extreme strength.

The snow had fallen harder with each passing moment. In the distance, The Deadly Spray Forest slowly disappeared from view. Now, before us, was a blur of white.

"Aevion, how much farther?" I yelled.

All I heard was a mumbled response as the small dark-skinned boy struggled through the deep snow, which had now reached his waist. If it were much longer, he would be buried alive.

"What?" I shouted back.

"It should be just up ahead," Phillip responded in my head.

It startled me. You think I would be used to that by now.

Then, like walking under an umbrella, the snow cascaded off the branches of a thirty-foot tall tree. As I walked underneath the snowdrifts became very small, only a few inches deep.

I looked to the sky and saw the skinny tree's trunk twist and turn into the air. It bent near the top at a strange angle like it was attempting to straighten itself. Then, almost at the top of the tree was the umbrella-like top. The branches were more like vines that intertwined and locked to form knots. Each group of branches also had thick carpet-like bushes sprouting from them. Even though some snow flurries leaked through, the trees created a roof over the forest floor. Now, for the first time since we arrived back in Mistasia, I could see the ground in some spots.

"Creepy," My sister said. "It's so quiet in here."

When looking into The Deadly Spray Forest it was like a series of saltshakers had been turned upside down as small amounts of snow trickled through the thick, dense tree cover and sprinkled onto the ground below in little circles.

"We are here," Aevion announced.

He didn't seem very comfortable with that either.

"What next?" Phillip asked our guide.

"I am not certain, Phillip the Frog. I was only supposed to bring you to the forest. This was the meeting point," Aevion nervously explained. It was obvious that he expected Grace to be here waiting for us.

"Phillip, try to talk to her," I said. He was able to speak to Grace through telepathy, something the elves in Mistasia shared with my best friend.

Phillip's big circular red eyes disappeared behind his green frog eyelids. He stood completely still for only a few moments. Then, he began to sway like a gust of wind pushed against him, but the air was completely still in The Deadly Spray Forest. Next, his face began to contort and he started to mumble like he was having a nightmare. Suddenly, he crumpled to the ground and landed in a heap.

"Phillip," Rachel screamed and rushed to his side.

I joined her, and we helped Phillip sit up.

When he opened his big red eyes he looked dizzy.

"Are you gonna throw up?" I asked him. Believe me, I have seen that look before and it almost always ended in Phillip barfing.

"Whizzy!" Rachel scolded. "He's not gonna throw up...are you, Phillip?" She didn't sound as confident after looking into his eyes which starting rolling back into his head.

Aevion stood completely silent directly behind us. He just anxiously watched to see what would happen next.

"What did you see, Phillip? Is Grace in danger? Is she okay?" I urged him to answer, but he just couldn't get any words to come out.

Phillip struggled to move his mouth. The last time I saw him like this I had accidentally hit him in the head with a soccer ball in my backyard. And yes...he threw up that time.

We spent a couple more minutes trying to pry information out of him, but no luck. Then, Aevion stepped up between my sister and me. He just placed his hand in front of Phillip's face and snapped his fingers.

"Grace!" Phillip croaked.

Aevion backed away quickly. Rachel and I did, too.

Phillip gasped for air like he had just come up from underwater. Then, he swallowed before calming himself down.

"Grace is in trouble. Something has her."

Phillip was afraid. That was the look I saw on Phillip Harper's face for as long as I had known him. He was afraid of a lot of things, but as Phillip the Frog I had never seen him so terrified.

"Where is she?" I demanded as I stood up and gripped my wand tightly.

Rachel grabbed my wrist, "Calm down."

"Grace needs our help, Rachel! That's why we are here." I was revved up. A surge of adrenaline shot through my furry body. The hairs on the back of my neck stood up like an electrical charge built up inside me. "Where is she, Phillip?" I demanded again.

"Whizzy, there is something evil in this forest." Phillip looked pale for a guy that was green. The color in his face had faded.

For a moment I could see Phillip Harper from Greenville emerge. He was shaken and scared.

"We are the saviors of Mistasia, Phillip...remember? Grace sent Aevion to find us! Not bring an elven army or creatures from Mistasia...you and me." I reminded my best friend.

"Me, too," Rachel added.

I looked at her for a moment then replied, "Yeah, I know." I was trying to forget that part. "Wherever Phillip is...I'll find you, too." Rachel seemed hurt by my jab, but I didn't care at the moment. This was about saving Grace. "Now, where is she, Phillip?"

I could see how reluctant my best friend was, but he fought against his fear and began running deeper into the forest. I dashed after him with Rachel and Aevion trailing behind me.

SHRIEKING IN THE DEADLY SPRAY FOREST

11

You know that feeling you get after you've made a bad choice? You know that sinking feeling in the pit of your stomach followed by the obvious reaction of wishing you hadn't done whatever it was that you just did?

Well, I had that exact feeling about three minutes after I started to run deeper into The Deadly Spray Forest.

I caught up to Phillip quickly. We ran side by side. Rachel and Aevion were still behind us. We ran between two tangled trees, each of which stood over forty-feet tall. I passed through first with Phillip directly behind me.

I'm not sure if I had ever said these words before in my life, but it just slipped out.

"Holy mother of crap!"

Phillip didn't say anything recognizable. It kind of sounded like his mouth began to speak a foreign tongue. I'd repeat it for you, but I wouldn't come close. Just understand it didn't make any sense at all. My statement had pretty much summed it up.

Rachel burst from between the trees and skidded to a stop. The three of us now stood in a small clearing within the forest.

Inside was a village. Small huts made of bark, wood and sticks were hanging in the air from the trees...dozens of them. That wasn't the most unbelievable part.

Across the clearing was a tall, thin and yellowish-looking creature. Its bony body dangled upside down in the tree next to a hut. It had black eyes and no nose, just two small holes. Its ears were round and floppy. Suddenly, I noticed these things were everywhere.

Maybe they're elves. I hoped.

I could hear shrieking and scratching. Then, I noticed a few other traits. These creatures had claws where they should have hands. Suddenly, one of them reached its arms above its hairy head, exposing wings that attached to their elbows and sides. It jumped from the tree and swooped down slightly before climbing into the air and landing in a nearby tree.

"That thing just flew," Rachel whispered.

We all began to walk backwards. Somehow, we hadn't been noticed.

My heart was pounding like a drum. It thumped so loudly that I swore one of those creatures could hear it. I placed my hands over my chest in a silly attempt to quiet my pounding heart.

"What in the world are those?" Phillip asked. His mouth was wide open in shock.

"Vampire bats," Aevion responded in a quiet yet blunt tone.

"You have to be joking?" I blurted out still holding my chest. "Are they good or bad?" I added.

"They look bad," Rachel quickly responded.

"Shh!" Phillip was frightened as a vampire bat swooped past directly in front of us. It shrieked an awful sound that hurt my ears. "Bats have great hearing."

"Actually, these vampire bats are not much different from elves, Phillip the Frog. They do have good hearing, but it's unidirectional." Aevion explained.

"What does that mean?" I asked.

"They won't be able to hear unless you are talking in their direction. If you are facing away from where the vampire bats are, their ears won't hear your sound waves. However, if you speak, even at a whisper, in their direction...they will hear you."

"Whizzy these creatures have Grace!" Phillip spoke to me using his 'special' powers.

I hadn't really mastered the way to respond back without speaking out loud yet, so I nodded instead. With my wand in hand, I stood up and started back into the clearing through the twisted trees.

Aevion reached out and grasped my wrist, "Don't attack them, Whizzy. They won't hurt you."

I gave him a quizzical glance. **If they won't hurt me than why are we hiding from them?** I thought.

"Good question," I heard in my head. Phillip stood next to me with a smirk on his big green face. His two large red eyes gazed at me. I hadn't realized until now just how large his eyes were. They were bigger than the headlights on my parents' car.

"Then, why are we hiding?" I finally asked.

"I don't know, Whizzy the Wizard Fox. You and your friends were standing here when I arrived," Aevion replied.

"Oh!" I didn't know what else to say.

I peeked back through the trees and noticed a group of vampire bats flying in a circle directly overhead. They appeared to be playing. One would screech and then they would dart off in different directions, as one vampire bat would chase them. I watched curiously as it chased down another vampire bat and jumped on its back. These two began to scuffle with each other, biting and clawing at one another while falling toward the forest floor. At the last moment, they separated and flew back up into another circle. The whole thing started again.

"I think they are playing some game," I announced to Rachel, Phillip and Aevion, who all stood behind the trees.

They followed me into the clearing again. This time it didn't take long for them to notice us. Quickly, three vampire bats descended upon us. They landed in front of us. Vampire bats may be thin, but they are quite tall. Phillip only came to their chests and he was over six-feet tall. Their faces were hideous. Now that they stood on their feet, their ears drooped back and their faces appeared wrinkled. They looked like they were hundreds of years old.

"Can they talk, Aevion?" I asked our guide.

"I'm not certain," he replied as he hid behind Phillip.

My heart was racing again. Aevion had said that they wouldn't hurt us, but I had my doubts. He had also conveniently forgotten to explain the eel-fish in Red River; maybe he forgot that vampire bats were bad.

I summoned up the courage to speak. "Do you know where Grace Tallon is?"

The three vampire bats looked at one another, but didn't make a sound. Suddenly, the creature on the right noticed my wand and shrieked. Dozens of his brethren in the trees took to flight in the forest.

I asked again, "Grace Tallon...have you seen her?

The tallest of the three vampire bats bent over and stuck his scary face in mine before responding, "Who are you and why have you entered our forest?"

VOICE IN THE SHADOWS
12

The vampire bats grizzly voice was followed by the most disgusting smell. It was like sweaty feet and cooked spinach. My stomach gurgled, and I felt myself getting sick. This wouldn't be very good if I barfed all over him.

"Wow, that breath's awful."

I heard Rachel and Phillip gasp behind me, and I suddenly realized that I had just said that out loud.

The vampire bat's face crumpled in anger. He stood upright again and shrieked.

Before I could realize what was happening, the vampire bats snatched the three of us off the ground and leapt into the air.

I struggled to free myself from his bony claws until I saw how far above the forest floor we were. My red and black fox legs dangled in the air.

We flew high into the air and then dipped down. My stomach flipped like on a roller coaster. Then, we did a complete spin like we were trapped in a washing machine. I was certainly glad that I hadn't eaten lately.

Phillip and Rachel were right behind us. The vampire bats flew to the end of the clearing and headed straight for a tangled group of trees.

"Oh no!" I yelled as it looked like this vampire bat was going to crash us into them. At the last second, he tilted sideways and slipped through a gap. It was dark, but I could hear the trees whizzing past us at great speed. A small sliver of light was up ahead. It grew wider and taller each second until it opened up into a large room.

The vampire bat swooped across the wooden floor and let me go. I hit the floor and slid into the wall.

"Ouch!" I yelled as I hit my paw against the hard wall. Then, I heard Phillip and Rachel screaming.

They were flying through the air right at me. Phillip bounced on his rear, flew over me, and landed face first into the wall. He slithered to the floor like a snake. Rachel landed on her side and began rolling toward me. I jumped to avoid her, but she clipped my legs and knocked me on top of her. The three of us rested in a heap. I struggled to keep my eyes open as the room spun. Rachel and Phillip were both out cold. It wasn't long before I joined them.

When I awoke, my head was throbbing. A dull noise echoed in my ears. Rachel was still passed out lying on her stomach. Phillip was laying over her in a painfully awkward fashion. His legs were underneath Rachel, but his body was bent backwards over her like a pretzel. I checked them to make sure they were both still breathing.

"They are alive, Whizzenmog." A familiar voice rang out.

I struggled to find where it was coming from. The room still moved uncontrollably in my vision. From my hands and knees, I crawled away from my sister and best friend.

"Where are you going?" The voice laughed. His voice seemed to be coming from everywhere, like I was inside it.

I slowly felt the room begin to stop moving. The pounding in my head had ended. After taking a deep breath, I pushed myself to my feet. Stumbling backwards I crashed to the ground again. Dizziness had trounced me. From my back, I noticed there was no ceiling in this room, just darkness. I rolled to my side and again attempted to stand up.

"You are persistent," The voice mocked me. I could recognize it. It was hateful and mean.

Laughing again he said, "I could watch you struggle forever, but that would be a waste of valuable time. Pick him up!" He barked in a deeper tone.

The vampire bat's claws gripped me once again and picked me off the ground. Hanging in the air, fear began to take over. I struggled to loosen its grasp, but the creature was much too strong.

That is when I realized that my wand was gone. I had dropped it when the vampire bat had thrown me into the room. I was helpless. I felt like I was back in Greenville fighting a schoolyard bully.

My vision had become much better, but I still couldn't see where the voice was coming from. The room looked empty. Torches lit the room along the wall, which was round and brown.

We must be inside a tree trunk. I thought.

"Do you remember me, Whizzenmog?" His voice taunted me.

"No!" I replied. **Phillip, wake up!** I tried to reach my friend. Hopefully, he would wake up and hear me. **Phillip, wake up!** I said in my mind.

"You really don't remember me?" The voice asked again. Suddenly, his face appeared before me out of darkness.

"Ah!" I screamed. "LaCroiux!"

Standing before me was Sorcerer Pierre LaCroiux.

"The last time I saw you King Cragon had banished you from the castle," I added.

"Yes! I guess that would be the last time you would remember." LaCroiux looked even older than before. His eyes were sunken deep into his skinny skull. Black circles surrounded them, swallowing up the whites of his eyes. It was frightening to look at. It almost looked like his eyes were missing. His white beard was even longer than before, but still braided. It looked like an icicle hanging from his chin.

"I was banished because of you and your sister. My king punished me because I failed to get rid of you two," LaCroiux began to explain.

"He isn't king anymore, LaCroiux!" I growled. The longer I was being held the angrier I was becoming. My frustration was setting in.

"Yes. I guess it seems you took care of that too." He just stared at me with those blank eyes. "It has been thirteen years since you defeated me. I have been waiting for the king to return to power, hoping that he would forgive me...take me back."

"That will never happen!" Rachel suddenly bellowed from behind me. She had both wands in her paws. "Let him go!" She demanded.

The vampire bat placed me back on solid ground, but refused to let go.

"Well, it appears we meet again, Rachel and Michael Whizzenmog...the last wizards of Mistasia. You do realize that while you were away, sorcery increased its popularity in these lands. Cadieux Castle is becoming weaker. Soon, your queen will no longer be in power," Sorcerer LaCroiux explained.

"Not if we have anything to say about it," Rachel retorted while raising her wand toward the sorcerer's heart. "We'll stop you just like we stopped your precious king."

"Ah...ah...ah, my dear, I wouldn't do that if I were you." LaCroiux said in a fatherly tone. "You have no idea what you are involved in, child. This isn't a game. Lives are at risk."

Rachel stepped forward and LaCroiux suddenly disappeared into a mist. She angrily pointed her wand at the vampire bat holding me prisoner.

"Let go!" She vented.

It shrieked and exposed its fangs, but then backed away.

"This will not end well, Whizzenmogs. I promise you both that," LaCroiux's voice echoed.

Rachel tossed me my wand. Phillip now awoke and joined us. The three of us stood in the middle of the wooden room, back to back, searching for any sign of LaCroiux.

"What's going on? What are we looking for?" Phillip requested.

"It's Sorcerer LaCroiux!" I answered.

"He's back?" Phillip croaked. "That can't be good." I could hear his stomach flip. That's the Phillip I knew, uncomfortable and afraid.

"Show yourself, you coward," I growled.

Suddenly, LaCroiux's face appeared before me. "BOO!" He yelled.

I flicked my wrist and shot a white bolt of lightning out of my wand. Just then his face disappeared and the bolt slammed into the wall. It scorched the wood, which smoldered.

"I have a present for you!" He laughed. "Follow the light, Whizzenmogs."

"It's a trap, Whizzy," Rachel urged.

"I know."

"Whizzy, Grace is here," Phillip said trying to remind me why we were here.

I began to walk down a slim hallway. As I walked, it felt like the walls were closing in on me. Rachel and Phillip followed, but so did the vampire bat. It stalked slowly, following Phillip. When I reached the end, there was another small room. The ceiling was very low and the area was no larger than Phillip's bedroom in Greenville.

Once inside I stopped. I could hear mumbling, but no one was there. Rachel stood beside me. Phillip bumped into me, almost knocking me down, as he backed into the room. The tall hideous creature creeping up behind him kept him preoccupied. The vampire bat stopped just outside the room.

Suddenly, I had a sinking feeling in my gut. Again, I heard a mumbled voice call out.

"Grace?" Phillip responded and then he turned around.

Right in front of us was Grace Tallon and Aevion. She had her mouth covered with some sort of clear paste that kept her from talking. Aevion looked terrified and had his hands behind his back.

Then, a loud bang echoed from behind me. The door had closed. I turned and fired a spell at it, but nothing happened. We were trapped.

I FELT SOMETHING FOOLISH COMING ON

13

"I told you it was a trap!" Rachel yelled. "Darn you, Whizzy." She frantically looked to find any way to open the door. "I can't find it!" She shouted.

"What?" Phillip replied. "How can that be? Whizzy, there is no door!"

"It's black magic...evil and treacherous." Aevion replied. "You can't escape."

"Watch me," I boasted. I walked over to where the door had been; motioned Rachel and Phillip to move aside and readied my wand.

"Your magic won't work! You cannot escape this room." LaCroiux's voice boomed. "I have been waiting for this moment. Never did I believe that it would be so easily accomplished, but thankfully you aren't as smart as everyone believed," Sorcerer LaCroiux sneered.

A pale-skinned hand poked through the wall where the door had been as if the wall wasn't even there.

I heard Phillip gasp with astonishment. Then, he mumbled something. I couldn't understand him, but I'm sure it wasn't good.

The hand easily moved through the solid wooden wall, followed by an arm and then Sorcerer LaCroiux's ugly, sagging face. He almost looked like the vampire bat creatures. When LaCroiux had completely stepped through the wall, his minion followed.

"How is that possible?" I blurted out. "Are you a ghost?" I added. After I said it, I wished that I hadn't because it sounded like a dumb question.

LaCroiux just smiled. He was completely enjoying every minute of this. It was like he had been planning this exact moment for the past thirteen years and now he was so satisfied he couldn't help but gloat.

"No, I am certainly alive, Whizzenmog," His reply was in a patronizing tone.

I could feel a division in the room, like a line was drawn on the floor. Phillip, Aevion, my sister and I stood on one side all wondering what was to happen next, while Sorcerer Pierre LaCroiux and his vampire bat stood on the other daring us to try and escape. He was challenging us...the saviors of Mistasia...without even saying a word.

"Whizzy, what do we do?" Phillip whispered into my ear.

What could we do? I wondered to myself. Grace was the strategist. She would have a plan...GRACE!

I darted around and startled Phillip. Pushing past Aevion I looked for Grace, but she was gone. There was no trace of her.

"But she was just here!" I shouted.

"Who?" Aevion questioned.

"Grace," I started when LaCroiux rudely interjected.

"Ah yes, my boy. Grace Tallon. Another one of Queen Merran Cadieux's great warriors."

A surge of warm blood began to boil in my chest. I could literally feel it moving through my veins and entering my entire body. My legs and arms began to swell with hatred. Frustration had always been one of my biggest weaknesses...it always forced me to do foolish things. Right now, I felt something foolish coming on.

When I turned to face our enemy, I caught a single glimpse of a smile on Aevion's small mousey face. He hadn't come close to smiling at any point in our journey. Since I had known him, he had shown nothing but fear. Why would he be smiling at the very moment I was about to explode and start a battle? Why wasn't he afraid now?

"Whizzy!" I heard Grace's voice leap into my head. She was using her elven abilities to contact me. She hadn't ever done that before. That was something only her and Phillip shared.

During this whole time while my foxy mind was wondering, Sorcerer LaCroiux had been babbling on. Right about now, I felt the sudden urge to shut him up!

"LaCroiux!" I yelled. "Release us!"

He cocked his head sideways and growled, "Make me."

Suddenly, the room was ablaze with wands and sorcery. Phillip dashed to the corner grabbing Aevion along the way.

Rachel and I attacked the sorcerer from two sides. He was very powerful, even more than I remembered. Blasts of color zapped from the tip of my wand.

LaCroiux knelt down and ran his hand across the floor like he was drawing a line. He snapped his arm upward and the floor cracked and bent, forming a wooden shield. My spells harmlessly splashed against it like watercolor paints on paper.

Rachel attempted to freeze him just as we had King Cragon Cadieux, but Sorcerer LaCroiux was expecting that. He produced a flame from his pocket. It lunged toward Rachel and collided with her freezing spell. When they touched, it produced a violent reaction. Thick smoke filled the room.

Everyone stood completely still for a moment. An evil laugh eerily pierced the silence. A stream of light sliced through the smoke like a sword cutting it in half. Then the light spread out and tore the cloud of smoke apart into opposite corners of the room, and in the middle stood our enemy.

"You will have to do better than that," He sneered and then stepped forward slamming his foot on the ground. It shook the room knocking Rachel and me to the floor.

A shrieking sound blasted out from next to me. The vampire bat now stood over me, and it looked angry...much angrier than normal. It spread its wings and began to reach out for me.

I went to hit it with a spell, when a green foot flashed across my face. It smashed into the vampire bat's chest and sent it disappearing into the smoke.

"Phillip!"

My best friend had just saved my rear.

"That was awesome, Phillip."

We both knew what we had to do next. Rachel was in trouble. The sorcerer had backed her into a corner. She did everything she could to fight him off, but he had become too powerful since we last fought him.

Phillip just snapped. He leapt across the room and landed on LaCroiux's back. Covering the sorcerer's eyes allowed my sister to escape. It wasn't long before Phillip was shaken off. He bounced across the floor and crashed into the wall. I saw him try to get up and then fall flat on his stomach.

LaCroiux just glared at me and smirked. He slowly glided toward us. His robes covered his feet so it appeared as if he was hovering in the air. When he approached us, LaCroiux stopped just a few feet away.

"This will have to wait until another time, Whizzenmogs. I have another matter to attend to," he said before standing up straight. The smoke in the room cleared.

From behind, two vampire bats grabbed Rachel and me. They had snuck up behind us during our battle. Each managed to pry our wands away from us.

"Don't worry! I will come back and finish you both, but for now I will leave you here with my friends." He pointed to the two vampire bats that held us captive. "You haven't had the opportunity to be properly introduced. I figure now is the time, since you will be spending all of it with them until I return. Rachel and Michael Whizzenmog, meet Goren and Vella. They are the rulers of The Deadly Spray Forest.''

Before either of us could say anything Sorcerer Pierre LaCroiux disappeared through the wall in a blur of light and was gone.

FINDING GRACE TALLON
14

Leaning against the wall in defeat I slowly slid to the floor. I hated to lose at anything, but this wasn't a game. This was real...the queen was in danger. We were all in danger.

I felt the energy leaving my body and was upset with myself for allowing LaCroiux to get away, for allowing us to become trapped in this room and mostly for losing my wand to these ugly creatures.

My head was buried between my furry knees. Staring at the floor, I heard a whimper.

For a split second, I thought it was Phillip. When I lifted my head, he was sitting next to me holding onto Rachel. He looked upset, but wasn't crying, and neither was Rachel.

Where is that coming from? I thought.

"I don't know," Phillip responded.

"Do you always have to be up there? It's not a garage sale you know. My brain isn't free for you to play around in, so stop poking around!" I snapped.

"Whizzy, calm down. Phillip isn't hurting anything," Rachel began to defend him.

"I'm tired of him in my head. It's already messed up enough; I don't need him driving me crazy."

"Fine! I'll stop talking to you, Whizzy."

"Good!" I yelled back.

"Fine!" He yelled back.

"Great!" I growled.

Rachel gave me the mom glare and shook her head at me. I knew I was wrong to yell at Phillip, but I was just so sick of him using his 'special' powers on me. It was creepy to constantly hear someone else's voice in my head.

It made me feel like I was going crazy, and I didn't need any help when I was in Mistasia...here, I always felt like I was crazy!

I must have been exhausted, because before I realized who was crying I was fast asleep. Dreams to me are useless. I almost never remember them, and when I do, they are always crazy. For example... one time I was dreaming about flying through the air as a pop tart, specifically a frosted strawberry pop tart. I had no arms or legs just eyes, at least I think, because I could see. I was flying over a lake of milk, and when I finally crossed it, there were orange and purple cows dancing without music. When I woke up, I understood why. I had fallen asleep in the basement with the television on. In my hand, was a frosted strawberry pop tart and all over my shirt was the milk I had been drinking. I'm still not sure where the colorful cows fit in.

However, tonight was much different. I found myself having the most intense dream of my life. The room was spinning. It stopped and in the corner I saw Grace. She was unable to speak at first, but then her voice began to echo in my head. It was so loud. Her words were muffled, and then became so loud she sounded like a broken speaker crackling and buzzing. I felt like I was floating in the room. I tried to yell for her to stop, but nothing came out. Suddenly, all noise ended. It was scary. I got chills up my spine, like I had just seen a ghost. Then, I heard her speak, "Whizzy, help me!"

I startled awake. My body shook, and I fell to my side. My large fox ear was against the wood floor. The banging of a large drum pulsed in my ear. It took me a second to realize that the banging was my heart against my chest.

Phillip and Rachel had shocked expressions on their faces.

In the opposite corner Aevion sat crying. It had been him I heard whimpering earlier. Beside him were Goren and Vella, the vampire bats. They hadn't moved since LaCroiux had left.

I tried to gather myself.

Phillip kept his word and refused to speak to me. Rachel, however, blurted out one question, "What the heck is wrong with you?"

That was the sister that I had known...before Mistasia. I struggled to stand up. My legs wobbled and my head swam. I felt so dizzy. I mustered the strength to get to my feet and yelled, "Grace!" Something was really wrong with me. I started to fall over when Phillip grabbed hold of my arms.

"Jerk," He simply said.

"Hi, Phillip," I replied. "I need to sit down."

Phillip carefully placed me back on the ground.

"Phillip, Grace is still here. I saw her in my dream.

"This isn't like the pop tart cow dream is it, Whizzy?" Phillip crassly responded. I had forgotten that I told him about that.

I could tell he was still upset with me. "No. There was something real about this dream. Like nothing I had ever felt before. I think Grace was calling to me. She was calling for my help." I attempted to explain but started to wonder if I really was going crazy.

"Why hasn't she contacted me, Whizzy? She could just as easily talk to me."

Phillip was right. Grace hadn't contacted him. It would be easy for her to speak to him. They shared the same ability. Maybe Sorcerer LaCroiux was playing a trick on me.

"No!" Aevion's small mousy voice crackled from across the room. "You are not crazy, Whizzy the Wizard Fox." The fear in Aevion's eyes had returned. He was shaking with it now.

The vampire bats, Goren and Vella, began to make strange noises toward the small dark-skinned boy.

Aevion cringed.

"Leave him alone," Rachel yelled. She stood up and ran to him.

The second she placed her arms around Aevion the vampire bats began to shriek and howl. Goren spread his wings, which looked like they belonged on a jet. Vella's claw-like hands clicked as she tapped her razor sharp fingers together.

"Release him," Goren demanded. "He does not belong to you, wizard." Goren puffed up his chest and opened up his wings to their fullest in an attempt to intimidate Rachel.

Aevion suddenly pushed her away and scurried back toward Goren before sitting on the floor next to him. He placed his head between his knees and covered his face with his arms.

Phillip shook his head in amazement. He couldn't understand what was happening.

"Why do you keep frightening him? He is just a child. Leave him alone?" Rachel defiantly barked at the vampire bats.

"Whizzy, I'm in here," Grace's voice shot into the room for everyone to hear.

"Grace where are you?" I shouted.

"I am here."

"Where is 'here'?" Phillip questioned with a frustrated tone.

"Hidden from sight by LaCroiux's powers," she answered.

Goren and Vella began making noises again. They seemed to be trying to cancel out her voice.

I covered my ears to block their painful sounds.

"Ahhhh!" Phillip screamed. "That's it." He just snapped. My best friend hopped across the room in one leap and attacked. Rachel bravely joined him even without her wand that Vella held in her clutches. I couldn't believe what I was watching and stood motionless.

Phillip dodged a swing from Goren and hopped in the air, landing on the floor behind the nasty creature. When Goren turned to face Phillip, a green webbed foot smacked him in the chin and knocked him down.

Rachel must have realized that she was defenseless against Vella without her wand about five seconds after she confronted the bony beast. Rachel was amazing as she maneuvered her way out of getting clobbered. She ducked and dodged a series of swings from Vella's claws. Then, Phillip jumped into the air and landed squarely on the vampire bat's back knocking our wands loose and into the air. Rachel dove and caught hers. Mine landed on the floor and rolled directly to me. It stopped against my left foot.

I reached down and grabbed it. A swell of power came over me. Just as I looked up, Rachel finished off Vella with a freezing spell. Goren was next. My sister gracefully spun on her toes like a ballerina. When she stopped, Rachel was in a dancer's pose with her wand extended at Goren. She fired, hitting him in the chest. Now both of our captors were frozen solid, in motion, like a stone statue.

Aevion screamed, "No! Let them go. Leave my parents alone!"

VAMPIRE PARENTS
15

Aevion was crying as he caressed Vella's frozen face. She looked frightening. Her mouth was open wide with her fangs jutting out. Her eyes bulged from their sockets.

We all stood motionless. Our mouths hung open in shock.

"Did he say parents?" Phillip questioned as his voice cracked.

Aevion didn't respond. He just sobbed. Rachel reached out and placed her paw on his shoulder, but Aevion shook it off.

"These aren't your parents, Aevion," Rachel tried to explain. She must have thought he was just confused. "They can't be. You are an elf." She looked at him with pity. His back was still turned toward her.

Finally, Aevion gathered himself long enough to speak, "She is my mother, Rachel the Wizard Fox. They are my parents."

Aevion turned around. He looked different. His eyes had changed. Aevion's entire body began to change shape. Suddenly, standing before us was a small childlike vampire bat-a miniature version of Goren and Vella.

Rachel gasped and stepped backward, bumping into Phillip. He yelped as Rachel stepped on his webbed foot.

"No way!" I recalled saying. "You were one of them the whole time."

We had been fooled, tricked by LaCroiux into believing that Grace had sent Aevion to bring us back to Mistasia in order to help her, but he was setting up a trap here in The Deadly Spray Forest the entire time. Grace knew nothing about us coming back. She was bait for the trap.

I gripped my wand so tightly that I thought it might splinter and break in my paw. I felt so stupid.

"Why did you trick us, Aevion? WHY?" I barked.

The small vampire bat recoiled and hid behind his frozen mother. His beady little eyes and one droopy ear peeked out from her side.

"Answer me. Why are you working with him?"

This time Rachel didn't protect him. She looked just as angry as I did. Raising her wand in the air, she gritted her teeth and said, "Speak or you'll join your parents."

"I...I had no choice. Please don't hurt me." Aevion started to sob again.

Rachel lowered her wand, but I raised mine.

"Whizzy," She said with a sympathetic tone in her voice.

I wouldn't even look in her direction. I was too angry to forgive him. I so badly wanted to zap him with a spell right now.

"I'm sorry, Whizzy the Wizard Fox. I had no choice. He had my parents. He said he would let them go if I went to get you from your world," Aevion stammered between sobs.

I lowered my wand slightly. "Let them go?" I didn't understand. "What do you mean, 'Let them go', Aevion?"

"He has them under his dark magic," Aevion explained.

"Sorcerer LaCroiux is controlling them?" Phillip asked.

Aevion nodded his head from behind his mother.

"Dark magic," Rachel said to me as she grabbed my arm holding my wand and pushed it to my side.

I didn't stop her. She was right. Aevion was being tricked, too. Sorcerer LaCroiux was using all of us against each other.

"Aevion, where is Grace?" I asked, hoping he knew where Sorcerer LaCroiux was hiding her.

"I do not know," He continued to cry. "My parents might know."

I shot my wand back in his direction.

"Whizzy, don't," Rachel screamed.

"Don't try to trick me," I stared him in the eyes. Then, I tried to contact Phillip without speaking. **Is he lying, Phillip?** I questioned.

"I don't know. She could know, but I have no way to ask her while she is under this spell," Phillip said.

I directed, "Rachel, free Vella only."

Rachel stepped toward Vella and raised her wand.

"Wait!" I demanded. "If this is a trick, Aevion, you will regret it. Only release Vella. After she takes us to Grace, then we will free Goren."

Rachel hesitated, "Uh...how do we know that they aren't still under LaCroiux's power?" She looked to me for an answer.

We all looked to Aevion.

"I will talk to her. I have changed so maybe she changed, too."

"Right. Okay then...here it goes." Rachel fired a counter spell, freeing Vella.

The mother vampire bat was very angry. She lashed out as if we were still in the battle from earlier.

We all backed away and lowered our wands as Aevion jumped in front of us.

"Mother!" He yelled with tears streaked across his pale face.

Vella's anger seemed to melt away when she saw her son. "Aevion?" She reached out and grabbed him. "You have returned." She sounded different...happy.

Aevion explained to Vella our deal. We would free Goren if she told us how to find Grace. Holding her son tightly, she whispered to him. They both spoke in their vampire bat shrieking tones before Vella turned to me and answered.

"She is in the far corner hidden by shadow. The sorcerer has many tricks wizard. It is in the eyes this time." She pointed behind us into the darkest corner of the room.

I dashed over with my heart racing. I called out for Grace. Muffled noises bounced against the walls. It was so hard to find where they came from.

"Whizzy, she said something about eyes, right?" Phillip said as he searched around the seemingly empty room.

"Yes. 'It is in the eyes this time'. That was what she said," I turned back to see if Vella was trying to attack us from behind. She and Aevion knelt in front of Goren. It appeared they were praying.

"Close them," Phillip shouted.

"What?" I asked.

"Your eyes. Close them."

"How can I see her with my eyes closed, Phillip?" I said, thinking my best friend had forgotten how it worked.

"Bats back home don't have very good sight," He explained.

"Yeah, that's right, Whizzy," my sister interjected. "They use sonar waves to see everything."

"If LaCroiux is using his sorcery to hide her from our sight, we need to use our hearing to find her. That's why Vella knows where she is." Phillip sounded very confident.

Finally, I understood, "She can't see Grace, she can hear her movement."

"Exactly!" Phillip yelled with excitement.

I closed my eyes tightly and listened for her. At first I heard nothing except Phillip's webbed feet on the floor.

"Stand still!" I commanded.

The muffled voice became clearer. It started to become louder. I reached out my hands and began feeling around. My hands searched for anything. They landed against the wooden wall. I slid them around side-to-side and then up and down. Finally, I felt something that didn't feel like wood.

"Whizzy!" I heard Grace call in my head.

"I found her!" I yelled.

When I opened my eyes, she was sitting on the floor with her mouth covered in the clear paste I had seen earlier. She was also tied at the hands and feet.

I used my wand to free her. She leapt to her feet and hugged me so tightly I could barely breathe. I nearly passed out.

As I held her she felt small. When we let go I noticed her face...she looked so tired. Her usually light, gray-colored eyes were darkened, almost black. When she walked over to grab her sword and bow and arrow from against the wall, I realized just how tiny she had become. Her arms and legs looked weak and frail. Long white hair flowed around her face as she turned back toward me. She still looked beautiful.

We had finally found her. Vella had given us the information needed to find Grace. Now, we had to honor our bargain and release Goren.

Rachel approached Vella and Aevion. The young vampire bat touched her arm.

"Please, let me daddy go," He pleaded.

Rachel smiled at him and nodded. She reversed the spell, freeing Goren.

He fell to the floor. Aevion dashed to his father and hugged him. Goren was confused. It took him a moment to realize that his son had returned.

Grace Tallon wasted little time. She quickly challenged the rulers of The Deadly Spray Forest, Goren and Vella, to help us stop Sorcerer Pierre LaCroiux before he could reach the castle.

"You have an army at your command, Goren. Use them to help us stop LaCroiux before it is too late," She pleaded with him.

Aevion clung to his father's leg like a young child. His face still had the expression of fear. It made him almost look human, unlike his parents.

Goren seemed afraid to challenge the sorcerer. Vella, however, was fuming mad. "He must be stopped, Goren."

"Once he reaches the castle it will be nearly impossible to stop him. We must leave now. He will return, Goren. When he does, what will you do to stop him from taking over your home?" Grace sternly questioned the leader of the vampire bats.

Goren looked at how frightened his son was and realized that he couldn't allow Sorcerer LaCroiux to come back.

"We will help you."

"Now, how do we get out of here?" I asked.

Grace looked up. It was pitch black. She just pointed and said, "The sky."

Rachel grinned from ear to ear. She knew exactly what Grace wanted. Reaching her wand toward the darkness, she blasted a white-hot bolt of lightning skyward. It disappeared into nothingness. My heart sank. Phillip groaned. Rachel turned to look at Grace, but Grace just kept staring at the ceiling. Rachel returned her gaze skyward just as the bolt hit the roof and punched its way through. A loud explosion rocked the room. Light poured in, stinging my eyes. Strange sounds assaulted my ears, like rushing air and fast moving objects, followed by a series of thuds. I opened my eyes when Goren shrieked! A group of vampire bats had flown into the room when the roof blew off.

Goren then spoke to them, "Brothers! It is time to stop this sorcerer. We must help the elves of Cadieux. Now take to flight. We go to fight!" He yelled.

Each of us found ourselves flying through the open roof and into the sky upon the backs of the vampire bats. Grace and Goren were together at the lead.

Snow was still falling outside The Deadly Spray Forest, and we were off to Cadieux Castle.

BATTLE IN THE SKIES
16

Flying through the cold Mistasian air was amazing. It would have been better, but I had a pointy claw sticking me in the ribs. I could only imagine how badly Phillip's stomach felt right now. He was probably about to throw up.

"Whizzy! This is awesome!" He yelled at me.

I guess I was wrong. He had the biggest smile I had ever seen on a frog's face. It would

have been from ear to ear, but frogs don't have
ears...which I'm sure you already knew, so I'll
move on.

The vampire bats followed in a strict
formation behind Goren with three on each side.
Vella flew in the middle behind Goren as she held
Aevion tightly. Apparently, the little guy couldn't
fly.

We quickly moved away from The Deadly
Spray Forest, and now flew over a vast open
land. There was nothing but white snow ahead of
us.

"Where are we?" I shouted to Phillip.

"We are over the Mastodon Lands," Grace
answered.

"Mastodons?" Phillip replied. "Like hairy
elephants?"

Grace gave Phillip a peculiar look. She had
no idea what an elephant was. "Efalant?" She
questioned.

"No an el-a-fant!" Phillip tried to
pronunciate.

"Phillip!" Rachel scolded. She just wanted him to stop talking. They could barely hear each other over the rushing wind. "Grace, are they dangerous?"

"Yes!"

"Great!" I muttered. Thankfully, they were on the ground, and we were in the air. That, however, wouldn't last long.

"Dragons!" Rachel warned.

Headed straight for us were five large scaly dragons. They ranged in color and shape. There was a red dragon with a large fan-like shield behind its head. Its tail was long and thin and pointed like a sword. A purple-colored beast flew next to it. That one was smaller in size but had spikes sticking out of its tail. Two golden dragons flew side by side. They had boils all over their skin and were very fat. The last dragon trailed behind the others. It was the largest of them all and dark green...like a lizard back home in Greenville. It looked the scariest, too. I could see its sharp fangs and forked tongue.

My first thought was which one breaths fire. I tried to remember which dragons could in Mistasia.

The vampire bats began shrieking, and the dragons screeched in response. It was awful.

"Grace!" I yelled over all the noise.

"What!"

"Which one breaths fire?" I screamed.

It was so loud I couldn't hear her answer.

"What?" I was now screaming like a scared little girl, as the dragons got closer. Gripping my wand tightly in my right paw, I aimed at the bright red dragon barreling down upon us. Before I could fire, Goren dove down, and we all followed.

A harsh rush of wind blasted my furry face. My eyes closed tightly. I could feel my cheeks being pushed against the wind and suddenly warmth surrounded me. Opening my eyes, I saw a dark reddish fireball was about to engulf me. I turned my head when the vampire bat released his grip. I fell to the ground and landed in a fluffy pile of snow.

My body had sunk from the impact, but my legs, arms and head were all above the snow.

"My wand? Where's my wand?" It was gone. I had dropped it when I landed in the snow.

A loud thud startled me. Snow swirled around me, making it hard to see. When it cleared, the same bright red dragon I had been targeting earlier was creeping toward me.

It had blazing yellow eyes. I felt like they could see inside me. I searched for my wand as the dragon approached.

Finally, I spotted it near my right foot, but I was trapped in the snow, helpless. The dragon opened its mouth.

A shriek blasted in the air and a gray blur whizzed past me crashing into the dragon. Snow again whipped into the air. I could hear fighting.

I struggled to free my body. Twisting side to side, I wiggled my way free and grasped my wand as the dragon reappeared with a vampire bat riding him. I pointed my wand at them when they took to the air over my head, knocking me backwards into the snow again. Jumping to my feet, I searched the sky.

Above me, raged an amazing battle. The vampire bats and dragons danced about the sky like ballerinas on stage swirling in and around each other.

I heard footsteps in the snow.

"Whizzy, you're alive!" Rachel shouted as she wrapped her arms around me.

Grace and Phillip were right behind her.

"Whizzy, we must go," Grace commanded. "Goren will give us time to escape. These lands aren't safe with the dragons among us. There are few places to hide."

"Where do we go from here?" I questioned.

"Come this way." Grace grabbed my hand and ran. Phillip and Rachel followed as the sky above cried out with the sounds from angry beasts.

The purple dragon swooped down upon us. It was very low to the ground and gaining quickly. Its spiked tail stuck straight up like a hammer waiting to slam down on a nail. I really didn't want to be the nail.

Before it could attack Vella landed on its head and grabbed its horns. She twisted the dragon's head causing it to turn and crashed its wing into the snow. As the giant purple dragon tumbled through the snow, Vella leapt back into the air and rejoined the other vampire bats.

"That was way too close!" Phillip croaked.

Grace continued to drag me through the snow. She was so fast it took all the energy I had left to just keep from falling. Rachel and Phillip attempted to keep pace. I had no idea where Grace was going. Suddenly, she stopped. I slammed into her backside and tumbled into the snow, face first.

"Watch out, Whizzy." Grace mocked me.

Rachel and Phillip caught up. Phillip was breathing so hard I could hear him wheezing.

"Why... did...you stop?" Phillip said between deep breaths.

Grace spun around and glanced into the sky. "We don't have much time. Rachel, we need a place to hide!" She demanded.

"Like what?"

"Something that will cover us. Just do it quickly before the dragons see us. We need something to create a visual shield." Grace pressured.

"An igloo!" Phillip shouted. "Make an igloo out of the snow."

Rachel smiled at him then held her wand out and began to move it in the shape of a circle. The snow swirled and created a dome. The half circle wasn't very large, but would be almost impossible to see from the air. The igloo blended in to all the snow surrounding us.

"Quickly! Get inside," Grace pushed me.

"But it's so small," Phillip whimpered.

Rachel slid inside the small opening. I followed. It was very small. The sunlight from outside was faded through the thick snow walls, but there was enough to allow me to see Rachel jammed into the back corner. I crawled over on my hands and knees. Snow was stuck in my fur. It looked like little balls of popcorn stuck all over my body. I stopped for a second to try and turn around, but Grace started pushing me further into the igloo.

"Hey, cut it out, Grace!"

"Get in!" She barked at me.

It really made me mad when she yelled at me, but right now I couldn't do anything about it anyway. I was crammed between Rachel and the ice-cold snowy igloo wall. My legs were twisted like a pretzel and then Grace sat on them.

"Ouch!" I cried out.

"Get in here, Phillip!" Grace called in a panicked voice.

That was definitely not something I was used to from Grace. She was normally cool under pressure. This situation must have been far more dangerous than I even understood.

Phillip's green legs and froggy butt wiggled into the igloo. His webbed foot smacked me in the face. Grace and Rachel started to pull him in as he started to scream.

"I'm stuck. I'm stuck!"

The girls pulled and pulled, but Phillip's large green head was stuck in the entryway. The walls began to crack and snow began to fall into the igloo's entrance.

"Wait!" Rachel yelled to Grace. She pointed her wand at the entrance and it slowly began to widen.

Finally, it was large enough for Phillip's head to slide through. Once inside, the hole shrunk again.

I took the deepest breath I had ever taken in my life. This igloo wasn't going to provide much protection, if any of the dragons found it, but maybe we would get lucky and the vampire bats would be able to fight them off before that happened.

My eyes were so tired. I fought to stay awake as Grace and Rachel talked about escaping the Mastodon Lands. The last thing I heard was Grace explaining how Sorcerer LaCroiux must have realized that we had escaped from The Deadly Spray Forest.

"The dragons have always worked with him. Sorcerer LaCroiux must know we have escaped."

THAT JUST MADE HIM ANGRY
17

"Whizzy!" a voice screamed in my head. It startled me awake. My eyes popped open so quickly that everything was hazy and unfocused, like looking in the bathroom mirror after a warm shower. I could hear a drum pounding in my head. It was my heart thumping. Shaking my head to try and wake up, I realized that Rachel and Phillip were looking out the small opening of our igloo.

"Close the opening, Rachel!" Grace demanded as she drew her sword.

I knew that wasn't a good sign. Jumping to my feet, I stumbled and Grace grabbed me.

"Wake up, Whizzy. We need to be alert." Grace was desperately trying to listen to something.

"What do you hear?" I whispered.

"Shh!"

Phillip and Rachel turned to see what Grace was doing. I remained as silent as I could.

We could all hear noises from outside the igloo, but nothing sounded familiar. Grace's elven ears, however, could make out much more than ours. She definitely was listening to something going on outside.

Phillip leaned against the cold snowy wall; placing his head to the wall, he concentrated to hear what was going on outside, too.

"Dragon?" Rachel mouthed.

Phillip didn't respond.

"Phillip, get away from there!" I screamed. Right about now, I was thinking that my best friend was an idiot, because if there was an angry monstrous dragon on the other side of that wall, he was going to get burnt to a crisp.

"I don't think it's a dragon?" Phillip responded. "Maybe it's a Mastodon?"

A deep inhaling sound echoed through the small opening in the igloo.

I looked at Grace hoping for a better explanation of what was going on outside than what Phillip thought.

"Get back!" She yelled at Phillip.

A horrid sound began outside like a jet's engines kicked into motion. The side of the igloo started melting. The snow darkened in color, and then a blast of red flames cut through the wall and shot across the igloo. It crashed into the wall next to me.

I let out a high-pitched squeal as the flame singed my tail. Jumping into Grace's arms, I fell onto the snow, taking Grace with me. I was lying on top of her when she pushed me off and gave me a dirty look.

A large hole had been burned into the side of our igloo. We had been found by the largest of the dragons that had attacked us...the scaly dark green beast.

One large, oblong orange eye peered into the igloo. A vicious roar shook its icy walls. Snow began to fall from the cracking ceiling.

Rachel ran toward me with her wand out. I thought she was going to zap me when the tip of her wand lit up bright white. I ducked to avoid her blast when she cast a spell against the wall behind me. The bolt exploded into the wall and shot a doorway for us to escape.

Rachel dashed through first, followed quickly by my best friend; both left me behind to face the angry dragon. Grace grabbed my arm and pulled me to my feet. I flew into the air like a ragdoll as she yanked me outside.

The dragon spit fire again melting the igloo as we escaped.

Grace led our way through the snowy field. There was no place to hide and the dragon began to chase us. Luckily, he wasn't very quick. The beast's large paws made the ground tremble like an earthquake with each step. We had nowhere to go...nowhere to hide. It was obvious that we were going to have to stand and fight the dragon. That was when we stopped running.

Grace Tallon stood next to me with her sword at her side. She was breathing heavily. The wind blew her long white hair back from her face. Her cheeks were red from the cold and breath curled out from her pink lips.

Rachel stepped up on the other side of Grace, and Phillip stood beside me. The four of us now faced the slowly approaching enemy. A puff of smoke slithered out from the dragon's mouth. Its blood-red forked tongue ran across its top lip like someone that was about to eat dinner.

I didn't want to be anybody's dinner and especially this stupid dragon's. I was getting tired of things attacking us in Mistasia so I fired a spell to freeze the dragon. It was one of the few spells I felt worked well...but this time it didn't.

The dragon winced when my spell slapped it in the face. It angrily shook its head like attempting to rid itself of an annoying fly.

"Why did you do that?" Rachel snapped. "All you did was make it angry."

She was right...the spell hadn't worked and the dragon looked really angry.

"What now?" I replied.

Grace unexpectedly stowed her sword into its holster.

"What are you doing, Grace?" I pleaded for an answer. "Giving up isn't a great option. I don't want to be this guy's dinner!"

"Phillip, wait here. Rachel and Whizzy, get on either side," Grace commanded.

"What are you doing?" Rachel seemed worried.

"Phillip, be ready to jump," Grace added. Then, she sprinted away toward the dragon.

It roared and spit fire. Grace dodged the first blast by leaping to the right. The dragon attempted to hit her again, but she avoided that shot, too.

Rachel slapped my shoulder and began to run. I followed. While the dragon was distracted with Grace, my sister and I were able to position ourselves on each side of the giant lizard.

Phillip still stood looking confused in the same spot. He watched Grace in amazement as she danced around the dragon's attempts to burn her.

Grace jumped onto the dragon's shoulder and climbed onto its back. "Bury it!" She yelled.

Rachel and I began forcing snow up and over the dragon's body. It thrashed around kicking snow back at us with its thick massive tail.

A scorching fireball shot from the dragon directly at Phillip. I panicked as it flew toward my best friend in slow motion. I stopped what I was doing to watch in terror. This dragon wanted frog legs for dinner.

Phillip leapt straight up and over the fireball. He flipped in a somersault and landed on the dragon's back next to Grace.

That was awesome! I thought.

"Whizzy!" Grace yelled snapping me back to reality.

Rachel and I continued to force snow over the dragon's body, like waves crashing onto the beach.

The beast tried to turn its large head toward Rachel. She moved a wave of snow directly into its scaly face. When the snow hit the dragon, it stumbled to its knees. As the snow began to pile up, it began to struggle to stand. Suddenly, the giant beast roared again and pushed its massive wings skyward sending snow flying into the air. It looked like a blizzard.

Grace pulled her sword out and handed it to Phillip. She grabbed her bow and arrows. Phillip slashed at the dragon's right wing while Grace pierced its scaly skin with arrows.

The beast screamed in pain and began thrashing around in the snow again. Phillip was tossed off. He landed hard in the snow not far from me.

"Phillip!" I yelled.

He got up quickly and just ducked the dragon's whipping tail.

A swell of anger overtook me. I dug my feet into the snow and summoned all the strength I had to attack the dragon. I reached down and pushed my paws into the snow, then pulled up into the air like lifting a blanket. A huge pile of snow raised into the air creating a wall. The dragon disappeared behind it.

"Ahhhhh!" I yelled releasing all my anger and all the snow toward the dragon. It crashed in a powerful wave. When it settled, the dragon was gone, buried under nearly six feet of snow, but so were Grace and Rachel.

BURIED ALIVE

18

"Whizzy, what have you done?" Phillip cried. He ran toward the hill of snow where the dragon was buried. Phillip shouted as he fell into a hole between the new snow pile and us.

"Holy moly, this is a huge hole! Look at this!" Phillip called from below. He stood on brownish-green grass, something we hadn't seen this whole time in Mistasia. I had dug the hole when I used magic to toss snow onto the dragon. This entire area had shifted and now Grace, Rachel and the dragon were underneath it on the other side.

"Rachel." I became scared as I realized she was missing. "Phillip!" I yelled to my best friend.

We ran to the hill and began searching for Rachel and Grace. Using my paws, I dug through the snow. Phillip did the same. It was taking too long. They wouldn't be able to survive at this pace.

I held my wand out like a shovel and began to dig. Each time I flicked my wand snow flung off the pile. I frantically tossed snow searching for them, even hitting Phillip with some snow.

"Hey, Whizzy, watch out!" He croaked at me.

"I have to find them, Phillip."

"Wait! Wait!" Phillip yelled. Then he said nothing.

"What?" I growled back.

"Be quiet. I can hear Grace!" Phillip was concentrating.

I was breathing very heavily. Each breath exploded from my mouth like fire from, ironically enough, a dragon.

Phillip walked around like a puppy searching for where it had buried a bone in the backyard. I slowly followed behind him in anticipation.

Just show me where do dig! I thought.

"There!" He pointed to a small pile near the top of the snowy hill.

The sun was setting and it was becoming very cold. We needed to find the girls and get to shelter quickly.

"Phillip, go find Rachel!" I pleaded and my best friend hopped off to where we last saw her.

I began shoveling again using magic. It wasn't long before I found Grace's leg. I stopped shoveling and began to dig her out by hand. She gasped for air when I freed her from the snow. After a few seconds she was completely free.

"Grace, are you okay?" I asked.

She punched me in the chest knocking me into the snow and then jumped on top of me.

"I should pound you, Whizzenmog!" She was furious. Just as she raised her fist, Phillip shouted.

"I found Rachel!"

Grace leapt off me and dashed to help. I quickly joined them.

The three of us eagerly dug her out of the snow. She wasn't breathing when Phillip pulled her free. He began to perform C.P.R. to revive her. Phillip placed his webbed hand under her neck and lifted slightly to open her airways. Then he moved in.

"What are you doing?" Grace sounded horrified. "This is no time for that!"

"What?" Phillip replied.

"No, it's okay," I told Grace.

The elven warrior gave me a confused expression as I motioned for Phillip to continue.

"He's trying to save her...not kiss her." I explained to Grace who thought that my best friend was trying to use this moment to make the moves on my sister. "He is trying to resuscitate her."

Phillip took a deep breath and then placed his clammy frog lips over Rachel's mouth and snout and exhaled. The first attempt didn't work. Grace placed her hand on my arm. I would have felt something, but I was too numb with fear. Phillip tried again and nothing.

"Rachel!" I muttered.

The sun had completely set now and it was very dark. The moon didn't shed much light tonight.

Tears started to form in my eyes. This couldn't be happening. She couldn't be dead.

Phillip placed his hands over her chest and began pushing down.

"One...two...three," He counted to himself. Then he waited a second and did it again. Phillip looked at me. All I could see was his bright red eyes in the darkness, but I knew he was crying, too.

"No!" was all I could say.

Grace looked at us not quite understanding what was happening. "Is she dead?"

"NO! Rachel you can't die!" I shouted. "Try again, Phillip!" I demanded. "Don't give up." I joined him by placing my paws over her chest. He did the breathing, and I pushed on her chest.

Phillip started to place his mouth over Rachel's again when she coughed and rolled to her side. She gasped for air.

"Rachel!" I yelled with excitement. I didn't even let her sit up before I hugged her. I had never hugged my sister so hard in my life.

DO YOU SEE WHAT I SEE?
19

Rachel had survived. I felt horribly...not
that she had survived. I was grateful my sister
was still alive, but that I had almost killed her
and Grace because I wasn't able to control my
anger. The powers I had in Mistasia made me
dangerous to my own friends and family. I began
to wonder if I should even stay with them.

It wasn't long after we saved Rachel from
her snowy tomb that we began to move toward
Cadieux Castle again.

"We cannot stay here," Grace said. "The
night will provide us with cover to move. We
have to go now. It is our best opportunity to try
and reach Cadieux Village by morning."

Phillip carried Rachel in his arms. He held
her so tightly. I could tell that he really cared for
her. It had bothered me so much that he and
Rachel were getting close after all these years. I
felt like I was losing my best friend, but I'm

really not. I'm gaining the sister I never had. Phillip had been able to bring Rachel and me closer. I should be thanking him.

His red eyes looked like two m&m candies floating in the air. I walked beside him, and Grace led the way. She seemed to be headed somewhere away from the castle.

"Grace, where are we going?" I questioned.

"Mastonia."

"Ah...excuse me. Mastonia?"

"The realm of the Mastodons, Whizzy." She replied with a laugh.

"I thought you said they were dangerous," Phillip questioned while he gazed at Rachel, who slept in his arms.

"Yes, they are to outsiders," Grace responded. "If you three entered Mastonia alone, they would be very angry. However, I will be with you."

She sounded very confident that these large hairy elephants wouldn't harm her.

"What does that mean?" I angrily snapped.

"Watch your temper, Whizzenmog. You don't want to bury us in snow again." She poked at me. "Besides the queen has protected these creatures. They will honor our treaty and help us. We can use them to travel to Cadieux Village tonight."

"Like ride them?" Phillip sounded uncomfortable with that idea. He probably imagined himself falling off and getting trampled.

"Yes, Phillip. We will need to ride one."

"One?" I was shocked. "They must be very large."

Grace never responded. She just gave me a sly smirk and kept walking. The moonlight led our way. To where I had no idea, but our guide most certainly knew where she was headed.

The moon had grown quite large in the wintry night sky. It had also become very bright. The Mistasian moon seemed to brighten as the nighttime moved along. We had been walking for what felt like an hour when Grace suddenly stopped. She placed her hand out behind her to stop us.

"Don't move," She whispered. She was watching something only she could see...which didn't make me feel any less uncomfortable about it.

"What do you see?" I asked because there wasn't anything in front of us but white fluffy snow...or so it appeared.

In the distance, was a large gorge hidden by the snow. From where we stood my eyes couldn't see the sliver of difference between the two sides of the gorge along the ground, but Grace could. We slowly crept up to it. She positioned herself down on her stomach and crawled to the gorge's edge. I followed.

When my head poked past allowing me to see into the gorge, I gasped. Grace slapped her hand over my fox mouth.

She shot me a disgusted look. "Be quiet, Whizzenmog. I don't need you blowing this. If you anger them, so help me, I will feed you to the dragons myself."

I couldn't believe what I saw below us. In the gorge was a huge city. Not like anything we had in Greenville or in Cadieux either. It was more like a jungle. There wasn't any snow, just bright green vines and trees and grass. Massive huts made from bark and tree limbs were lined up on one side. Then I saw one...a Mastodon. It was the biggest living thing I had ever seen, nearly the size of a cruise ship.

I turned around, "Phillip, you have got to see this!"

Grace grabbed my shoulder and pushed me into the snow. Her face appeared upside down over mine. "Maybe I didn't make myself clear...shut it!" She looked around for a way to get down into the gorge. "Stay here!" She commanded. Then Grace stood up, grabbed her bow and fired an arrow with a rope tied to the end. It flew through the air and slammed into the far side of the gorge. She pulled out her sword and stabbed the snowy ground before tying the loose end of the rope to its handle.

"I will be back soon." Then, she began to walk across the rope.

I watched in amazement. She never even stumbled on the thin rope. When she reached the other side, Grace jumped off onto a nearby rock and began to descend into the gorge. Quickly, she made her way down and finally disappeared behind the massive Mastodon huts.

"What if she doesn't come back, Phillip?" I asked.

"Grace will be fine, Whizzy. Don't worry."

"I'm not worried about her getting hurt...what if she leaves us here? We are helpless." Suddenly, I had the sinking feeling that someone was playing a practical joke on us, and we were going to be left stranded in a Mistasian snowstorm to die.

"She wouldn't do that. Would she?" Phillip suddenly didn't sound so sure either.

All I knew now was that the three of us were stuck up here in the cold, and Grace Tallon was below in the seemingly warm gorge attempting to get a Mastodon transport. Was this really happening?

MASTODON RIDERS
20

Rachel awoke just a few minutes after Grace had gone down into Mastonia. She was tired and confused, but still managed to be very mad at me. I should have expected that...I mean I did almost suffocate her under a mound of snow. That would have been difficult to explain to mom...where's my sister, you ask? Well, mom, she was being attacked by a giant fire-breathing dragon so I used my wizard powers to bury them both in snow. What's that? I'm grounded for life?

Well, maybe it wouldn't go exactly like that, but thankfully I don't have to explain any of this to our mom. She already thinks there is something wrong with me. Any stories about Mistasia and she'll put me on a funny farm.

I watched for any sign of Grace. It wasn't easy to see as the snow had begun to fall again. Somehow, the snow melted as it went below into the gorge. I could tell that the grass below was wet, so I knew that the snow must have been turning into rain as it hit the warmer air down below.

Right about now, I wished I had gone with Grace. Even with this thick fur, I was feeling the chill of winter in my bones. Rachel didn't look much better. Phillip was starting to turn a shade of bluish-green. We wouldn't last much longer.

A rumbling noise started, followed by trembling in the ground around us.

"Earthquake?" Phillip asked.

"I don't know," I replied.

"No, look!" Rachel pointed to a whitish-brown hairy Mastodon approaching us. Grace was perched on its back.

My mouth dropped open as my head tilted back to try and see her all the way up on top of the Mastodon. It was like she sat on top of a three-story building.

The Mastodon stopped and grunted. Then it lowered its trunk into the snow.

"Climb on," Grace urged.

Phillip helped Rachel up onto the beast's trunk and then joined her. The Mastodon lifted them up into the air and let go, tossing them down on its back. I could hear Phillip scream as he fell.

"Rachel! Phillip! Are you alright?" I shouted worried that they had been hurt. Then, I heard them laughing.

"We're fine, Whizzy!" Rachel replied with a huge grin on her furry fox face.

"Let's go, Whizzenmog!" Grace barked at me.

I tried to move...but I just couldn't. Instead I found myself staring at this gigantic furry elephant standing in front of me. Its leg was like a tree trunk, except where the leaves would have been was a sharp pointy tusk.

"What? You scared?" Grace teased me. She began to giggle...Rachel, too.

Phillip just looked at me. "Come on, Whizzy. It's cool. Don't be afraid." He spoke in my head so the girls wouldn't hear. I appreciated that he didn't add to my humiliation, but it didn't solve my worries.

487

"I'm not afraid," I lied. I was terrified. This creature was huge, and I hadn't had the best experiences with creatures in Mistasia this time around. **Do they remember the dragon? Or the eel-fish?** I thought.

I huffed over to the front of the Mastodon and waited for it to extend its trunk. Its two black eyes blinked at me. I wasn't about to be tossed around like a rag doll, so I took off at full speed, running up its trunk between its eyes and across its head, sliding to a stop in front of Grace.

"Nice," Phillip responded.

The girls stopped laughing. Grace smiled like she was actually impressed.

The Mastodon lifted its trunk into the air and trumpeted a tune, signaling our departure. We were off to Cadieux Castle on the back of a Mastodon. I hoped that this part of our adventure would end quickly and without anyone trying to eat or burn us.

The slow trip to Cadieux Castle was pretty boring. I know...everything up to this point had been exciting to say the least, but the last three hours had moved along like the Mastodon...painfully slow and uneventful. Don't get me wrong, that was fine with me. I would have been enjoying this part of our journey much more if it weren't snowing so hard that I felt like I was in one of those snow globes that sit on the mantle around the holidays with a snowman in them. You know the one's that you shake and snow flies all around inside, but your mom won't let you touch because you broke one when you were four years old, and she still doesn't trust that you can handle them?

Anyway, the snow made it very hard to see anything, so I hoped that this monster we were riding on knows where it's going.

Even worse was the horrible smell. This thing stunk so badly...I thought maybe Phillip had farted, but he never smelled this awful. I started to believe that the brownish color fur on the mastodon was actually poop stained. It was that bad!

Phillip agreed. Rachel wouldn't even talk about it. She just tried to ignore it, but I caught her holding her nose at one point, so I knew it was bothering her, too. Grace, however, seemed unaffected by it. Maybe she had no sense of smell. That had to be it because there was no way she could stand it otherwise. The smell was overpowering. It reminded me of when I am under the covers and I fart and then I move around and the covers fluff up. That sudden burst of horrid odor that hits me makes it hard to breathe. It was like that only it never ended.

I'd rather fight the fire-breathing dragon right now.

"How much longer?" I asked Grace with my nose plugged.

She shook her head in disgust. "You are so childish."

A gust of wind blew by, swirling the snow into a frenzy. The Mastodon stood still as the snow danced around us. It only lasted for a few moments, and when it stopped, the nighttime sky cleared.

The snow had stopped. Cadieux Castle was straight ahead in the distance. Lights from the village lit the way like an airport landing strip. It wouldn't be much longer until we reached the castle and faced Sorcerer LaCroiux once again.

THE EMPTY BEDROOM
21

We ran through the village to Grace's house. Inside we dashed down the hallway to the secret passage that we had used to enter the castle on our last visit. Grace grabbed a torch and led the way through the same tunnel into the castle where we entered through the door in the floor just like before.

I couldn't believe that we were here again. It felt like we had just been in this room, the princess's old bedroom, a few months ago, but it looked like it hadn't been slept in years.

"Thirteen years!" Grace reminded me. She must have been reading my mind.

It looked exactly the same. The bed and dressers were in the same place.

"The queen doesn't live here anymore?" Phillip questioned as he wiped his finger across the top of a dusty cabinet. He held it up for me to see that his green finger was now discolored from the dirt.

"She lives in another part of the castle," Grace responded.

"Why doesn't the queen let you live here? It is a lot bigger than your house?" I replied without thinking. Grace had told us last time that elves didn't live in large homes. They preferred the outdoors.

"This room is for the future children of the queen," she answered. After an awkward silence she added, "I like my house."

"I know," I responded. I felt like an idiot. Sometimes I wished that I would just think before I said things.

"We need to find Queen Merran," Grace announced as she opened the door.

Without warning, a flash of light exploded into the dark room. I could hear screaming and then the sounds of something hitting the floor.

Boom! Boom! Boom! It echoed against the stone walls.

I tried to yell for Grace, but nothing came out. The light was so bright that my eyes burned. I felt a zap against my chest. It began to hurt. It felt like my heart was beating a million times a second. The light began to fade. My legs started to tremble and I stumbled to my knees. I couldn't breathe. Gasping for air, I grabbed my throat.

Am I dying? I thought.

I fell to the floor. The sound of footsteps echoed in my ears. Two feet stopped next to me. I rolled over to see who it was. Sorcerer LaCroiux stood over me with an evil grin and then everything went black.

LACROIUX'S MASTER PLAN
22

"LaCroiux!" I yelled after gasping for air. Warmth surged through my body. I jolted to my feet and pointed my wand at a shadowy figure in front of me.

"Whizzy! It's me!" My sister cried out. She had awakened the others and me with a spell.

"What happened?" I asked her.

"I don't know. When Grace opened the door and the light burst in, I just used a spell to shield myself. Whatever came in slammed me against the wall. I must have hit my head. When I woke up, you were all knocked out on the floor. I tried to wake you up...that was when I realized that it must have been LaCroiux. His dark magic was keeping you all from waking up," Rachel explained.

"He's already here?" Grace sounded uncomfortable.

"It must have been him. Who else could have done this?" Rachel questioned.

"The queen!" Grace dashed from the room and down the hallway.

We all followed her toward the queen's new chambers. Grace slid to a stop. The hallway we were in split.

"What's wrong?" I asked Grace while trying to catch my breath. "You don't remember which way?"

"Why did he come here?" Grace demanded.

"What? What do you mean? LaCroiux...are you asking what he came for?" I didn't understand why she wasn't running to the queen. She was the queen's protector. "What are you waiting for?" I asked.

"Which way, Grace?" Rachel interrupted.

"Phillip!" Grace yelled, startling my best friend.

"Yes!"

"I need you and Rachel to protect the queen!" She commanded.

"But...okay!" Phillip seemed unsure as to Grace's plan. "But where are you going?"

"Whizzy and I are going to find LaCroiux."

She directed Phillip to the queen's quarters down the hallway to our left. Grace grabbed a wooden stool that sat in the hallway and flipped it upside down.

"Get on!" She yelled.

I jumped in between the stool's legs.

"Grab hold and don't let go," she smiled as she tied a rope to the stool and then her belt.

Grace took off down the hallway in the opposite direction from where Rachel and Phillip had gone. We sped down the halls and around corners until she cut one corner too closely. The stool swung out and smashed into the wall. Two legs broke free. I grabbed hold of the front stool legs and Grace dragged me along the ground. We finally reached our destination and the wooden stool slid to a stop.

My hands hurt from gripping so hard.

"I never want to do that again!" I told Grace, who smiled. I think she enjoyed seeing me suffer. "Where are we, Grace?" I asked as I struggled to stand. My knees had stone burns...if that is even possible.

"This is where Cragon Cadieux is held. LaCroiux is here."

"How do you know?"

"I can feel his presence," Grace answered.

"If you can feel him, how did you not know he was outside the door earlier?"

Grace didn't answer immediately. She seemed ashamed. "I let my focus leave me. You asked me about my home. It bothered me...and I couldn't concentrate."

I didn't really know what to say to that. After a moment, the silence made me uncomfortable, so I blurted out the first nice thing I could think of.

"You have a nice smile." Sometimes I wish I couldn't talk. It would probably make things easier.

Grace shook her head like most girls at Greenville High School. Her expression was a cross between frightened and ashamed. Then she looked me in the eyes and began to laugh.

"You are something else, Whizzy."

I smiled back. I think that was actually a compliment.

"So what do we do, Grace?" I asked redirecting our attention to the fact that we now stood outside the door where the former evil king, Cragon Cadieux, had been held for more than a decade.

She pulled out her sword. It sparkled against the flame of a torch on the wall. "We go inside."

Grace reached for the handle, and the hairs on the back of my neck stood up. Time seemed to move in slow motion as I saw a spark leap from the metal handle and jump into Grace's skin.

I tried to stop her but wasn't quick enough. When I reached for her wrist to stop her, the spark zapped her. Grace flew backward into the stone wall opposite the door. Her eyes were still wide open and she lay on the floor twitching.

"Grace!" I yelled in a panic as I rushed to her side.

She was still breathing, but she couldn't talk. Her mouth moved, but there was no sound. I began to feel that violent building of aggression in the pit of my stomach. It swept through my body like a forest fire in the heat of the summer. My brows sunk around my eyes and I gritted my sharp fox teeth.

I snapped up straight, pointed my wand at the door and fired. A blue flame shot like a missile from a jet fighter across the hallway and exploded into the door. Shards of wood shattered across the floor and the door creaked open before falling from its hinges and crashing to the floor. Quickly, I moved through the opening with my wand at the ready.

"LaCroiux!" I growled. It was impossible to see anything in the windowless room. The tip of my wand began to glow as I thought about light. Being a wizard definitely had its advantages; being able to create light whenever I needed it was just one of them.

The room seemed empty as I scanned it with the stream of light produced by my wand's tip. Sounds of dripping water and the scrapping of sharp nails on the stone floor echoed inside. A large brown rat appeared in my light. Its movement startled me. That just made me angrier.

"Dumb rat!" I muttered.

"You're too late, Whizzenmog!" A strong voice boomed.

"Show yourself, sorcerer!" I demanded as I whipped my wand around trying to find where LaCroiux was hiding. "You can't hide forever, you coward!"

A sinister laugh began to grow. It became louder with each second. The voice echoed against the walls making it nearly impossible to figure out where it was coming from.

"Don't move!" LaCroiux barked as a bright circular object, looking like a hula-hoop my sister played with back home, came flying toward me.

I tried to dodge it but the hula-hoop just followed. It wrapped around me and tightened until my arms were pinned to my sides.

"I want you to watch me overturn everything you have worked to create." Cried Sorcerer Pierre LaCrouix.

A flame burst in the corner to my right and then another to my left. Now fires blazed all around me, brightly lighting the room. Standing before me was LaCroiux. He knelt down beside a black object with no particular shape. It didn't look like much of anything.

I struggled to free myself, but with every movement the hula-hoop-like lasso tightened more. My arms began to hurt and my hands tingled like they had fallen asleep.

"Whizzenmog, do you recognize this man?"

I didn't reply. I knew exactly who it was...Cragon Cadieux, Queen Merran's evil uncle who had ruled Mistasia before my sister, Phillip and I had overthrown him during our last trip to Mistasia.

"You probably don't see it do you? It's the face of the rightful ruler of Mistasia." LaCroiux said with anticipation in his voice. A flame appeared in his left hand. It danced like a belly dancer in the palm of his hand. Then, he slowly waved his hand across the stone black objects frame to reveal Cragon Cadiuex's monstrous expression. The expression he had when Rachel and I had frozen him solid during our battle. All the rage he had at that exact moment was still there staring at me through his icy tomb.

"Don't do it, LaCroiux! Did you forget he banished you?" I attempted to reason with the sorcerer.

He started to laugh as though I was telling him a funny joke. "Boy, that was long ago. He will forgive me once I've saved him from this icy prison and helped him to reclaim his throne!" He empathically replied.

The flame in his hand began to grow as he placed it against Cragon's face.

"NO, DON'T!" I screamed. When I started to move again, the binds around me tightened once more. The pain shot up my back and I fell to the floor. "Don't do this. You are making a mistake!"

I watched as the flame engulfed Cragon's body. The ice melted away quickly, and the former king's figure emerged. He collapsed to the floor.

"My Lord?" LaCroiux said as he pulled Cragon Cadieux's limp body from the puddle on the floor. "You are free."

The moment LaCroiux uttered the word 'free' Cragon's face came to life. The same evil smile he had ruled with returned.

"Ahhhhhh!" Cragon screamed releasing thirteen years of frustration. The force of his voice shook the room.

It also freed me from the sorcery that LaCroiux had been using to hold me captive. I wasted no time as I jumped to my feet and dashed out of the room. When I returned to the hallway...Grace was gone!

THE RUNNING FIRE

23

"Grace!" I yelled as a rumbling noise came from behind me. I turned around to see a fireball steaming toward me like a train. I jumped away at the last second. The fireball scorched the stone wall where Grace had been when I entered the room.

I ran as fast as I could yelling for Grace the entire time. **Where did she go? What happened to her?** I thought.

Another rumbling came up the hallway behind me. I was terrified to look back. When I did, I saw a strange fiery creature with no eyes charging at me. It was gaining on me. Its roar sounded like nothing I had ever heard before; the closest thing I could imagine was a cross between fingernails on a chalkboard and a crackling fire. The heat burned my feet, which made me run faster yet. I could barely breathe. My fur was wet and heavy. I wasn't going to make it.

Up ahead was the place where we had left Rachel and Phillip earlier. **Here was my only chance.** I thought. I mustered all the speed I could and dashed for the corner. At the last moment, I dove down the hallway to my left. The fiery creature went past bellowing in rage.

I slid along the stone floor until I slammed into the wall. It hurt badly, but at this point I would gladly settle for a few scrapes and bruises, if I could avoid being burned alive. I got up and walked back into the hallway again. Waiting for me just twenty feet away was the fiery creature. It snorted like a bull ready to charge a matador.

I whimpered like a two year old that had to go to bed early. I was sweating so badly now that I looked as though I had just gotten out of a swimming pool. Sweat dripped from my snout. Suddenly, I remembered my wand. I had been holding it the entire time. I was so frightened that I forgot I was a wizard.

"Hey, Red, did you know it is winter?" I said with a smile on my face.

The creature roared, shaking the walls so violently that dirt and pebbles fell onto my head from the ceiling.

I pointed my wand directly at where I thought its head was and fired. Nothing happened. I panicked and attempted a freezing spell again.

"Oh crap!" I gulped. The heat from this nasty beast was making it so I couldn't use my favorite spell...the one spell I had relied on most.

The fiery red monster shifted and two tentacle arms shot out from its side. They swung around like whips before the monster lashed out at me.

I ducked to avoid its first attempt, but the second landed on my tail. I screamed in pain and jumped into the air. Without thinking I swung my wand like a sword at the tentacle on my tail cutting it in half. The red monster cried out in pain. Now, we were even. I was shocked. I held my wand up and noticed a thin ray of light sticking straight out of the end creating a sword.

"Now, it's on," I yelled while running toward it crazily swinging my new weapon. This wand was awesome. I sliced LaCroiux's creature into a dozen pieces and then used my favorite spell to freeze all those little pieces before they could reform. The hallway now resembled a miniature mountain range.

I was impressed with myself. "That was pretty awesome," I announced. That was when I remembered that I was alone and no one had witnessed me defeating this fiery monster. "Great, now nobody's gonna believe me when I tell this story!"

Wandering the hallways of Cadieux Castle, I struggled to find Queen Merran's chamber. I also had no way to contact Phillip or Rachel, and my guide was missing. Walking through a hallway that looked identical to every other one in this castle, I noticed a pair of eyes on the ceiling.

"Don't move!" I pointed my wand at it. My heart was pounding. **What has Sorcerer LaCroiux sent now?** I thought.

"No, Whizzy! It is Aevion!" He pleaded.

"Aevion? How did you get here?" I was quite happy to see him. "Where are your parents?"

"They came looking for the sorcerer."

"Did they find him?" I asked.

Aevion didn't look happy. He began to cry. "He has them under his control again."

"Where are they now!" I commanded. I wasn't about to let him lose his parents again. "Follow me," he said.

Running through the hallways of Cadieux Castle had become somewhat of a new sport for me. It was so easy to get lost. Everything looked the same, but something was leading me somewhere. I wasn't sure where, but I knew that I had to get there...and fast.

Aevion tried to keep pace. He was flapping his wings and suddenly leapt toward the ceiling in an effort to catch up.

"Come on, Aevion. We will find your parents. I promise," I wasn't so certain but didn't want to worry him. He almost felt like a little brother. It was really strange. I instantly pictured him dressed up in my clothes playing in my basement back in Greenville. It made me smile. That would be a very weird conversation with my mom.

We approached a dead end, and I skidded to a stop. Aevion wasn't so slick. He slammed into my back and we fell to the hard stone floor.

"Ouch," I cried as I felt my knee throbbing. Blood trickled down my leg. The dark red blood mixed with the orange color of my fur. I wobbled when I stood up. A sharp pain shot up my leg.

"Where do we go now?" Aevion questioned as he stared at the stone walls before us.

"Why would this hallway end?" It made no sense to me. This hallway had come a long way to suddenly end. "There must be a hidden door," I mumbled. "Just like in Grace's home," I said to myself thinking about the trap door that lead us from her home into the castle.

"What?" Aevion replied.

"Whizzy, use your wand," Grace's voice echoed in my head.

A smile suddenly spread across my face. I pointed my wand at the stone wall and fired. A bright white bolt burst from the tip of my wand.

Aevion gasped.

The wall exploded and dust and light filled the air.

Aevion coughed and covered his face with his bat wings. I ducked my snout into my furry arm. When the dust cleared, another brightly lit hallway appeared, but this one was far different than any other in Cadieux Castle.

HIDDEN HALLWAY

24

"What in the world?" I gasped. I couldn't believe my eyes. It was like a totally different world behind this stone wall.

Bright light streamed through the broken stone wall. The walls were covered with brilliant green vines and colorful flowers. Warmth swirled around my body, like standing too close to a fireplace. There was no snow; I couldn't believe my eyes.

Aevion began to whimper and then screech.

"What's wrong, Aevion?"

"The light hurts!" He cried.

I felt a tingling in my paws, and injured knee; it's like that slight pain I feel when my feet are cold and I place them into warm water. It stings, but then I am just fine a few minutes later.

My vampire bat friend, however, didn't look well. His grayish-colored skin was glowing. Well, actually Aevion was transparent...I could see every bone in his body. I could even see his heart racing in his chest.

"Back away from the light, Aevion!" I yelled.

The young vampire bat's skin returned to its normal hue.

"I'll have to go alone."

Aevion looked scared.

"Your parents may be in there. I have to go. You will be fine. Just hide like you did before." I pointed to the ceiling and watched as he climbed up into the shadows until only his eyes remained. "I'll be back soon." Then, I took off running.

This new hallway seemed to go on forever. I stopped to catch my breath. My heart was pounding so hard, and I struggled to breath. The air was so hot it felt like I was breathing sand through my lungs. My throat began to close. I started to panic.

Laughter echoed through the air. It was Cragon Cadieux.

I couldn't see him. I tried to shout, but my throat hurt. Nothing came out.

"Having trouble are we, Whizzenfox?"
Cragon's voice boomed before he appeared
through the bright light. As he walked toward
me, everything behind him died. The trees
collapsed, vines shriveled and light disappeared.
It was as if he sucked the life from every living
thing around him. He slowly walked past me.
Vines shot up from, the now, dirt-covered floor
and tangled themselves around me. Cragon
circled me like a lion ready to pounce on its
prey. Almost all the light from the hallway was
gone. It was now gloomy and dismal like the rest
of the castle. The walls were moss covered and it
stunk like the boy's locker room at Greenville
High School.

"Well, Whizzenmog...it appears that you
definitely aren't the brains of your family. Like a
moth to the flame...you were simple prey."
Cragon Cadieux stared at me. His beard had
gray hairs sticking out. His eyes were cold and
harsh.

"You deserved what you got, Cragon!" I
yelled while struggling to free myself from the
vines tangled around my wrists.

"Deserved?" He yelled so loudly it shook the room. Cragon leaned in close and whispered into my ear. "Then let's see what you deserve!"

He slowly backed away from me. I didn't move...I was stunned. What could he mean? What would he do?

I saw motion in the darkness behind Cragon. Out from the shadows came Sorcerer LaCroiux and Grace. She was bound with her arms behind her back.

"Grace!" I yelled.

"Don't do anything he says, Whizzy!" She said to me in my head to avoid Cragon or LaCroiux overhearing.

"Grace Tallon. Protector of the queen," Cragon spoke with sarcasm. "Oh...where is the queen? Have you lost her?" Cragon and LaCroiux began to laugh.

"Whizzenmog...have you ever heard the phrase 'eye for an eye'?" Cragon asked. He had a smug look on his ugly face.

I didn't respond.

"That's right; how silly of me...you're not the smart one. I'll explain."

The sound of his voice made me very angry, but the more I struggled to free myself the tighter the vines twisted around my wrist.

"You remember when you and your sister cast a spell on me...freezing me? Now, you get to watch me do it to her." Cragon pointed his finger at Grace. Then, he opened his hand. A blast of icy mist shot from the palm of his hand and covered Grace.

"NO!" I yelled, but it was too late. She was now frozen solid, just like Cragon had been just an hour ago.

"Eye for an eye!" Cragon walked up to me again and whispered into my ear. "Your sister is next."

A jolt of rage fired through my entire body, "NO! Cragon I will stop you!" I screamed.

Cragon grabbed me by the neck and squeezed. He looked very angry. "Don't waste your breath, Whizzenmog. You can't stop me this time. Soon enough you will join them all. I will save you for last, and then when I'm finished...I'm going to place you all around my

514

castle as statues to commemorate my great victory and reclaim my throne."

"Not...if...I...have...anything...to...say...about ...it," I struggle to speak as he held my throat.

Cragon released his grip on me and took a step back. A wicked smile brushed across his bearded face. Then, he walked back into the darkness and disappeared into the shadows.

ALONE WITH A STATUE
25

This trip to Mistasia was beginning to feel more like a horrible nightmare. I just couldn't escape. I found myself hoping that when I reopened my eyes I'd find myself laying on the couch in the basement of my parents' house back in Greenville. I would give almost anything to be relaxing there right now...not caring about anything else, just watching some stupid TV show and trying to not fall asleep early.

Unfortunately, I wasn't there. "Grace?" I muttered when I reopened my eyes. The only thing I could see in the room was her figure staring at me helplessly. Her eyes looked like a scared child that had lost her parent.

A tear rolled down my furry cheek. I found myself crying alone with a frozen statue, which just happened to be a friend of mine.

I struggled to free myself from the vines that tangled around my wrists. I was helpless. My wand lay on the ground between Grace and me, but there was no way for me to reach it.

Tears streamed down my face. I hadn't cried since I'd lost my favorite toy when I was five years old.

Grace made me feel something that I had never felt before. I needed to help her.

Sorcerer LaCroiux reappeared from the shadows. He slowly walked by Grace and placed his hand on her head. He tapped his fingers on her like on a tabletop. Then, he turned and looked at her face.

"Uh," He said in disgust. "Not a good look for an elf."

"Shut up. LaCroiux!" I barked.

He just smiled. It was obvious that he was trying to make me angry.

"Where are your friends, Whizzenmog? You should be saving this girl! Hurry; don't wait!" LaCroiux mocked my situation. He laughed heartily.

I couldn't do anything to save her. Phillip and Rachel were nowhere to be found, and I couldn't reach my wand.

"Sorry, Whizzenmog, it's too late." Sorcerer LaCroiux smiled and swirled his hands over Grace Tallon's frozen figure. A whirl of wind and light entered the room and funneled around her like a tornado. A flash of light exploded into the dark room. Then, they were both gone.

A LITTLE TOO LATE
26

I screamed at the top of my lungs. My frustration made it hard to think. LaCroiux knew my weakness...it was me. I had always been my own worst enemy. Right now, I had to figure out how to escape, find Phillip and Rachel, and save Grace.

"Whizzy!" I heard a familiar voice cry out. It was my best friend, Phillip. Following behind him was Queen Merran, my sister and our new vampire bat friend, Aevion.

Rachel freed me using her wand. I fell to the floor. My body hurt badly. It felt like I had just lost a boxing match. Phillip helped me back up.

"Whizzy, where have you been? Rachel and I have been looking for you everywhere!" Phillip excitedly explained. His skinny arms wrapped around me while hugging me so tightly I nearly couldn't breathe...which was now the second time that had happened in this room.

"Where is Grace, Whizzy?" Rachel questioned.

I couldn't answer. How would I tell them she was gone?

"Gone?" Phillip said as he released his grip on me.

I just looked at him. There weren't any words left. My heart sank when I saw the image of her face in my head. I knew that Phillip would see it too.

My best friend gasped. "No! How did it happen?"

"Cragon!" Queen Merran empathetically responded.

Our journey had been so crazy I hadn't realized that this was the first time I had seen Queen Merran since we arrived back in Mistasia. She hadn't changed at all, despite the thirteen years that had passed since our last visit. Her rosy cheeks kept her youthful appearance. The only different was her hair was tied on top of her head beneath her crown.

I shook my head as another tear rolled down my cheek. I was too distraught to speak to the queen.

"Cragon's free?" Rachel yelled as she grabbed my arm and spun me around to face her. "Whizzy, talk to me! What is going on?" She was frantic.

I explained to them how Sorcerer LaCroiux had released Cragon Cadieux, captured me and turned Grace into a frozen statue.

"He plans to reclaim the throne," Queen Merran calmly spoke.

"They were too strong. I couldn't stop them alone."

"We were too late!" Rachel said. She looked so sad.

Phillip was in shock. He seemed to be waiting for someone to tell him what to do.

"We need to find Grace. She must be somewhere around the castle." I began to run back through the hallway. It looked vastly different than when I first entered. Slimy, brown vines clung to the walls that were stained and gross. The floor crackled underneath my paws from the dried leaves and vines. The smell was awful, like rotten potatoes.

"What makes you think they would put her outside?" Rachel questioned my sanity more than the actual fact that Grace would possibly be outside. "Anyone could see her."

"That's why. Cragon plans to reclaim the throne. So taking the queen's bodyguard prisoner and placing her exactly where everyone in

Cadieux Village would see her would frighten them all. No one will challenge him then."

I lead them through the halls back to where I had fought with the fiery beast earlier. Up ahead was a corner. I slid to a stop. The others did, too.

"What is it, Whizzy?" Phillip whispered in my head.

I placed my finger over my mouth to tell everyone to be quiet. Rustling noises came from around the corner. It sounded like knives scrapping along the stone floor.

I gripped my wand tightly. My heart pounded. Right now, I hoped it wasn't LaCroiux. Two elongated shadows appeared on the floor. Reaching back, I used my arm to block my sister from being noticed.

"What is that?" Phillip again spoke to me using his telepathy.

"I don't know."

CRAGON TO GREENVILLE
27

The figures jutted out from around the corner like two mountaintops peaking against the setting sun as they blocked the light from the torches on the wall.

Aevion whimpered as Queen Merran Cadieux held him closely while standing behind Phillip. He curled up into a small ball under her arm.

Rachel and I caught eyes. She and I had been at odds for almost all our lives...now we stood together ready to fight whatever was about to attack us. It was funny how things had changed in our lives over the past six months. Mistasia had given me one very important thing...the sister that I had always wanted. A smile spread across my face.

Rachel seemed surprised by my sudden state of joy. I could tell she believed that I had just gone completely insane at that exact moment. I winked and turned back to face our oncoming foe.

The figures came around the corner. They were very thin and tall. Rachel and I jumped to our feet and pointed our wands at them. When the tips of our wands lit up to fire, we realized that it was Vella and Goren who stood before us.

"Mom!" Aevion screamed.

"Goren. Vella. Where have you been? Aevion said that you were captured by LaCroiux," I was surprised to see them walking the hallways...alone. "Who is with you?"

"We are alone, Whizzenmog," Goren replied. "We escaped from the sorcerer."

"Great. We could use your help," I began when Goren interrupted me.

"You all must leave this castle immediately."

"But...what?" I said completely confused. "We have to find Grace."

"I will send my friends to find her, Whizzenmog. You must come with us now." Goren was determined to get us away from Cadieux Castle, which was concerning me until he finally explained.

"Goren, we can't leave yet. Cragon escaped and this castle is under attack!"

"I know. He is in Wolverine Forest."

Phillip and I shared a concerned glance.

"Where is he going?" Rachel anxiously asked.

"He is headed from where you came."

"Greenville?" We questioned together.

Goren nodded.

"How do we get out of this castle?" I demanded.

Queen Merran led our group to a hidden doorway near her quarters. It led us down a set of narrow hallways. They were extremely dark and wet. Queen Merran came upon a wall. She searched along the dirt-covered wall for a way to release the door. When she grabbed hold of a thick tree root she pulled down and the wall lifted upwards.

A rush of crisp cold winter air flooded the hall. It slammed against my body and sent a chill up my back. My fur rustled against the air.

We all escaped out into the village. We were in an unfamiliar area at the base of the castle. A small path allowed us to wander back into nearby Cadieux Castle. There, we encountered something no one expected.

The crowds in the village were panicked. They were all running and screaming. When we entered an opening in the square in the middle of Cadieux Village, we instantly noticed why.

Cragon's war had begun. A group of trolls were running amok. Rachel dashed off to save a little elven girl. She grabbed the girl just before the troll's large foot slammed down into the snow.

Phillip rubbed snow on his legs. The friction heated the snow making it melt. The water quickly absorbed into his amphibian skin. It gave him unbelievable strength. Phillip the Frog leapt into action. He hopped onto the head of one troll. A second troll noticed him and swung its massive club-like hand punching the other troll directly in the face. Phillip jumped away just in time. The troll tumbled and fell onto a house crashing through the roof and hitting the fireplace. Flames quickly spread through the small house, which now was ablaze.

"Phillip! Watch out!" I yelled as the troll closed in on him.

The troll slammed its fist like a hammer. Phillip leapt away again, but the force of the troll's punch was like an earthquake. It shook the frozen snow-covered dirt causing a massive crack in the ground that sped directly for me.

I didn't move quickly enough and fell into the small crack up to my waist.

Goren reached down and snatched me up by the scruff of my neck. He sped across the snow and grabbed Queen Merran. Suddenly, more vampire bats appeared in the sky. They swooped down and attacked the trolls in Cadieux Village. One grabbed Rachel. Another snatched Phillip by his webbed feet.

We were soaring through the sky and moving back toward Wolverine Forest. With the battle behind us now, I could see fires raging in the village against the white wintry background.

Phillip hung upside down next to me. "We have to go back!" he yelled at me.

"Goren, we have to help them!" I pleaded.

The vampire bat leader calmly responded, "You are needed elsewhere. Cragon must be stopped."

Suddenly, I remembered what Goren had told us earlier. Cragon was headed to Greenville, and we definitely had to stop him before he traveled to our world.

My mind raced as we flew toward our destination. I hoped that Cragon was alone. Rachel, Phillip and I had to figure out how to stop him before he entered the portal to Greenville.

EYES IN THE TREES

28

My paws landed so hard on the ground that it sent a sharp pain into my neck and back. Stumbling, I struggled to keep my balance when Goren grabbed hold of me.

"Thanks," I said.

We stood at the edge of Wolverine Forest, the same place where we had begun our journey nearly seven days ago. We had unfinished business here in Mistasia. I had no intention of leaving tonight.

Rachel walked beside me, with Phillip directly behind me. The vampire bats had gathered around Goren and Vella, but Aevion, who had traveled here with his mother, was now standing with the queen.

"Cragon?" I called. "Show yourself, you coward."

"Those are brave words for a child," the former king answered. "You definitely have heart, Whizzenmog. However, that is why I have had a change of heart."

Rachel scoffed, "I doubt that."

"Where are you, Cragon?" I called out again. He was nowhere to be seen, and now neither were our travel companions. "Where's Goren?" I asked my sister.

"That can't be good," Phillip gulped.

"Mom!" Aevion screeched. The queen held him tightly once again.

"Something is very wrong, Rachel" I pointed out just as I saw two wicked blazing eyes hiding in Wolverine Forest. "Wolverines!" I cried out.

Cragon's voice boomed through the air, "No...something far worse." Then, he chuckled like a deranged clown. "I see you have brought the fair princess with you tonight, Michael Whizzenmog!"

"Queen!" Phillip croaked.

"Not anymore, Phillip Harper!"

Cragon Cadieux appeared from the darkness of Wolverine Forest. His dark figure silhouetted against the white snow.

"My crown please, niece!" Cragon reached out and the crown flew from her head and into his outstretched hand. As he walked toward us he placed the golden crown upon his black-haired head.

Rachel fired a spell at Cragon, who blocked it with ease. I tried my best to stop him too, but Cragon deflected my blast as well.

He began to chant in a deep voice. It was utterly frightening. The ground started shaking and the snow began to swirl around us. It was a blizzard within seconds.

I could barely see anyone else. Reaching out, I grabbed Phillip's arm. He did the same to Rachel. We had all grabbed a hold of each other in the white out.

Cragon's voice bellowed one last time over the rushing wind, "I return you to where you belong."

My feet lifted from the snow. I felt a violent tug on my body and suddenly everything was spinning like I was trapped in a washing machine.

Everyone screamed as we flew through the air. When it stopped, we found ourselves lying on the carpet in my parents' basement.

I sat up quickly as the sunlight shined through the sliding glass door, which had already changed back from the portal to Mistasia into the window to our backyard.

Cragon had won. He had managed to trick us and send us back from Mistasia. Now, he was left to rule Mistasia all alone.

RAINER WHIZZENMOG

29

My breathing was heavy and my heart was racing against my chest. I felt sick to my stomach, partly because of the roller coaster return from Mistasia but also because of how we had left things.

Searching around the basement to see how many had returned with me I quickly saw my best friend lying face first on the carpet. He was still passed out. Phillip didn't travel well, so he was probably going to throw up when he awoke. Rachel was next to him. That was when I noticed that they were holding hands. A brief smile came over my face, which was no longer furry. I must have been okay with it, because normally I would have felt the urge to punch Phillip in the head.

I struggled to stand up. I was so tired. My whole body hurt. I mean places that had never hurt before, like the inside of my feet and ears, were throbbing.

"Where is Aevion?" I muttered to myself. I couldn't remember what he would turn into in our world. **Was it a bat? Maybe a rat?** I thought to myself. I reached down and shook my sister to wake her up.

She gasped and shot up slamming her head into mine. "Agh, Whizzy!" She barked at me.

We both rubbed our head in pain. Now, I could add something else to the list of things that hurt on my body.

"Are you trying to scare me to death?" Rachel continued to verbally assault me.

"Rachel, Whizzy?" our mom called from at the top of the basement stairs. She sounded surprised to hear our voices.

My sister and I panicked. "What do we do?" It had been about seven hours since we had traveled to Mistasia and it must be early in the morning. Rachel and I...well mostly me, weren't morning people so it would definitely be weird that we were up...and dressed!

"You two are up mighty early! You do realize you're on winter vacation, don't you?"

Our mom continued as she walked down the stairs; she was still in her pajamas and bathrobe.

Rachel and I gave each other a scared glance when she noticed Phillip sleeping on the floor.

"Michael? Why is Phillip sleeping on the floor?"

"Ah." I was not even sure how to answer. My mind searched for a response that would fit.

"Oh, you know...he is such a klutz that he fell off the couch," Rachel told our mom. She gave me a strange look and then elbowed me in the arm. "Right, Whizzy?"

Mom was giving me a questioning look, probably because Phillip was nowhere near the couch. **Thanks a lot, Rachel!** I sarcastically thought.

"Oh...yeah. He fell and he must have been having a dream and he was crawling away from a monster and then the monster attacked and he sprawled out on the floor to pretend he was dead so the monster would leave him alone and..." I was rambling out of nervousness. Rachel looked like she was going to slap me. Her eyes nearly popped out of her head. I nervously started laughing and said, "I mean...um...yeah, he fell."

My mom just shook her head. She had always thought I was weird, but this conversation wasn't changing that. "Okay, Michael. I'm gonna go have a cup of coffee. You kids come up for breakfast. Okay? Your grandfather will be coming later today, so I'll need your help cleaning up the house."

After my mom went back upstairs, Phillip finally woke up and he did get sick. It wasn't pretty.

"Phillip! You are cleaning that up, man," I barked.

"I know," he replied as he went upstairs to get cleaning supplies.

Meanwhile, Rachel and I searched the basement for Aevion and Queen Merran.

"What did Aevion change into again?" I asked my sister.

"A mouse!"

"Mouse! That's right."

"Mouse!?" Mom yelled from the top of the stairs.

"On the TV, Mom! We are watching cartoons," I shrugged my shoulders after Rachel gave me a strange look. "It was the first thing I thought of!"

"I found him," Rachel announced as Phillip reentered the basement.

"Now, we just have to find Queen Merran. What do you think a queen would become?" I asked.

"Cat!" Phillip answered.

"Really? I would think something cooler like a giraffe or a zebra." I jokingly responded.

"You're an idiot. Do you think a giraffe would be hard to find in this basement?" Rachel snarked.

"I was just kidding."

"No, guys, look. A cat," Phillip pointed at a pure white cat with a black-tipped tail and bright blue eyes standing at the sliding glass door.

"We don't have a cat," I said and then immediately wished I hadn't.

"You need to stop talking because you're gonna hurt yourself, Whizzy." Rachel looked tired, frustrated and ready to physically hurt me.

Phillip picked the cat up and held it to his face. "Queen Merran?"

"I'm afraid I am no longer queen, Phillip Harper."

Phillip's face frowned when he heard the now princess's voice sadly reply to his question.

"Well, we all made it here safely." Rachel summed up our current state. "Now how do we get back?"

We all looked at each other blankly.

"Aevion, you brought us to Mistasia before; you can do it again!" Rachel pleaded.

"I'm sorry Rachel Whizzenmog, but I do not have any more of the mushrooms that I used to open the portal." He replied with a sad tone.

"Hey, Princess...can you take us back? We don't know how to open the portal. Someone always comes to get us." I said hoping she had an answer.

"I cannot open the portal to my home, Michael Whizzenmog, but there is someone in your world that can."

"Really?" Phillip replied.

"Who?" Rachel and I questioned in unison.

"Your grandfather, Rainer Whizzenmog," Princess Merran replied.

A GRAND GIFT

30

"I can't believe that we forgot," Rachel groaned as she punched me in the arm.

"Forgot what? Rachel, I don't understand," Phillip said as the crease between his eyes formed. It always appeared when he was trying to remember something he thought he knew.

"Our grandfather brought our family to Greenville," I instantly remembered.

"Yes. Rainer Whizzenmog created the portal between our worlds many years ago. He is the link. Your grandfather will be able to open the portal and send us back," Princess Merran explained.

"Mom said he is coming today!" Rachel excitedly announced.

"That is unbelievable," I said.

"Yes, that is a grand gift of fortune. Your grandfather was an extremely powerful wizard. He could help turn the tide in our favor," the princess said. "You must convince him to help us."

Princess Merran and Aevion remained hidden in the basement as Phillip, Rachel and I helped clean the house.

That afternoon my grandfather arrived. I couldn't wait to get him away from mom and talk to him about Mistasia. He would understand. Each hour that past in our world was another day that King Cragon Cadieux ruled in Mistasia. The longer he reigned the harder it would be to remove him.

I had always admired my grandfather. He was a strong man, with a salt and pepper beard and short white hair. I never really knew what he did for a living. Rachel and I had never asked, but we always imagined it was something cool and important, but never would we imagine that he was a wizard from another world.

After dinner, I was becoming much more anxious. Rachel and I nearly dragged him downstairs as Mom and Dad cleaned up the kitchen.

"Grandfather, we have something to show you in the basement," I pressed.

"What do you have for me, Whizzy?" He replied while sitting on the couch in our basement.

"Something amazing happened to us this past summer," I began to explain. "Rachel, my best friend Phillip, and I traveled to another world."

"Well, that sounds exciting," Grandfather giggled. "Tell me about it." He moved forward in his seat to listen.

"Where did you go, Whizzy? Don't keep it a secret, my boy." He chuckled again.

"Ah...well, we went to..." I stammered. **Just say it, Whizzy!** I yelled at myself. Suddenly,

I was very nervous. I feared my mom finding out about Mistasia, thinking she would put me in the loony bin, so telling my grandfather seemed like breaking some family rule or something.

"We have been to Mistasia!" Rachel blurted out.

"What?" Our grandfather's expression harshly changed. "You've been where?"

"Mistasia," I softly replied. I was beginning to regret this conversation.

"No." His eyes searched us over as if he thought we were joking.

"We have been there twice, Sir," Phillip added.

"Yes, we were just there. We returned only this morning, Grandfather," Rachel excitedly burst out.

I was hoping for a much better reaction, but we definitely hadn't gotten one.

"Grandfather, are you okay?" I asked, as he remained silent for a while.

He slid back in the couch and took a deep breath before exhaling. A tear rolled down his left cheek and then a smirk hit his lip. When he turned to face us, he asked, "Wasn't it the most wonderfully beautiful place you've ever seen?"

"Yes," I answered.

"It's been so long that I have almost forgotten what it looks like." He fought back more tears.

"You could go there again," Princess Merran said from Phillip Harper's lap.

My grandfather's head turned so briskly I thought he had snapped his neck.

"Excuse me?" He laughed.

"This is Princess Merran Cadieux, Grandfather. She was queen until her uncle, King Cragon, sent us back here. He has taken over Cadieux Castle," I explained.

"Yes, and we need your help to get back to Mistasia," Rachel added as she grabbed Grandfather's hand.

"How?"

"You must reopen the portal to Mistasia, Rainer Whizzenmog. It is time you return to your home and reclaim your proper place in our world," Princess Merran urged.

He sat silently for a moment; a glimmer in his eye began to shine and a smile gleamed across his face.

Then, he spoke, "Yes...I believe you're right."

Phillip & Whizzy Trilogy

LAST EMERALD

Christopher M. Purrett

www.Purrett.com

CHAPTERS

RACHEL WHIZZENMOG

1

My name is Rachel Whizzenmog, and I have an unbelievable story to tell you. It all began last summer when I was kidnapped by a snake and dragged off to another world called Mistasia. I know that's not what you were probably expecting to hear from a fifteen-year-old girl, but it's true.

Mistasia is a beautiful and dangerous world that I enter through the sliding glass door in my basement. My grandpa once lived in Mistasia long ago as the protector to the King.

In Mistasia, my twin brother, Michael, who we call "Whizzy", and his best friend, Phillip Harper, saved me from the evil King Cragon, who turned out to be a sorcerer.

That's not all...six months later, just before Christmas we all traveled back to Mistasia. When we arrived, it was winter there too and awfully cold...oh, did I mention my brother and I turn into foxes and Phillip becomes a frog in Mistasia?

Phillip, Whizzy and I were brought back to Mistasia by a young vampire bat named, Aevion. The sorcerer, Pierre LaCroiux, was controlling his parents, Goren and Vella. They tricked us and helped King Cragon return to power.

Now, Phillip, Whizzy and I found ourselves trapped, but not in Mistasia...in our hometown of Greenville. We needed to get back and help Queen Merran reclaim her throne from her uncle, the king. It seemed almost hopeless until we realized we had a secret weapon coming over for Christmas holiday, our grandpa...Rainer Whizzenmog.

A LITTLE PRIVACY

2

I looked into the bathroom mirror.

I look awful. I thought to myself.

My eyes were red like I had been crying for days and my hair was a complete mess. Grabbing the nearest hairbrush from the drawer I started to tame my hair. Suddenly, I caught a frightening scent. My clothes were damp and smelled like Whizzy's sweaty gym socks. Yikes!

I need to take a shower before Phillip thinks I'm some wild animal. I told myself. That was probably the best idea I'd had in some time. I needed to relax and unwind. The tension in my neck was causing me to hunch over. I just kept thinking about the poor helpless creatures of Mistasia and the awful things that King Cragon was doing to punish them now that he was back in power. Princess Merran was correct...we needed to get back right away. Every hour we waited here in Greenville, another day passed in

Mistasia. Cragon wouldn't wait very long to take his revenge.

The hot water from the shower felt great. It was definitely much better than the cold air in Mistasia. Stepping from the shower, I reached for my towel and quickly wrapped it around me.

I heard a creaking noise while I was drying my hair and quickly stopped. The door was slightly open.

"Whizzy!" I yelled, thinking my stupid brother had opened the door to let in a cool draft. He was always doing dumb things like that to make me mad. I made sure the towel was wrapped around me tightly and stuck my head out into the hallway to yell at him, but there was no one there.

I scoffed. Maybe I just hadn't closed the door tightly enough. This was a very old house and the doors would sometimes creak open. Whizzy used to think it was haunted when we were kids. Pushing against the door harder, I heard it click. Then, I locked it...just to be sure.

When I turned around, I screamed. Standing in the middle of the floor was a small black mouse.

"Aevion! I'm naked," I shouted angrily while pulling my towel close between my legs and crossing my knees.

The small black mouse was the same vampire bat that had taken us to Mistasia the day before. He had been sent back to Greenville with us when his parents, Goren and Vella, the leaders of the vampire bats, betrayed us. Sorcerer LaCroiux kept them under his control, which basically made Phillip, Whizzy and me Aevion's parents now.

"I'm sorry, Rachel. The princess has requested to see you," he spoke while staring at the floor and rubbing his tiny paws together nervously.

"This couldn't wait until I was dressed?" I quickly reached back, unlocked the door and pushed him outside with my hand. He covered his eyes as I slid him across the tile floor and onto the carpeted hallway. "Give me five minutes," I barked and then slammed the door.

I could hear him whimper and then
scurry down the hallway towards my bedroom
where Princess Merran was hiding.

Standing back in front of the mirror, I
wiped away the condensation from the glass. My
wet hair clung to my face, and my eyes were
still red. There was a knock at the door.

"I said five minutes!" I snapped thinking
Aevion had returned.

"Oh, I'm sorry, Rachel," Phillip's muffled
voice replied through the door. "But I really need
to go to the bathroom."

My heart started to flutter when I heard
his voice. It was very strange. Only a year ago I
wouldn't have cared if Phillip were here, but now
things were different. He made me feel weird
and I sort of liked it.

I took a deep breath, "Can't you go
downstairs?"

He didn't respond immediately. "Ah...well.
I'm not quite comfortable with that, Rachel," He
replied. "I had to borrow Whizzy's clothes and
they're...well, a little small."

I watched in the mirror as a smile crept across my face. I couldn't help it. I had to see this. Phillip was over six feet tall and Whizzy was shorter than me. Reaching out for the door handle I could feel myself begin to giggle. I stopped to gather myself and then grabbed hold of my towel across my chest and cracked the door open slightly to peer out. Catching a glimpse of Phillip standing there with an orange t-shirt that looked more like a tube top, I burst into laughter. His belly button was staring at me like a creepy eyeball. He also wore Christmas-themed pajama pants with Rudolph and Santa faces all over them. These were also too short and barely covered his knobby knees. He stood with his hands and arms covering his body as if he were naked. It was the strangest and funniest thing I had ever seen. It was kind of cute.

"Oh my gosh, Phillip. What did my brother do to you?" I was laughing pretty hard now and his face began to turn bright red. "Phillip...you look ridiculous."

"Can I go...please?" He begged as he danced on the carpet in his bare feet. "I'd go downstairs, but I can't let everyone see me like this."

"I'll hurry; just wait right there." I rushed back into the bathroom, finished drying off and hurriedly pulled on my night clothes...just an old t-shirt and sweatpants since I had long out grown the little girl night gowns. I didn't even dry my hair, but pulled it back in a ponytail.

Phillip was still hopping around like a frog in the hallway when I opened the door. His dance was quite silly, and it added to how goofy he looked in my brother's clothes. I so wished I had my phone to get video. The door slammed behind me, almost hitting my rear when I heard Phillip yell, "Thanks!"

In my bedroom, Princess Merran waited impatiently for my return. It was just like my mom would have done. Merran, a white cat, was curled up on my pillow with Aevion at the foot of the bed. She gracefully rose when I entered. The banished ex-queen was anxiously awaiting our return to Mistasia.

"Sorry I took so long...I was delayed, Princess," I started to bow then felt silly, so I stopped and then stumbled. It was really awkward which I am definitely glad Phillip didn't see...or my brother. Whizzy would have definitely made some joke about it. "What is it that you wanted to talk to me about?"

"Why does your grandpa wait to take us back to Mistasia, Rachel?" She was very forceful in her tone.

I was shocked to hear her so rude. That was not something she had ever done to me before.

"We need to return immediately!" She continued before I could answer.

"I know, Princess Merran. I want to go back too, but he said he wanted to wait until the morning when my parents are gone," I replied.

The cat tilted her head in a peculiar way. I instantly knew that she didn't understand why that was important.

"I fear that your grandpa has lost his courage, Rachel Whizzenmog."

"No...no, Princess. We can't just leave with my parents here. They will realize that we are missing. With my grandpa here, things are different. When it's just Whizzy and me, we have the freedom to...go play. So our parents expect us to be missing for some time. It is normal. They believe that we are just playing with friends. If my grandpa is missing, that would worry them." I wasn't sure if that even made sense to me so I was pretty sure that Princess Merran would probably be confused.

"It's like the difference between Grace and your servants at Cadieux Castle."

Her ears perked up.

"When Grace isn't at the castle you believe her to be off protecting it. When your servants are gone, you notice that there isn't someone taking care of your needs."

"Ah...I think I understand." She paused for a moment. "Does that mean your grandpa is your parents' servant?"

"No! No, I mean that he is someone that is expected to be around the castle and easily found when needed." I responded.

"Oh...I see."

"Princess, please. You must understand my grandpa will take us to Mistasia. I promise you that. He hasn't lost his courage," I added.

GREEN STONE

3

Later that night, I stood outside the door to the room where my grandpa slept. Whizzy and I had always known him as Grandpa, but he was the original Michael Whizzenmog. His middle name was Rainer. My dad is Michael Whizzenmog, junior, and my brother is the third.

There was a pounding in my chest as I stood, hesitantly, outside the door. I could feel my heart pumping blood through my body like a speeding roller coaster. It was something I had never noticed before our trips to Mistasia. Now everything seemed clearer...more noticeable. My senses were so focused. I wished I could be this focused in math class...maybe I wouldn't have gotten a "C" on my first semester exam.

It was 10:15 pm. Grandpa Whizzenmog was surely asleep, but I needed to know that he was still going. Something in my gut told me something was wrong. I could hear the sound of music from Whizzy's video game in the distance. I scanned the hallway before knocking. No one was around.

My body moved in slow motion. I softly tapped my knuckles on the door as if it was made of glass and afraid it would shatter.

"Why am I so nervous?" I muttered to myself. My hands felt sweaty. "This is ridiculous."

I felt like a criminal. All I wanted to do was talk with my grandpa about a secret magical world where an evil king has taken over and we are trying to overthrow him.

"Oh that's why I'm nervous…I sound crazy!" I answered my own question, which now I realize doesn't make me seem very sane in the first place.

The door opened.

I gasped.

"Rachel?" my grandpa questioned, sounding as surprised as I was to find me standing outside his door this late at night.

"Grandpa," I replied.

"Are you all right?"

I nodded, "Sorry to bother you. I'll go back to bed."

"My dear, come in." He placed his large hand on my shoulder. It seemed so light and delicate for something that resembled a bear claw in size.

He walked me to a single wooden chair at the desk along the wall. Then he sat on the bed. We remained quiet for a moment. I avoided his eyes, but I knew he was looking right at me. Instead I stared at a picture of our family sitting on the nightstand. It was my grandpa's. He had brought it with him on his trip. That is when I noticed this room looked like my grandpa had lived in it for years. The covers on the bed and curtains on the wall were the same, a dark orange like the leaves in fall. Yet, on the nightstand were his reading glasses and chrome-colored watch. His jacket was wrapped around the chair I sat in. I could smell his aftershave on its collar. He had made this room his home. That was when I saw a strange object sitting next to his glasses that I had never seen before. It was small and dark green, yet it glowed like a flame inside lighted it.

"Grandpa, what is that?"

"Ah...that is an emerald. It is a very rare gemstone."

"Did it belong to Grandmother?" I questioned. I couldn't remember her ever talking about it, but she had died nearly five years ago. Maybe I had just forgotten.

My grandpa changed the subject. "Rachel, what brings you to my door at this hour?" He raised his eyebrow.

I still couldn't look in his eyes. This whole situation was making me very uncomfortable. Was I really about to ask my grandpa, a man I loved and admired, if he was a coward? I must be insane to even believe Princess Merran for a second.

The emerald glimmered in the corner of my eye. Suddenly, I couldn't stop thinking about it. It was mesmerizing.

"Rachel!" My grandpa sternly called. "You are acting strangely...like your brother."

I laughed. I was acting very strangely, but lately everything in my life was strange. "Grandpa, why didn't you return to Mistasia?"

"Love," he answered without hesitation. "My priorities changed. I met your grandmother, had a family and moved far away from that life." He didn't appear to have any regrets, but tears formed in his aged eyes.

I didn't know if he was thinking about Grandma or Mistasia.

"Didn't you ever wonder what had happened in Mistasia?" I wanted to know how he left it behind so easily. I had been a wreck since we left and it had only been a few hours!

"I always knew it would find me."

"Find you?" I asked. "Why were you hiding?"

"Mistasia had changed. Everything had changed, my dear." He rubbed the back of his neck.

"How had Mistasia changed? What made you leave?" I needed to know. Mistasia was dangerous now, but only because my grandpa had left it unprotected.

"Sometimes one choice is all it takes to alter the course of everything, Rachel. Just one." Then he stopped explaining. He seemed very upset.

We sat together silently for a few moments as my grandpa struggled to regain his composure. He rubbed his hand over his mouth and took a deep breath.

Finally, I spoke out, "It is time to return, Grandpa."

He nodded. "Off to bed now. We have quite a journey ahead of us tomorrow."

LEAVING GREENVILLE
4

My alarm began blaring at 7 am that following morning. I am sure that I don't have to explain how early that is when there is no school. Yet, my excitement drove me like it was Christmas morning. I leapt out of bed and dashed to my closet. Quickly changing out of my pajamas, I got dressed, grabbed my wand and went to leave my bedroom when I nearly tripped over Princess Merran. She stood at the door like she was waiting for me to open it. When I did, she gracefully exited. I rolled my eyes at her antics and headed for Whizzy's room.

Grandpa Whizzenmog met me in the hallway outside my brother's room. He, too, was dressed and ready for our trip.

"Do we dare enter?" He said with a smile.

"We had better knock," I replied back with a slight giggle.

He knocked on Whizzy's bedroom door three times. There was no reply.

"Whizzy! Phillip! It is time to go," I called so they would hear me through the door.

My grandpa reached for the door handle.

"Stop!" I blurted out. "Please, don't do that. What if he isn't...decent?"

"Whizzy? My dear he's been indecent since the day he was born." Then he rubbed my back to calm my nerves. "Just wait right here."

Then Grandpa Whizzenmog opened the door, stepped inside, gave me a sly wink and closed the door behind him. Next, his booming voice erupted from the bedroom. "Michael Whizzenmog, wake up!"

I could hear shouting, followed by crashing, and I think someone farted. The commotion continued for a few minutes. Then my grandpa came into the hallway and quickly slammed the door. He was covering his nose and mouth with his shirt. The door handle violently wiggled; then Phillip and Whizzy pounded on the door. They were trying to get out like some hideous creature was attempting to eat them alive.

"What is wrong? What happened?" I screamed in a panic.

"Open this door, Grandpa!" Whizzy yelled in a fit of rage.

"You must pay the penalty for keeping us from our departing time, Michael Whizzenmog." Grandpa chuckled heartily with his nose and mouth still covered within his shirt. His eyes were watering when he looked at me.

I gave him a shocked expression and shook my head.

"It was Whizzy's alarm...do I have to pay the penalty, sir?" Phillip cried.

"Sorry, my boy. Guilt by association." He cackled like a high school freshman.

"What did you do?" I scolded.

"Just gave the boy some of his own medicine."

"Did you fart?" I was most disgusted to imagine my grandpa intentionally passing gas and then trapping my brother and Phillip inside the room to suffer. "Open the door!"

His laughter was growing with every second.

"Now!" I shouted like my mom.

The door flung open causing Phillip and Whizzy to crash to the floor gasping for air. Phillip crawled down the hallway.

"What did you eat?" Phillip squealed in a girlish voice.

"That...was...awful," Whizzy said between deep breaths of fresh air. "I'm gonna get you back, Grandpa."

"Son, you can't beat the master," my grandpa replied, patting Whizzy on top of the head.

"I hope that isn't your power in Mistasia," Whizzy blurted out. "Well, actually that would be pretty cool." He pointed at our giggling elder. "Just don't use it on us...remember, we are on your side."

"You two are embarrassing," I yelled. "Let's just go, please. We have to get to Mistasia and you guys are screwing around."

It was December 16th and my parents had gone to finish their holiday shopping. They would be gone all day. It made today our best opportunity to travel to Mistasia and hopefully return before my parents could realize that we had disappeared.

"We have around ten hours in Greenville," I explained.

"Good that gives us about ten days in Mistasia then," Whizzy replied. "That isn't too bad."

We had gathered in the basement...that was, everyone except Grandpa Whizzenmog.

"Where is your grandpa, Rachel?" Princess Merran questioned.

As we looked around, he finally appeared at the top of the stairs. We watched as he slowly maneuvered the staircase and walked across the basement to the sliding glass door that had served as the portal to Mistasia for our previous trips.

I watched as he adjusted his gloves and then grabbed the handle to the door.

"What are you doing?" I asked.

"I am opening the door," he said with a smart tone.

Whizzy and I shared a confused glance.

"But we have to go through the door," Whizzy said before I could.

"That is the portal to Mistasia, Rainer Whizzenmog," Princess Merran added.

"Well, we can't really go back through the same way you came out can we? Weren't you all banished?" He slid the door open and walked out into the cold winter air.

Phillip was the first to follow. Then we all proceeded to walk out into our wintry backyard.

I carried Princess Merran in my arms, and Aevion sat on Phillip's shoulder. We didn't talk much. Instead we just followed my grandpa as he walked through the backyard and into the forest.

It was cold and slightly windy. It had apparently snowed last night, as a fresh layer of white fluffy snow hung on the tree branches above our heads. A pile of snow slid off one tree and landed directly in front of Phillip.

"That was close," Phillip said, sounding relieved it didn't land on his head. Then more snow tumbled from the same tree and hit

Whizzy. Phillip and I laughed at Whizzy as he brushed the snow from his hair.

"That's not funny!" my brother yelled. He looked up into the trees. They swayed in the wind. More snow began to fall toward us. Phillip, Whizzy and I dashed away just in time.

"Where are we going, Whizzy?" Phillip spoke out the side of his mouth. He looked worried. "Your grandpa isn't gonna smoke us out again, is he?"

How disgusting...boys and their bodily functions. How could someone be so proud when they make a room smell so badly that no one can even breathe?

"I know; it was like rotten cabbage and dead animals!" Whizzy laughed.

"Don't say dead animals," Phillip gulped. "We're all gonna be animals when we get back to Mistasia, and I don't wanna be dead!" He cried.

We were silent again. I knew we all were thinking about what Phillip had just said. Everyone looked worried.

"I don't think we can just walk to Mistasia," Whizzy snarled in an attempt to be funny and lighten the mood.

It didn't work.

"No, we cannot, Whizzy. It is just up ahead," Grandpa Whizzenmog responded.

"The river?" I muttered. "But it is frozen over."

"Water makes for a strong magical conductor, Rachel," Grandpa Whizzenmog explained.

"Condu-what?" Whizzy showed how little he paid attention in science class.

"A conductor, Whizzy. It is something that allows another force...in this case magic, to flow properly. Even with the water being frozen, it will let the magic in my wand through...sometimes even magnifying its power," Our grandpa elaborated as he stepped up to the river's edge.

"I'm not really liking this whole jumping into a frozen river idea," Whizzy whined.

"Then you don't have to come," Grandpa Whizzenmog replied. "You can stay home and help your parents wrap gifts." He turned back and smiled at me. I loved it when he picked on Whizzy.

Grandpa Whizzenmog adjusted his snowcap and then pulled a straight wooden stick from his boot. It was his wand. He studied it longingly. It must have been decades since he used it. Running his fingers along the length of his wand, he inhaled deeply.

"Let's see if I remember how to use this," he said.

FLUSHED AWAY
5

I stood impatiently behind my grandpa as he looked out across the frozen river. Drifts of snow swelled on the far side of the river, but there was very little at our feet. Phillip and Whizzy were standing on either side of me as the wind blew at our backs, sweeping the snow across the ice. It slithered along the frozen river top like a snake in the sand. The sun was very low and dim in the sky.

I squinted to see what Grandpa Whizzenmog was doing as he reached into his pocket for something. When he found it, he quickly moved onto the ice.

"What is he waiting for?" Whizzy crassly remarked.

I didn't have any idea. No one did, because none of us responded.

Phillip, Whizzy and I stayed back on shore.

"Do not follow me, kids. I will make sure it is safe first." He stopped only a few feet away from us when a strong gust of wind swirled around and engulfed him in snow.

"Grandpa!" Whizzy yelled then started to run on the ice.

I grabbed him by the arm, "Wait! Don't move!"

The snow blew into the air and Grandpa Whizzenmog reappeared. He had huddled and covered his face.

"I'm fine. Please, stay there," He commanded while wiping snow from his eyes and beard.

The winds had caught us by surprise. Phillip was cuddling Aevion to his chest and I knelt down and huddled around Princess Merran. Snow was flying around like we were in a winter tornado. It was somewhat difficult to see until my grandpa pulled something from his pocket.

A bright green light made the fluffy white snow seem to disappear. It shot rays of dark green light into the river.

"What is that?" Phillip croaked. He seemed very nervous. I didn't like it when he was nervous...I liked him better when he was confident.

My grandpa raised his arm into the air. He was chanting something, although I couldn't hear him, I could see his lips moving. The light from the object in his hands grew brighter and brighter just before he slammed it onto the frozen river with a loud grunt. A circle of green light rippled out from the object, shaking the ground like a tremor when it passed us by.

"That was wicked!" Whizzy shouted.

Grandpa stood up and backed away with his wand still in his left hand. He eagerly studied the small green object now sticking out from the ice.

"It's the emerald!" I shouted above the rushing winds.

"What?" Phillip asked.

Whizzy and Phillip each listened intently, "A green emerald. I saw it in Grandpa's room last night," I explained as my hair whipped against the increasing winds. "I asked if it belonged to Grandmother, but he didn't say."

Small cracks began to splinter in the ice. They stretched out from the center where the emerald had pierced the ice. The river began to change colors like it was melting rapidly. A large circle formed near where my grandpa now stood.

"Hurry!" Grandpa Whizzenmog shouted as he emphatically waved us toward him.

We dashed onto the icy river and slid to a stop next to the only person who seemed to have any idea what was happening beneath us.

I saw the water bubbling and swirling under our feet. It changed colors directly below us, from a white to clear like the sliding glass door in our basement.

"Hold on!" I heard my grandpa's voice shout, as he firmly grabbed a hold of my arm.

A sinking feeling came over me. Now I knew how Phillip felt almost every single day in school. My stomach flipped and I suddenly felt sick when I watched the icy river-top disintegrate under my boots.

I screamed as I fell into the river, which now swirled like a whirlpool. The water was all around me, yet I wasn't wet or cold. We were in a portal. Grandpa had done it...he had opened the portal to Mistasia.

An orange fish flew past my face. I screamed and then covered my mouth for fear of drowning, but I could breath.

I watched as Whizzy flipped around doing somersaults. He smiled so widely that I almost didn't recognize him. Phillip, however, looked terrified.

Colors began to fade. My brother and Phillip grew smaller until I could no longer see them. Then everything went dark.

Thud!

MY BROTHER AND THE STUPID, FAT DRAGON

6

"Are we in Mistasia?" Whizzy blurted out. It was the first thing I remembered after landing on the frozen ground.

When I opened my eyes, I was no longer human. My skin was covered in golden fur...I was Rachel the Fox, but we appeared to still be in Greenville.

"It didn't work," I sadly stated.

Everything looked identical to the snow-covered river in Greenville...except us. Everyone had returned to their Mistasian forms: Whizzy was a reddish-orange fox, Phillip, a brightly-colored green tree frog with bright red eyes, Aevion a smallish, almost transparent vampire bat, and Princess Merran a blonde-haired, fair-skinned Elven girl.

I searched our landing spot for my grandpa, but couldn't see him. Whizzy and Phillip joined me.

"Are we back?" Whizzy yelled to me.

"We must be! Look at us!" I shouted. I knew that Greenville and Mistasia shared similarities, but the wintry conditions made it very difficult to tell the difference between them now.

There was so much snow piled very high. It had been nearly a month in Mistasian time since we were banished by Cragon Cadieux and the snow had continued to build up.

"Grandpa!" I yelled.

Whizzy placed his hand over my mouth and pulled me down into the snow.

"Be quiet," he mouthed without speaking.

A ferocious roar bellowed out from the forest in the distance behind us.

"Dragons," Phillip said, confirming my fear. "We are definitely back because I didn't see dragons in the trees on the way here." Then he began rubbing snow on his froggy thighs. "Do you have your wands?" He said with a glimmer in his eye.

"Phillip? What are you thinking?" I scolded. His confidence had returned. Water gave him power, so rubbing the snow on his thighs would allow him to absorb the water and strengthen his legs.

That was when I realized Princess Merran and Aevion weren't with us anymore. "Where are they?" I blurted out stopping Phillip in his tracks.

"Out there," Phillip pointed in front of us.

"What?" I replied with confusion. "No, Phillip, not the dragons. Where are Aevion and Princess Merran?" I replied with concern.

"Oh, crap," Whizzy said as he pointed into the open area where we had landed after exiting the portal from Greenville. "They're right there."

Flying in from above, like low cruising airplanes, were two large dragons with Wolverine riders. Aevion began shrieking with fear at the sight of the large scaly beasts.

The dragons roared back in a vocal battle. Any second, I feared that the dragons would blast them with fire and burn them to a crisp. This trip to Mistasia was not starting off very well at all.

"Aevion!" I screamed to draw the dragon's attention without properly thinking the situation through.

"Rachel!" Whizzy barked.

"Here it comes," Phillip yelled in excitement.

The large red dragon swooped down toward us. Its bright yellow eyes glared at me as smoke smoldered from its mouth.

Whizzy and I gripped our wands and pointed them directly at the dragon. Phillip dashed off at a full sprint straight for the angry beast.

"Phillip!" I screamed. I liked his confidence, but this was ridiculous...and now he was in the way! Whizzy and I couldn't use magic without hitting Phillip. "Where is he going?" I asked my brother.

"I think he's going after that dragon," he replied.

Phillip was on a collision course with the flying beast when it spit fire. The heated blast melted the snow at Phillip's feet causing a plume of steam to hang in the air like a fog over a lake.

I screamed, "NO!" The thought of Phillip being melted flashed into my mind.

Phillip shot up out of the steam and landed on the dragon's head.

"Phillip!" I yelled in relief.

He stood on the red beast's snout, between its glowing eyes. The dragon scowled and snorted. Then Phillip ran across its head, jumped over the Wolverine rider, and continued across its back before leaping skyward again. He flipped and landed in the snow just a few dozen feet away from Aevion and Princess Merran.

The second dragon was purple and fat. It appeared to never pass on any meal. Unfortunately, that meant we were on his dinner menu. Its large belly dragged in the snow as it lumbered back and forth keeping Aevion and Princess Merran from escaping. The dragon was taunting them.

Phillip ran across the top of the deep snow to help Aevion and the princess.

The purple dragon's Wolverine rider pulled hard on the reigns, causing the dragon to stand up, exposing its large white underbelly.

Phillip leapt into action, launching himself toward the purple beast. His webbed feet collided with the dragon's belly, only to bounce back like jumping on a trampoline. Phillip was flung into a snowdrift. Crashing violently, he was knocked unconscious.

Whizzy and I ducked behind some snow as the red dragon buzzed by, kicking snow over us like an ocean wave crashing onshore. It trapped my legs and covered most of Whizzy's body. I struggled to free myself, before using my wand to toss the snow aside. Then I freed my brother. We ran to help Aevion and Princess Merran against the purple dragon.

Whizzy shot a freezing spell at the Wolverine rider atop the purple dragon, but missed. I attempted to hit it with an electric shock, but only winged the dragon, causing it to squeal in pain and begin stomping around, flinging snow.

We all scattered. Aevion barely dodged the purple dragon's tail as it slammed down beside him. Princess Merran ran to Phillip, who was still unconscious in the snow. Just before she reached him the red dragon scooped her up in its claws. Whizzy and I attempted to avoid the purple dragon's large feet, which danced around like it was standing in fire instead of cold snow.

A stiff gust of wind pushed Whizzy and me off our feet. As I lay on my back in the snow, I saw the red dragon fly over me with the princess clutched in its grasp.

Quickly, I rolled over and pushed to my feet. I started running after them with my wand pointed at the red dragon's pointy tail.

"Hold still," I said to my target while closing one eye. I aimed and fired a stunning spell at the red dragon just as I was hit in the stomach by the purple dragon's tail.

All the air in my body escaped me. It hurt even more when I landed on my back. I struggled to regain my breath.

"Princess," the word fought to escape my lungs.

Whizzy continued to fight with the fat purple dragon. He had become angry, as Whizzy tends to do. Snow began swirling around him. He slid one leg back and bent his front leg like doing some sort of yoga position. Whizzy swung his right arm back, holding his wand firmly in his paw, and let out a tremendous growl. A blue bolt of lightning erupted from his wand. A thunderclap exploded in the air when the bolt hit the large dragon. It wavered slightly and then crashed to the ground. The vicious beast's horned head landed just a foot from Aevion, who was shaking with fear. The purple dragon's long sharp fangs jutted out from its closed mouth.

Whizzy punched it in the snout, "Stupid, fat dragon."

I gasped at the sight of the huge beast's head lying in the snow next to Whizzy. My brother was so small compared to it, but he had managed to defeat the purple dragon anyway.

"Rachel?" Whizzy asked with concern.

I replied, as I thought how lucky we were to escape this battle alive, "Whizzy, I'm really beginning to see why Grandpa didn't want to return to Mistasia."

"Grandpa?" Whizzy and I both called out. He was still missing.

CRACKS IN THE ICE

7

I had no idea exactly how long we had been back in Mistasia, but I knew that we were in serious trouble already.

Princess Merran had been captured by a dragon that was no doubt working for King Cragon, Phillip was injured in battle and lay unconscious in the snow, Aevion was so scared that he just shivered, and worst of all...Grandpa Whizzenmog hadn't been seen since we arrived.

What if we can't find our grandpa? I thought. **What would we tell our parents?**

Then Whizzy questioned as if he could read my mind, "What do we do if we don't find, Grandpa?"

"We will find him, Whizzy. Trust me," I stated emphatically trying to convince myself more than my brother. "Just keep looking. He couldn't have just vanished. Think. Just think," I yelled in frustration.

"Where are we?" Whizzy asked.

"You have to be kidding. The giant flying dragons didn't give it away. I'm positive we are in Mistasia, Whizzy." I really didn't want to talk to my brother anymore. I suddenly recalled why I didn't speak to him in middle school.

"Shut it, Rachel. You don't have to be a stupid-head," Whizzy replied.

I couldn't believe what I had heard. "Did you just call me 'stupid-head'? Are you five years old?" I questioned. It was the weakest comeback I had ever heard him use.

"I know we're in Mistasia, Rachel. I am asking you where in Mistasia, genius?" Whizzy barked at me.

"Oh." I looked around again now that the commotion had ended. "I have no idea."

"Aevion, where are we exactly?" Whizzy asked the frightened vampire bat, but Aevion only shook his head in reply.

"Well, let's think about this, Whizzy. There is a forest over there." I pointed behind the slain purple dragon.

"And they had Wolverine riders," Whizzy began and suddenly stopped. He was intently staring at something. He spun his wand in his hand like a gunslinger and then raised his arm and pointed the wand at the dragon again.

"Whizzy, are you going crazy? That dragon is dead." My brother was always weird, but this wasn't the time to be goofing around.

"But not his rider," Whizzy replied.

Just then a hairy black figure moved out from behind the large purple dragon's body. It was the Wolverine. Whizzy had dealt with them before, the first time we had traveled to

Mistasia. They tried to attack Whizzy, Phillip and Grace as they moved through the forest to save me.

The nasty monstrous Wolverine glared at us with its evil eyes. Spit dripped from its mouth while its shoulders bobbed up and down with each breath like an apple in water. Then, it charged.

Whizzy fired. The red blast zipped from his wand and slammed into its target. The Wolverine stopped dead in its tracks. Whizzy flicked his wand and tossed the hairy monster. It landed with a sickening crack.

Whizzy smiled victoriously.

Aevion, Whizzy and I ran over to the Wolverine. It lay motionless. I pointed my wand at it.

"These things are really ugly," I gasped.

Whizzy kicked it, "Not so tough are ya?"

"We're on ice," I said aloud.

"What?" Whizzy replied. He still had a smile on his dumb face.

"It's the river! Whizzy, this is Red River," I shouted with excitement. "We always come into

Mistasia in what would be our backyard, because we go through the portal in our basement. The backyard would be on the other side. This time we went to the river in Greenville...and so we arrived at the river here in Mistasia."

"So that is Wolverine Forest behind us?" Whizzy questioned.

"Yes! Oh, no. That means the dragon was flying south...to Cadieux Castle," I suddenly felt a sinking feeling. "Whizzy, what if he adds the princess to his statue collection?"

"We'll rescue her, Rachel," my brother promised. "Grace and the princess will be free. Once we find Grandpa...we will save them both," Whizzy replied as he grabbed my arm.

A crack began to form in the ice below our feet.

"Whizzy, watch out," I grabbed my brother and pulled him off the frozen river.

It quickly fractured and collapsed dragging the Wolverine down below. The river swallowed the beast whole.

A strange noise began to gurgle up from the river. Large chunks of ice shot up into the air and crashed down exploding and tossing fragments of ice at us.

A green light began to glow from below the bubbling water's surface. The ground shook and vibrated, making it very hard to stand. Suddenly, a figure burst from the water.

Landing before us was a tall gray-haired fox with black ears and bright blue eyes. He was completely dry despite coming from the river. In his left paw was a green emerald and in his right a straight stick.

"Grandpa?" I asked hopefully.

A sly smile crossed the gray fox's face as he replied, "Yes, my dear."

MAGICAL RIDE

8

I ran and jumped into his arms, giving Grandpa Whizzenmog the biggest hug I could.

"You're alive!" I said while choking back tears of joy.

"Yes, Rachel. I am most certainly alive," Grandpa Whizzenmog replied with a hearty chuckle. "And it appears that you've had quite the encounter." He pointed his wand at the slain purple dragon lying in the white snow.

"Grandpa, Princess Merran has been captured," Whizzy informed him.

The gray fox didn't respond. He stood up straight and looked painfully at the glowing green emerald in his left paw. Then he waved his wand over the stone in a circular motion. It glowed even brighter and then flashed like lightning. When my sight returned to normal, I saw him placing something around his wrist. It looked like a bracelet bearing the same color as the emerald.

"Grandpa," I began when he interrupted me.

"We must make our leave of this place. The castle is still a good distance from here. Princess Merran needs our help." Then the gray fox briskly walked away signaling the end of our conversation.

I watched him walked directly toward our friend, Phillip. Grandpa zapped Phillip awakening him. "We must go, Phillip." Then the gray fox moved on again.

Phillip looked at me with a confused expression. He quickly noticed the fat purple dragon lying in the snow and began to smile.

"Did I do that?" He asked.

"No," I quickly retorted.

Phillip, Whizzy, Aevion and I trekked behind Grandpa Whizzenmog as he walked passed a single tree amidst the deep snow.

"The Friendless Tree," Whizzy whispered to me as he pointed at the lonesome tree that appeared to have run away from the great forest behind us.

I looked it up and down trying to figure out how it ended up by itself. Phillip had his mouth open wide as he gawked at the same tree.

"What is so special about this tree?" I asked. Sometimes I completely forgot that Phillip and Whizzy had this amazing adventure through Mistasia without me. That they experienced fighting dragons in Wolverine Forest, Mermaids on Lake Dragon and so much more when I was held captive by King Cragon's henchmen, Ethan Whizzenmog, in Cadieux Castle.

I was jealous for not getting to experience those same adventures and angry for being held prisoner against my will. Those emotions were long forgotten. Suddenly, they all came flooding back like it was yesterday. Really it had only been six months in our world, but here in Mistasia, it had been more than a dozen years. The difference between our time and that in Mistasia was starting to make it very difficult to keep track.

Whizzy replied to my question about why this tree was so special. "We were here once before. Phillip, Grace and I fought a couple of

Wolverines right there," Whizzy said with pride in his voice. Then he looked me dead in the eyes, "It is when I first used my power as a wizard." He beamed from big red ear to big red ear.

"Yeah, Whizzy was awesome!" Phillip responded and then the two gave each other a "high-five" and began to laugh.

I saw Grandpa turn back to watch the commotion. He grinned at me and then came toward us.

"It sounds like you boys have had some amazing adventures here in Mistasia." He patted Whizzy on the shoulder. "We will have plenty of time to tell stories once I have finalized our travel arrangements." He explained while giving me a wily glance.

"Travel arrangements?" Whizzy questioned. "Aren't we walking?"

"Just wait right here, Whizzy, my boy. Your sister and I will be right back."

Grandpa Whizzenmog and I didn't have to go far. We walked only a few feet as Phillip, Whizzy and Aevion stood behind us watching curiously. The crafty gray fox stared at The Friendless Tree.

"What are you thinking?" I asked.

"I'm thinking what would be the best mode of transportation across Lake Dragon," Grandpa responded with a gleam in his eyes. "This tree will do nicely."

"Really?" I was not fully certain that my grandpa hadn't experienced some sort of brain freeze when he was trapped in the icy river. "'Cuz that looks an awful lot like a tree," I finished my thought aloud.

Grandpa Whizzenmog laughed like I had just told the funniest joke he had ever heard...and I was pretty sure what I had just said wasn't funny at all.

"Rachel, my dear...you are absolutely right. However, you need to open your eyes. This is much more than a tree in Mistasia. The powers that you and your brother possess are a gift almost greater than life itself. When you open your mind to the possibilities, your eyes will show you what may truly be done with those powers." He spoke like a schoolteacher, telling all his most treasured secrets. "Watch and I will show you."

Holding his wand in his right hand, the elderly fox mustered up his strength. He gripped the wand tightly and then slashed at The Friendless Tree's trunk. The wand sliced past the bottom of the tree, yet nothing appeared to happen. Grandpa stood up straight and paused for a moment.

I turned back to my brother giving him a look of bewilderment. He shrugged his shoulders in response. Neither of us understood what was about to happen next. Suddenly, Phillip's red eyes bulged out even further than normal. When I turned back around, Grandpa was pushing the tall tree to the ground. It creaked and snapped before falling and sending the fresh powdery snow into the air.

Phillip, Whizzy, Aevion and I watched in utter amazement as Grandpa Whizzenmog used his magical powers to transform the tree into a wooden ship. The trunk was hollowed out for us to sit in, branches turned into sled rails, and the leaves bonded together to form a large green sail.

"Please, step inside," The tall gray fox proudly proclaimed.

"This is amazing," I announced while climbing aboard.

"Cool," Phillip said as he hopped up.

"You have to teach me how to do that, Grandpa," Whizzy said while Phillip helped him into the ship.

Once Aevion was on board and huddled in the corner Grandpa turned to me and said, "Rachel. This is where you come in. I need you to summon the wind to direct us toward Cadieux Castle."

"Okay." I stood at the edge of the wooden ship and closed my eyes. In my mind I repeated the words "**steady winds**." Slowly, gusts of wind blew through my fur. My ears bent backwards with each passing gust. The winds increased and before long its strength did too. Within just a few minutes I felt the ship beneath me move. The shift startled me, causing me to open my eyes and the winds died.

"What happened?" Whizzy yelled to me from the other end of the ship.

"Don't worry, Rachel. Focus. Just relax and let your mind work," the gray fox instructed.

I again closed my eyes and began to speak the same words in my mind, "**steady winds.**" Once again I felt the stiff cold breeze against my furry face and the ship began to slide across the snow. I kept my eyes closed tightly this time for fear of losing focus again. The wind rushed quickly now, forcing the wooden ship to glide faster and faster in the snow.

"That's it, Rachel. You've done it!" Grandpa Whizzenmog proudly called out over the wind.

I could feel the surge of adrenaline moving through my body. It was great. I was controlling the wind, forcing it against the green-leaf sail and pushing us toward Cadieux Castle much quicker than we ever could have traveled on foot.

"Open your eyes, my dear," the calming voice of my grandpa called to me.

I exhaled slowly and peeked out of my left eye. The ship continued to race across the frozen, snow-covered Lake Dragon. A smile burst across my foxy face while I opened my right eye.

"This is awesome!" I squealed in excitement, which must have been really loud, because when I saw Phillip, he was giving me a strange look like I had just grown a second head...it was sort of embarrassing.

The next hour we continued across Lake Dragon and into the realm of Cadieux Castle

The sun had completely disappeared behind the massive dark winter clouds in the usually beautiful Mistasian sky over Cadieux Castle, which was now peeking up in the distance.

Phillip and Whizzy slept while snoring all huddled together. Phillip was spooning Whizzy...I so wished I had brought my phone to get a picture of that. Besides the fact they were animals, I would so be able to use that as blackmail when we got back to school. Aevion was still cowering in the corner of the ship. I sat next to Grandpa Whizzenmog as he steered the wooden ship using a branch from The Friendless

Tree that was attached to a large flat stick hanging off the back of the ship. He moved it from left to right, causing the ship to change direction and avoid trees, rocks or large chunks of ice sticking up from the ground.

The emerald bracelet on his wrist wasn't glowing as brightly as it had before. It was almost black now.

"Where did you get that emerald?" I finally mustered up the courage to ask.

Grandpa looked at me for a moment and then quickly focused his eyes on the world in front of the ship.

"It was a gift from King Steven," He solemnly replied, but offered no further explanation.

"Who was he?" I asked, hoping to find out more information about the emerald.

The gray fox suddenly seemed upset, angered by my question. He shook his head and exhaled deeply.

I wasn't sure what to say.

Then the gray fox answered. "He was Princess Merran's father. King Steven Cadieux was the ruler of Mistasia, and I was his wizard guardian."

"Merran's father?" I responded.

"Yes. What do you know about the princess's parents?" Grandpa questioned me.

"I don't know very much, just that they went on a trip and never returned. That was how Cragon became King," I announced. A light went off in my head, "King Cragon had his own brother killed?"

"He was a part of the plot against King Steven, but he was not the only one," My grandpa began to explain. Then his bright blue eyes grew wide and shock took over his face.

I stood up to see what he was afraid of. "What's wrong?" I yelled over the rushing wind.

"Stop the winds, my dear, or our journey may end quicker than expected," he demanded.

MAGICAL SHIELD

9

My golden-colored furry arms were stretched out in front of me as I chanted, "Cease momentum!"

"Focus on the winds, Rachel, not the ship!" Grandpa Whizzenmog yelled.

My arms fell to my sides. I stared at my paws, hoping for them to show me which spell to use. My mind was racing, and I couldn't think straight, just like at school when I took my math test. I struggled to focus my mind...it was spinning around a million miles an hour. I could feel the lack air in my chest, like I had forgotten to breathe.

I heard the elder fox shout, "Rachel, hurry!"

Phillip and Whizzy had awakened now.

"What's going on?" Whizzy yelled.

"Look at those snow drifts," Phillip said in amazement.

I could see them...huge piles of snow reaching into the sky, like tentacles on an octopus. There was no way the snow should have been piled up like that...it looked like the snow was climbing a wall, but there wasn't anything there.

"What is that?" Phillip croaked.

"What's going on here?" Whizzy squealed again in a high-pitched voice.

"Rachel, now!" Grandpa yelled.

"STOP!" I screamed in frustration. The wind ceased immediately and the previously taut leafy sail drooped down, but the ship was still moving rapidly.

We approached the snowy tentacles too quickly.

Grandpa Whizzenmog pulled hard on his steering branch. He grunted as the paddle cut into the snow.

A white spray made of powdery snow gushed from behind us as the paddle sliced into it.

I dashed to help and grabbed hold of the steering branch with my grandpa.

"Hold on!" The struggling fox growled as the ship turned sideways.

The ship hit a rock, which broke one of the sled rails away, causing us to pitch to the side. Snow cascaded over the side and knocked me down. The steering branch snapped in half. Grandpa stumbled and fell on top of me. Our wooden ship began to widely swing around.

"Cease Momentum!" I shouted in an attempt to stop the ship from crashing into whatever was out there, but it was too late.

Crash!

When I woke up, I was frightened to see Aevion's ghoulish vampire bat face hovering over me.

"Rachel, are you okay?" He whimpered.

"Ahh!" I screamed in his face, causing him to screech back at me and then run away. "Aevion, wait! I'm sorry," I called out to him. A sharp pain shot down my right leg, when I tried to stand up. There was blood in the snow where my furry fox leg stretched out in front of me. A large splinter from our wooden ship was sticking in my thigh. It hurt really badly.

"Rachel!" Phillip's voice rang out. He hopped to my side and hugged me tightly.

I winced in pain.

"You're alive," he happily declared.

"Yes, Phillip. Aevion too," I replied. "Where is Whizzy and Grandpa?" I asked in panic.

Phillip tried to help me up when he saw the splinter in my thigh.

"Rachel, you're hurt," he said while looking me in the eyes. Without hesitation, he lifted me off my feet and into his arms.

"Phillip, don't. What are you doing? Put me down!" I shouted.

"What is going on?" Whizzy barked while lying on his backside.

Phillip walked us over to my brother, who laid sprawled out on his back in the snow staring into the sky.

"Can you ask a different question?" I snarled.

"Not until someone answers my first question!" He snapped back. Whizzy sat up. Snow was stuck in his reddish-orange fur.

"A magical shield, Whizzy," Grandpa Whizzenmog answered in a breathless tone. He struggled to stand and was obviously having trouble breathing. His paw was against his chest.

"Grandpa," I cried while struggling to break free from Phillip's grasp. I managed to get down, but a stabbing pain in my leg knocked me to the ground.

"Rachel, you are injured?" Grandpa asked with remorse.

"Don't worry about me," I replied as I hobbled over to him.

Whizzy ran to help me walk the exhausted gray fox to a large piece of the wooden ship remaining in the snow. He sat down and took a deep breath. I sat beside him.

"I'm sorry, my dear," Grandpa Whizzenmog replied, sounding sad.

"I'll be fine."

"Let me help you," he said and removed the emerald bracelet from his wrist and

wrapped it around my thigh. Grandpa grabbed
the splinter sticking out of my fur and said,
"This will only hurt for a moment."

Grandpa yanked the wooden splinter
from my thigh.

I screamed in pain, but quickly covered
my mouth with my paws. Tears streamed from
my eyes. It was the worst pain I could remember
in my entire life. It made getting a shot at the
doctor's, feel more like a pinch.

Phillip, Whizzy and I watched as the
emerald bracelet began to glow again. It
suddenly was alive with bright lights inside,
swirling and dancing around. My leg began to
glow as well. A warm sensation entered my
entire leg, like when it falls asleep and I get that
prickliness. I started to laugh...it felt really weird.
When it was over, my leg was healed.

Grandpa smiled at us. He took the
emerald bracelet back and wrapped it around
his wrist once again. The color faded back to
black.

"That emerald is wicked," Whizzy replied.

He isn't the most intelligent 15-year-old boy in the world...but he is the only brother I have.

I couldn't stop staring at the spot where the splinter had been. I rubbed my paw across it. It was as if the wound never existed.

"How was that possible?" I blurted out.

Everyone stopped and turned to gawk at me.

"Some things cannot be explained, my dear," Grandpa responded. "This emerald...this last emerald of Mistasia is a very powerful gem. It can perform miraculous feats...or destructive acts, if it falls into the wrong hands."

"Then let's make sure King Cragon doesn't know about it," Phillip replied.

I saw Grandpa glance at Phillip, but say nothing. He moved away from us and reached out like he was feeling for something in the air.

I hobbled next to him. My leg may have healed, but it was extremely sore.

"King Cragon already knows about the emerald doesn't he," I whispered to the tall gray fox.

He stopped his hands for a second...then continued without answering.

"I take that as a 'yes'," I replied now, realizing that we had another problem. We were trying to get into Cadieux Castle to save our friends, yet bringing the one thing that the evil king wanted most...the last emerald. With it, he would be even more powerful.

"What is going on?" Whizzy asked for the fourth time.

"I'm gonna punch you in the nose," I growled.

"Well that isn't very lady-like," Whizzy responded in a silly voice.

I balled my paw in a fist and reached back to slug him, when Grandpa spoke.

"This is a very powerful dark magic," he muttered.

"Excuse me," I asked with my fist still ready to fly.

I saw Whizzy take two steps backward from the corner of my eye.

Grandpa closed his eyes and placed his paw against an invisible object. He began to mumble under his breath. I couldn't understand what he said. It sounded like he was speaking in another language.

His paws started to glow. The light stretched out into the air. As it moved outward, shapes began to appear. Before our eyes, a wall emerged. It was made from a series of tangled vines and branches that covered the entire castle and some of the surrounding village, like a protective bubble.

"Well...now I know what happened," Whizzy said and immediately looked at me. "So I'm done. Promise." He said with his hands up, like he surrendered.

I growled at him and put my fist down.

"How do we get inside?" Phillip asked. "Can we use the emerald?" He added.

"No. I am afraid not. The emerald does have extraordinary powers, but it also has its limitations. The gemstone stores energy from everything around it. It absorbs from this world...but once it has been used, it will take some time to restore the emerald's power,"

Grandpa said while examining the wall in front of him.

"So what do we do?" Whizzy said finally, asking a different question.

"It's about time," I teased him.

"Find a weakness," Grandpa responded.

SAVING GRACE

10

It grew very dark outside as angry clouds now hung over Cadieux Castle. A few lit windows in the distance peeked through the void, like eyes watching our every movement.

I felt the hair on my neck stand on end as I thought about King Cragon plotting against us as he looked through those same windows. He would most definitely do his worst.

Grandpa studied the magical shield that kept us from entering Cadieux Village. If he was frustrated, I couldn't tell...he seemed so calm. I would have been a mess, and my brother would be throwing a temper-tantrum by now.

"Is there anything I can do?" I offered my assistance to our leader.

"I'm open to any and all suggestions, my dear," He somberly responded.

"Couldn't we try cutting it open?" I asked, trying not to sound too obvious.

"Watch," Grandpa slashed at the tangled mess with his wand the same way he did when he cut down The Friendless Tree only a few hours earlier. Nothing happened. "It is dark magic and very strong."

"Any other suggestions, Sis," Whizzy teased.

"Well, what is your idea, brainiac?" I challenged.

"Dig underneath," He smartly replied.

"That won't work!" I shouted. "Will it?" I whispered to Grandpa so Whizzy wouldn't hear.

The gray fox shrugged his shoulders.

Whizzy used his magic to dig a hole under the magic shield, but with each inch of snow he removed the shield stretched to cover it back up.

"See," I scoffed. "Told you it wouldn't work."

"What about fire?" Phillip added.

Whizzy, Grandpa and I glanced at each other. No one seemed to know what would happen.

Grandpa Whizzenmog asked us to stand back. He shot a large fireball directly at the magic shield. It quickly caught fire. The vines and branches were burning. With each passing second, the wall shriveled up and crashed to the snow. Grandpa blew out the flames with a blast of cold air. Left behind was a hole torched in the sorcerer's magical shield.

"Phillip, you were correct," The elder gray fox spoke in amazement. "And you're not even a wizard. How about that?"

Phillip smiled.

We all entered Cadieux Village through the small hole. Running through the snowy village, we dashed to the edge of the castle grounds.

As we approached, I began to have a bad feeling. It had been so easy to get to the castle. Other than the dragons at Red River, we hadn't had to fight anyone. I quickly looked for Phillip.

One of his abilities here in Mistasia is clairvoyance, or visions that appeared to him when he was dreaming...but he hadn't slept since we arrived.

Phillip and I ran to the edge of the field leading to the castle. There, we stopped and stood side by side. Whizzy was on the other side of Phillip, and Grandpa was beside me. Aevion was hiding behind Phillip.

"I have a very bad feeling we are walking into a trap," Phillip said to me.

"You, too?" I replied.

He reached out and grabbed my paw. I felt a tingle in my arm. Then my hand felt damp. I pulled my paw away.

"Sorry, sometimes I forget I'm an amphibian," Phillip apologized.

"It's okay," I replied. I felt warmth in my cheeks. Hopefully, Phillip couldn't tell; I was probably blushing.

"Hey, love birds...we've got company," Whizzy pointed at the sky above the castle.

"I don't see anything," I said.

"Neither can I," My brother replied with his eyes closed. "But I can hear their wings."

I closed my eyes. My fox ears quickly picked up a flapping sound in the distance. "Vampire bats."

"I hear them too, Whizzy." Grandpa chimed in.

In the distance, a light began bobbing in the darkness. It moved briskly toward us and then stopped. The light grew brighter by the second until we could see the image of a man standing in the snow between the castle and us.

"LaCroiux," Grandpa said empathically.

"Rainer Whizzenmog," Sorcerer Pierre LaCroiux sneered. "After all these years you have finally returned. Unfortunately, it is far too late."

"We will see," Grandpa responded.

"No, Rainer...I will show you."

The grounds lit up as if the sun had exploded from behind the gloomy storm clouds, yet the dark gray sky still remained. That made it even more frightening.

Sorcerer LaCroiux stood alone in the snow, but in the distance was a more menacing force. Three great trolls stood along the castle walls, Vella and Goren circled the skies above with nearly a dozen more vampire bats, and slowly marching to the sorcerer's side were nearly two-dozen wolverines.

"Oh, crap," Whizzy blurted out.

"I think I already did," Phillip whined.

"Welcome back to Mistasia," Sorcerer LaCroiux blasted. "King Cragon sends his regards." The smug white-bearded villain replied. "ATTACK!"

The Wolverine Army roared toward us, while the vampire bats swooped in from above.

"We need to split up," Grandpa calmly spoke. "Rachel and Whizzy you must find your friend, Grace. Phillip will come with me. Aevion...hide," He demanded.

I watched as the gray fox and green frog ran toward the Wolverine Army.

"This is insane," Whizzy barked as he grabbed my hand and ran away.

"No stop, Whizzy! We can't leave Phillip and Grandpa behind," I cried as my brother dragged me through the snow.

"We have to find Grace!" he yelled at me.

"She's that way," I pointed at the castle.

"We can get into the castle from her house, remember!" Whizzy said, referring to the underground passage we had used in the past.

Goren and Vella crashed down beside us and screeched. I flicked my wand at Vella hitting her with a stunning charm. She was tossed backwards. Goren became very angry and swatted at me. Whizzy punched him with a spell, spinning the vampire bat around before he fell into the snow, ugly face first.

My brother and I ran as fast as we could to Grace Tallon's quaint home in Cadieux Village, but before we could reach it, two more vampire bats snatched us off the ground and circled back to the castle. As we flew by, I saw Phillip jumping around like crazy. He bounced up and down landing on one wolverine and then crashing into another. Each angry hairy beast fell to the ground in pain. Grandpa cut a path to the castle by blasting his foes with different spells. A fury of various colors exploded from his wand. It resembled a firework show.

A pit grew in my stomach as we approached the castle. We couldn't let these vampire bats take us there. Nothing good could possibly come of arriving at Cadieux Castle before our grandpa.

I still gripped my wand in my paw. To my left I could see Whizzy. I began to wiggle. Suddenly, the vampire bat's grip on me loosened, and I began to fall. I turned to face the sky and shot at each vampire bat, hitting one in the face. The second shot slammed into the wing of Whizzy's captor. The vampire bat squealed and dropped my brother.

We landed only a few feet from each other. My leg was throbbing now where the wooden splinter had been. I could barely stand up, and then my brother grabbed me and pulled me up out of the snow.

"We gotta go," he screamed.

A massive tree trunk crashed into the snow where I had just been. As I followed the length of the big wooden object, I found a hideously large troll at the other end. It had a small head with beady eyes and ears that stuck out like targets on either side. His face was covered in warts and thick hairs just stuck out in random places. He even had one on the tip of his nose.

"Kids," Grandpa called as we had somehow met up with him and Phillip in the middle of this battle. "Are you all right?" He questioned while fighting two wolverines and a vampire bat at the same time.

"No," I began when Whizzy interrupted.

"There!" He shouted.

I looked at the spot where he was pointing atop a tower on Cadieux Castle. There, Grace Tallon stood frozen in motion as a stone statue.

"We need her," Grandpa urged us to complete our task. "You must save her!"

Whizzy and I dashed off immediately leaving Phillip and Grandpa Whizzenmog to battle King Cragon's Army.

FLIGHT OF THE FOX

11

I followed directly behind my brother as he whisked through the battlefield. He blazed a trail in front of us with his wand.

I struggled to keep pace as my leg felt like someone was stabbing me every time I placed my right paw down. It would send a shockwave up my thigh, through my back and into my brain. I thought the emerald had healed me...it only masked the injury. Maybe that was what my grandpa was trying to do.

Some type of sorcery from Pierre LaCroiux still brightly lighted the field surrounding Cadieux Castle. I saw a shadowy figure peering from one of the lit windows of the castle...it must be King Cragon. He is too cowardly to actually fight his own battles, yet he found the time to watch them from a safe distance.

It was so loud. The roar of wolverines, the screeching of vampire bats, then an explosion of magic slammed into my highly tuned fox ears. It sounded like a cross between the Fourth of July celebration and the Greenville Zoo.

Whizzy and I had almost reached the castle when we ran into a very large problem...literally.

The smelly foot of another grotesque troll crashed down in front of Whizzy just as he reached for the handle on the castle's front door. Whizzy's face planted into the anklebone of the troll, and pin-balled to the ground. I slid to a stop, only inches away.

A large droplet of goober splashed into the snow at my feet. I gulped and then looked up to see the absolutely stomach- turning face of our latest enemy.

"AHHHHH!" I screamed like a little girl.

"ARRRGGGG!" the troll screamed back.

I think I actually frightened him too. Unfortunately, this troll must have had a winter cold, because greenish-yellow snot oozed from his nostrils. The troll reached out to grab me with its chunky dirty fingers.

I stumbled backwards and fell. I was trapped.

"Whizzy!" I screamed.

My brother cast a spell to control the troll's wooden club. Whizzy swatted the troll in its thick melon-head repeatedly, while shouting, "Leave my sister alone. You ugly...smelly...snot-nosed...turd!"

After somewhere around 15 swats in the head, the troll finally stumbled. Its eyes rolled back in its head and then it fell backwards into the castle door, smashing it open.

I had taken one step toward the open door when I felt two sharp claws grab my waist and yank me off the ground. It was Vella. She had found us and couldn't be happy with me for zapping her with a spell earlier. Whizzy was gone. I couldn't see him as Vella sped skyward into the dark gray clouds.

I could instantly feel the chill of the air increase around me. Frost formed on my whiskers and snout. Once we reached the storm clouds, Vella stopped. I thought I was dead. The

sudden thought of her dropping me from this
height sickened me.

"Rachel Whizzenmog," Vella's voice
sounded different. "Do you know where my son
is?" She questioned sadly.

"Yes." I could see in her eyes that Vella
was somehow different...frightened. "He has been
with us the whole time."

"Is he here now?"

"Yes. He is hiding until the battle is over."
I suddenly realized that when I hit her with a
spell earlier I must have broken the hold that
Sorcerer LaCroiux had over her.

"Will you take me to him?" Vella asked
humbly.

"Of course, Vella, but I need your help
first." This was my chance. She could fly me to
the tower where Grace Tallon was kept.

Vella gave her consent, and I told her my
plan. Together we flew through the clouds and
burst out directly above the castle. I pointed to
where Grace was being held and she took me
there.

We landed safely atop the tower. There Grace Tallon stood, eerily frozen in stone. I wasted little time, and began firing spells to free her. Nothing worked...I couldn't break the magical secret that turned her into stone.

"I can't free her," I said, disappointed in myself.

A rustling of footsteps sounded just on the other side of the door leading out to where we stood atop the tower.

"Hide," I shouted to Vella who jumped into the sky leaving me alone. I searched for a place to hide, but it was a wide-open tower with nothing to hide behind.

The door handle jiggled, but the door was locked. I sighed in relief, just before it exploded. Splinters and chunks of wood flew toward me.

"Protectum," I whispered trying not to draw attention to myself. An invisible shield formed, blocking me from the wooden pieces.

A small figure entered the tower. It was Whizzy. I had never been so excited to see my brother in my whole life.

"Whizzy!" I shouted.

"Rachel!" He hugged me.

"You're hugging me," I said in amazement.

"Yeah, sorry. Got carried away," He replied, quickly letting me go.

"Whizzy, I tried to free Grace, but nothing I tried worked."

My brother just ignored me and began blasting Grace's statuesque figure with an array of magical charms and spells.

After a few moments of frustration, Whizzy threw his wand onto the stone ground.

"As I was saying, I tried to free her before you got here and nothing worked. What are we gonna do, Whizzy?" I was out of ideas.

My brother had developed a crush on Grace. She was very special to him. He stood as close as he could, resting his forehead against hers.

"I watched him do this to her, Rachel. I couldn't help her. It was like I was that helpless little kid back in Greenville," Whizzy tried to hold back his emotions. He placed his paw on her cheek. "Look at how scared she is."

"Whizzy," I wanted to tell him it would be okay. I wanted to tell him that Grace would be fine. I also wanted to tell him that we were running out of time...but I couldn't say anything.

"I'm sorry," Whizzy softly spoke. Then, my brother moved in and placed his lips on Grace's cheek giving her statue a kiss.

My eyes nearly popped out of my head. "Whizzy," I muttered to myself in shock. The only thing I had ever seen my brother kiss was his pillow. I could feel the cold winter air rushing into my mouth as it flopped wide open.

Whizzy stepped back. Grace Tallon's face began to shimmer. A glow moved down her body until it completely covered her. The shimmering light grew brighter and more intense, but I couldn't stop staring. The stone seemed to melt away. All of a sudden, standing before us was Grace Tallon, the Elven warrior, protector of Princess Merran Cadieux, and our friend...and she was free!

Grace began to fall to the ground. Whizzy caught her.

"Grace," he called to her in a panic.

She smiled at him, "Whizzy, you came back for me," she replied in a weak voice.

"Yes," he replied with a sniffle. "I'm so sorry, Grace."

The Elven warrior lifted her head and looked to the edge of the castle tower. "What is that noise?"

DISAPPEARING ACT
12

Grace looked awful. Her usually pretty white hair was dirty and grimy. Her cheeks were dry and cracked and eyes bloodshot.

"Can you stand up?" I asked her, wondering if she would have enough strength to escape with us.

Struggling to her feet, the willful Elven warrior now stood beside her rescuer, Whizzy.

"Thank you, Whizzy," Grace spoke in a humble tone. Then she walked to the edge of the castle tower to witness the battle below.

Phillip and Grandpa Whizzenmog continued to fight off King Cragon's Wolverine Army. The vampire bats had disappeared and the trolls had been defeated.

"We must aid them," Grace commanded.

I knew it wouldn't be long before she returned to normal. It was just her nature to be a leader...and so she led us down the staircase, through the castle halls and out through the broken front door where the troll Whizzy had knocked out still lay unconscious. The commotion in the field around the castle was exciting and frightening at the same time.

We sprinted across the open field to help Phillip and Grandpa Whizzenmog ward off the ferocious wolverines.

"Phillip, behind you!" I yelled to warn him as a wolverine snuck up to grab him. He turned around and dodged the wolverine's attack.

I fired a spell directly into the hairy beast's chest causing it to fall to the snow.

"Thanks, Rachel," Phillip replied with a smile. "Grace!" He called out with joy.

"Great job, kids!" Grandpa Whizzenmog praised. He punched one wolverine in the face and then zapped another. "We need to retreat to the village!" He ordered. "I will afford you some time. Now, go!"

"What about Princess Merran?" Phillip reminded us that she too had been captured.

"We must regroup in order to save her," Grandpa gritted his teeth as he grappled with another beast. "Go!"

I grabbed Phillip by his webbed hand and began to run away from the castle. Whizzy and Grace followed. Grace Tallon quickly overtook us as she flashed passed.

Grandpa continued to keep our enemies at a distance. A green light crept from the tip of his wand, like a whip. He would fling it at any wolverine that approached, cracking the whip loudly.

We nearly reached the edge of the field when we realized the magical shield was still there. Whizzy pointed to where the opening had been burned earlier for us to enter and we ran toward it.

A loud crack of thunder rumbled behind us, causing all of us to stop immediately. Sorcerer LaCroiux had returned. He twisted his braided white beard with his left fingers.

The heinous Sorcerer LaCroiux and Grandpa Whizzenmog locked eyes. Neither spoke a word. LaCroiux just sneered.

"Grandpa, no!" I shouted. It was too late.

The evil sorcerer and wizard fox were locked in battle.

I found myself stuck in the snow completely unable to move as I watched our grandpa brawl with LaCroiux. My legs just didn't work. They felt like heavy cement pillars dug deep into the ground.

"You never should have returned," Sorcerer LaCroiux challenged while waving his hands over the snow stirring it into a blizzard. He disappeared behind the whitewash.

Grandpa split the snowy wall by using his wand as a sword. The slick gray fox maneuvered through the gap sliding on his left side and shot a spell directly at his foe.

LaCroiux deflected the wizard's attempt. "Rainer, you must be rusty. I expected better than that," he mocked before lashing out and knocking Grandpa Whizzenmog down with a wave of snow.

The gray fox jumped back to his feet and dodged two move waves of snow by somersaulting backwards. He retaliated, zapping LaCroiux with a paralyzing spell.

The elderly sorcerer fell to his knees and shouted in disgust, "You are weak." Then he raised his arms slowly and all the snow around him ascended. "I will show you strength!" He boasted and then flung his arms at his target, pushing all the snow at him. It was too much for the nimble fox to avoid. Grandpa was overtaken by the avalanche and covered in thick, cold snow.

I gasped as my grandpa disappeared from view.

"No!" Whizzy barked from behind me.

It was as though my legs had been released from the heavy weight I felt before and now I was running to help my grandpa. Whizzy

followed behind me. I thought I heard Grace call
to us, but I didn't care...I was going to help him.
Phillip joined us. Grace must have decided to as
well because soon she ran up beside me. The four
of us approached when Sorcerer LaCroiux swept
in front of us riding a wave of snow.

"Going somewhere?" He bellowed.

"Get out of the way!" Whizzy yelled while
pointing his crooked wand at LaCroiux.

The sorcerer immediately responded by
knocking my brother down with a blast of wind.

I kept moving toward Grandpa.

Grace pulled an arrow from her backpack
and swiftly fired, but the evil sorcerer deflected
it with ease and fought back, sweeping her aside
with the wave of his hand.

"Phillip!" I called out. "Give me time!"

"I'm on it," he replied.

But before Phillip could even attempt to
battle Sorcerer LaCroiux, I felt a strange
sensation against my fur. The world seemed to
be slowing down. Sounds stretched in my ears. It
was like I fell down a tunnel. Snowflakes hung
motionless in the air before me.

Then a wall of orange light began to move across the field. I watched it engulf Whizzy. When it passed by, my brother was gone. Then it swallowed Phillip and Grace. Next, the orange light attacked me. I was only a few feet away from where Grandpa Whizzenmog was buried alive in the snow when the orange light blinded me.

Then, everything went completely black!

WORKING FOR THE WICKED MONSTER
13

"Grandpa!" I screamed when I felt my body hit the ground. Immediately, something was very different about Mistasia. It was unexpectedly warm. The chill removed from my fur-covered body and was replaced with dampness, like when I just leave the shower. My chest was sore from my heart racing so quickly. I placed my paw against it and opened my eyes.

"No. No, no, NO!" Panic began to set in. This wasn't Mistasia. At least not the one we knew. **What happened? Where did LaCroiux send us?**

I picked myself up and found I was standing in thick blades of dark green grass that reached over my head. They had to be nearly eight feet tall. There was no snow, only dirt in my paws.

Noises echoed all around me, as it grew harder to breath, but not from the lack of oxygen, just fear.

Where are we? I thought.

"Rachel," Phillip's voice sounded off in my head.

I spun around to find him, but could see nothing but green grass, standing like trees, surrounding me.

"Phillip!" I called out, but it was no use. The blades of grass blocked my voice from escaping.

"Rachel, where are you?" Phillip asked me again using his ability of telepathy. He and Grace shared that power here in Mistasia. That meant that wherever we were was at least still Mistasia.

I tried to calm myself down. There was so much noise in my head between Phillip and my own heart pounding. I took a slow deep breath and closed my eyes.

Phillip, I am here! I thought, hoping to be able to speak to him. He could hear my thoughts, so I would be able to contact him.

"Rachel," Phillip said aloud as he grabbed my arm.

"Ahhh!" I screamed and then punched him in the face just below his big red eye.

The tall frog stumbled and fell backward, toppling over some blades of grass. Behind him was a path in the dense jungle that he had used to find me.

"Phillip, I'm so sorry." I leaned in and gave him a kiss on the cheek where I had socked him. It was really red...I couldn't tell if it was because I punched him or he was embarrassed to be hit by a girl. After helping him back to his webbed feet, we rejoined Grace and Whizzy.

"Where are we, Grace?" Whizzy demanded to know.

She mumbled sometime in elfish that sounded a lot like swearing, and then checked her backpack for weapons.

"Grace, where are we?" I asked, hoping she would give me some information, if she wouldn't answer my brother.

Again she continued to ignore us and shuffled through her collection of arrows. Finally, she blurted out, "Twenty-two."

"Great, now that you have counted your arrows, can you tell us where we are in Mistasia?" Whizzy barked.

"We have been banished to The Colossal Lands," Grace looked shaken and afraid.

"Okay, I get that. Really big grass. Big...colossal," Whizzy reasoned while waving his arms in the air. "Why are all the names here so cheesy?" He turned to Phillip and me for answers.

His best friend shrugged his shoulders.

I did what I have done for most of my life, ignored the fact he said anything at all and moved on.

"Grace, how do we get back to Cadieux Castle?" I asked while placing my paw on her shoulder.

She shrugged it off and stood up. "That is impossible, Rachel the Fox. We are a great distance from Cadieux Castle. It would take a great deal of time to travel back." Grace aggressively shoved her arrows back into her pack.

"Why is there no snow?" Phillip added.

I shot Phillip a dirty look for asking such a stupid question.

"This land does not experience winter like we do. It is perpetually warm in the Colossal Lands." Grace replied as she slung her pack onto her back.

Phillip, Whizzy and I gave each other a nervous look. We had never seen Grace so distraught before. She had fought wolverines, vampire bats, trolls and even sorcerers so bravely, but now she was as frightened as Phillip on the first day of school.

The Elven warrior readied her bow and arrow, "Now we must find a way to stay alive."

Grace had my brother and I dig a trench using magic. Meanwhile, Grace and Phillip built weapons to protect us at each end of the trench. She said it would allow us to survive the night. That sounded like a great idea to me.

I walked past Phillip as he assembled a crude looking weapon. "What are you making?" I asked.

"Grace showed me how to build a slingshot out of blades of grass and roots from the ground. She is gathering pebbles and stuff for us to use to defend ourselves."

"From what exactly? Because she hasn't really explained of what we should be so afraid." I was starting to become upset that Grace was leaving us in the dark about The Colossal Lands and its dangers. "Maybe she's working for LaCroiux too," I added.

Phillip's eyes grew wide.

Then, I heard rustling behind me. Grace ran at me just as I turned around, pulled her sword on me and pinned me against the wall.

She held the sword at my face and yelled, "I would never side with that heartless, wicked monster! He has taken everything from us. EVERYTHING!" She spit those words in my face, like a fire-breathing dragon.

"Grace, I...I didn't. You wouldn't," I stammered as the blade of her sword shined in my eye.

"Grace, let her go," Whizzy commanded. He pointed his wand at the back of her head. "Don't make me do it, Grace." His voice was now much softer.

"We need to stick together," Phillip croaked. "This is exactly what Cragon and LaCroiux want...us fighting each other."

Grace continued to stare me down. She had so much hatred in her once beautiful eyes. Now they seemed dark and dangerous.

"Grace, I'm sorry," I cried. It was a simple gesture, but I truly meant it.

Suddenly, the elf changed, like a light switch had been turned on, and her eyes instantly flashed back to their original beauty. She released her strong grip on my fur, and pulled the sword back to her side. Grace slowly walked away. Her rage was now shame.

"Forgive me," she pleaded and then ran away into the grass beyond our safety trench.

I slid down the dirt wall where she had pinned me and sat on the ground. I began to cry.

"Rachel, are you okay?" Phillip asked as he reached out in an attempt to console me.

"Why did I say that? I knew she couldn't be a traitor." I continued to cry.

Whizzy shook his head in disappointment, and then went out after Grace.

I was exhausted. Phillip sat down beside me and wrapped his arms around me. His chest pressed up against my ear. It wasn't long before the steady beating of his heart put me to sleep.

My sleep was restless. Phillip told me that I thrashed around like I was still fighting in the battle. He said that I kept calling out for my grandpa. I don't remember much from my dreams; however, Grandpa Whizzenmog being buried in the snow was one of them.

I was startled awake by the vivid image of Grandpa falling beneath the snow. His dirty gray paw being the last thing I saw. When I awoke, I was still crying and Phillip was still with me.

He looked concerned.

"Phillip," I gasped while trying to catch my breath. It felt like I had just run a hundred miles.

He smiled back at me and then rubbed his webbed hand across my furry cheek to wipe away the tears.

My head throbbed between my eyes. It made my vision blurry. I searched around the trench attempting to focus my sight. It was very bare, mostly dirt with a few roots and a pile of grass and rocks next to Phillip where he had been building a slingshot for Grace.

Grace? I thought.

Phillip's expression changed. He looked concerned.

I again searched the trench for Grace and my brother before asking the question.

"Phillip, where is my brother?"

SPIKY GREEN BLOB
14

"Where is Whizzy, Phillip?" I screamed at him.

"He is with Grace, Rachel. Relax. Please!" He pleaded with me.

By now, I was pacing around the trench, huffing and crying. It wasn't very pretty.

Phillip tried to calm me down, but every time he tried I would just grow more worried...and frustrated.

"We have to go after them, Phillip!" I demanded.

"I'm not going out there?" Phillip gulped.

"What? Why not?" I demanded an answer. "He's your best friend!"

"Yes, and he has a bodyguard," the red-eyed tree frog reminded me.

I paced around for a few more seconds running scenarios of how to save Whizzy in my head.

I could make wings out of blades of grass and fly to him.

Maybe I can dig an underground tunnel below him and when I do he'll fall in the hole and I can drag his whinny butt back here.

"That's a good one," Phillip laughed.

"Are you reading my mind?" I barked.

"Or how about I use a slingshot and shoot Phillip's big head into the air as a signal so Whizzy can find his way back!"

"That's not funny," Phillip replied with a sour look on his green face.

"Stop reading my mind!" I growled in my head.

"Then talk to me, Rachel," Phillip pleaded still using his powers of telepathy. "I just want to help you."

"I know, Phillip. I'm sorry."

Just then Whizzy burst through the tall blades of grass and tumbled down the side of the trench. He rolled to a stop at Phillip's feet.

"Hey, Whizzy...where's Grace?" Phillip calmly asked.

Whizzy was breathing very heavily.

"You jerk!" I yelled; then I punched him in the shoulder.

He was terrified. I hadn't seen him that afraid since he hit Billy Lawton in the family jewels with a dodge ball in gym class back in the seventh grade.

"Run!" Whizzy shouted at me.

Funny...that was what he did in gym class too.

"Whizzy...wait what's wrong?" I pulled on his arm trying to keep him from running away.

"Let go?" He yelled and pointed his wand at me. He was crazed.

My heart began thumping. I couldn't believe it, but my own brother was about to zap me with his wand. I was frozen with shock. Whizzy's bright blue eyes grew wide, and his mouth opened exposing his sharp front teeth. His face was frightening. The tip of his wand began to light up. I started to yell. Phillip did too. Before I could react, a hot white flash zoomed past my head and exploded behind me. Phillip slammed into my brother knocking them and me to the ground.

"No, don't eat me!" Whizzy screamed.

"Eat you?" I said with a mouth full of dirt.

When I turned around, I squealed in terror.

Above us was the biggest, fattest, spiky green blob I had ever seen.

"What is that?" I yelled to Phillip.

"I don't know," he replied with no emotion, like he was in a trance.

We untangled ourselves from one another and ran. A ground-shaking thud rumbled through the dirt below us. I stumbled and fell. Phillip did too. Whizzy somehow managed to keep running.

"Whizzy! Don't leave me," I yelled.

My brother skidded to a stop and stared at the green blob with hundreds of sharp spikes like a porcupine, jutting out from its body inching toward us.

A rush of wind echoed in my ears. I rolled over onto my back to see Grace Tallon flying into the trench on a glider made from roots and flower petals.

"You have to be kidding me," I said in amazement.

The Elven warrior landed hard on her feet between the hairy blob monster and me. She drew her sword to protect me and put out her hand.

I grabbed hold and she pulled me up.

"Thanks," I said gratefully, now standing next to her and gripping my wand. "Grace...what is that?"

She replied, "That is Kiefer."

"Excuse me?"

"Kiefer the Caterpillar," Grace replied with a smile.

I stopped for the first time and looked up at the sloppy green blob moving slowly across the dirt. Upon its face were two enormous flat circles for eyes and nothing else. The long spikes sticking out all over its body were more like hairs. It was a scary image, like something out of a Halloween nightmare.

"A caterpillar?" I said hoping not to sound stupid. "We are running away from a bug."

"Well, this bug just might eat you for dinner," Grace frankly stated.

"But don't caterpillars only eat plants?" Phillip asked.

I waited for Grace to answer as Kiefer made his approach. She was taking too long to answer.

"Well?" I shouted.

"Maybe they do where you are from, but in Mistasia Kiefer eats whatever he wants to," Grace replied, now pointing the tip of her sword directly at Kiefer the Caterpillar, who had apparently slithered his way across the trench to dine on us. It was obvious he didn't avoid too many opportunities to snack.

"I don't wanna be that thing's dinner!" The thought of being swallowed up by this smelly, disgusting blob was not how I wanted things to end.

My wand began to glow.

"Rachel! Don't fire," Grace commanded. "Let me talk to him."

"Talk to him...he doesn't have a mouth!" Whizzy snarked.

The tension was heavy on us all. What if she couldn't talk Kiefer into not eating us like treats...would our magic be strong enough to stop something so big. He was like a house, a very green and disgusting house.

"Kiefer, in the name of Princess Merran Cadieux, I order you to not eat us," Grace strongly protested the monster's hungry impulses.

Kiefer lurched upward pushing its massive head skyward. Underneath the caterpillar's round head I could see its grotesque mouth with tiny teeth and hairs protruded out. It was sickening. I felt my stomach flop. Then the noises began. It was a strange array of sounds between a belly growl and a blender spinning at high speed.

We all took a few steps back.

Grace Tallon moved to protect us. She was only a few feet from the green beast when it bellowed again.

"Kiefer, you leave me no choice," she yelled.

"This is crazy," I overheard Whizzy whispered to Phillip.

Grace pulled her sword back, and widened her stance, preparing to strike the caterpillar in the abdomen.

Kiefer lunged at the Elven warrior and she stabbed him in the belly. The caterpillar let out a horrifying high-pitched squeal and flopped onto the dirt. Dust flew into the air blocking our sight.

Phillip grabbed my wrist. I reached out for Whizzy and found his paw. The three of us waited for the dust to settle. Grace's silhouette emerged in the dust cloud. It began to grow darker as the dirt settled back to the ground. Lying next to her was the giant caterpillar named Kiefer.

"She did it," Phillip called out in amazement.

Whizzy and Phillip gave each other a 'high-five' like they had just saved us.

I ran over to Grace and hugged her. "Thank you for coming back, Grace. I am so sorry."

"You were really awesome," Whizzy said to Grace.

Phillip and I began to laugh.

"What?" Whizzy said, giving us both a peculiar expression.

"Okay, so what's for dinner?" A nasally voice overtook the laughter.

We all looked up to see the large green caterpillar hovering directly above us. A string of spit hung from its mouth.

Phillip and I screamed. Whizzy made some strange noise...I don't know if it was him crying or wetting himself, but it was definitely not manly.

"Good job, Kiefer. You really got them," Grace smiled.

"Wha-u-sa?" Whizzy couldn't fully express himself. He had the dumbest look on his face as he tried to figure out what had just happened.

"This was a trick?" I blurted out.

"Kiefer is the one friend I know in The Colossal Lands," Grace explained. "I went out to find him. If anyone can help us escape unharmed, it's him."

"But he's a caterpillar," Phillip stated the obvious, sounding as confused as Whizzy appeared.

My brother still stared ignorantly at Kiefer, possibly hoping that he would magically disappear at any moment.

"Yes, and you're a frog. I like this game. Who's next?" Kiefer's large eyes now directed themselves to me. "And you're a fox." He continued.

"Yeah," I uncomfortably responded. This was quickly becoming one of the top 'strange moments' in my life...right up there with being dragged to another world by a talking snake.

"So he's not going to eat us?" Whizzy finally spoke looking for clarification on the current situation. His right eye began to twitch slightly.

I knew that wasn't a good sign. It meant that my brother was going to either explode in a rage or fart, and neither would be very pleasant right now.

"Oh, no!" Kiefer the Caterpillar responded. "Foxes give me bad gas."

"Oh, Whizzy this guy's right up your alley," I snidely remarked. "Wait a minute. When did you get a sense of humor?" I asked Grace.

She smiled. "I guess I've spent too much time with your brother," She jokingly responded.

"So when do we eat?" Kiefer asked again.

"If he is gonna protect us, we'd better feed him before he slims down. So where do we find a six-foot cricket?" Whizzy joked.

SORCERER'S NEW APPRENTICE

15

I haven't had too many normal moments in the past six months of my life, so a sixty-foot talking green caterpillar is just another oddity in what had become my irregular teenage life.

It had already been two days since we arrived back in Mistasia at the banks of Red River, which gave us eight remaining days to stop King Cragon, and return to Greenville before our parents came back home.

Grace and Whizzy had designed and built this amazing wheeled wagon using grass, roots, flowers, tree bark...basically anything found in the forest, and magic. We had fastened it to Kiefer allowing him to pull us along behind him. Grace stood on the great caterpillar's back weaving between the hairy spikes.

The trip was very slow moving. Kiefer wasn't necessarily the quickest moving bug. So we had to be patient, which wasn't working out well for me. The more time I had to sit and think the sadder and more distraught I became. I felt a weakness throughout my body.

All three of us had a weakness. They came from emotions, which I guess is pretty common at our age, but it had a different effect on each of us; Phillip's was confidence. In Greenville he was bullied and weak. He would let people put him down. Whizzy's was his temper. Being small all his life had made him angry and resentful. That turned into something almost uncontrollable lately. He could just explode at any given time. Mine had always been my lack of focus, just like in school. My parents always told me I was smart, but I just needed to study more. My grandpa had stressed the importance of keeping myself focused; it allowed me to gather my strength and increase my power as a witch.

I missed my grandpa so much. The image of his paw in the snow just kept replaying in my mind.

"Rachel?" Phillip sat down next to me and smiled.

I struggled to return a smile.

"Whizzy and I have been planning out an attack on the castle. Do you want to hear it?" Phillip eagerly explained.

An uncomfortable laugh escaped me. It was the only way I could keep from crying. "Phillip, not now."

"Oh...well, okay. Maybe later then," He got up and moved across the small-wheeled wagon to sit next to Whizzy.

Phillip leaned over and whispered something to my brother. Whizzy's face curled up in anger when he finished explaining that I didn't want to hear their plan.

"So you have a better idea, sis?" Whizzy challenged. "Are we too stupid?"

"Whizzy, not now."

My brother wondered why the girls at school never talked to him...this was why. He just doesn't understand them. Phillip wasn't much better, but at least he tried.

"Whizzy, I'm sorry, but I just can't handle that right now. I need to rest. We'll go over your plan after I wake up, okay?" I bargained with him, hoping to calm him down so I could rest.

He smiled, signaling he was pleased, so I immediately closed my eyes. I could feel the wagon rolling up and down over the uneven ground below. We swayed side to side slightly, but enough to make me feel uneasy. The horrid smell of sweaty gym socks and rotten milk hung in my snout. It rolled back to us from Kiefer. He was disgusting. I don't know how Grace could stand the smell from up there. I tried to relax, but every time I came close to falling asleep, something would wake me.

First, Phillip and Whizzy yelled when they watched a flying bug swallow another bug whole in mid flight. Next, we rocked so hard it tossed me up in the air, and I landed hard onto my stomach in the middle of the wooden wagon. Then, Whizzy belched. I don't think I even have to explain anymore, but those two knuckleheads giggled for like an hour afterward. Finally, Philllip and Whizzy fell asleep and it had grown quiet and peaceful enough that I drifted off myself, but not for long.

I awoke to absolute mayhem. An explosion had tossed the wagon sideways causing the three of us to fall out. I landed on Phillip, with his amphibian foot in my face. My heart nearly leapt from my chest.

Kiefer was thrashing around and making horrific high-pitched noises. Whizzy and I placed our paws over our sensitive fox ears. Phillip hopped up.

"Phillip!" I yelled and pulled him back down just as a bright red blast scorched the wheel off our wagon, sending it zipping across the field behind us, decapitating the tops of the tall blades of grass.

Phillip placed his hands around his neck realizing that could have been him. He gulped, "Thanks, Rachel."

We scrambled to find Grace in the commotion. When we found her, she pulled her sword out and sliced through the ropes holding the wagon to Kiefer. The giant caterpillar, once freed, began to roll to the left toward whatever attacked us.

Grace led us into the thick grass. She had stowed her sword, but now held her bow and arrow at the ready.

My brother and I joined her with our wands.

"Grace, do you mind?" Phillip pointed at her sword. "I'd like to use that."

Grace gladly handed over her sword, and ducked down as low as possible.

I joined her along the dirt-covered forest floor. "What do you see, Grace?" I asked knowing her Elven sight would allow her a much better view of the situation than mine.

Kiefer rolled back to the right as he took a direct hit to the side. The red-hot blast scorched his thick green skin, turning it black. The hairy spikes fell to the ground where he was burned. Our giant caterpillar friend roared and fired back, launching a series of spikes from his body like missiles into the air.

It went silent.

I took a deep breath. Had Kiefer struck our attacker? I attempted to stand up when Grace grabbed me.

"Wait," she spoke to me telepathically. "It is an elf," Grace spoke with astonishment.

"LaCroiux?" I whispered.

She shook her head. Grace squinted her eyes to see across the opening.

The broken wagon lay on its side smoldering in front of us, making it hard to see. Kiefer huffed in disgust. The black spot on his side began to ooze a white puss. In only a few seconds, the puss began to sizzle and bubble around the black wound. It quickly ate away and dissolved the wound until Kiefer's side was completely healed.

"That was amazing," Whizzy whispered,
still aware that we were trying to not be found.

No, that is disgusting. I thought.

Suddenly, Grace bolted up and out
through the grass into the open, with her arrow
drawn.

"Whizzy," I yelled as my brother followed.

Grace let the arrow loose just as a small
masked figure burst through the thick green
blades of grass on the other side. The figure
deflected the arrow causing it to glance off its
shoulder.

Whizzy reacted, "Helar!" A light blue ray
of light illuminated the darkened forest and
covered the small figure's body.

The masked goon placed his arms in front
of his body and pulled his knees to his elbows. A
shield emerged, protecting him from Whizzy's
freezing spell.

Grace fired again, but it slammed into
the shield too and snapped in half.

Suddenly, our attacker landed on the
ground, tumbled over and punched toward us
with his fist, but didn't strike anyone. A wave of

light jumped from his extended fist and knocked Whizzy and Grace to the ground.

Kiefer took a chance to protect Grace. He fired three more spikes. The masked figure dodged each, performing flips and jumps; it was amazing.

"Atar," Whizzy angrily fired another spell causing roots to burst through the dirt and wrap themselves around our enemy.

The mysterious enemy struggled to escape, but each second another root would grab hold.

Phillip and I joined Grace and Whizzy. We all stood together as the masked figure stood between Kiefer and us along the narrow trail.

"Who are you?" Grace commanded.

No response. The roots had covered the entire body of our attacker from its neck to knees.

"Don't let go," Grace said to Whizzy.

"I've got it," my brother proudly replied.

Phillip grabbed my paw. I didn't even realize at first, until I felt the cool dampness from his skin. A smile moved across my face.

"Who are you?" Grace shouted louder.

The captured figure refused to respond.

I was done playing games. I blasted the mask off to reveal the face of a young Elven man with oddly cut black hair and evil green eyes.

"Javid?" Grace said with disappointment.

"You know him?" I asked.

"Yes." Grace replied. "He is my brother."

MEET THE GRIMMIADS

16

"Your brother?" Whizzy shouted, causing the roots tied around Javid Tallon to loosen.

I quickly intervened and strengthened the magical hold around the evil elf.

"How could you?" Grace asked. She raised her bow and pointed its arrow directly at her brother's heart.

"Grace, don't," I attempted to reason with her.

I could see her rage beginning to overflow. Grace's usually steady hands were shaking, her voice different, softer, like she was ashamed to speak.

"You have disgraced our family, Javid. You will be banished from Mistasia," Grace stated as a tear rolled down her cheek.

"You are wrong, sister. I am not going anywhere. I work for the true ruler of Mistasia. It is you that will be banished," Javid scolded.

"He works for LaCroiux?" Phillip asked in an attempt to keep up.

"Maybe he is under a spell?" I whispered to Grace. "LaCroiux could be controlling him."

Javid began to laugh.

Grace gritted her teeth. "No. That's impossible."

"It has to be," I began when Grace interrupted.

"NO!" Grace shook her head in defiance.

"Elves are too strong willed for sorcerers to use their powers on them," Grace explained. "My brother acts of his own will." Grace lowered her bow and arrow and walked away briskly.

I followed her. "Grace, stop. Wait. Why would he betray your family like this? Wait. Grace!" I yelled her name.

She finally stopped, but before she could speak, her brother attacked.

I had been controlling the spell that held Javid captive, but when I turned to walk after Grace, I forgot about the spell, which allowed the roots to weaken.

"Arrrhhh!" Sorcerer LaCroiux's new apprentice bellowed, as he broke free.

We had no time to react. He caught us with our guards down. Javid summoned the winds. They whipped in through the grass, bending the blades to the ground. Javid Tallon spun like a tornado and rose into the air. The winds raced passed us so quickly that they began to pull us toward him.

I tried to call out to my brother, but nothing came out, like something had placed my voice on mute. The wind roared in my ears as if I stood next to a jet engine.

Javid raised his arms into the air and then everything stopped. The winds vanished and

Javid came crashing down. When he landed, the ground shook like an earthquake, knocking us all down. Then the ground beneath Javid Tallon split. The crack grew and spread across the field in an instant.

Suddenly, the dirt beneath us let loose and collapsed. We all fell into the darkness below.

I screamed as I tumbled into the unknown. It didn't last long...only a few seconds before we landed nearly twenty feet below the surface. Phillip and Whizzy were only a few feet away from me. Grace managed to land on her feet, as did her brother.

We began to gather ourselves. Javid and Grace were in a standoff. They were in the center of the hole we had fallen into and the light from above shone on them like a spotlight for everyone to see.

"Are you quick enough to hit me? Your arrow won't be able to pierce my shield," Javid challenged his sister. "Come on, Grace. Shoot. Do it!" He taunted her.

Grace pulled her bow back further than I had ever seen. She gripped it so tightly that her skin began to turn whiter than usual.

"You aren't even worth it," Grace replied. "I should have known you wouldn't be able to resist his temptation. You were always weak, Javid."

A few small rocks fell into the hole from above.

"Grace, I'm alone up here." The nasally voice of Kiefer the Caterpillar called down to her.

"Oh, no," Whizzy gasped.

"Kiefer back up," I shouted as the very large and heavy caterpillar hung dangerously over the side of the hole that we had all just fallen through. Kiefer was teetering on the edge and about to fall in on top of us.

Javid's wicked smile grew when he saw our friend hanging above. The Elven sorcerer swung his arm across the ground gathering rocks and stones in one swipe and launched them toward Kiefer.

"Run!" I yelled.

The rocks collided with the ground beneath Kiefer, causing it to crumble. The big green blob slipped and plummeted down toward us.

The crash was tremendous. It sounded like 500 drums banging in unison. My head rang so much my eyes rolled in my head like dice.

A dust plume rose into the air making it impossible to see. I just heard screaming and yelling. The commotion was startling. My heart was racing a million miles a minute. The dirt flying around caused me to cough.

When the dust settled, Kiefer's massive body occupied most of the area we had fallen into and Javid Tallon had disappeared.

Phillip was hurriedly tossing rocks and dirt aside like he was digging for buried treasure. That was when I heard him yell.

"Whizzy!"

My brother was trapped under the sixty-foot caterpillar that had just crashed down on top of us.

I ran to help Phillip.

"Whizzy. Whizzy!" my voice sounded strange. I just kept yelling frantically until I reached Phillip.

"What!" My brother snapped as he too, feverishly dug in the dirt under Kiefer.

"Oh, Whizzy, you're okay!" I hugged him

He pushed me away, "Get off of me!" He growled.

I looked to Phillip for an answer as to why my brother was being so rude.

"Grace," was all he replied.

Suddenly, I realized that not all of us had made it out. Grace and her brother Javid must have both ended up underneath Kiefer.

"Grace!" Whizzy excitedly yelled just before he dove into the small hole he and Phillip had dug beneath the large green caterpillar. "Phillip, grab my feet!" His muffled voice called.

Phillip began to pull at my brother's feet. I helped too. Each of us yanked on Whizzy's stinky paws. We dragged him out and he emerged clutching Grace's dirt-covered body with him.

"Is she breathing?" I asked Whizzy.

He placed his ear over her small Elven mouth.

"No!" He yelled.

Whizzy immediately began to resuscitate her. He pushed on her chest and then leaned in to breathe into her mouth. Just as his lips reached hers, Grace's eyes shot open.

She pushed Whizzy away, "What are you doing?" Grace demanded in a weak voice. She had a green-colored liquid running down her forehead and arm.

"You are injured, Grace," Phillip pointed to her forehead.

She reached up and touched the green blood coming from her head. The Elven warrior stood up. She looked very dizzy.

"Where is he?" Grace asked about her brother. The injured elf fell to her knees and spit blood.

"We think he's trapped under, Kiefer," Phillip explained.

Grace laughed for a second before spitting blood again.

Whizzy reached out to console her, but she swatted at him.

"Leave me alone. I am fine," the proud elf claimed as she attempted to stand up a second time. Once again, she stumbled to her knees and grabbed at her head.

"What do we do?" Phillip asked me.

"When did I become a doctor?" I harshly responded. "We've gotta get outta here."

How are we going to get back up there? I thought. Wherever we were was quite dark, except for the spot in the middle where Kiefer lay. I couldn't even see the walls.

My fox ears could hear many sounds; dripping water on something metallic, a whirring similar to mother's dishwasher, and scratching.

"Kiefer, where are we?" I asked the one creature that lived in these lands.

"The Grimmiad Tunnels," he replied in a pained voice.

"Are you okay?" I asked after realizing he was in pain.

"Something is stabbing me in the gut. It really hurts, Rachel the Fox," the big green blob whined.

I walked up to Kiefer's face and placed my hand out to comfort him. His eyes widened as he roared in agony, causing me to be tossed onto my back.

"It's raining," Whizzy crassly remarked.

"I don't think this is rain, Whizzy," Phillip said as he whipped the liquid from his froggy face.

"It's blood," Grace shouted. "Kiefer!" she cried out.

Kiefer's large head slumped. Then the great big bug let out a moan.

"What's happening to him?" I shouted to Grace Tallon.

Just then my question was answered as the wicked sorcerer emerged from Kiefer's midsection. He was covered in liquid too. His hair matted to his small head.

"Grace!" the enraged Javid Tallon called out to his sister. He punched the ground sending a wave of dirt directly at her.

She tried to leap away but was too late. The dirt whipped her legs, sending her flying through the air. When she landed, her bow slid to me. I grabbed it.

Javid quickly focused his evil little eyes on me. Running up the side of Kiefer's limp body, the elf sprung into the air soaring over my head and landing behind me. One quick punch landed in my chest when I turned around to face him. I flew backward and bounced off Kiefer.

I was unconscious for only a few minutes after hitting my head. When I awoke, I remembered seeing Grace when I lifted my head. She was too badly injured to continue to fight. Whizzy and I would have to battle her brother without her.

Phillip, get Grace away from here. I spoke in my head, hoping he would listen.

The green frog's glowing red eyes spotted me in the dimly lit tunnel. He dashed to Grace and swept her up off the ground. She didn't fight...she could barely move. Phillip leapt up and over our fallen friend, Kiefer, and disappeared.

Javid tried to stop him, by whipping stones from the ground, barely missing.

I pointed my wand at my target and attempted to hit Javid Tallon with a spell to slow him down, but he narrowly escaped. The fleet-footed elf danced around, dodging each blast Whizzy and I cast at him. Javid was far faster than anything we had ever seen before...even faster than Grace.

He began to run circles around us. Whizzy and I stood back to back as the elf whirled around us so quickly that he spun up a funnel of dust. We were trapped.

Whizzy began to randomly fire spells into the funnel of dirt hoping to hit his target. Luckily, one did. Javid tumbled and crashed into the wall.

"Nice shot, Whizzy," I exclaimed.

My brother spun his wand in his paw like a drumstick.

"It only took twenty shots," I joked.

Javid pushed himself up to one knee. He was breathing very heavily. Green blood trickled from his bottom lip.

"That was a lucky shot," Javid warned.
"You will not be so fortunate again." He started
toward us.

In the distance a low rumble began.

The fuming sorcerer's apprentice
hesitated at the new noise.

"Is this some trick?" He blasted.

Whizzy and I looked at each other with
confusion. We had no idea what was making the
noise either.

The rumbling grew louder. Stones and
pebbles at my feet began trembling to the
rhythm.

"Whizzy?" I called to my brother, hoping
he wasn't as scared as I was. One look answered
my question. My brother's eyes were huge, like he
had just seen a ghost.

Even Javid had turned his back to us,
looking into the darkness of the tunnel.

"Which one of you is doing this?" He
yelled in fear.

The rumble sounded like a marching of
footsteps. It was shaking the entire tunnel now.

I grabbed Whizzy's arm and pulled, tugging him toward Kiefer. We used his body to shield us from whatever was coming up the tunnel at us. Just then I remembered that I had sent Phillip and Grace in that direction only a few minutes earlier.

"Grace and Phillip," I gasped.

"What did you do, Rachel?" Whizzy blamed me for sending them fleeing into the dark and dangerous tunnel.

"How could I have known? It didn't look much safer here!" I shouted at him.

Then the noise completely stopped. It was eerily quiet. I could hear the wind blowing through the hole above us. I was more scared now. The silence was torture.

Whizzy and I held our wands across our chests and our backs against the now brownish-yellow skin of our lifeless caterpillar guide. Kiefer's color was fading.

"Where is that stupid, elf?" Whizzy peeked out. "I can't see him."

"I'm more concerned about Phillip and Grace."

A strong hand reached around my waist and yanked me away from my brother.

"Whizzy," I called out.

"Chede!" an angry voice blasted from behind me.

I felt a chill in my throat. A puff of smoke escaped my mouth, like when I exhale in the winter air. I couldn't speak! My throat was frozen.

Twisting my body I caught a glimpse of my kidnapper. It was Javid, but he had covered his face with his hideous mask once again. Now up close I noticed the black mask was painted with red streaks, like blood ran down his face. It had two small rectangular holes for his eyes, and an opening for his mouth and chin. He continued to drag me out into the open.

Whizzy ran after us, but Javid tossed him aside with a gust of wind, like a crumpled up piece of paper. The sinister elf held me so tightly that my ribs began to hurt. It was difficult to breath and my vision was becoming blurry.

We stopped so that Javid could easily see into the tunnel, but there appeared to be nothing there.

"Show yourself!" The frightened little sorcerer exclaimed in his deepest voice. "Come out and fight me!" He barked.

A series of tiny yellow dots appeared in the distance. At first I thought it was the lack of oxygen to my brain, until Javid took a sharp deep breath. Then I realized he must have seen them too.

"What deception is this, witch?" He whispered into my ear.

But I couldn't answer. His spell made it so I was unable to talk. It didn't matter because Phillip and Grace were gone and Whizzy was unconscious after bumping his head on the ground when Javid attacked him.

More tiny yellow dots appeared with each passing moment. There were hundreds. It was creepy. The hairs on my furry neck began to stand up.

"Are you afraid of me?" Javid Tallon challenged the yellow dots. "Show yourself!" He screamed.

That was when the rumble from before returned...this time it was even more thunderous.

Emerging from the shadows were hundreds of squatty, hairy humans. They ran towards us with axes and swords. More and more brutish creatures continued to escape the shadows of the tunnel and flood into the moonlight that shone in from above.

Javid released his grip on me. I fell to the ground gasping for air. The chill in my throat disappeared.

I felt helpless against these new creatures, but I quickly realized I didn't need to fear them.

THE GREEN GLOW
17

The small, hairy looking humans stampeded by me chasing after Javid Tallon.

Sorcerer LaCroiux's brash apprentice scurried up the tunnel wall, like a spider, and burst into the night sky. He landed in The Colossal Lands above and disappeared from view.

A small, but thick-fingered hand appeared next to my face. I followed the short arm up to a dirt-covered and hairy smiling face. It appeared to be a very small man, who only came to my chest, with short and spiky, yet thick, coarse black hair.

"Thank you?" I said, not quite knowing what else to say.

"You are welcome, Rachel Whizzenmog," the gruff, yet obviously female, voice surprised me.

"You know my name?" I replied.

She laughed. "Yez, we know who yuz are...we have long zince been knowing the Whizzenmog family. We Grimmiads have fought many battlez with yuz. I Gellna Grimmiad."

"It is nice to meet you, Gellna. And thanks again for saving me. Have you seen my friends?"

"Friendz? Do yuz mean the elf and the frog?" She began to heartily roar.

The many Grimmiads surrounding her joined in with a short burst of raucous laughter. Then, they all suddenly stopped.

Whizzy was startled awake by the commotion. "Rachel!" He yelled like the battle was still going on.

It's a good thing that he has red fur, because I could tell he was embarrassed after noticing that we were not alone.

"What's going on, sis? Who are the dwarfs?" Whizzy joked.

"Grimmiads, Michael Whizzenmog!" Gellna forcefully responded.

"Sorry. I didn't know," Whizzy rolled his eyes at me. "What's a Grim-nod?" my brother whispered in my ear.

"You're an idiot!" I replied.

"What?" He shrugged his shoulders.

"Whizzy has this problem where he sometimes forgets to use his brain and his mouth runs amok," I explained to Gellna and the other Grimmiads. "I'm sorry to be in such a hurry, but we need to return to Cadieux Castle. Can you take us to our friends?"

"Yez, we will take yuz to them." Gellna began to lead the way when she stopped to place her hand on Kiefer's face. She closed her eyes and began speaking in a language I didn't recognize.

"Short and funny. I like these people," Whizzy glibly spoke.

I swatted him in the chest.

"Castle ride soon yuz will have, Whizzenmogs," the Grimmiad leader declared as she rubbed Kiefer the Caterpillar's peaceful face.

She led us down the tunnel a short way to where Grace and Phillip were being protected by another swarm of Grimmiads.

"Phillip!" I ran and hugged him. I was so relieved to see him alive.

Whizzy just stood uncomfortably at Grace's feet not knowing if he should speak. It was then I realized that the last time they were together she awoke to him kissing her...sort of.

"Grace, are you okay?" Whizzy mustered up the courage to ask.

"I'm fine, Whizzy." She replied in discomfort.

"How are we going to get back to the castle now?" I asked referring to our Elven guide's injuries and Kiefer's passing. "Is there another way back to Cadieux Castle, Gellna?"

A vibrant smile came over her face. "Yuz will be in Caduz sooner than yuz realize," she boasted. "Coming event will make it so."

I had no idea to what she was referring, but Gellna Grimmiad had recently saved my life so I wasn't about to argue with her...and her hundreds of Grimmiad fighters so I sat down beside Phillip and waited.

The Grimmiads hustled about the tunnel. Some carried weapons and others food. They appeared to be gathering supplies.

"What do you think they are doing?" Whizzy snidely remarked, pointing at three peculiar-looking Grimmiads directly across from us.

One had a silver helmet on his head that covered his ears and nose. His fat cheeks burst out in front, and he was also missing a few teeth. The second had streaks of gray in his hair, which reminded me of our grandpa. Suddenly, I felt sad again. The third was rather thin and a few inches taller than the others. He was actually close to my brother's height. He had a very long braided beard and long hair that resembled tentacles in the back. His eyes were yellow, like his friends', but appeared sharper.

They huddled around a pile of axes, arrows and swords. The Grimmiad wearing the silver helmet pulled a thick, but short sword out from the pile and slashed it back and forth. It produced a strange sound as it cut through the air. The others chuckled, while he made a goofy face.

The bearded Grimmiad then grabbed an axe and swung it about like a baton twirler in a marching band, almost striking his friend in the head.

They all began to laugh again.

"It looks like they're trying to kill each other," Phillip replied. Then he started laughing and Whizzy joined him.

Grace and I gave each other an annoyed glance.

"We can't just wait here forever. I'm not even sure how many days we have left?" I was getting worried that we wouldn't return to Greenville in time...or with our grandpa.

"Six days," Phillip responded.

"How do you know that? Can you be absolutely sure?" I challenged.

"Yes. I am sure. We have had four sunsets since we arrived. One on our journey to the castle, another at the castle and now two here," Phillip explained.

We all looked at him like he was crazy.

"I can feel the moon," he added.

"You're mental!" Whizzy shouted. "Feel the moon. That is ridiculous."

"He is correct, Whizzy. I can feel the moon's power. It is nighttime," Grace Tallon replied.

"How is that possible?" I asked Grace. "Why would Phillip be able to feel the moon in the sky?"

"The tide!" Phillip muttered. "The tides control the water, and water gives me strength."

"So?" Whizzy blasted, not understanding anything his best friend was explaining.

"Do you ever pay attention at school?" Phillip snapped back. "The moon controls the levels of water. When it is up at night, the water levels rise due to gravity. So that must be why I can tell when the moon has risen even without being able to see it. Its control over water is like when I become stronger around water. That's the connection."

"I have no idea what you just said. There were words coming out of your mouth, but I only heard 'water'. The rest of it was kinda...not so much!" Whizzy jokingly replied.

"Whizzenmog, you must make your family proud," Grace jabbed.

I started laughing but then I noticed Phillip's eyes glued to something directly over my head.

"What?" I shouted afraid there was a giant spider dangling between my fox ears. The image of a sixty-foot spider jumped into my head.

Phillip pointed behind me. When I turned around, there were dozens of Grimmiads clustered together with their backs to us. A commotion rose from them. Phillip, Whizzy and I stood up to see.

A bright green light shimmered on the tunnel wall. The strange light was getting brighter and began swirling around like the water draining in a toilet.

The rushing wind sounded like a vacuum cleaner stuck on a carpet floor. A flash leapt into the once dark underground tunnel.

The Grimmiads erupted in cheers. Standing amongst them was an image I never thought I would see again.

A smile beamed across my face. I gasped at the sight of the gray fox towering over the Grimmiads.

"Grandpa!" Whizzy spoke in disbelief.

Grandpa had returned. He was clutching his wand and the powerful gem that had allowed him to escape the snow outside Cadieux Castle, the Last Emerald.

THE LAST EMERALD

18

Grandpa Whizzenmog hunched over in pain. The Grimmiads caught him before he fell. The short but strong dwarves helped Grandpa walk over to us. He used them like crutches.

I was so excited. My emotions swamped me. I started hopping around like a five year old on Christmas morning ready to open presents. My eyes welled up with tears. I wanted to hug him so badly but was afraid to touch him. He looked so fragile.

"Rainer Whizzenmog, what took you so long?" Grace Tallon interrupted my joy. She sternly glared at him.

"I am sorry, my dear." My grandpa rolled his eyes at me. "She thinks this is easy," he whispered.

"I heard that, Rainer," the Elven warrior replied.

The old fox just smiled. The Grimmiads helped him to the ground, where he sat beside me. He exhaled deeply like a huge weight had just been lifted from his shoulders.

I watched as he turned the gem into a bracelet by waving his wand around it in a circular motion. He struggled to place it around his wrist.

"Let me help you," I said as I reached out to grab the green bracelet.

Grandpa Whizzenmog pulled it away quickly and then winced in pain.

I was shocked. Why would he pull it away from me? I wasn't going to steal it.

My grandpa quickly noticed my expression, and responded with, "Rachel, I know you just want to help, but...I cannot allow you to put yourself in such danger. I am sorry, my dear."

We sat in silence for a few seconds. At that time, I noticed that the Grimmiads had once again resumed their strange behaviors from before. They tested out weapons on each other, laughing all the while.

These guys are weird. I thought.

I searched for Phillip to see if he was possibly listening to my mind again, but he wasn't. He and Whizzy had begun playing with the Grimmiads' weapons as well.

I wondered how long it would be before one of them sliced off a limb. My money would be on Whizzy...doing it to Phillip.

I was just about to ask my grandpa if we could use magic to reattach body parts when he suddenly began telling me about the Last Emerald as if I had asked him a question.

He had a guilty look on his face when he spoke, "This is a magical stone, Rachel." The green bracelet stuck out against his gray-colored fur. He bent his wrist to show me...as if I hadn't seen it before or watched him place it on his wrist seconds before. "In Greenville, it is only a visual piece of art, nothing more." He continued to explain. "However, here in Mistasia it has many powers. You have already seen some of what the beholder of this gemstone is capable of...but it has far greater powers than anything I have demonstrated." Grandpa was now speaking in a whisper and had leaned in uncomfortably close even for a family member. "In this world, an emerald like this could be used to change the face of everything we see, control all the creatures, and reshape the world. If Cragon Cadieux is allowed to possess this emerald, Rachel...Mistasia would be lost forever."

The sudden flash of thoughts in my head unsettled my stomach. Imagining what Cragon Cadieux could do with a magical weapon like that. It was horrifying. The pain and suffering would be so wide spread that Mistasia would be destroyed.

"What do we do? How can we keep him from stealing it?" I asked in a panic.

"We will have to destroy it," Grace Tallon interjected.

I saw my grandpa's face contort in pain as he shifted uncomfortably next to me, but he didn't respond.

"Is that possible?" I asked, looking between Grace and my grandpa for a response.

"He could do it!" Grace answered before Grandpa was able to catch his breath and respond.

Grandpa Whizzenmog and Grace Tallon silently glared at one another.

"What do you mean he could do it? Can you do that?" I found myself feeling a lot like Whizzy right now as my frustration level grew with each new question I asked.

"I take it you haven't told them yet, Rainer?" Grace spoke with an odd tone in her voice. It sounded like sarcasm.

Grandpa attempted to swallow and then replied. "Yes." He wouldn't look at me.

"Yes? Yes, what? To which question? Is that possible? Can you do it? What?" I began shouting, drawing my brother's and Phillip's attention as well as a few hundred Grimmiads.

Suddenly, our once private conversation had developed into a large-scale meeting.

Grandpa leaned close to me and whispered, "To both."

I didn't exactly know how to take that. "If this emerald is so powerful and so dangerous if Cragon gets hold of it, then why haven't you destroyed it?" I sternly questioned my grandpa.

"There are many reasons, Rachel."

I waited for him to elaborate, but he didn't. "That's your answer? Many reasons? We are risking our lives for that?"

"What's going on, Rachel?" Whizzy finally joined in the conversation.

"Yeah, why are you so upset? I thought you'd be happy to see your grandpa alive," Phillip added while twirling a Grimmiad sword in his webbed hand.

"I did too," I replied and then stormed away.

I was furious. It seemed so selfish that he kept the emerald, like a trophy when destroying it would make Cragon so much easier to defeat. I spent the next few hours alone trying to understand my grandpa's reasoning. It didn't help. I couldn't.

Later that day, a commotion rose from the area of the tunnel where we had fallen in the day before from The Colossal Lands.

I ran back towards the hundreds of Grimmiads chanting and roaring in unison. Phillip, Whizzy, Grace and Grandpa were standing together behind the Grimmiads, watching them dance around. At the center of this celebration, was Gellna. She had her stubby arms raised above her head as she barked out unfamiliar words into the sky.

"Chun...ba...rune! Ramme...varoon!" The Grimmiad leader chanted repeatedly.

It was a few moments before I realized that directly behind the cluster of short, hairy Grimmiads was a large, dark brown pile of dirt.

"Did they bury, Kiefer?" I asked Phillip.

"They must have," he replied.

As the Grimmiads sang and danced in the tunnel, the rumbling grew.

"Did that just move?" I wondered out loud, referring to the pile of dirt.

"Ahhhh, I think so," Phillip answered, as he scratched between his big red eyes.

I watched intently as the massive lump of dirt shifted and stretched like something stuck inside a sack. Suddenly, it burst at the top.

Liquid flowed out like a broken water balloon. A slimy colorfully winged creature emerged.

"What is that?" Whizzy shrieked like a frightened child. He stepped behind his best friend for protection.

I remember thinking he was acting like a pansy, but didn't get the chance to tell him before I realized something.

"Is that...?" I started.

"It can't be," Phillip defiantly replied.

"That's a freaking huge butterfly," I shouted.

"It's Kiefer," Grace responded.

"What?" Phillip, Whizzy and I yelled.

RUMBLING IN THE DISTANCE
19

"Now that is magical!" Grandpa Whizzenmog boasted with a chuckle. He was grinning widely. "Mistasian nature."

The Grimmiads continued to dance around between the massive butterfly and us that had suddenly emerged from the dirt cocoon.

Kiefer spread his wings, which had strings of slimy goo stretching from them to his body. He flapped them, slopping the gooey liquid all over the tunnel. The Grimmiads were covered in Kiefer's slime, like he had just sneezed upon them. The Grimmiads only cheered louder.

Gellna Grimmiad began to grunt and her followers did too.

Grace smiled as she looked up at the flying creature.

Kiefer was nearly as big as a jumbo jet but far more colorful. I couldn't wait to see him up close. I ran and Phillip followed. Dodging piles of slime, I dashed to our revived friend's side.

"Kiefer, you look amazing!" I shouted with joy. "I completely forgot that caterpillars turn into butterflies. This is amazing."

I began to examine his beautifully colored wings. The morning sunlight from above shone into the dark tunnel and directly on Kiefer. It made his wings shimmer. The colors swirled and spiraled around on his wings. Red turned to yellow and then green. Dozens of vibrant blue circles covered his wings too. His body was bright yellow now and fuzzy like a peach.

Phillip was rubbing Kiefer's furry side when the giant butterfly spoke in a deeper voice.

"Rainer Whizzenmog, we must move quickly. The evil sorcerer is headed our way."

"Thank you, Kiefer," Grandpa responded. He appeared worried.

"We will aid yuz, Rainer Whizzenmog," Gellna told our grandpa.

The gray fox bowed his head in response. He was standing in the center of a mass of followers.

Phillip, Whizzy, Grace and I were with him without a doubt. The Grimmiads had given their word to fight with us too, and now Kiefer had been reborn as a butterfly. We definitely had weapons at our disposal...and in this battle we wouldn't be as badly outnumbered as we had been at Cadieux Castle. Yet, I still felt sick to my stomach, like that nervous feeling I get when I have to take a math test...except when I answer incorrectly at school, an evil sorcerer doesn't zap me.

"We can use The Colossal Lands to our advantage," Grace spoke. "Kiefer and Gellna know these lands better than anyone."

"Yeah, this time we're gonna kick his butt!" Whizzy shouted.

The Grimmiads cheered!

I still felt sick.

"All right everyone, let's go!" Grandpa suddenly shouted, exciting the Grimmiads into a frenzy.

The little people began to scurry about the tunnel gathering weapons. Gellna shouted instructions to them as Grandpa called us together.

"Grace, in battle I want you to stay with Whizzy. Phillip, stick close to Rachel. We all will fly out on Kiefer. They won't be expecting that!" Grandpa explained with a sly smile.

Our grandpa leapt upon the great butterfly's back with the flick of his wand. A gust of wind lifted him skyward and safely landed him on Kiefer's fuzzy body.

"Cool," was my brother's simple response.

I was just glad the gust of wind was magic and not a fart like back in my parent's house.

Whizzy was next to join Grandpa. Then Phillip wrapped his arms around Grace, who was still sore from her battle with Javid, and leapt skyward with great force. A whoosh sound buzzed my ears as he jumped past. I took a deep breath and whispered, "Catapult." My body was flung upward. My heart began pumping so fast. Kiefer's brightly colored body whizzed past me, and then his wing and suddenly I was flying out of the Grimmiad tunnel and landing in the thick green grass of The Colossal Lands. I had overshot my target because of my excitement.

Phillip called to me using his telepathy, "Rachel are you all right?" His voice resonated with fear in my head.

"Yeah...I just used too much magic," I replied with embarrassment as the ground around me began to tremble.

The rocks at my feet bounced around like the crowd at a concert. Wind gusts blew dirt into my face and through my fur. Kiefer emerged from the hole in front of me.

I ran and jumped onto his back as he rose. Phillip and Whizzy grabbed me. My right paw slipped on the butterfly's fur, causing me to dangle off his side. Whizzy struggled to hold on to me. I could feel his grip slipping.

"I can't hold her!" Whizzy yelled for help.

"Help me!" I screamed as Kiefer continued to climb into the air. I looked down and saw the long drop into the dark tunnel. "Whizzy!"

"Phillip, pull," my brother barked at his best friend.

"I am!" Phillip replied, as his voice trembled while he struggled to keep his grip on me.

My hand slipped from Whizzy's, causing my body to swing like a clock pendulum and slam into Kiefer's side.

"Rachel!" I heard my brother's voice.

My heart skipped a beat. I gasped at the sight of the drop to the green grass.

Suddenly, I felt a tug against my body like a pair of large hands wrapping themselves around me and lifting me up to place me down safely on Kiefer's soft fuzzy back.

When I looked up, Grandpa Whizzenmog smiled at me. "You are safe, my dear."

I hugged him so tightly. My grandpa had saved me. He hadn't panicked. He used his magical powers to pull me to safety. I was still mad at him about the emerald, but very glad he was here.

After my heart slowed back to normal, my eyes caught a glimpse of our future. In the distance was a massive field of waving green grass. It spread out far into the distance. As the grass swayed, black blurry images emerged...hundreds of them!

"Wolverines!" Whizzy growled as he pointed to the same figures I saw. "Look...see! In the grass,"

"I see them Whizzy!" I cracked back.

"What's that sound?" Phillip croaked.

A mechanical whirring shot up from the ground below and could be heard over the flapping of Kiefer's wings. Large chunks of grass were being cut down in strips to allow the Wolverine Army to easily pass through The Colossal Lands. The paths looked like cracks in the green fields and they all were coming directly toward us.

Grandpa instructed Kiefer to hover in one spot.

"What's our strategy, Whizzenmog?" Grace smugly questioned our leader.

"To stay alive!" The stern voice of Grandpa Whizzenmog replied.

A TANGLED WEB
20

That phrase, 'To stay alive', hung in my brain like a spider web in the corner of our basement. It dangled there swaying in the wind, unable to fall...catching every horrible thought I could possibly have about our impending battle.

"Right now, I wish I'd never come back!" Whizzy blurted out.

It was exactly what I was thinking...I just didn't have the courage to say it because we were all the hope that remained for all of Mistasia.

The Wolverine Army amassed in great numbers. Meanwhile, the Grimmiads were nowhere to be found. They had promised to help us, but I couldn't find them anywhere.

"This isn't looking very good," Phillip commented on the large number of enemy soldiers in the distance.

"How are they getting here?" Grace questioned.

"I have no idea?" Grandpa responded. He squinted his aged eyes in an attempt to see clearly. "Can you see anything, Grace?"

The Elven warrior focused her powerful eyes at the wolverines. "I can see flashes of light. Then they just appear in small groups."

"LaCroiux?" Grandpa growled.

"No, it's Javid!" Grace gritted her teeth in disgust.

"Who?" Grandpa asked.

"My brother."

"You have a brother?" Grandpa replied.
Grace nodded.

"And he works for LaCroiux?" Grandpa sarcastically questioned.

Grace tilted her head slightly and rolled her eyes. "Yes."

"So you're not gonna invite him over for dinner anytime soon," Grandpa cracked.

I smiled.

"No, but I'll give him something to eat," she replied clenching her fist.

"You'll get your chance," I added watching the Wolverine Army begin to move closer. "Where are the Grimmiads?"

"We can't wait much longer," Whizzy stated the obvious.

"Then we are going to have to stop them on our own," Grandpa calmly replied. "Grace, are you up to this?"

Grace nodded and grabbed an arrow from her backpack. "Just tell me when, Rainer."

"Good. I will go down and attack them from the ground using the grass as cover. I need the rest of you to take Kiefer and stop Javid

700

from bringing anymore soldiers here," our leader commanded.

"Kiefer, down!" Grace ordered.

"Wait!" Grandpa shouted to stop the giant butterfly from descending. "I have another way down." He winked at me with a sly smile on his face.

"Wingadom," the crafty fox spoke as he flicked his wand toward his chest. Grandpa held his arms out stretched from his sides. Under his arms a glowing light began to form wings that attached from his hips to his wrists like a bat.

Grandpa ran to the end of Kiefer's body and leapt. I watched in fear as he plummeted to the ground. His arms were held out and wings bowed against the rushing winds. Just before hitting the ground, Grandpa lurched back causing the wind to catch his wings and pull him skyward again. The gray fox did a full circle in the air and landed squarely on his paws.

"That was freaking awesome!" Whizzy blurted out.

"You would have killed yourself," Grace taunted the reddish-colored fox.

"Look out," I heard Phillip croak from beside me.

He pointed down at my grandpa. Wolverines were closing in on him quickly, and Grandpa was unable to see them through the tall grass.

"Call to him, Phillip!" I shouted. "Use your powers."

Phillip used his telepathy to warn Grandpa. I helplessly watched from above as Kiefer began to fly away with us on his back. We were supposed to stop Javid from bringing more soldiers here, but I couldn't leave my grandpa alone. I stepped to the edge of Kiefer's back and prepared to jump when Phillip's damp webbed hands grabbed me and pulled me back.

"Stop! Let go! I have to help him!" I screamed.

"He told us to stop Javid, Rachel. He can handle them!" Phillip shouted back as he struggled to hold onto me.

Just then the first wolverine approached Grandpa.

I gasped as it swung its large sword.

A flash of light erupted from the ground, and the wolverine was flung through the air and down into the large dark hole to Grimmiad tunnel.

Grandpa used his wand like a sword to fend off two more wolverines. He slashed at one enemy and dodged the attack from the other. More and more wolverines converged on his position. Their thick black fur was beginning to overtake the green of the grass surrounding him. They used their machines to cut the grass to the ground. Now a large section had been destroyed around them. Grandpa stood in the middle with dozens of wolverines all around him. He was trapped.

"Kiefer go back!" I yelled.

Phillip didn't try to stop me this time. He watched in terror as Grandpa tried to fight them off.

A large wolverine stepped up through his brothers and approached the gray wizard fox. He was the tallest and most muscular wolverine I'd ever seen. He carried a club that resembled a tree.

Grace Tallon pulled back hard on her bow. She fired, missing the huge wolverine that prepared to attack Grandpa. It whizzed by and struck another black-haired beast, which fell to the ground in pain.

A loud roar erupted from the ground below. It was becoming harder to see and the sun had almost set. That was when a thundering noise began.

"A storm?" Whizzy said searching the clouds above.

There didn't appear to be any storm, but we knew that in Mistasia anything could happen and probably would. A tornado could instantly spring up out of one of the wolverine's rear-ends and I wouldn't be surprised.

A familiar voice grunted. It was Gellna Grimmiad as she burst from the hole in the ground behind my grandpa. She was riding a huge black spider with ugly yellow eyes.

"Oh, yeah!" Whizzy yelled as he pumped his fists with excitement. "Get 'em!"

The Grimmiads had kept their promise and emerged from their tunnel, riding large spiders. The Wolverine Army was no match for the arachnids.

Gellna rode up to Grandpa quickly. Her spider spit a web entangling the largest wolverine, which seemed small compared to the spiders.

Grandpa took the opportunity to strike and zapped his enemy. The wolverine froze and then crashed backwards to the ground. "Go! Stop Javid!" The angered fox called to us.

TALLON CHALLENGE
21

It was a frightening sight, like something out of a horror movie. Giant spiders scurried below...their glowing yellow eyes targeting their prey before shooting webs like nets, trapping wolverines in thick cocoons.

My heart was racing...partly because of the scene below and partly because my adrenaline was pumping. I felt strength surging through my body. The momentum had swung in our direction.

Kiefer swooped down. Flashes of light pointed us in the right direction to find Javid as the sun had completely set and nightfall had arrived.

Our butterfly friend moved in close and hovered above the flashing lights.

"Where is he?" Whizzy yelled over the flapping of Kiefer's wings.

The sorcerer's apprentice answered with a scorching fireball, before any of us could respond.

Kiefer howled in pain as the flame singed his belly.

"We're hit!" Grace announced.

Kiefer began to spin uncontrollably toward the ground. His left wing was ablaze. The wind rushed by my face, causing my whiskers to point to my ears.

I reached for Phillip's hand. He pulled me tightly into his chest as we braced for a crash landing. I closed my eyes and wrapped my arms around him too.

Just before smashing into the ground, we came to a halt. Kiefer's large body hung in the air as if strings from above were holding him.

"What happened?" Kiefer's strangely normal voice asked.

I opened my eyes to see my brother standing in the middle of Kiefer's furry back. His entire body shook as if he was cold, but it was very warm in The Colossal Lands.

"I...can't...hold...him," Whizzy struggled to speak.

Whizzy had stopped Kiefer from crashing.

"Set us down, Whizzy." I was very impressed, but knew that setting down an object this large wouldn't be easy.

We dropped suddenly. Kiefer bounced on the ground, tossing us into the air like ragdolls.

Phillip's hold on me was broken. He extended his webbed hand, but I couldn't grab hold. We separated and fell to opposite sides of Kiefer's body.

I landed on my back on Kiefer's wing, and slid backward to the soft grass below. Grace was laying face down to my left. I wasn't able to see Phillip or Whizzy.

"Grace, are you okay?" I reached out to touch her arm. Grace didn't respond, but stood up and walked by me.

I chased after her. She didn't seem right. When I saw Kiefer's face I understood why. Javid Tallon was awaiting his sister on the other side. Before I could reach her, Grace pulled two arrows from her pack and drew them back in her bow. She pointed them at Javid.

Phillip and Whizzy were standing at Kiefer's wing, Phillip holding a Grimmiad sword and Whizzy pointing his wand at the evil little sorcerer.

"Drop them," Javid demanded. "Now!" he barked.

"No, Javid! Surrender; we have you!" Grace pleaded.

Javid smiled and raised his left hand.

"You underestimate me, Grace," Javid said.

"You can't control me, Javid!" Grace explained, as she believed her brother was trying to use his sorcery on her.

Her bow began to vibrate, causing her to fire her arrow, and she nearly clipped Whizzy.

"Hey, Grace, watch it!" Whizzy growled.

The Elven warrior's bow jumped from her hands and hung in the air.

"No, but I can control your weapon." Javid moved the bow and pointed it at Grace. An arrow leapt from her pack, entered the bow and drew back.

"Stop it," I screamed and pointed my wand at Javid.

"Don't point that at her!" Whizzy shouted.

The arrow's tip glimmered in the moonlight.

"As you wish, fox!" Javid snidely remarked and then abruptly turned the bow and arrow toward Phillip and Whizzy.

The evil elf taunted Whizzy. "You care for my sister, don't you Whizzenmog? Then maybe you'd take an arrow for her?"

"I'd rather not," Whizzy snarled.

Javid fired, but Whizzy deflected the arrow into the ground with a simple spell.

"You'll have to do better than that," Whizzy replied feeling very confident.

Javid zipped into action whirling around and crouching to the ground, holding out his left arm and swiping it across the ground. The grass turned bright white before Javid slammed his right hand down like a hammer, sparking the grass into a wall of flame that raced toward Phillip and Whizzy. The two best friends split in opposite directions to avoid the flames.

Grace reached out and placed her hand on her brother's shoulders. Javid spun around and wrapped the bow around her neck. He began to choke her as Grace struggled to free herself. They wrestled for a moment when I pointed my wand at Javid.

"You'll hit her!" He yelled. "You wouldn't want to do that would you, Whizzenmog?"

Whizzy and Phillip approached Javid from opposite sides. I held my wand as steady as possible. Javid appeared to be assessing his situation. His shady eyes shifted back and forth between all of us. Then he attacked Phillip, lifting him from the ground in a funnel of wind and tossing him at my brother. Phillip's large frog head slammed into Whizzy's furry white chest. They tumbled to the ground.

I took the opportunity to fire a spell at Javid's shoulder, hoping not to hit Grace. Her brother turned at the last moment and pulled Grace in front of my spell.

It hit her directly in the face. Her eyes crossed and closed. Her body slumped in Javid's arms. The crooked little elf smiled at me and then released his hold on Grace.

Javid backed away as I approached him with my wand now fixed on his heart. I gritted my teeth in anger.

"It's over, Javid. Give up!" I ordered.

Phillip and Whizzy joined me. Whizzy pointed his wand at Javid, too. Phillip held his Grimmiad sword.

"Three against one. Those are good odds for you. However, I am up for the challenge.

In the distance, I could still hear the patter of the spiders rumbling around. I heard the sound of webs shooting from the spinnerets of spiders like a laser in a sci-fi movie, and then the howling from another captured wolverine.

"Listen. Your army is losing!" Whizzy growled. "We have won!"

Javid started to chuckle. His bright white teeth emerged from his darkened face. "Not yet!" He zipped between us in a flash, knocking me to the ground.

Phillip and Whizzy chased after him.

When I got back up, I saw Phillip hopping around dodging Javid's attempts to burn him to a crisp. Whizzy just stood confidently with his right leg forward and his left leg back, like a swordsman, as he continually fired blasts.

"Stand still, you twerp!" Whizzy growled.

Javid stopped for a moment with a confused expression.

Phillip reacted and pounced, kicking the elf in the head. He landed on top of Javid.

"Yeah, Phillip!" Whizzy shouted with excitement.

I had joined them as we began to celebrate our accomplishment.

"Ahhhhh!" Javid screamed in anger. He clenched his fists.

Phillip's eyes grew. He knew whatever was about to happen wouldn't be good.

The sorcerer's apprentice smashed his fists into the ground, driving into the green -covered grass and flinging shavings into the air. The sheer force produced a crack of thunder. Javid used the momentum it produced to kick his legs up and knock Phillip from his chest. The little Elven sorcerer spun and landed with his feet wide apart and one hand on the ground. He exploded toward Whizzy who suddenly had a wide-eyed and panicked expression on his face.

"Oh crap!" Whizzy gasped.

Javid whistled past Whizzy, ran up the side of Kiefer jumping into the air. With his legs pointed skyward, Grace's brother held his hands extended over his head and fired two sonic blasts into the ground between Whizzy and me.

The ground began to distort. It resembled waves on the ocean until the ground began to spin. It happened all in a few seconds. I couldn't watch.

A familiar screech stabbed my ears. When I turned back around, a ten-foot tall portal spun directly in front of me and dozens of vampire bats swarmed the sky.

SUMMON THE SORCERER
22

Boom! That was the sound that Javid's feet made when he landed back on the ground. He had a wicked smirk like he had just won the battle.

I didn't agree! I showed him by casting a spell to wrap him up with blades of grass like an Egyptian mummy.

Javid wiggled like a worm in an attempt to free himself, but I wasn't letting him go.

Vampire bats continued to circle above us but didn't attack. They appeared to be waiting for something.

Grace rustled. She stood up in pain, holding her face. Blood trickled from her nostrils. She dabbed her fingers at the blood.

"Why am I bleeding?" Grace asked no one in particular.

"Ah...that was me," I answered.

She gave me a sour look.

"Your brother used you as a shield," I angrily defended myself.

It was only an instant, but that was all Javid needed. As I verbally battled his sister, I lost focus...just for a split second and Javid used that opportunity to break the magical binds with which I held him.

I tried to hold him off. I cast spell after spell. The grass blades reached out and grabbed hold, but Javid kept snapping them and pulling himself free.

It was chaos! The vampire bats dove into action. Goren swooped in and slashed at me. I ducked. That was all that Javid needed to free himself completely. He spun, creating a whirlwind. At that same moment, Grandpa

Whizzenmog appeared behind Whizzy. Debris from Javid's tornado slapped against his face.

I covered my eyes with my arm.

Phillip braced for the impact; Javid's wind funnel crashed into him flinging him like a sock into the air. I heard the sound of the air escaping his lungs as he bounced on the ground behind me.

My wand slipped from my hand and was sucked up into the vortex.

"NO!" I screamed.

Grace fired two arrows into the funnel, but nothing happened. It crept along, crackling like a flag whipping in the wind.

Goren continued to dive-bomb us, swooping down and just missing Whizzy with a swipe of his razor sharp claws.

My brother immediately shot back, zapping Goren out of the sky. Goren spun uncontrollably before crashing. Then Whizzy turned his anger on the vortex produced by Javid as it was bearing down on him.

Whizzy knelt down to brace himself before unleashing a bolt of lightning. It hit the tornado, which lit up from inside. The winds immediately slowed and the whirlwinds disappeared, revealing the injured sorcerer. Javid spun on the ground a few more time before sliding to a stop curled in agony.

The bolt had struck him in the leg. A large wound was easy to see. Javid writhed in pain, grunting and screaming.

Whizzy kept his wand fixed on its target. I joined him, as did Grandpa. Even Grace held an arrow to her brother...and I was certain she would fire first.

"It's over, Javid," Grace announced. "You have lost."

The injured elf continued to roll around in agony. "Master! Master!" He yelled like a lunatic.

"Shut up, you crazy..." Whizzy began to bark but our grandpa stopped him.

"Let him. Maybe he will summon the sorcerer we need," Grandpa explained.

It happened so quickly that I am still not sure how he arrived, but Sorcerer Pierre LaCroiux was suddenly standing before us. He wasted little time speaking. The wicked henchmen of Cragon Cadieux went directly after Grandpa...the strongest of us.

I just saw my grandpa's shadow fly across the nighttime skyline before hitting Kiefer's body with a loud thump. The impact knocked his wand clear from his paw. Grandpa landed on his stomach then rolled over on his back.

Whizzy didn't stand a chance either. He had turned to watch our grandpa's flight, courtesy of LaCroiux, when he too was tossed through the air.

I sprinted to Grace and pulled her behind Kiefer for cover. LaCroiux simply lifted the giant butterfly from the ground with the wave of his hand and sneered at us as we cowered behind our friend.

He had become so powerful...and vengeful. I could sense his hatred. It was in his eyes how much he despised us all. A deep red flame burned in his eyes.

He pulled roots from the ground to tie my hands and feet. He did the same to Grace and Phillip. Phillip was still woozy from his earlier battle with Javid's vortex.

Sorcerer LaCroiux vanished and then instantly reappeared above me.

I screamed.

"Oh...my poor dear, do you fear me?" the evil sorcerer chuckled as he tormented me. He held out his hand and moved it directly over my face without touching me. I could feel the heat from his palms...the energy within him waiting to come out. It was frightening.

"LaCroiux, you must face me!" Grandpa Whizzenmog proclaimed.

He and my brother remained free.

I had never been so afraid in all my life when a smile overcame that wretched, evil elf's face.

LaCroiux slowly turned and challenged my grandpa. I could still feel the chill in my body from the smile on his face even after he had turned. It was too sinister to explain.

"I believe you are right, Rainer," LaCroiux calmly replied before turning over his right hand and casting a spell on Whizzy.

My brother's fox face contorted in pain. His body became limp, and he crumpled to the ground. Then roots exploded from the ground and wrapped around his ankles, wrists and neck.

"Let's see if you can defeat me before your grandson runs...out...of...air," LaCroiux challenged.

Grandpa wasted no time lashing out.

SHRUBBERY BOMBS
23

Flashes erupted followed by thunderous claps as a powerful wizard battled against a dangerous sorcerer. They attacked with ferocious strength as their bodies blurred in motion.

Grandpa Whizzenmog's eyes glowed in the darkness. The gray fox sprang into the air, flipped over Pierre LaCroiux, fired a spell and landed gracefully on the other side.

The sorcerer blocked the wizard's attack with a swat from his bony hand, and pivoted on his leg to face Grandpa as he landed. LaCroiux turned both hands palm up and pulled upward as if he was holding something heavy.

The ground beneath Grandpa lifted sending the wizard tumbling backward. He caught himself before falling. Grandpa dropped to one knee and flicked his wand like he was cracking a whip. Then he yanked back causing Sorcerer LaCroiux's legs to come out from underneath him.

The crafty old elf summoned a gust of wind to catch him. LaCroiux dangled in the air a few feet above the ground.

Grandpa Whizzenmog took the opportunity to zap the roots holding Whizzy. They crumbled and fell from his neck allowing Whizzy to breathe again.

LaCroiux got back to his feet, but began to run away from Grandpa.

My grandpa furrowed his brow and yelled, "STOP!"

The evil sorcerer didn't respond. I struggled to break free from the thick, strong roots holding me hostage, but without my wand I was helpless.

Grandpa chased after LaCroiux, who had run a short distance and stopped.

"Where do you think you're going?" Grandpa Whizzenmog demanded.

The elderly sorcerer still refused to acknowledge Grandpa. He began to reach to the sky as though he was pulling on a rope.

"I have a surprise for you, Whizzenmog," LaCroiux mumbled.

A whistling noise grew.

"What is that sound?" Whizzy called out to me.

The high pitch sound grew louder and closer. Then an explosion between Whizzy and me tossed fragments of grass, leaves, dirt and rocks all over us.

Grandpa whipped back around when the sound hit his ears. "Children?" He shouted.

New whistling sounds hung in the air followed by a series of explosions.

"Bombs!" Grandpa called out as he ran back to free us. His battle with LaCroiux would have to wait.

The gray fox nimbly dodged the exploding shrubbery. I watched in amazement. Grandpa Whizzenmog dashed from side to side avoiding the bomb's impacts. A circular shrubbery bomb headed for a collision course with the fleet-footed fox. Grandpa noticed it at the last moment and slid underneath the fast moving bomb. It detonated only a few feet behind Grandpa.

When he reached me, I was free within seconds. He moved quickly and freed us all.

Sorcerer LaCroiux continued to create havoc summoning his shrubbery bombs. They scattered throughout the battlefield.

One slammed into the face of a nearby spider. It splattered leaves across the spider's eyes, blinding it. The hairy arachnid stumbled and collapsed, causing its Grimmiad rider to topple over and fall to the ground.

"We have to stop, LaCroiux!" Phillip shouted.

"Ya think?" Whizzy crassly responded. He was breathing heavily and rubbing his neck. "This guy is really starting to bother me."

"We will have to do this together," Grandpa commanded. "He has become too powerful to defeat on my own."

Sorcerer LaCroiux continued to assault the Grimmiads with his magical shrubbery bombs, exploding throughout the grasslands.

The vampire bats had returned and swarmed directly above us. Goren screeched loudly and dove directly at me.

I panicked. My heart was racing. I froze. At the last second, Phillip jumped and knocked me out of the way as Goren swooped past swiping his razor sharp claws at me.

I landed hard on the dirt. When I rolled over, Goren was nowhere in sight, but many other vampire bats were. Dozens circled over us in the night sky, like airplanes waiting to land at a busy airport.

"Where's, Goren," I yelled while searching the skies above.

"There!" Phillip croaked as he pointed.

Goren had reappeared; he was perched atop a nearby wolverine soldier's shoulders. He hissed at Whizzy and me. The bone thin vampire jumped down and began throwing rocks in our direction.

Whizzy quickly responded by firing a spell, freezing the grass blades next to him. He grabbed hold and snapped one of the grass blades. Whizzy spun around and swung the frozen blade, like a baseball bat, with all his might, hitting one stone right back at Goren.

The vampire bat ducked as the rock zoomed by this head, but it sliced his ear.

"AHHHHHRRRGGGG!" Goren yelled in pain and then jumped skyward disappearing from sight in the night sky.

The spell wore off and the blade of grass became limp in Whizzy's hands.

"That was pretty impressive," Grace Tallon complimented the reddish-orange wizard fox.

"You know it was," Whizzy brashly responded. A smile beamed across his furry face.

Grace scoffed at the fox's brazen reply.

I saw her smile when she walked away from my brother.

"Look out!" Phillip shouted.

A shrubbery bomb crashed down in the middle of us. It detonated with great force, throwing me, Whizzy and Grace.

I landed on my back. The stars in the sky above me blurred on impact. Everything was out of focus, like being cross-eyed.

I could hear Whizzy call out in pain.

I tried to get to my feet but couldn't. I had hit my head when I landed. A green fuzzy blob grew larger in front of me.

"Stop!" I shouted, placing my hand out in front of me.

A green hand grabbed hold of mine. It was Phillip's. I could tell because it was damp and clammy.

"Rachel, it's me, Phillip." He rubbed the back of my hand with his.

I closed my eyes and inhaled deeply.

Phillip pulled me close to his chest and wrapped his arms around me tightly. I could feel his heart pounding against my cheek.

"It's gonna be ok, Rachel," he spoke in a semi-reassuring tone. I could tell he was trying to convince himself too. "I found something that belongs to you." He held out his webbed hand.

Even with my eyes closed I knew immediately that it was my wand.

Before I could say thank you, another explosion erupted behind me. My eyes opened. I could see clearly again.

"Whizzy! Behind you!" I screamed to my brother as a large wolverine soldier raised its sword above its hairy head.

My brother rolled to avoid being sliced in half as the metal blade sparked against a stone in the dirt when it slammed into the ground. Whizzy had barely escaped. He scrambled backward on his backside to get away.

Meanwhile, Grandpa and LaCroiux had started their quarrel again.

The sorcerer twisted his white braided beard around his finger as a sinister smirk crept across his dirty face.

"Come on, sorcerer. Make your move!" Grandpa Whizzenmog challenged. He stood prepared for the sorcerer's attack.

Pierre LaCroiux reached down and tore two blades of the tall dark green grass from the ground. He began swinging them around like massive swords.

Grandpa backed away from the sorcerer's attack.

"It's time to see what you're made of, Whizzenmog!" LaCroiux laughed as he swung at the gray fox. "Hold still...and I promise this will be over quickly, Rainer!"

"We have to help them!" I pleaded with Phillip. My brother and my grandpa both needed our help.

"I'll help Whizzy," Phillip said as he pulled a Grimmiad sword from its sheath at his hip.

I ran to help my grandpa when I felt the hairs on my neck stand up. Something was following me. Just as I turned to see, a vampire bat grabbed me. It was Vella. I zapped her, causing us to crash. We tumbled along the ground. I landed on top of Vella, when she finally stopped.

My head was swimming. "I can't keep doing this," I cried. I tried to stand up, but fell back down. Everything on my golden foxy body hurt from my paws to my pointy ears. It was even painful to grip my wand, but that was the best protection I had so there was no way I was going to let go.

Vella didn't look any better. Blood trickled from her nostrils and mouth. She had a laceration across her cheek that bled onto the grass beneath us.

Phillip was faring better in his attempt to help my brother against the wolverine soldier. He was swinging away at the hairy beast from Wolverine Forest. The two enemies were trading swats...each ending with a clanging of metal.

Whizzy had gotten back up on his fox paws and pointed his crooked wooden wand at the wolverine, but couldn't get a clear shot as Phillip dodged a strike from the beast's sword.

"Get 'em, Whizzy!" Phillip yelped.

"Move outta the way!" Whizzy shouted back.

Grandpa continued to back pedal from the dangerous grass blades that Sorcerer LaCroiux spun above his head like a helicopter.

The elderly sorcerer flung the blades at Grandpa, who leapt away just in time. The blades sliced into the ground and spun back into the air. They returned to their master like a boomerang. LaCroiux caught them easily and targeted his prey again.

I fired a spell to freeze the sorcerer, but he redirected the blast with his spinning blades. The bright blue bolt zapped a vampire bat, causing it to fall from the sky and crash into a wolverine and spider battling each other.

I kept firing, hoping something would hit him. It was at least keeping him from throwing that wicked grass blade back at my grandpa.

Grandpa Whizzenmog had regained his composure and aimed at the sorcerer once again.

"LaCroiux!" He barked, gaining the sorcerer's attention. Just then, Grandpa blasted a thunderous spell from his wand. It almost knocked him down.

Sorcerer LaCroiux deflected the blast. The force from its collision jarred the whirling blades free. The blades spun into the ground and fractured. LaCroiux was knocked down as the blast scorched across the battlefield.

It slammed into the wolverine battling Phillip and Whizzy. The beast groaned before falling to the ground with its eyes wide in pain. The massive creature fell forward and crashed down at the feet of Phillip.

"Did you do that?" Whizzy questioned his best friend.

"Ahh...no." Phillip shrugged and glanced at me.

I pointed to my grandpa with a smile on my face.

Our enemy was lying on the ground...wounded. His right arm was bleeding badly. He made awful noises as he attempted to get back to his feet.

"You were lucky, Rainer!" LaCroiux grunted in pain while holding his arm.

"And your luck has run out, LaCroiux." My grandpa raised his wand.

I did the same.

Whizzy and Phillip were walking toward us. My brother held his wand pointed directly at the nasty sorcerer.

LaCroiux's eyes jumped from wand to wand.

"He is trying to decide who to attack first," Phillip announced after reading the sorcerer's thoughts.

LaCroiux's face grimaced. He made a small movement toward the tall green frog.

Phillip grabbed his neck like he was being choked and fell to his knees, struggling for air.

Whizzy was enraged. He screamed without hesitation, "Signa." It was a spell that paralyzes the body.

I fired too, a freezing spell. "Ica!".

Grandpa fired at the same time I did, "Zeus!" A lightning bolt zipped from the tip of his wand.

I could see the spells racing toward Sorcerer LaCroiux. Three streams of magic were converging on the same target.

Whizzy's bright red spell hit first. LaCroiux's face turned rigid and pained. My bright blue freezing spell hit just a split second later turning the heinous elf's body a slight shade of blue. Grandpa's white-hot lightning bolt pierced LaCroiux's chest a moment later. The scorching bolt surged through the sorcerer's paralyzed and frozen body. His skin began to sizzle. Smoke rose from his head. A flash of white light brightened up the night. A zapping sound roared through the air like a fly got caught in an electric bug zapper.

Sorcerer LaCroiux was completely motionless...his hand still reaching out to choke our friend Phillip. His skin had changed to a dark gray color of a statue.

We gawked at Cragon Cadieux's henchmen. Suddenly, a gust of wind rushed across my back and slammed into LaCroiux. His body began to fall apart and fly away with the wind.

I gasped.

Sorcerer Pierre LaCroiux was gone.

WORDS OF WARNING
24

Grandpa Whizzenmog stood motionless. His face held a look of concern.

Whizzy excitedly pumped his fist in the air in celebration, "We did it!" He swung his fist like punching an enemy.

I couldn't speak. I didn't know how to react. We had just defeated Sorcerer LaCroiux...I should've been happy. Something immediately felt different in The Colossal Lands; there was a calmness.

"Is he dead?" Phillip asked as if he couldn't believe what he had just witnessed.

I was having the same feeling.

Goren swooped in and landed where the evil sorcerer had last been standing. He placed his razor sharp claws on the ground grabbing a claw full of dirt and dust.

"He has been returned to Mother Mistasia," the leader of the vampire bats explained. "You have freed us, Whizzenmogs." He spoke with a tone in his voice that sounded like gratitude.

The Wolverine Army had retreated. We found ourselves on a winning battlefield.

A cheer rose from behind. The Grimmiads began dancing around in celebration.

Phillip and Whizzy were doing some strange hi-five hand dance. They looked ridiculous. I couldn't help but smile at them. Phillip ran over and wrapped his thin amphibian arms around my waist and picked me up off the ground.

"We did it!" He yelled with a huge smile on his face.

My snout rubbed against his green cheek causing him to realize he was very close to me. Phillip set me back down and stepped back awkwardly.

"Sorry!" He apologized as he slightly blushed.

I could tell I was blushing too.

The gleeful frog ran away screaming excitedly, celebrating our apparent victory.

That was when I noticed Grandpa staring down at the spot where Sorcerer LaCroiux had been. While everyone else cheered like fools...he did not.

"Grandpa?" I called to him. I reached out and touched his forearm. "Is everything okay?"

He gave me a halfhearted smile and wiped away a tear from his furry cheek.

"Yes, my dear," he replied. My grandpa smiled and then he hugged me tightly.

The party continued on through the night. There was a joy in Mistasia that I hadn't seen since we last defeated Cragon Cadieux.

Grace Tallon was the only one that didn't celebrate. She walked to her brother's side, as Javid remained sitting injured in the grass. He was too weak to use his sorcery to escape.

The two were arguing, but I was too far to hear them. I suddenly wished that I had Phillip's powers of telepathy so I could eavesdrop on their conversation.

As I approached, it became clear that Grace was challenging her brother to rethink his choice of supporting King Cragon Cadieux, the last remaining sorcerer... besides her brother.

"How could you think fighting for him would make you stronger?" Grace scolded Javid. Her tone was cutting and abrasive.

"I have discovered things that few elves have ever learned. LaCroiux taught me the ways of a sorcerer...something you will never understand," Javid blasted back.

"No! I can't understand, and I don't want to, Javid! Our family fights to protect Cadieux Castle not rule it!" Grace replied.

"Rule?" Javid scoffed. "I don't want to rule, sister. I want to survive," the injured Elven sorcerer revealed.

Grace hesitated. She was trying to grasp what her brother could possibly mean.

Javid continued to explain, "King Cragon will rule Mistasia. I've chosen to follow him in order to survive. Anyone against him will be captured or destroyed, Grace," Javid appeared to be pleading his case in an attempt to convince his sister to join his side of this battle.

"No! How could you turn your back on those we are supposed to protect? We fight for this reason...to keep rulers like King Cragon Cadieux out of power." Grace gripped her sword handle at her side.

"How is that working out for you?" Javid crassly asked, since Cragon Cadieux was currently the king.

"Merran Cadieux is the rightful ruler of Mistasia, Javid. She will be once again," Grace defiantly boasted.

"I believe that you are fighting a losing battle. There is no defeating him," Javid's voice changed. He was scared.

"Look around, brother. Does this look like we are losing?" Grace pointed to the jubilant group of Grimmiads celebrating in the grasslands behind her. "Your powerful teacher is gone. How do you think King Cragon will react now?"

Javid simply replied, "You will find out soon enough."

TO CATCH A KING
25

The celebration in The Colossal Lands of Mistasia after the defeat of the terrible Sorcerer Pierre LaCroiux felt like they would have lasted all night, but one frightening moment brought it all to an end.

Grace had rejoined Phillip, Whizzy and me. Grandpa was again examining the dusty remains of LaCroiux like he was waiting for the elder sorcerer to instantly return before our eyes in a flash of light.

The vampire bats had gathered together, as did the giant spiders of The Colossal Lands with their dwarf-sized Grimmiad riders.

"Is this going to be a problem?" Whizzy wondered referring to the two groups huddling about on opposite sides of the grasslands as if waiting for the perfect time to strike.

"I don't think they like each other," I replied.

The wind rustled the once tall grass that had been crushed and trampled during the recent battle. Heavy gusts lifted the blades up off the ground.

A trembling began at my feet.

"What's happening?" Phillip asked with his large red eyes searching for an answer in the night sky.

"King Cragon?" Whizzy asked, gripping his wand against his chest to keep the wind from ripping it from his paw.

The ground near Grandpa Whizzenmog began to spin.

"A portal," the gray fox shouted over the winds. "Get back!" He motioned for us all to move away as he ran toward us.

The thunderous roar of the winds seemed to cancel out all other noise. It hurt my sensitive fox ears. Placing my paws over them, I attempted to block the rushing wind.

A shadowy figure appeared in the portal.

The wind suddenly stopped and all noise disappeared. It was eerily silent. A pressure entered my ears. Nothing moved as if someone had pressed 'pause'. Then a blast of sound knocked everyone to the ground. The portal had disappeared.

"Whizzenmog!" A deep growling voice called into the night. The once shadowy figure gained its shape directly before our eyes.

"Cragon!" I gasped. The king had ventured from his castle. He must have really wanted the emerald badly to risk coming here alone. He appeared tall and strong. His beard was beginning to show some aging as tiny gray hairs showed like imperfections on his well-groomed face.

Within an instant, vampire bats swarmed the king. He knelt and braced himself against the rushing winds from their wings.

The vampire bats continued to assault him. Loud ear piercing screeches erupted into the air.

I covered my ears. Whizzy did too. That was when I noticed that Grace and Phillip both held their swords at the ready. I could see Phillip's chest pounding as his heart raced. Mine was too. I didn't know what was worse...the booming from my heart or the high pitch noise echoing in my ears from the vampire bats.

King Cragon held his hands over his ears. He was wincing in pain.

Grandpa now stood beside me. He was covering his ears as well. His eyes never broke contact with the monstrous leader of Mistasia. I could tell he was waiting for the opportune moment to strike.

The vampire bats had afforded us the chance to prepare while the evil king was wounded.

The slick gray fox released his grip on his large ears and readied his wand. With the flick of his wrist, Grandpa sent a wide bright green flash across the ground. It spread out underneath his target.

The hundreds of blades of grass stood up off the ground and marched toward the king as he struggled against the painful noise. He lashed out, knocking a single vampire bat out of formation, sending it crashing to the ground behind Whizzy and me. The green blades of grass, which now were half their original height, began wrapping themselves around Cragon Cadieux's limbs. First they attacked his arms and legs, and then encased his body until the defiant ruler was tightly held.

Grandpa fought to hold King Cragon captive.

"Grimmiads, now!" My grandpa shouted.

Three giant spiders rumbled toward the struggling king.

"Fire!" Gelna Grimmiad commanded. The three ugly, hairy black spiders began spitting webs.

The vampire bats narrowly escaped being captured themselves as the thick, wet, silken webs launched through the air and landed on the king, rendering him motionless.

GRANDPA'S SECRET

26

My grandpa's eyes were bloodshot and wet. He gritted his teeth so hard I could hear them cracking. I had never seen him so upset.

"Cragon!" Grandpa shouted as he hastily approached the restrained king.

The dark-haired, bearded elf had always resembled a human more than any other creature in Mistasia. His eyes were burning with aggression. A vein began to protrude from his forehead, as his face grew red from distress. Cragon Cadieux continued his attempt to free himself.

"Give me the emerald, Whizzenmog!" The pompous king demanded.

The gray fox zapped him.

I called out, "No!" I was shocked. "Grandpa, don't!" I pleaded with him to stop.

Whizzy grabbed our grandpa from behind, stopping the gray fox from continuing to torture the defenseless king.

"Grandpa, please. He can't harm us now!" I continued to plead with him.

Everyone was still on edge, despite King Cragon's current predicament. Phillip and Grace continued to hold their swords in defense. Whizzy and Grandpa held their wands pointed

744

at their enemy. Even the Grimmiads and Vampire bats seemed restless and uncomfortable.

I, however, felt at ease for the first time since we arrived. All three sorcerers were accounted for and currently subdued. LaCroiux was dead, Javid was badly injured, and now Cragon Cadieux was captured.

"Give it to me, you cowardly fox. It belongs to me," Cragon shouted.

A strange silence fell over everyone. We had all heard him, but awaited my grandpa's response.

"It never belonged to you, Cragon!" Grandpa lashed back.

"The emerald belongs to my family, and you stole it!" The captive king revealed.

Grandpa zapped him again. Cragon yelled in pain. I stepped in, but the spell hit my arm.

I fell to the ground in pain.

"Rachel," Phillip shouted. He reached down and grabbed me.

I could feel a burning heat surging through my body like I was on fire inside. My legs and arms trembled. This was not normal magic...it was a dark, sinister magic!

"Grandpa!" Whizzy shouted.

"Control your emotions, Whizzenmog!" Grace scolded the elder fox.

Grandpa's eyes suddenly changed. His normal appearance returned, like a demon had left his body.

"Rachel, my dear, I am so sorry." Grandpa fell to his knees at my side and placed his hand on my face. He closed his eyes and began mumbling something.

The burning sensation quickly disappeared. A cool feeling took over like a blast of winter air rolled across my body.

When he opened his eyes, he must have seen the fear in mine.

"What did he mean, grandpa?" I asked. "Did you steal the emerald?"

Grandpa Whizzenmog didn't answer. The anger reappeared. He snapped to his feet and once again held his wand at the king. Its white-hot tip was glowing in the darkness.

"I was protecting the Cadieux family...something you wouldn't understand, Cragon!" The sheer rage in my grandpa's voice was frightening.

"Protect?" King Cragon continued to challenge the gray fox. "Then you are a worldly failure, Whizzenmog!"

Grandpa's wand tip brightened.

"No!" I cried.

For an instant, Grandpa peeked over his shoulder at me. His wand dimmed again but remained lit.

"You couldn't do it then, and you won't now, Whizzenmog," the sorcerer sneered as his bright white teeth glowed amidst his thick black beard. "It's time you come clean, wizard. Tell your grandchildren of the hero you are. Tell them about your greatest triumph."

"No," my grandpa whispered as tears formed in his eyes. He lowered his wand, which was now pointed at the ground. Grandpa lowered his head as well, but said nothing.

"Remember, Whizzenmog. I certainly do. It was one of the greatest nights of my life,"

Cragon Cadieux continued to pressure the gray wizard fox into spilling the story. "It was the night I first became the King of Mistasia."

"Enough, Cragon!" Grandpa shouted. He raised his wand once again.

"You can tell us, Grandpa," Whizzy said in a reassuring voice. Then my brother looked to me to see if I agreed.

I nodded, hoping what we would hear next wouldn't be as horrible as it seemed.

"Not able to recall your greatest moment as the protector of the king and queen of Mistasia, Whizzenmog? Then let me refresh your memory. After all it has been many years since you ran away." Cragon smiled again.

Grandpa just glared at the evil king. He appeared ready to allow Cragon Cadieux to unlock whatever secret Grandpa Whizzenmog held so tightly for all these years.

Suddenly, Grandpa broke his silence and interrupted the captured king before he could reveal the story.

"I knew I couldn't trust you, Cragon. Your brother knew too. Steven Cadieux was truly a great ruler and king...something you will never accomplish. But I never believed that you could corrupt so many minds." Grandpa paused as King Cragon grinned widely, showing pride in his devilry. "When I positioned Ethan to guard the Cadieuxs that night...I never thought. I never imagined the betrayal...from my own brother."

"It was pure genius to use Ethan Whizzenmog," Cragon began laughing.

"My own brother," Grandpa's rage erupted again. "AHHHH!" He screamed as he zapped his prisoner again.

King Cragon yelled in agony and fell to the ground, but resumed his laughter when the spell subsided. The Cadieux crown fell from the head of the king and rolled to his side. It shimmered slightly with the moonlight.

I placed my paws over my mouth and began to cry. Phillip hugged me.

"It was easily accomplished," Cragon chuckled as Goren pulled him off the ground.

"What?" Grandpa asked. "What was easily accomplished?"

"I know what you want to ask me, Whizzenmog. How did I corrupt your darling brother?" Cragon leaned forward slightly and whispered, "It...was...easy!"

"You are the most evil being I have ever met," Grandpa said.

"Why? Because I had my own brother killed so I could claim the throne! You would do the same." Cragon explained.

"No. No, I would never," Grandpa replied defiantly.

"Your brother did," Cragon responded.

"My brother was a fool to trust in you, Cragon. You are a deceitful and treacherous snake!" Grandpa Whizzenmog emotionally shouted.

"A snake." Cragon's face beamed with glee. "That reminds me of your brother, Whizzenmog. Do you know how he died?" The sinister king goaded the wizard fox into asking.

"No. How did he die?" Grandpa questioned.

A sinking feeling entered my stomach. I caught eyes with Phillip. I could see the fear in his red eyes.

"At the hands of your grandchildren's friend...the frog," Cragon revealed to the unsuspected gray fox.

Grandpa had been in Greenville then. That was when Ethan Whizzenmog appeared as a snake in our home. He captured and dragged me here. It was the first time Phillip, Whizzy and I came to Mistasia. He was Sorcerer LaCroiux's original apprentice. We had battled him in Cadieux Castle. Phillip eventually killed the corrupted Whizzenmog with Grace's sword.

"Phillip was protecting me, Grandpa," I explained.

Grandpa unexpectedly smiled. "For decades I have lived with the regret of those days. I never knew how deep your wickedness went Cragon. I just knew that when the king and queen were killed, you had everything to do with it! So I removed the last emerald from Cadieux Castle, opened a portal to leave Mistasia, and hoped that someday I could return to see your demise," the wizard fox declared. "My grandchildren have come to Mistasia to turn that wish into a reality. They will end your rule over these creatures, Cragon Cadieux. Your time is coming to an end."

MIND IMAGES
27

Grandpa Whizzenmog conjured up a spell that encased Cragon Cadieux, the current King of Mistasia, in a magical bubble to hold him securely.

The sun had begun to rise in The Colossal Lands. That meant we were another day closer to returning home before our parents could discover we had disappeared.

I felt at ease. We were all together—Phillip, Whizzy, Grandpa and I. We were all uninjured, and we had finally captured the king. All that remained was to find Princess Merran Cadieux, free her from the sorcerer's magic and once again aid her in becoming Queen of Mistasia.

Vampire bats now stood watch over Cragon Cadieux. The captive king was eerily calm like he was meditating.

Whizzy slept on a makeshift bed of grass. Grace stood guard over her brother, Javid. The injured Elven sorcerer hadn't moved in hours, but Grace was making certain he didn't try to escape. Grandpa hovered around Cragon Cadieux, keeping a close eye on the powerful sorcerer king. Phillip and I sat together next to Whizzy.

"Thank you, Phillip," I said.

"For what?" He replied with an uncomfortable giggle.

"Just for being here with me. I know that I didn't always treat you very well in the past...I'm sorry," I had truly been awful to Phillip Harper for years. He was always my brother's annoying best friend. That was until last summer. It is amazing how differently you can see someone that you have known for years after just one experience with them. I never even considered that I could have feelings for him, but now I do.

Phillip played with some dirt with his left hand, while avoiding eye contact. "Don't worry about it. That's okay." He replied.

"No, Phillip...it isn't." I placed my paw on his cheek and turned his head to face me. I looked into his big red eyes and smiled. My heart fluttered, then he surprised me with a kiss. It was quick and wet...he is a frog. I was just happy he didn't use his tongue.

Phillip quickly looked down again, but I placed my paw on his cheek again. He turned his head on his own this time and we kissed again.

"Hey! Stop that! Gross, Phillip," Whizzy shouted. He pelted us with chunks of grass. "I don't wanna see that ever again."

"Whizzy?" I started to argue, but he just pointed his wand at me.

"I'll zap you!" He joked.

The three of us sat in uncomfortable silence on the ground with Phillip in the middle. Out of the corner of my eye I saw my brother hold up his paw. Phillip punched it in celebration, like boys do when they do something cool. A smile came over me. My brother had finally realized that if anyone was going to date his sister...it should be his best friend. At least I wasn't dating Billy Lawton.

It had been almost six hours since my grandpa and King Cragon had verbally battled. In that time we had watched the sun rise and Phillip had kissed me, two things that I would have normally enjoyed, but by now I was becoming fidgety.

"We need to return to the castle," Grace said, startling Phillip and me. Whizzy just turned around and waved like an idiot.

"Hi, Grace," he said.

"Your grandpa sleeps, when we need to be moving to free the queen," Grace demanded.

I hadn't realized that our grandpa was sleeping.

"He isn't sleeping. He's standing up, Grace!" Whizzy pointed to Grandpa Whizzenmog, who stood up facing King Cragon like a watchdog...or watchfox.

"I think he is sleeping, Whizzy," Phillip added backing Grace. "I can't reach him. I tried to speak to him, but there is no answer."

"He isn't a phone, Phillip. There won't be a voice message. Maybe he just doesn't want to talk to you," Whizzy snarled.

"Okay, but it's different in the mind of someone who is asleep. It is like a jumbled mess of words and sounds. Images swirl around like being in a toilet after you flush," Phillip graphically explained.

"Oh, nice, Phillip. That is disgusting!" I suddenly got a vivid picture of a flushing toilet.

"Like right now I can see images in your mind, Rachel."

"Really? What do you see?" I eagerly asked.

Phillip paused for a moment, "Ahhh...maybe I'll just do Whizzy's mind," Phillip said bashfully.

"No, I don't ever want to know what is going on in this Whizzenmog's mind," Grace said before urging Phillip to answer my question.

"Err...I can see us kissing. I feel warmth and happiness," Phillip replied as he blushed.

I suddenly couldn't stop smiling.

"Phillip, that's your mind, you twit. Try someone else," Whizzy demanded.

"Oh, this is ridiculous. I'll just go over there." I got up and walked over to my grandpa. He stood perfectly still. His chest moved in sequence with his breathing. He was very peaceful.

I didn't speak for fear that he would awaken. When I saw his face, I noticed that his eyes were wide open but glazed over. He didn't blink. It was like no one was there. I waved my paw in front of his face and had no reaction, like he couldn't see me.

I shrugged my shoulders in reply back to my brother. Grandpa definitely appeared to be sleeping. When I started to walk away, a flash of green light caught my eye. On my grandpa's wrist was the green emerald bracelet. I peeked at his face to see if he was watching, but he continued to stare at King Cragon. I placed my paw over the emerald bracelet. Warmth flowed through my paw and up my arm. It pulsed into my ear. I pulled my arm back and again looked at grandpa. He didn't react. The power surging from the emerald was tremendous. It was drawing me to it like the emerald was calling me to take it. Again I reached for the bracelet. When I touched it, a spark shot from its center. I fell to the ground.

My grandpa awoke violently, stumbling to his knees. He shook his head. The green bracelet went completely black and fell from his wrist into the grass.

"Rachel?" Grandpa looked at me with confusion in his now normal eyes.

A feeling of panic came over me.

He realized something was wrong immediately after looking at me. "What is it, my dear?" Then, he noticed the bracelet was gone. "NO!" He shouted. "Where is it?"

The magical prison holding the devilish King Cragon had vanished. In an instant the calm atmosphere of The Colossal Lands turned into a terrifying horror.

The evil sorcerer king had been waiting for the moment he could break free, and this was it. He tore through the spider webs holding him in seconds.

Grandpa jumped in front of me as the king punched the ground sending a tidal wave of debris in our direction.

I didn't have time to react. I wouldn't have even known what to do, but grandpa raised both arms, forming a wall with the grass blades that were on the ground around us. The debris slammed into it like a monstrous wave from an ocean. Its power was tremendous, but Grandpa's wall held long enough to save us both. Grandpa was knocked down from the impact, landing next to me.

King Cragon Cadieux reached to the ground and picked up his crown, placing it on his head. Next, he summoned a tiny funnel of wind that danced around beside my grandpa and me. It sucked the bracelet up and brought it to King Cragon.

Grace Tallon shot arrows at the unsuspecting king. The first sliced across his chest tearing his robes but only scratching his skin. He easily deflected the other into the ground. He raised his fist. When King Cragon opened his hand, a gust of wind knocked Grace to the ground. He held the bracelet in his hand as it morphed back into the shiny green emerald. He smirked at Grandpa Whizzenmog and then vanished with a loud clap of thunder.

King Cragon Cadieux had escaped with the last emerald.

MAKE THE RIGHT CHOICE
28

Chaos reigned in The Colossal Lands. The Grimmiads were loudly chanting, vampire bats swirled in the skies above us, Grace and Grandpa began arguing, and to top it all off King Cragon must have conjured up a terrific storm as the winds picked up and began whipping around us. Within seconds the clear sunny morning Mistasian sky changed violently. It was now dark and frightening. Flashes of lightning leapt from the clouds racing in all around us. They were on a collision course directly over us. Then the rains began, which was nothing like I had ever seen in Greenville. Drops of rain exploded on the ground. They hit with such force it hurt.

"Kiefer!" I yelled to our winged friend. The giant butterfly landed and opened his wings to protect us from the winds and rain.

"You know we have to destroy it!" Grace yelled at Grandpa resuming her argument.

"I won't do that elf!" He barked back in a disrespectful tone.

I had never heard my grandpa speak so rudely toward anyone before. It shocked me.

"If you don't Whizzenmog, then I will!" Grace gave an ultimatum. She gripped her sword handle at her side.

"Stop it!" I yelled.

"I don't take orders from an elf," Grandpa growled at Grace Tallon while ignoring my plea for them to stop arguing.

The two combatants were mere inches away from one another. Whizzy and Phillip stepped in to pull them, but Grace and Grandpa continued to argue.

"Shut up!" I screamed over the winds and pouring rain.

Suddenly, everyone stopped.

"We need to get to Cadieux Castle. Save your anger for the enemy that deserves it." I was frustrated and fed up.

"She's right," Grandpa Whizzenmog conceded. He looked ashamed of his behavior. "Kiefer, can you get us there?" He asked of the large butterfly shielding us from the weather.

Before Kiefer could respond, Grace interrupted. "I think I have a better solution." She walked away briskly and pulled her sword from its sheath to point it at her brother, Javid. "You will open a portal to the castle!" She demanded.

Javid scoffed. "Not likely, my sister."

Grace pushed closer. The tip of her sword touched Javid's Elven skin at the neck.

"Your master left you here...all alone, brother. He abandoned you."

"He...but...he couldn't," Javid stammered to explain the king's actions.

"You mean nothing to him. You are just another servant. Disposable. Replaceable," Grace jabbed verbally. "Here is your opportunity to make this right, Javid. Brother...open the portal."

"But I don't have the strength," he answered.

"I believe you do. You always did, but you were just waiting for him to save you. You knew it would be too difficult to escape alone. You knew that he would come for the emerald, but you were mistaken in thinking you would leave with him." Grace continued to explain the errors of Javid's trust in the Sorcerer King of Mistasia.

Javid's bottom lip trembled with anger. He knew that Cragon Cadieux had abandoned him.

"You can do this, Javid. It is the right choice." Grace lowered her sword and stowed it back in its sheath. Then she held out her hand.

Javid just looked at the extended hand of his sister for a moment. He grabbed hold and pulled himself up. Grace half smiled, and whispered something to Javid. She took a few steps backward allowing her brother room to work. He squatted down and winced in pain. The Elven sorcerer closed his eyes and put his arms out straight in front of him. He moved his hands in a circular motion.

As the rains continued, Javid conjured a small portal. It looked weak and unstable. Javid was exhausted. "Hurry!" He shouted. "I can't keep it open for long!"

"I don't trust him, Grace!" Whizzy shouted.

"Then trust me," she replied before grabbing Whizzy and pulling him into the portal with her.

They disappeared instantly.

"Whizzy!" I shouted.

"Come on, Rachel!" Phillip yelled. He grabbed my paw and hopped in to the portal, dragging me with him.

The ride was quick but rough. Phillip and I were tossed out on the other side. We landed in a fluffy, cold and deep snow pile.

Grandpa landed just behind us, but on his feet. Only four vampire bats managed to pass through the portal before it collapsed and closed.

"He did it," Grandpa acknowledged with surprised.

It was cold again in Mistasia; we had returned from The Colossal Lands back into the wintry weather outside Cadieux Castle. Snow was stuck in my fur, so was Whizzy's as I saw him and Grace walking toward the silhouetted image of the castle in the distance.

We had returned in the exact spot we had left a few days earlier during our first battle with Sorcerer LaCroiux when he banished us to The Colossal Lands. Now a blizzard, probably compliments of King Cragon, raged.

"We have little time," Grandpa called. "I need to get that emerald back!"

"We must destroy it, Rainer!" Grace emphatically demanded.

"I will not discuss it, elf!" The elder gray fox scowled as snow built up along his cheeks and eyes.

"Stop it," I pleaded again.

"Look," Phillip pointed to a green hue lighting a window atop Cadieux Castle.

"The emerald," Grandpa replied.

We lumbered through the snow as quickly as we could. It was becoming increasingly more difficult with each passing second as the snow grew deeper and deeper. As we reached the walls of the castle the drifts of snow reached nearly twelve feet high. It aided our entrance into the castle. We would be able to climb the snow and enter through windows along the second floor instead of using the main entrance where King Cragon would most certainly have guards awaiting our arrival.

Grace led the way to the room where we had seen the green light from outside. Grandpa followed close behind. Phillip and I stayed close together as Whizzy brought up the rear.

It wasn't long before we encountered the first of the King's minions sent to stop us.

A single troll blocked the hallway. His body was so large it consumed everything. The dumb-looking creature's pear-shaped head rubbed along the ceiling.

Grace didn't even break stride as she pulled an arrow from her pack and launched it from her bow, piercing the troll's neck. The ugly monster roared. Grace leapt. She bounced from the stone wall higher into the air landing on the troll's shoulder.

"Phillip!" she yelled. Grace grabbed hold of the arrow stuck in the troll's neck and pulled hard.

The troll cried in pain and leaned back.

Phillip winked at me, then hopped into action. He bounded at the troll-webbed feet first. Phillip landed with all his strength against the troll's chest sending it toppling over and crashing to the ground.

We dashed past the falling creature. Grace performed a back flip from the falling enemy's shoulder and landed next to Grandpa. She resumed the lead and directed us through the stone hallways of Cadieux Castle toward King Cragon.

We passed an unlit hallway when a low rumble began behind us.

"We have company!" Whizzy shouted.

"Wolverines!" I added after turning around.

There were four wolverines chasing us.

"I've got them," Whizzy called. "Keep going!" He shouted to Grace.

I skidded to a stop to help my brother. Phillip did too.

"Rachel?" Phillip started to ask.

"Keep going...I'm gonna help Whizzy." I held my wand directly at the lead wolverine as it closed in on us.

"Whizzy, duck!" I shouted. "Bombastic!" I called as my wand exploded in a bright yellow flame.

Whizzy leapt to the side as the spell closed in. It impacted the lead wolverine knocking it backwards, crashing into another.

The remaining two wolverines were very angry and ignored Whizzy as he lay on the floor in order to charge at me.

When they passed by, my brother stepped up and blasted them from behind with the same spell.

"Bombastic!" I heard his voice call out, followed by a bright yellow light.

I closed my eyes and slid to the wall to avoid the flying wolverines. The two beasts crashed to the floor in a heap.

They didn't look good when we ran past to rejoin our friends. Phillip was waiting for us just around the corner.

"They went up these stairs," Phillip said as he led the way.

Before us was a dark staircase. We slowly climbed when I lit the corridor with my wand. At the top was a heavy door. Phillip slowly pushed it open. Standing in the middle of the room was our enemy, King Cragon Cadieux, and he seemed to be awaiting our arrival.

KING'S PROCLAMATION
29

The room was poorly lit and empty. There was nothing but stone floors and walls, except a single statue in its center.

"Princess Merran," I gasped.

"Let her go, Cragon!" Whizzy heroically barked.

The sorcerer king only smirked. He was calm and arrogant. It was obvious that he believed that he had won. He did possess the emerald, and held the future queen captive in the castle she was supposed to rule, but there were five of us and only one of him.

"Give up, Cragon. You don't stand a chance," Grace confidently demanded.

The king inhaled deeply. A plume of white smoke flowed from his mouth when he exhaled into the room. It hung in the air, floating toward the Elven protector to the princess. It began to change form and take shape right before us. The cloudy formation stretched and grew into long tentacles. It wrapped itself around Grace.

The three wizards, Grandpa, Whizzy and I immediately focused our wands at Cragon Cadieux.

"Release her!" Grandpa commanded.

"Whizzenmog, come now. You know that is not going to happen. She is my prisoner," Cragon replied.

Grace attempted to break free. Phillip helped by pulling on the white tentacles, but couldn't get a grip.

"Just like her," Cragon placed his hand on the stone figure in the center of the cold room.

He leaned closer and held out his left hand in which a flame emerged. Cragon blew at the flame causing it to touch the stone figure of Princess Merran's face. Suddenly, her appearance changed. Princess Merran's normal face appeared, though her body was still stone.

She gasped for air like she had been trapped underwater.

Grace Tallon finally freed herself from the king's sorcery. "Princess?" She called to her leader.

Grandpa started to move forward.

"Don't move!" Cragon demanded. "You stay right there," he said as he cast a devilish charm on us all.

The floor began to melt and cover our feet, trapping us in place.

"Uncle, what have you done?" the frightened princess questioned of her family member.

"Merran, I am just doing as I always have," he said in a sarcastic tone. "I'm doing what is best for Mistasia. Now, I want you to see this for yourself."

"See what?" she began to become upset.

"I want you to watch me destroy them." The evil king whispered into her ear. "With this." He held the last emerald in his hand.

The normally shiny green jewel looked dim and black in the sinister hands of the king.

Princess Merran composed herself. "You can't do that, Uncle. These are good creatures. They will do you no harm if you set me free," she attempted to reason with an unreasonable mind.

King Cragon had no intention of letting anyone in this room go. He couldn't if he wanted to remain ruler of Mistasia.

"I am the unquestionable ruler of Mistasia, and now with the Cadieux Emerald in my possession I am unstoppable," Cragon boasted. "You will remain my prisoner forever. Just like you planned to do to me," he reminded her. "How quickly you seem to forget that I was frozen in a dungeon...trapped in this castle for thirteen years, while my niece pretended that I didn't exist. You would have left me there to rot!" He spat his words at the statuesque princess.

"That is no trinket you hold, Cragon," Grandpa Whizzenmog reminded the king.

"Whizzy, you must destroy it," Grace whispered to the red-haired fox.

"Do you understand the consequences of destroying this jewel, fox?" King Cragon scolded. "You would lose your life."

I pointed my wand at the brooding king, "Don't threaten him again!"

"He isn't, Rachel," my grandpa replied. "The lore of the emerald states that anyone who destroys the gemstone will lose their life," Grandpa explained.

"Then I'll do it," Grace yelled as she drew back her bow and let an arrow fly.

King Cragon calmly snatched the arrow in his hand. "Your services are no longer needed in this castle, elf!" he replied. Cragon lifted his leg and then slammed his foot on the stone floor. The stones cracked and crumbled opening a gap in the floor, which Grace fell through and disappeared.

Our feet had been released when the stones began to crack. We were free. The four of us instantly attacked.

DEMISE OF A WIZARD
30

King Cragon Cadieux gripped the emerald tightly while defending himself. We attacked him from all four corners of the stone walled room. He seemed to anticipate each move, deflecting our attacks and using them against us.

Grandpa nearly took a blast from my wand in the face after the king redirected it with his hand. Whizzy fell to the ground when his own paralyzing spell was catapulted back at him. It hit his left leg. Phillip too barely dodged a rouge spell from Grandpa's wand. It singed the stone wall behind him.

I saw the gray figure of my grandpa running toward the king as he battled me. I tried everything I could imagine to keep him occupied, but the powerful king crushed each spell.

King Cragon punched the ground. The shaking caused me to tremble to my knees. I had only half stood up when I witnessed the tall black robed leader of Mistasia turn and hit my grandpa in the chest with his fist...the same one that held the emerald. A flash of green lit the room.

I screamed, "NO!"

My grandpa's face looked horrified. He cried out in agony and collapsed to the floor.

Cragon stood over him and raised his arm to finish him off.

Phillip leapt into action landing on King Cragon's back. The strong king's legs buckled slightly. Phillip jabbed his sword into the king's shoulder.

"Arrrg," King Cragon Cadieux cried in pain. He grabbed his wounded shoulder, when Phillip reached back again.

My grandpa suddenly sat up, wand in hand, and fired a spell at the emerald in King Cragon's right hand. The light from Grandpa's wand pierced the dim jewel, causing it to light up and shoot rays of green light shot across the room.

"No!" the wicked king bellowed.

Phillip swung his sword again cutting King Cragon's hand holding the emerald clean off.

The king fell to the ground in agony. Phillip began to fall too. King Cragon Cadieux reached out for the now glowing white emerald. The moment the king wrapped his fingers around the emerald, it exploded.

Phillip and grandpa where thrown in opposite directions. Each crashed into the stone walls. The light was so bright. It engulfed the entire room.

Then silence.

A female voice called my name. I could feel a soft hand rubbing my shoulder.

Grandpa! I thought and suddenly I was awake again.

Princess Merran Cadieux was kneeling before me. She looked distressed.

"Rachel, wake up!" she shook me vigorously.

Grace ran into the room. "Princess!" she called out with her sword drawn. "You are alive!" Grace happily replied after seeing Princess Merran still alive.

"Yes, Grace. I am alive," she replied solemnly.

The room was a disaster. Chunks of stone where scattered around the room.

My heart was beating so quickly. I was breathing heavily. Finally, I spotted my brother.

"Whizzy!" I shouted.

He was covered in a dusty powder from the crumbling stone scattered around him.

"Rachel," he coughed. "Where is Phillip?"

We instantly searched for the distinct green-colored skin of our frog friend.

"There he is!" I shouted with excitement.

Phillip was sprawled out in a far dark corner. He was amazingly uninjured.

"You are so lucky," I said as I hugged him tightly.

"Rachel," Whizzy called my name.

The sound in his voice told me everything I needed to know. He had just seen our grandpa...and it wasn't good.

When I turned around, Whizzy was on his knees uncovering our grandpa who lay underneath hundreds of fragments of stone.

Phillip and I joined him as we all frantically worked to free Grandpa Whizzenmog.

I gasped when Whizzy pulled away a chunk of stone to reveal our grandpa's face. It wasn't the gray fox that I expected. Underneath the dust and dirt was the aged human face of our true grandpa, Rainer Whizzenmog from Greenville. The one we had know all of our lives until the past few days in Mistasia.

"Is he alive?" Phillip gulped.

A began to cry as I covered my mouth with my paw. "He can't be dead."

"He has lost his life," Grace coldly remarked.

"Shut up!" Whizzy cried.

"No! He isn't dead," I yelled at Grace, hoping that would change everything.

"He has lost his life in Mistasia," Grace said again. "Your grandpa chose to sacrifice his life as the wizard fox. The image you see before you is no longer alive here in this world, but he has not died," Grace continued.

"I don't understand. Is he dead or alive?" my head was beginning to ache.

"Grandpa, wake up; it's Whizzy?" my brother said while crying.

I couldn't remember the last time I saw him cry.

"His life has ended here in Mistasia, Rachel. Your grandpa will be waiting for you in your world," Princess Merran reassured.

I couldn't begin to explain how happy I felt hearing that my grandpa would be waiting for us back home. I didn't know whether to cry or celebrate. I was so proud of my grandpa. He had shown such bravery. He sacrificed his life as Rainer the Wizard Fox to save us from the evil of Mistasia and in doing so destroyed the last emerald of power and the heinous Cragon Cadieux.

GRAND HALL TAPESTRIES
31

Queen Merran Cadieux once again was the ruler of Mistasia. My heart swelled with emotions to see her seated in the throne in the Grand Hall of Cadieux Castle. To know that we were the reason she sat there felt so rewarding.

Preparations for tonight's celebration were being made. A memorial for my grandpa was being created for tonight as well. Elves scurried about the castle hanging decorations, cleaning floors and preparing food as Phillip, Whizzy and I entered the Grand Hall.

It was a massive room with twenty-foot ceilings from which many large oval-shaped lanterns hung. The stone room was different from all the others in Cadieux Castle. It had a brightness, without any windows.

"Are these floors made of gold?" Phillip wondered. He looked at his webbed green froggy feet against the yellowish stone floor.

"They can't be," I laughed.

"This entire room is covered in gold," Grace's voice answered from behind us.

"That is friggin' awesome!" Whizzy so elegantly expressed.

Queen Merran and I caught eyes across the large room as she directed her Elven staff. She smiled at me.

I smiled too. It was so good to feel the calmness in Mistasia had returned. This world was so beautiful when the queen held the throne. Now that the sorcerers of Mistasia had been destroyed, maybe peace would remain.

"What are these?" I asked Grace pointing to dozens of long colorful decorative cloths hanging from the walls.

"Tapestries," Grace replied. "Each shows an important moment in our history."

"They are so beautiful," I said while looking at a picture of a red fox slaying a purple dragon. "Is that Whizzy?"

"That is your grandpa," Grace responded.

"He looks so much like, Whizzy?" I said with surprise. I had never imagined what grandpa would have looked like when he was a young fox protecting the king and queen before coming to Greenville.

"He was a lot like your brother then."

"Really? Like how?" I wondered.

"Angry and comical," Grace replied with a smile.

I started to ask Grace if she and my grandpa had been in love, but she must have read my mind because she immediately stopped me.

"I was very close to Rainer. He was very important to me...to all of us here at the castle. That was why it was so hard when he left," Grace revealed. "We missed him dearly."

It was the most emotion I had seen Grace
show...other than being angry at Whizzy.

"Who is that?" I asked after noticing
another fox-like figure in the background of the
same tapestry where grandpa battled the
dragon. I pointed to the small golden fox casting
a spell on another dragon.

"That is Ethan Whizzenmog," Grace sadly
replied. "They were once so close...Rainer and
Ethan. It destroyed your grandpa when his
brother betrayed him. By the time you and
Whizzy arrived in Mistasia, Ethan Whizzenmog
was far removed from the striking fox he had
been long ago."

During my conversation with Grace,
Phillip and Whizzy had wandered around the
Grand Hall looking at the other tapestries. Now
they were across the room closest to the
memorial that was being made for Grandpa
Whizzenmog.

"Rachel! You've gotta see this!" My
brother excitedly yelled.

I hurried across the golden room. Whizzy
was pointing at a black tapestry behind him, and

Phillip was hopping with excitement. They both had big smiles on their faces.

"What is it?" I asked.

"Look. It's us! All of us! We are all in this picture," Whizzy frantically tried to explain.

"Wow," was all I could say. The tapestry looked brand new.

"It was made in honor of your family's triumph," Queen Merran Cadieux proudly boasted.

"Cool," Phillip said.

"Awesome," Whizzy replied.

"It's beautiful. Thank you so much," I was amazed at how quickly it had been crafted.

The image was the battle we fought against King Cragon Cadieux. In it, Phillip was on Cragon's back holding a sword, while Grandpa shot a spell to destroy the emerald. Whizzy and I were also on the tapestry pointing our wands at the sorcerer.

"The entire Whizzenmog family of wizards, plus Phillip the Frog, will forever be honored in the Grand Hall of this castle," Queen

Merran proudly spoke. "I am forever grateful for everything your family has done for mine."

Grace and the queen left to attend to the preparation for the celebration. Phillip, Whizzy and I now stood together. I reached out and held their hands. The memorial for Grandpa Whizzenmog was completed. A life size, colorful statue of the elder gray fox casting his final spell stood before us. He would continue to be at the queen's side in the Grand Hall forever.

ELVEN SURPRISE
32

Our return home was far different than the last. When we set out from Cadieux Castle the following morning the sun was shining brightly in the Mistasian sky. It was quite warm for a winter day with no clouds in the sky.

We were cheered from the moment we left the front of the castle until we reached the Whizzenmog house just beyond Wolverine Forest. Creatures of every kind we had ever encountered in Mistasia awaited our arrival. We saw Goren,

Vella and Aevion, the vampire bats, Kiefer the Butterfly, and the Grimmiads. It was like we were in a parade.

Grace accompanied us. When we finally reached the spot we would return to Greenville, I felt sad.

"I will miss you, Grace," I said holding back tears.

"And I you, Rachel Whizzenmog." Grace hugged me. "You keep your brother out of trouble."

"Hey, I can keep myself out of trouble," Whizzy said sounding offended.

"I'm sure you can't, Michael Whizzenmog," Grace said jokingly to the red-haired fox. She leaned close and kissed Whizzy on the cheek. "Never forget me," she whispered into his ear.

Whizzy blushed as he smirked. "I won't."

Phillip pulled his sword from his sheath and extended the handle to the Elven warrior. "I guess I won't be needing this any longer."

"You can keep it," Grace replied.

"Ahhh...where would I keep a sword?" He looked at Whizzy and me. "I don't think I could begin to explain a sword to my parents," Phillip joked as he handed it to Grace. They hugged each other goodbye.

"How do we open the portal? The emerald has been destroyed," Whizzy bellowed.

"None of us know how," Phillip added.

"We need a sorcerer," Grace responded.

"What?" Phillip, Whizzy and I said in unison.

"Each time you came to Mistasia in the past...without your grandpa that is...you were brought here by a sorcerer's hand. Sorcerer LaCroiux to be exact." Grace stopped speaking for a moment to turn around.

Emerging from the Wolverine Forest was a small dark hooded figure. It walked toward us.

Whizzy pointed his wand at the small hooded figure.

Grace placed her hand on Whizzy's arm and lowered his wand. "This one is with me."

The figure stopped and pulled back its hood.

I gasped.

"Javid?" Phillip croaked. "I want my sword back, please!"

Grace hugged her brother. "Thank you for coming, brother."

We were all in shock. This couldn't be the same brother that had been helping Sorcerer LaCroiux because Grace seemed to be completely happy to see him.

"Grace, what's going on?" Whizzy asked. "Have you lost your mind?"

"No, Michael Whizzenmog. I have learned to forgive and forget...for the sake of my family. Seeing you and your sister together provides hope for us," Grace replied.

"So, are you ready to return?" Javid asked us.

Phillip and Whizzy didn't answer. Finally, I did. "Yes!"

"Have a safe trip," Javid smiled.

Suddenly, I had the urge to stay, but before I could change my answer the portal was stirring behind us.

Grace nodded to me and smiled.

I turned and leapt into the swirling portal and left Mistasia.

WHIZZENMOGS
33

I landed first. Phillip seconds later, and my brother bounced onto the snowy ground outside our sliding glass door in the backyard last.

It was a clear, sunny day in Greenville too. A soft wind blew against my human skin like a kiss. I exhaled. A puff of white hung in the cold air in front of my face.

We entered the house through the same door we had left from earlier this morning. It had been seven hours since we had left. Our parents wouldn't be home, yet from holiday shopping.

The house was eerily quiet.

"Grandpa," I called, but there was no answer.

Phillip and Whizzy followed me up the basement stairs. We had no idea where Grandpa Whizzenmog would be...we only hoped he was alive like Grace and the queen promised us he would be.

I went upstairs to the bedrooms. My heart was racing. I grabbed the handle to the room where he had slept. The door creaked. Whizzy was standing right behind me.

We walked into the room. In the bed something was definitely laying under the covers.

I grabbed hold and slowly pulled them back. I was terrified of what would be underneath them. I stopped when Grandpa Whizzenmog's face appeared. I gasped and then whipped the covers back completely.

"Is he here?" Phillip called from the hallway as he entered the bedroom.

Grandpa Whizzenmog appeared in the bed laying as he had in the castle after fighting Sorcerer Cadieux.

"Oh, no," Phillip cried as he covered his mouth. "I'm so sorry."

"Grandpa?" Whizzy placed his hand on Grandpa's shoulder. He stood on the opposite side of the bed.

I stared at my grandpa's face. He looked so peaceful...happy. I wiped away tears from my cheek with my sweatshirt.

"Rachel?" Whizzy looked at me confused. He was upset. "but Grace said..." He couldn't finish his sentence.

I leaned close and kissed my grandpa's forehead. "I love you," I whispered.

Suddenly, Grandpa began to stir. His eyes fluttered. Grandpa Whizzenmog awoke and shot up in bed.

We all froze.

"What just happened?" Phillip screamed in a high-pitched voice.

Whizzy and I wrapped our arms around our grandpa.

"Kids, you are all right," He sounded relieved. He hugged Whizzy. Then, he hugged me so tightly I thought he would never let go. "Ahh, my dear, Rachel. It is so good to see you all safe." He had tears in his eyes when he pushed back.

"We are safe. Everyone is safe. You did it Grandpa," I excitedly cried.

"Oh, it was so cool. After you...ahh, well...I mean when you were gone," Whizzy stammered. "We were at the castle with Queen Merran and Grace. They have this awesome room with stuff hanging on the walls." Whizzy animatedly explained.

"Tapestries, Whizzy," I interjected.

Grandpa Whizzenmog eagerly listened to everything. He had the proudest smile on his face.

"Yeah, and they had pictures on them," Whizzy kept going.

"You were on them," I told Grandpa Whizzenmog.

"And we were too," Whizzy said.

Grandpa began to laugh, because Whizzy was so excited.

"Ahh, it was awesome." Whizzy hugged our grandpa again. "I'm so glad you're alive!" He shouted.

"Well, I am too, my boy," Grandpa chuckled.

Phillip laughed.

The mood of the room calmed. Grandpa Whizzenmog and I smiled at each other.

"I'm so proud of you, Grandpa."

"And I of you, my dear."

I pulled his wand out of my back pocket and handed it to him. He gave it a peculiar look.

"It's your wand?" I said thinking he didn't recognize it.

"Not any longer," he sadly replied.

"Will you miss, Mistasia?" I asked him, knowing he wouldn't be able to return after sacrificing his powers to stop King Cragon.

Grandpa stood up and pulled me close. He took a deep breath and kissed my forehead. Then, he waved Whizzy over and held us both before he said, "I believe I have everything I need right here."

EPILOGUE

My life has experienced many changes since we first went to Mistasia just six short months ago. I feel like I've grown up so much. I've entered high school, grown closer to my brother, Whizzy, learned a great deal about my family history, and most importantly, I discovered sometimes the best things in your life are right in front of you...even if he is your brother's best friend.

Whizzy and I are closer than we have ever been. Our experiences in Mistasia made us realize just how important we can be to one another. Together we can accomplish anything.

My grandfather is doing very well too. He doesn't really talk much about Mistasia, but I think he misses it. In the meantime, Grandpa is spending a lot more time at our house than he used to. It is really nice having him around. He even gave Whizzy his wand. Grandpa told him, "A Whizzenmog shouldn't cast spells with a crooked wand."

The morning after we returned, Phillip Harper asked me out. I couldn't believe it. He had changed more than any of us. Like I said, it is funny how the best things in life are right in front of you. I had known Phillip almost all my life, but never thought he would become my boyfriend. Whizzy seems to be handling it pretty well. At first, he tried to tell Phillip and me we could only see each other on Wednesdays and Thursdays...because he had shows to watch on television those nights so 'his best friend' would be free then. We're still working on the schedule.

So what is next for me? I guess high school, then college and someday a family. But will I ever get to go back to Mistasia again...only time will tell. Maybe someday in the future Grace Tallon will reappear as an eagle at the basement sliding glass door ready to take all of us on another amazing adventure through the Land of Mistasia. Until then...we will have to wait.

GOSSAMER PEN

AVAILABLE NOW @ PURRETT.COM
FREE WEB COMIC